Joey

 CORAL CANYON COWBOYS

LIZ ISAACSON

ISBN-13: 978-1-63876-432-8

The Young Family

Welcome to Coral Canyon! The Young family is BIG, and sometimes it can be hard to keep track of everyone. **This is updated through Joey (April 8, 2025).**

Here's how things are right now:

Jerry and Cecily Young, 9 sons, in age-order:

1. TEX

Wife: Abigail Ingalls

His son: Bryce (32)

Children he and Abby share: Melissa (13), Carver (9), Pippa (7)

. . .

2. TRACE

Wife: Everly Avery

His son: Harry (26)

Children he and Ev share: Keri (7), Clay (5), Avery (2)

3. BLAZE

Wife: Faith Cromwell

His son: Cash (24)

Children he and Faith share: Grace (8), Celeste (7), Tyrone (4), Harmony (6 weeks)

4. OTIS

Wife: Georgia Beck

His daughter: Joelle (Joey / Roo, 22)

Children he and Georgia share: OJ (Otis Judson, turns 11), Anaya (8)

5. MAV

Wife: Danielle Simpson

His daughter: Beth (19)

Her son: Boston (22)

Children he and Dani share: Lars (12), Emilia (8)

6. JEM

Wife: Sunny Samuelson

His kids: Cole (17), Rosie (15)

Children he and Sunny share: Ladd (7), Skye (almost 2)

7. LUKE

Wife: Sterling Boyd

His daughter: Corrine (16)

Children he and Sterling share: Ryder (7), North (5), Mattie (2)

8. MORRIS

Wife: Leighann Drummond

Children he and Leigh share: Eric (15), Rachelle (10), Skip (6), Ridge (2), Remington (Remi, 2)

9. GABRIEL (GABE)

Wife: Hilde O'Dell

His daughter: Liesl (16)

Her daughter: Lynnie (25)

Children he and Hilde share: Canyon (8), Brant, Cort, Tanner (5)

10. BRYCE

Wife: Codi Hudson, due just before Thanksgiving with their first baby

. . .

11. HARRY
Engaged to: Belle Graves

OTHERS TO KNOW ABOUT:

12. Reggie and Kassie Avery - Ev's brother and Bryce's best friend; they live at Rising Sun Ranch and help run it; they're due with their first baby just before Christmas

13. DENZEL AND MICHELLE DRUMMOND - LEIGH'S brother and sister-in-law
Children: Daniel (6), Hazel (4), pregnant and due this coming summer
Denzel has a service German shepherd: Scout

14. SHAWN AND ENID AVERY - EV'S BROTHER AND sister-in-law
Children: Isaac (3), Thomas (1.5)

15. WADE AND CHERYL INGALLS - ABBY'S BROTHER AND sister-in-law; they live right next door to Tex and Abby
Children: Bennett (12), Wyatt (8)

1

J oelle Young carried a clear plastic tote up the wide steps at Uncle Morris's house. "Keep going, Ana," she said to her younger sister, who carried two grocery sacks. One had a loaf of bread and a bag of hot dog buns in it, and the other had two bags of chips.

The girl had just turned eight years old, and she exuded spunk and sass. She loved ponies, coloring, and hula hooping, and Joey loved her with her whole heart.

"In the kitchen," she said to her sister as she crossed the threshold of the house. The tote she carried had been labeled "office," and Joey detoured to the left just off the foyer of this great big mansion that Uncle Morris and Aunt Leigh had built for their family.

It sat on the northern highway of Coral Canyon, just inside the city limits, and had taken them almost a year and a half to get to today—moving day. Everyone in the Young family had been recruited to help move five children and two adults, as well as a pet lizard, a *secret* pet snake—that Uncle Morris and Aunt Leigh had found out about and steadfastly refused to move from their other house—and a hot tub.

Joey barely weighed a hundred pounds, but she'd tied back her white-blonde hair and was determined to help her aunt and uncle however she could. She usually ended up doing something with the kids to keep them out of the way, and she didn't mind that.

Today, she went back and forth with OJ and Ana, each of them carrying something light that someone had set in a pile for movers just like them. *Many hands make light work*, as Grams said, but sometimes it could also put a lot of bodies in a small space, and that didn't help anybody.

Joey had moved back to Coral Canyon after her first and only year at the Culinary Institute in New York City, and she had been working two jobs and living with her grandparents since. She told herself she was only twenty-two years old, and she didn't need to have every step of her life mapped out.

She liked working at the bakery and had graduated from being a roller-skating runner of orders to a baker. That meant she had to be awake, dressed, and alert by four a.m. so she could have pastries ready to be bought and picked up when Cake Bites opened at six.

Her boss, a woman named Miriam, was a smart businesswoman. She had built and opened her bakery right next to a coffee shop. Aunt Michelle owned Daily Grind, and the two ladies often ran specials for each other's shops. Aunt Michelle had stopped her own in-house baking and simply purchased from the bakery next door.

Joey's new baker position meant she had to quit at Michelle's coffee shop. She didn't mind working in the food service industry; she loved to cook, after all.

To fill her evenings, she had gotten a job with Ev's brother, Shawn. He owned a catering company called Pork & Beans and had expanded it to a single restaurant in Coral Canyon. Joey worked on the catering side, which meant she didn't have to interact with people very often, and she once again got to put her cooking skills to use.

When she wasn't working in either of those places, she tested recipes in her granny's kitchen, fed her grandparents, and kept them company while spending afternoons with her tablet, taking them for walks, or lying in bed watching crime documentaries.

She wondered if her life would simply be baking cupcakes in the morning and smoking meat in the afternoon. *It wouldn't be a bad life,* she told herself as a commotion broke out in the kitchen.

"I told you now wasn't a good time to do this egg experiment," Aunt Leigh said, handing Eric a roll of paper towels. "Clean them up and get out of here." She sounded stressed, and Joey wanted to help.

She waited while Eric muttered his apology and started cleaning up the broken eggs that had fallen to the floor—their brand new, pristine tile floor.

She met Aunt Leigh's eyes. "Can I take the kids some-where where we could help you unpack?" she asked.

Aunt Leigh ran her hands through her hair, pushing her bangs back as she sighed. "Yes. Why don't you take the girls into the sewing room? Rachelle helped me pack it up, and she'll be able to help you guys get everything put away."

Joey nodded and glanced over to Eric, a gangly fifteen-year-old who'd been making messes since he was a little boy.

"Eric's going to go outside with all of Luke's kids and Uncle Gabe. They're working on setting up the shed out there." Aunt Leigh gave her son a severe glare, and he tossed the ruined paper towels in the trash and stalked out.

"All right," Joey called. "Rosie, you're with me. Corinne, Rachelle, Liesl, Grace, Celeste, Melissa, Carter, Pippa, Keri, and Clay. Let's go unpack the sewing room."

That was basically every child between the ages of five and twelve in the Young family, and Joey led the way down the hall to the room where Aunt Leigh had put all of her sewing things. Joey had underestimated how many boxes there would be, and she and all the kids could barely fit in the room with them.

"Okay," Rosie said, whipping a pocketknife out of her back pocket. Joey simply blinked and stared at her. She wasn't even sure if she'd ever *held* a pocketknife before, but in Rosie's hand, it looked like a natural extension. Rosie was all wild cowgirl, while Joey was more of a stay-indoors-and-read type of girl.

Rosie had started riding horses by age four, following her daddy, her cousin Cash, and her brother into the rodeo.

She'd just started training to ride the barrels, and Joey actually couldn't wait to see her do it at next summer's rodeo.

"Rachelle, you get up here and help," Joey said. She turned and found the wall to her right completely full of built-in shelves. "What do you think your mama wants to put over here?"

"Her fabrics will go there," Rachelle said.

Rosie lifted out patterns, set the box down so that smaller hands than hers could take the things out of them, and sliced open another box.

"Okay, everyone," Joey said. "You're going to take something out of the box, bring it to me or Rachelle, and we'll decide where to put it. Okay?"

Several *okay's* chorused back to her, and Joey had been part of the Young family long enough to be used to this sort of chaos. Her family hadn't moved since Daddy had married Georgia when Joey was only eight years old. Joey herself had moved to Jackson Hole to go to college and then to New York City to go to the Culinary Institute, and then back.

Always back home.

Where will you move next? she thought as she established one of the shelves for Aunt Leigh's patterns.

Rosie broke down the boxes as they went through them, which created more room. Joey opened the cupboards built into the other wall to reveal more storage, more shelves, more places to put things.

She thought of Bryce and Codi and Kassie and Reggie about to become parents. She thought about Belle and Harry and their recent engagement. Joey wondered if she'd

Liz Isaacson

ever meet that just-right man for her. She had dated a lot in high school and even had a couple of boyfriends in college. No one in New York City, as the enormity of that place had scared her more than she thought it would.

And no one here in Coral Canyon, though she knew some cowboys who hadn't left town after they'd graduated from high school. No one seemed interested, and Joey wasn't really looking for a boyfriend anyway.

She had just turned to tell Grace, Liesl, and Celeste to go put a sewing basket on the lowest shelf by the door, when OJ asked, "What about this, Joey?"

Joey turned and came face-to-face with a cupboard door that had not been open a moment ago, and she rammed it with her face. She cried out, and her hands flew up to cover her nose. She tasted blood on the back of her tongue, and tears flooded her eyes. Pain smarted through her sinuses and down her cheekbones, but Joey was more startled and embarrassed than anything.

She cried when her emotions got the best of her, and so it wasn't surprising to her that tears streamed down her face.

"I'm sorry," OJ said, and he really meant it. He was a sweet kid that wouldn't hurt a spider, but instead carried it outside so it could be free.

"It's not your fault," Rosie said as she closed the door. "We just gotta be careful, guys."

"It's fine," Joey said, her voice nasally and pinched. "I just need to go to the bathroom." She rushed out of the sewing room.

Behind her, she heard Rosie start to lecture Ana for

opening the cupboard door when Joey had been standing right there. Her nose stung and her heartbeat flopped in her chest for some reason.

She ducked into the bathroom, but her nose wasn't bleeding too badly. Thankfully, as she didn't handle the sight of her own blood very well. To her great relief, the bleeding stopped within a few seconds, but she couldn't stop sniffling.

"This is so stupid," she whispered as she tossed the tissue away so she didn't have to see the blood. She wasn't even sure why she'd completely lost control of her emotions.

Her uncles kept bustling by the bathroom with bigger boxes and items of furniture as they had to go past her to get to the stairs that led to the second floor where a lot of the children's bedrooms waited. Down the hall, she heard crying, which had to be Leigh and Morris's twins who had just turned two.

Suddenly, everything felt too big, too chaotic, and too fast. Joey rushed out of the bathroom, kept her head low as she ducked around the corner, and then went out the back door.

In the corner of the yard to her right, Uncle Gabe, Uncle Morris, and several of the older teen boys still wrestled with garden tools, a lawn mower, a wheelbarrow, several rakes and shovels, and other larger equipment waiting outside the shed for its proper placement.

Joey ducked to the left, away from them. Her chest hitched with every step, and she held a new tissue to her nose to check if it was bleeding. It wasn't. Aunt Leigh and

Uncle Morris had built a large house, and it seemed to take forever to gain the corner and duck around it.

The side yard over here wasn't very big, maybe only fifteen feet between the house and the fence beside it, and shade covered everything here. Joey pressed her back into the house and slid down until she reached the ground, her knees folded to her chest. She put her head against them and cried, hoping that this tsunami of emotions and this deluge of tears would subside, and she could get back and continue being helpful.

Several trees had been left on the property, giving Aunt Leigh and Uncle Morris a maturely landscaped yard. As Joey quieted, she listened to the wind rustle through the tall trees. The leaves had already started to fall, and in fact, most were gone as Halloween lingered only ten days away now.

She sniffled, but thankfully she wasn't outright sobbing anymore. She'd just checked to make sure her nose wasn't bleeding again when someone came around the front corner of the house, saying in a clipped voice, "I can't help that, Delaney. It's not my job to find you an assistant."

Adam Harmon. Glorious, gorgeous Adam Harmon.

The blond god of a man took two steps and then turned as he paced back the way he'd come. Clearly, he hadn't seen Joey. Her breathing turned shallow, because she didn't want him to find her there, pressed against the side of the house, bleeding and crying.

You're not bleeding, a voice whispered in her head. But she may as well have been, and Joey simply felt stitched together wrong right now.

Adam, however, had been cut from one of God's choicest cloths. He had hair the color of the warmest sandy beach Joey could imagine, and those broad shoulders.... Joey dreamt about them at night.

He wore a suit coat as well as he did a polo, and Joey hadn't realized he'd be there to help Uncle Morris move. In fact, Joey thought Adam had left Coral Canyon at the beginning of the month to start a new job with a new country music star in Nashville.

Her heartbeat thundered like a herd of stampeding mustangs as she heard his voice fill her ears. She couldn't even tell what he said, but he certainly didn't seem happy. She wondered who Delaney was.

Probably his girlfriend, she thought. Adam had to be a decade older than her, and she had no right to be crushing on the man at all. He'd helped her several months ago when a rude customer at Cake Bites had launched into her, that was all.

She'd fallen and skinned her knees, and oh, Joey couldn't handle the sight of her own blood, and she'd nearly fainted in Adam's car. He'd doctored her up and taken care of her, and she couldn't help but wish he'd come around the corner of the house to do the same thing again today.

He'd sit down on the ground beside her, put his arm around her, pull her close, and say, *Tell me why you're crying, Roo.* And she would, and he wouldn't judge her, and he wouldn't make her try to spell out why she felt the way she did.

He turned around again and started along the length of the house, and Joey held very, very still.

"I did not violate any contracts," he said. "I did not sign a contract, and as Mister Young has said, you're free to hire someone else. I followed everything to the letter of the law, and I never signed an employment contract. In fact, I *told you* eight days prior to the agreed-upon signing day that I would *not* be signing and that you would need to find someone else."

Joey's nose started to itch, and it felt like it might leak a trickle of blood at any moment. She lifted her hand as slowly as she could to press the tissue there.

Adam's eyes zoomed to her. He froze, suddenly silent and unmoving, his phone stuck in his ear and his mouth partway open still. Then he barked, "I have to go. If you need to contact me again, please call my lawyer." He lowered the phone and stabbed at the button. Then he marched toward her.

So maybe Delaney wasn't his girlfriend.

She almost flinched away from the angry storm of emotions preceding him. Then he softened right before her eyes—the muscles in his face, the set of his shoulders, the way he swung his arms, the anger in his step—it all melted away until he sighed as he sank onto the ground next to her.

"Are you okay?" he asked in a voice one-hundred-and-eighty-degrees different than the one he just used with Delaney on the phone.

To her horror, Joey sniffled, and that only triggered a

new floodgate of emotions to open. She managed to shake her head as tears flowed down her face once more.

2

Adam Harmon just wanted to go home. The problem was, he didn't have anywhere in Coral Canyon that truly felt like his. The rental he'd been living in since he'd moved here six months ago had been a blank canvas when he'd rented it, and it still held white walls, beige carpet, and zero personality.

Now that he'd be staying in Coral Canyon for the foreseeable future, he'd be buying something. But he hadn't had time to look yet.

He hated the sight of Joelle Young crumbled against the side of the house, sobbing. And he'd be an astronomical fool and a total tool if he didn't do something to comfort her. Therefore, he found himself doing the most natural thing in the world: he lifted his arm and pulled the weeping woman into his side.

He wasn't sure what had happened. She held a tissue,

but she didn't seem to be bleeding anywhere. This could be emotional trauma from something someone had said, or physical pain from stubbing her toe against any number of piles of boxes in the house.

No matter what, the fiercely protective and possessive streak inside him reared up. He would do anything to protect her and make sure that she didn't have to feel like this again. He hushed her and whispered, "You're okay. I've got you."

And he stroked her soft, silky hair over her shoulder, his heart screaming at him that it had been far too long since he'd held a woman like this. Years since he'd had a girlfriend for any length of time.

Morris's parents had just arrived at the house when Delaney Alabaster had called him, and he'd ducked out of the way. But Morris wanted to make the announcement that he would be retiring at the end of the year as Country Quad's manager...and Adam would be taking over. They'd work together for the next couple of months as Morris brought him up to speed on everything Country Quad had been doing for the past dozen years. And then Adam would be on his own to field all the concert requests, the emails, the interview calls, and all social media.

The four Young brothers, still mega country music stars in their own right, needed a manager, and Morris wanted to be a father. Harry had decided to manage his own career, which was just as large as Country Quad, but Adam had never really done business things for Harry. He'd handled Harry's personal affairs, and the young man simply didn't need him to run to the ATM, find him some reading glasses, or go pick up his take-out any longer.

All of the Country Quad brothers, plus Morris, knew of Adam's new job, but no one else did.

He felt like he'd swallowed a freight train that was trying to chug its way up a hill. The taste of metal and grease and smoke seemed to constantly be in his mouth, no matter how much he drank or how he tried to swallow it away.

He couldn't wait until this announcement was out, and he could find a house with a home office and get started in this new phase of his career. Band management wasn't quite the same as personal assisting, though his meticulous eye for detail and his excellent networking skills would certainly come in handy. Plus, he knew a lot of people in the country music industry because of his work with Harry for the past year and a half.

He tipped his head back and looked up into the sliver of sky that he could see between the rooftop and the tree branches and whispered, "Dear Lord, help me." Not only with his new job and the Young family, but specifically with Joey. He tilted his head down to look at her and she looked up at him.

Her pale blue eyes became the most beautiful thing Adam had seen in a long, long time. He'd had no idea that robin's egg blue was his favorite color, but oh, it was. It so was.

She blinked, and he swore the blue in her eyes darkened. It mirrored that of a lake now, and Adam wanted to dive into that crystalline-blue water. He'd even be okay if he drowned there.

His pulse bobbed in his neck, telling him that he wanted something with this woman. What, he wasn't sure, but he could start with something simple like coffee. He licked his lips and reached out to wipe the tears away from her left cheek. "You okay?"

"I don't know," she said.

"Did someone say something?" Because he would seriously find them and lay into them until *they* were the one crying out of sight on the side of the house.

She shook her head and wiped the other side of her face. "No, it was stupid. I just ran into a cupboard door."

"You're not stupid," he whispered.

"I just...." She trailed off and didn't continue. Adam didn't know her at all, so he couldn't presume to figure out why running into a cupboard had prompted her to hide from her family and sob into her knees.

"I didn't mean to hear your phone call," she said. "You came around the corner really fast, and you didn't see me at first."

"It's fine," he said. "It doesn't matter." He heard the hardness in his voice come back and he swallowed to get it to go away.

His phone chimed. Since he never let it get very far away from him, he heard it loud and clear. The weight of his device sometimes pounded him into the ground by noon, but he couldn't just leave it behind. He worked with celebrities, and they expected him to be on call twenty-four-seven. In fact, they *paid* him very well to be available at all hours.

As a band manager, it would be far easier because this was *retired* band management, and Adam might be able to get an hour away from his phone to go on a date, or get a massage, or simply go running up the canyon.

His life had definitely been a little bit out of control, though Harry had been one of his least demanding clients.

"Do you still work in that cupcake place?" he asked.

"Yeah," she said. "They promoted me to a baker." A hint of brightness entered her expression, and Adam smiled at her. Her eyes dropped to his mouth and quickly rebounded to his and then flitted away. Adam had seen other women look at him like this, and his heart grew a size and then sprouted wings.

Could Joey be interested in him too?

He shook the thought away, not sure what to do with it. His phone chimed again, and then again. Then it rang. He sighed the mother of all sighs and looked at it. Morris's name sat there, and reality came rushing back at Adam.

He had no idea what time it was, but it didn't matter. Morris had said he wanted to make the announcement when his parents arrived, and he'd likely gathered everybody into the main living room of the house to do exactly that.

With his right arm around Joey, he was slower picking up his phone and swiping to answer the call. But he'd moved too slow, and the call ended before he could tap it on.

He swore under his breath, and with his left hand, tried

to dial Morris back, but he wasn't as ambidextrous as he'd like to be. He couldn't quite do it before his phone started ringing again. This time Tex's name shone on the screen, and Adam managed to swipe on the call and say, "I'm on my way in."

"Yeah, we lost you, bro. Where'd you go?"

Adam looked at Joey, and she brought her gaze back to his.

"I got a phone call," he said. "I need a minute."

"All right," Tex said good-naturedly. "We're all in here waiting for you."

Adam could only imagine what Tex would look like when he walked in the house with Joey—probably ready to take a weed whacker and give him a haircut with it. He let Tex hang up, put his phone back down on the ground next to him, and said, "I've got to go in, baby doll."

He swore someone else controlled his body as he reached up, took her ponytail in his hand, and ran his fingers down the length of it, letting the hair slide through. She looked at him, and he gazed back at her, an invitation for coffee sitting right there on the tip of his tongue. He couldn't quite get the words to go out, and she sat up and leaned away from him.

"What did they want?" she asked.

Adam's brain misfired because he'd forgotten that she didn't know that he was going to be Country Quad's manager—*her daddy's manager*, he thought. Adam felt sick to his stomach.

No wonder God hadn't let him speak a dinner invitation

and make a complete fool of himself. He scooted away from Joey and got to his feet, then extended his hand to her. "Your uncle has an announcement," he said, donning his professional skin again.

He'd hidden feelings for women before. He could do it again. He and Joey's paths didn't cross that often, and she didn't even live at home. Besides, once he had a house and a home office, he'd call Country Quad to him. He wouldn't go to them.

She dusted off her backside, then turned and went around the back of the house where Adam had come from the front. He glanced back that way, then followed her instead. The backyard sat empty, the big lot extending out diagonally from the back of the house to include at least an acre of lawn. There were some apple trees back here, and a shed over against the fence where the cement pad ended. Tools and small yard machines still sat out in front of the shed, and Adam hated moving with everything inside him.

Of course, he didn't have a wife and five children, and a solitary move was far easier than what Morris and Leigh had to accomplish.

Joey slid open the sliding glass door about the time Adam realized that they'd be walking in and facing the entire Young family together, as if they were a couple. Before he could say anything, she stepped inside, and she'd barely moved out of the way before Adam did too.

He managed to stop then, but he'd already committed himself to the lion's den. Every eye came to him or Joey, and he felt the weight of their stares like gravity pushing, pushing, pushing him down into the ground.

"Well," Trace said in his homicidal cowboy tone. "Where have you two been?"

Thankfully, he didn't speak too loud, and Morris, who held a mic, said, "All right, now that everyone's here, we have an announcement to make." He nodded around the room and added, "Can I get Tex, Trace, Otis, and Luke over here?"

"What is going on?" someone demanded from Adam's left. Murmurs ran through the family, and Adam sidestepped behind a couple of teenagers, hoping to disappear completely from Joey's side.

She'd moved too, and he found her standing with Harry and Belle, which was the worst place possible for Adam. He wasn't sure how Harry would feel about him taking a job with his uncles and daddy, and Adam once again questioned the decision he'd made.

He hadn't felt like he'd made it irrationally or impulsively. Morris had approached him the moment he'd returned from Belle's meet-and-greet in Nashville. He'd said several of his contacts had told him how amazing the meet-and-greet was and how much they enjoyed meeting Adam specifically.

He'd outlined his desire to retire, be a full-time dad so he didn't miss his kids growing up, and Morris had offered Adam a contract with Country Quad as their manager. Everyone had already signed off on it, even Harry's daddy, though they hadn't told anyone.

It was a million dollars a year to live in small-town Wyoming and manage a retired band of four country music stars.

A million dollars.

Adam had had a few interviews in Nashville, only one of which had produced a job offer from an up-and-coming female country music star who'd landed a three-album deal. It would have been like working with Harry from the beginning, but she was spoiled and demanding, and Adam had not truly enjoyed their first interaction.

But he needed a job.

Rather, he needed something to do. Because in truth, Harry had paid him very well, as had some of his previous celebrity clients, and Adam had plenty of money in the bank. He simply wasn't an idle man. He wouldn't know what to do with himself if all twenty-four of his hours every day truly belonged to him.

"All right," Morris bellowed into the microphone. "Everyone settle down."

Luke said, "Dude, you're holding a mic. You don't need to yell."

That caused some in the crowd to laugh, and Adam told himself he better be happy. He better put on his professional celebrity skin. He better be ready to shake hands and hug and give explanations.

He paused at the end of the island where he could see Morris and the rest of Country Quad.

"Right, right," Morris said. "Sorry, but everyone just keeps talking."

"That's why you have the mic." Tex grinned out to everyone.

Morris ignored him and kept going. "We wanted to make a quick announcement. First, thank you so much for coming to help Leigh and I move today. We've ordered food from our favorite place, Pork and Beans. It'll be here in half an hour, so make sure you stick around long enough to get fed. Shawn's going to set up a tent out in the driveway, since it's kind of chaotic in the house."

"Yes, thank you!" Leigh yelled without a mic, and plenty of people heard her.

Morris grinned down the line of his brothers. "Country Quad is retired, but I didn't retire with them. I've still been working on managing their appearances, their requests, and their social media. They still get paid all the time. Someone has to manage that, and there's plenty that goes on residually even after someone retires." He paused and took a big breath, his dark eyes taking on a heaviness they hadn't had a moment ago.

"So they need a new band manager, because I'm going to retire at the end of the year."

Murmurs moved through the Young family crowd, and they definitely constituted *a crowd*. People started to chatter over each other, and Morris said, "Don't make me yell into this thing again," in kind of a yell.

Adam grinned at him and folded his arms.

"So, the five of us are all real happy to say we've brought on Adam Harmon as the new band manager for Country Quad."

The words sat there, echoing through the house from the amplification of the microphone.

Then someone shrieked, several people gasped, and Harry himself said, "You have got to be kidding me," in a voice definitely loud enough for everyone to hear without a mic.

"Come on up, Adam," Morris said, and Adam moved through the crowd of teens, adults, and children until he stood next to Morris. He smiled out at everyone and raised his hand as if they didn't know who he was. Of course they did.

"Good, yeah," Morris said, "Harry, make yourself useful and take our picture so we can announce our staffing change on our social media." Adam stood next to Morris with Tex and Trace pressing in on his right side and Otis and Luke pressing in on his left.

Morris lowered the mic, and Harry's wasn't the only camera held high taking pictures. Adam only looked at his, though, and when he lowered it, he met his best friend's eyes. Harry didn't seem like he'd commit murder in the next ten seconds, and Adam's gaze automatically fell to those who had been close to him, Belle and then Joey.

Now, *she* definitely looked like she was about to go postal and commit some sort of homicide here in this room.

She glared back at him, her arms folded, and one skinny hip cocked out, and he knew then that she wasn't going to commit homicide. She wanted to commit Adam-icide. She scoffed loud enough for him to hear, then turned and stomped out of the house.

Adam watched her go, noting that he wasn't the only one. In fact, her daddy said, "What's wrong with Joey?" which sent a tremor of fear right down to his heels that then rebounded up to the top of his head.

Then he got swarmed by other members of the Young family congratulating him, and he came face-to-face with Harry, who said, "You dirty dog. You did not say a word," before he grabbed onto him and hauled him into a hug. As he clapped him on the back, he said, "I'm so glad you get to stay in Coral Canyon."

Adam was too, or he had been until he'd seen that murderous look on Joey's face. He should just leave well enough alone. But he knew he wouldn't. He'd have to find her and ask her why him being the manager of Country Quad had upset her so much.

And maybe, just maybe, they could discuss it over coffee and cupcakes.

3

Now that she'd stormed out of the house, Joey wasn't quite sure what to do. She wished she had an array of wigs the way Codi did. She could simply put on another one and disappear for a while. She could walk right past people in the grocery store, and they wouldn't know it was her, wouldn't ask her questions about her family, or what she was doing with her life, or what she hoped for her future.

For a few brief minutes against the side of the house, she'd fantasized about having someone tall and strong to take care of her. Then she wouldn't have to know much more than she already did.

"He's managing your *father's* band," she said with plenty of disgust in her tone. She walked over to a garden rake and picked it up. Clearly, those who had been outside unpacking the yard tools had been called in for the announcement, as they littered the cement pad.

Joey's stomach growled as she started putting away garden tools, children's toys, and even a chainsaw in the big shed in the back corner of Uncle Morris's yard. She wasn't sure who had seen her stomp out of the house, and embarrassment swirled through her when she realized she'd have to face the group eventually. Her family very rarely let someone slip away, and surely someone had seen her leave the celebration early.

"Adam saw you," she muttered to herself, because his eyes had been glued to hers during the announcement.

No one came to get her, so Joey simply continued to work. When she heard voices filtering into the backyard from the front, she left the lawn mowers and leaf blowers and went that way.

She found Shawn and Enid setting up for the family luncheon, and since working outside would be better than going back in, Joey approached her boss and uncle.

"Hey, Uncle Shawn, what do you need help with?"

He flashed her a quick smile. "Hey, Joey." He gave her a side hug and nodded to the catering van. "You can get out the cart and start loading it. We should have the tables and tent done by then."

Joey nodded and walked over to the van that she'd driven around Coral Canyon for other events. Shawn had brought two other employees with him, and the three of them got the tent set up in Uncle Morris and Aunt Leigh's driveway. Enid covered the tables with ivory-colored cloths, and when Joey returned, she left the trays of smoked turkey, scalloped potatoes, and salad in the cart so she could help her aunt set up the heating elements that would keep the food warm.

A crisp October breeze ruffled the tent and kept extinguishing the flame that Enid got going. "Shawn," she finally said, turning toward her husband. "Can we put those flaps down? I can't keep this lit."

She sounded more irritated than the situation called for, but Joey certainly didn't know everything going on in her life.

"We're working on it," her husband said. Joey moved to try to shield the flame with her body. "Maybe if I stand right here," she said. "It will help."

Enid flashed her a grateful smile, got the burners lit, the tent flaps came down, and Joey helped Enid get the food on the tables. She didn't have to be told what to do, as she worked for Pork and Beans in their catering department, and she returned to the van to get the utensils, plates, and cups. Another employee, a man named Robert, came over and grabbed the lemonade, sweet tea, and coffee.

"Howdy, Joey," he said, tipping his cowboy hat at her. He smiled, a hint of a blush on his face, and Joey realized with a start that his simple cowboy greeting was actually him flirting with her.

"Hey, Robbie," she said brightly. She'd entertained no romantic feelings for the cowboy, and she had no idea how old he was—definitely older than her.

She turned away with the bin of creamers, sugars, and

stirring sticks for the hot drinks, and took it over to the table. She started setting everything out, refusing to look at Robbie again. She wasn't sure why, though. If someone was going to ask her out today, she wanted it to be Adam and not a coworker.

You're being delusional, she told herself. No one was going to ask her out today, not Robbie and not Adam. She'd known them both for months now, and neither had ever indicated that they wanted to be more than mere acquaintances.

Thankfully, the front door opened, and people began spilling out of the house. The garage door lifted, and more people arrived. Joey bustled around, finishing up with the catering, and then she fell out of sight again, standing next to Aunt Enid the way a worker would do instead of a family member. No one looked her way, and that only reinforced to Joey that she was invisible inside her own family.

She watched as aunts and uncles corralled their children and helped them pick up plates and start to load food onto them.

"You can take everything back inside," Aunt Leigh yelled. "We have couches, and our dining room table too."

That would still not be enough places to sit, and Joey wasn't surprised to see some of the older teens and young adults taking their plates into the backyard instead of the house. That would most likely be her group with Rosie and Cole, Boston and Eric.

There were still too many people in line, so Joey didn't move to get her food yet. She could wait until the crowd thinned a little bit. She looked toward the front door as one more person came out, and her eyes locked onto Adam. He chatted easily with Bryce on his right, and Harry followed them and pulled the door closed.

Adam looked up toward the crowd, and it took less than a second for him to scan it and find her. Joey wasn't sure what to do with his attention. She only knew it made her warm from the inside out, and she wanted to smile and lift her hand to acknowledge him.

At the same time, his gaze felt too powerful for her to hold, and her earlier embarrassment at sobbing into his chest, ridiculously hoping for a relationship to start, and then fleeing the scene once she found out he was the new manager of Country Quad, had Joey looking away again.

He, Bryce, and Harry continued toward them, and Joey knew Adam wasn't going anywhere. He did, somehow, manage to separate himself from her cousins, because she found them laughing in the food line without him. She looked up, hoping to locate him again, and flinched as she found him only two feet from her. He moved to her side effortlessly, now out of the way and almost out of sight.

Her heartbeat pulsed in the back of her throat, and she had no idea what to say. Besides, he'd come over to her, and surely *he* would start this conversation. She didn't know how. She didn't even know what she wanted him to say.

His pinky touched hers, and Joey gasped right out loud. Her hand swung a tiny bit from where he'd bumped it, and then he took her hand in his in the next moment. Joey had not held hands with a man in a while, but that wasn't why she suddenly felt like combusting. She knew she wouldn't feel like this if Robbie held her hand, and Joey found herself leaning closer and ducking her head as Adam murmured, "I can explain everything. Maybe over coffee?"

Joey liked coffee. She drank it every day. While she scolded herself and told herself not to create any more fantasies that would only get her hopes up where they should not be, she nodded.

"Great," Adam said, and he gently pulled his hand free. "I think I can get your number, and I'll text you."

With that, he stepped away, leaving Joey to wonder how he was going to get her number, and from whom.

4

Adam finished putting out the ice-cold cans of soda and frosty bottles of juice. He had a couple of lemonades still in the fridge that he could offer to the men in Country Quad when they arrived. His doorbell had already rung, and he hurried to answer it.

He needed a new house with a big front office where he could conduct his business, but for now, this rental would do. He opened the door to find Bryce and Harry standing there, both wearing big cowboy hats, blue jeans, and windbreakers.

"Howdy, fellas," Adam said, stepping back and pulling the door with him. "Come on in."

"Uncle Luke just got here," Harry said, hooking his thumb over his shoulder. "He had everyone with him."

"Great," Adam said. Once Bryce and Harry had gone

by, he stepped out onto the front porch to welcome his new team to his house.

He'd met with Country Quad previously, of course, and while technically they employed him and could be called his bosses, Adam never liked thinking of his clients that way.

Tex opened the back door and spilled from the truck, and then more cowboys simply kept coming out of it: Morris, Otis, Luke, and Trace. They all seemed to talk over one another, laughing and joking, even while Tex raised his hand in a welcome to Adam.

They definitely looked like brothers, though some of them had sharper features than others. Otis, in particular, came with a rounder face and shoulders, and Adam could see those same characteristics in his daughter.

You cannot be thinking about her right now, he told himself sternly while pasting a professional-manager smile on his face for her daddy. Never mind that he and Joey were meeting for coffee in only a few hours. He expected this meeting to run right up against it, and he hoped someone else would make an excuse to finish things up so that he didn't have to. He could probably count on Bryce for that, as his wife was due with their first baby in less than a month now. He wouldn't want to be forty minutes from her for very long.

The Young men arrived, and Adam started shaking hands and welcoming them to this, their first official meeting at his home. He entered last and pushed the door closed behind him, locking it as a habit of living in the city with celebrities. Country Quad definitely had achieved celebrity status, though they lived in a tiny Wyoming town.

Adam joined them in the back of the house, where the dining room blended seamlessly into the living room on the left and the kitchen on the right. Harry had taken a seat at the table, and that had prompted others to do the same.

"I've got sodas and water and juice," he said. "And there's some lemonade in the fridge, if anyone wants it."

"I'll take a lemonade," Luke said, and Adam detoured to get it for him. Once everyone had the things that they wanted, he joined everyone at the table, where he had put mini notebooks in the middle. He recorded all of his meetings with his phone and transcribed the notes later.

As he said, "Welcome, everyone," he tapped on his phone to get to the app that would do that for him.

"*Ahhhhh*," Otis said, really making a big show of drinking half his Diet Coke and acting like he loved it.

Trace threw Otis a dirty look, then folded his arms and looked at Adam. "Tell us why we're here."

Adam looked around at the men that had gathered there that day.

"Yeah," Luke said, "I thought we wouldn't have to have very many meetings."

"It's *one* meeting, Uncle Luke," Bryce teased. "The man just started working for you."

"We had three before this," Luke said. "I thought he would mostly be meeting with Morris."

"I will be," Adam said crisply, glancing over to the man who had come to him and offered him this job. Morris

Young looked tired, and Adam didn't blame him. He had just moved his large family into a much bigger house, and just because they had a lot of help for the initial transfer of items didn't mean that everything was settled and going well.

"Yep, we totally are," Morris said. "In fact, I thought one of the best ways to transition Adam into the role—" He paused, cutting off mid-sentence, and smiled.

"Oh, I don't think I'm gonna like this," Tex said, but he wore a jovial smile.

All eyes seemed to volley between Adam and Morris, but it was Bryce who said, "I told Harry here that I thought we should put on a charity concert series at the Rising Sun Ranch."

"That's right," Harry said, as if they had rehearsed this. "And I went straight to Adam and told him that I thought Country Quad, along with me as a solo artist, as well as Bryce—all six of us—could really raise some money and awareness for the horse rescue operations. Not just Bryce's, but around the country."

Adam smiled at his best friend, so grateful for the day that he had walked into that conference room in Nashville, Tennessee, and met Harry and his daddy.

"I immediately texted Morris," Adam said. "And we set up this meeting." He turned to the desk behind him, where he had prepared several folders. He handed them out as he continued, "Morris, Bryce, Harry, and I thought a five-concert series over the holidays would allow enough time for planning, as well as appeal to people in the giving spirit."

"You want to do a concert series in the winter?" Luke flipped open his folder without looking at it. His voice sounded like hammering nails out of staples, and Adam glanced at him. He'd been told that Luke was one of the grumpier brothers, but that he usually came around in the end.

Trace wouldn't say very much, and when he finally did say something, Adam would need to listen. Otis and Tex would talk the most and really hash things out.

Bryce had laughed as he said, "It takes them a while, but they get there—eventually."

Adam had hedged his bets as much as possible, questioning Harry, Morris, and Bryce relentlessly about whether the band members would go for this idea or not. They had all agreed that they would...eventually, and Adam had taken it as his job to get them to agree.

"A concert on Christmas Eve," Adam said, handing a folder to Tex, who had taken the seat at the head of the table. Harry had told him that most of the band members would go along with Tex, and that winning him over first was the smartest move. "Then Bryce wants to do one on his birthday a few days later."

"You forgot about OJ," Bryce said.

"Oh, right." Adam met Otis's eyes, and time seemed to stall completely. Images of Joey with her long, pale hair flashed through his mind, immediately followed by Otis's younger child, OJ.

"Bryce wanted OJ to do a number with him, and maybe you, maybe everyone." Adam suddenly felt like he was rambling. "On Christmas Eve, because that's his birthday."

Otis took the folder with a little too much force and switched his gaze over to Bryce, where he glared.

"What?" Bryce asked. "You don't want OJ to play the guitar? He's really good, Uncle Otis."

"Maybe he doesn't want to be a country music star," Otis said.

"Maybe he does," Harry deadpanned.

"You're not the boy's father," Trace said in a low voice, and Harry looked over to his daddy.

"We know that," he said. "This is just all a proposal. We're here to talk about it."

Adam glanced at the clock and handed the last folder to Morris. "Three additional concerts," he continued. "One on New Year's Eve, which we can pre-record and set to play as the clock hits midnight around the world. One on Christmas Day, which again, we can record in advance. And one on Three Kings Day. It rounds out the concert series and only takes thirteen days of your life."

Luke scoffed but said nothing, and Adam didn't blame him. Thirteen days of live appearances, sure. Thirteen days of massive social media, yes. Thirteen days of everyone talking about the concerts, absolutely.

But Adam knew that if Country Quad was going to play and produce five concerts in only two months' time, the work would have to start immediately.

He took a seat at the foot of the table and gazed around at everyone as they looked at the single sheet of paper in the folder. Adam knew that sometimes silence was the best motivator to get someone to speak, and he simply waited.

Bryce and Harry exchanged a glance, and Harry drew a breath, as if he would say something. Then he pressed his lips together and looked across the table to the three uncles sitting there.

"Looks like only Harry and Belle are doing a new song," Trace said, almost in an off-hand way, like he didn't care at all about anything happening right now.

"That's too bad," Otis said. "I've got some music in my mind that I think I could write for this."

Bryce ducked his head as a slow smile curved his mouth, but Adam remained stoic.

"You think you've got some music in your mind?" Luke repeated, putting a question mark on it. "Are you kidding me right now?"

Otis looked at him coolly. "Just because we don't tour anymore doesn't mean I've stopped writing songs." He looked over to Trace. "We just did three last week that are in negotiation for purchase by Sabrina Roundy."

"Oh, that'd be a good sale," Tex said.

Otis switched his gaze to his. "Yeah, it would be."

"You've got a different song for us?" Tex asked.

"Yes," Otis said. "And I think it would be great for all...." He glanced around the table, his fingers ticking up. "Seven of us."

Tex, Trace, Otis, Luke, Bryce, Harry, Belle.

"Not eight?" Bryce asked, with a grin, and Adam's gaze flew back to Otis.

Eight would be OJ.

Otis's jaw tightened, and he chose not to answer.

"So Trace picked up on the fact that this charity concert will all be previous songs," Adam said, moving things along. "I don't know what condition the recording studio is in, but Morris assures me that it's functional and ready to be used, and he says he thinks you guys would only have to practice a couple of times a week to have those twelve songs ready to go in two months."

"I can have these twelve songs ready to go tonight," Luke said. A beat of silence hit the table, and then every man there started to laugh.

Adam smiled, something he rarely did during a business meeting, but listening to the brothers fill his house with joy simply got to him.

"Great," Adam said as they quieted. "We know you're retired." He shot a look over to Bryce. "But everything is more expensive these days, from the feed Bryce needs for his rescues, to gas to go pick up the horses he finds. He and Kassie are both about to have a baby, and he doesn't want Rising Sun to suffer any more than it already has."

"What's the goal for the charity concert?" Trace asked.

Bryce leaned forward and looked past Harry to his uncle Trace. "I deliberately didn't set a goal," he said. "Because I'm not sure what's reasonable."

"I told him I thought we could get six figures," Harry said.

"And all of that is going into horse rescue ranches?" Trace asked. "Or your ranch?"

Bryce swallowed, a hint of nerves in his expression. "No, I thought we could do fifty-fifty," he said. "Rising Sun would take fifty percent of the profits, and we could collaborate on finding another ranch or horse rescue operation—or two or three—that could use the rest."

Trace nodded, and smaller conversations broke out among men sitting next to one another. Adam simply listened, hoping his app would get all of the voices and be able to distinguish them. In the end, he finally raised his hand and said, "Let's come back together and take a preliminary vote. Nothing has to be decided today."

He glanced over to the clock in the kitchen. "But I do have another appointment I need to get to."

Thankfully, no one asked him what else he had going on in his life. Surely he wasn't meeting with another client, but they didn't know if he had to go to the dentist, or the doctor...or coffee with Joey.

Tex had thrown his folder down long ago, and he said, "I'll take any opportunity I can to play with my son. And this is for a good cause; I vote yes."

"I need a new guitar," Trace said. "But barring that, I think I can do it."

Morris leaned back in his chair and folded his arms, his expression absolutely neutral. Adam tried to mimic him as he looked to Luke, who wore a frown.

"I was going to do winter camping with my kids this year," he said.

"So it's a maybe," Tex said. "Otis?"

"I've already got the song half-written," Otis said. He

pushed his folder into the middle of the table, and he clearly would not be taking it with him. "And I suppose I can talk to OJ about playing with us."

Bryce whooped, and Harry started to laugh.

Before things could get too out of hand, Adam stood up to end the meeting. "Thank you guys for coming," he said. "If you have any concerns or questions, feel free to text me privately. I want to make sure this is exactly what we *all* want."

He looked over to Luke, who hadn't said yes, no, or maybe—at least not from his own mouth.

"This is a great transition," Morris said. "It'll teach Adam how to work with each of you individually *and* plan a concert *and* work with streaming services."

Adam had done all of that with Harry, but there were definitely more personalities here to deal with than he was used to. The men stood up, and they took their sweet cowboy time leaving his house. So much so, that by the time Adam left, he was rushing to get to Joey's grandparents' condo, where she lived, on time.

He pulled up and bustled down the sidewalk, his phone out, as several texts had come in since he'd left his house on the other side of town: something from a potential client that he hadn't signed with, a couple of texts from Bryce and several from Harry—one about playing a new song with Belle, doing a solo, and then a trio with him, OJ, and Bryce.

At this point, Harry was going to be the death of Adam. He ignored all the messages and went to the ground-floor unit that Joey had specified.

He knocked on the door, expecting her to open it a moment later and step outside without letting him meet her grandparents. He had no idea what she'd told them, but she had allowed him to come pick her up, and that alone had surprised Adam.

It took several seconds for the door to open, and when it did, the beautiful blonde that had dominated Adam's thoughts for the past several days did not stand there. Instead, Cecily Young smiled at him and said, "Oh, hello, Adam."

"Hello, ma'am." He reached up as if he would tip his cowboy hat at her, though he didn't wear one. Now that he would be a permanent resident of Wyoming, he figured he better get one, and he'd been planning to do that this weekend.

"I'm coming, Grams," Joey called from somewhere in the house, and a moment later she rushed out of the hallway and joined her grandmother at the front door. She wore a beautiful brown dress with white lace accents along the arms, hem, bodice, and waist, and Adam could not tear his eyes from her.

"Everything's in for dinner," Joey said, a little breath-lessly. "And I'll be back in plenty of time to shred the chicken and make the noodles." She smiled at her grand-mother and swept a kiss along her cheek.

"Okay, dear," Cecily said, and then she trained her eyes on Adam again. "Will you be joining us for dinner, Adam? You should. Joey makes the best cream cheese chicken in the world."

"She sure does," a male voice yelled from further in the house.

Joey smiled over her shoulder and shook her head. "Grams, he can't stay for dinner."

Adam took it as a challenge, and he looked from Joey to Cecily and back to Joey, trying to figure out what to say.

"Of course he can," Grams said. "He doesn't have to work in the evening, now that he's working for your daddy and uncles. Do you, Adam?"

No, he did not. Adam swallowed. In the end, he found that he couldn't lie to Joey's grandmother, and so he shook his head. "No, I don't have to work tonight."

"Great. That's settled." Cecily gave Joey a little nudge, and she practically fell out of the condo to join Adam on the sidewalk. "We'll see you both for dinner then."

She started to bring the door closed, and Adam hooked his arm through Joey's and backed up, gently tugging her with him. He had no idea what had just happened, but joy and rejoicing moved through him that his coffee date would be a little longer than he'd planned.

5

Joey's adrenaline seemed to spike a little higher with every step she took. She had planned to meet Adam at the end of the sidewalk leading to her grandparents' condo, not to have him come all the way to the door. She knew her grandmother well enough to know that Grams would extend the dinner invitation that she had—but she hadn't known how Adam would respond.

He'd seemed very unsure at first, and he'd looked to her a couple of times. Joey could admit her mind had gone blank, and she'd left him to his own devices.

"It's okay if you cancel on dinner," she said.

"Do you want me to cancel on dinner?" he asked.

"It's up to you," she said. "I just mean, you don't have to feel like you have to come. It's chicken in a crockpot with some noodles. It's not that good."

He chuckled, but when Joey looked at him, he barely

had a smile on his face. She didn't think she'd ever seen him smile, and she found it quite the feat to laugh without doing so.

"You went to the Culinary Institute in New York City," he said. "I'm sure your chicken and noodles is extraordinary."

"You still don't have to come eat it," she said, frustrated with herself and the conversation. "Grams was just being nice."

"Was she?" Adam led her off the curb and over to a deep blue luxury SUV. Of course.

She'd managed to find out from Momma that Country Quad was paying Adam a million dollars a year to live in small-town Wyoming and manage their careers. She cast a glance over to her tan sedan, hoping Adam never had to see her drive it.

"I don't mind coming to dinner," he said. "But if it makes you uncomfortable, then I won't. I could make something up." He leaned closer, something dangerous riding in the air between them now. "Though my momma taught me not to lie."

Joey scoffed, because surely Adam had reached an age where he didn't consider what his mother thought of him. He opened her door for her and stood back so she could get in.

"You might not want to spend that much time with me," she said. "Isn't that why you started with coffee?"

The playful glint in his eyes extinguished, his jaw turning hard. "I suggested coffee," he said. "Because I always need a mid-afternoon pick-me-up, and I know you work two jobs." He nodded toward the door. "And secondly, I thought *you* might not want to spend that much time with *me*. So if you don't, just say so. I'm not into playing games."

Joey lifted her chin, energy buzzing through her veins like wildfire. "Good," she said. "Neither am I." She got in the car, and Adam closed the door behind her. She watched him walk around the front of it, a frown between his eyes and him muttering something to himself.

He got behind the wheel and said, "Look, I'm sorry. Sometimes I sound really harsh when I don't mean to."

"It's all right," she said. "Maybe I can...." She paused and thought for a moment, trying to find a way to say what she wanted without being dismissive or rude. "Maybe I can decide after we get coffee if I want you to come to dinner or not."

His jaw twitched just once. "Fair enough." He backed out of the space he'd parked in, and Joey expected him to take her back into town to Daily Grind. Her grandparents lived on the edge of the center of town, and it was only five minutes away. Instead, he headed south, and a slip of nerves moved through Joey.

"Where are we going?" she asked. "I don't really care. I'd just like to know."

He glanced over to her. "There's a great coffee shop that just went in on the south highway," he said. "It's called Sip and Stay. They have a cute little storefront and lots of tables inside."

She nodded and looked down at her phone. She didn't

need to check to make sure that her location was turned on. She reminded herself she didn't live in New York City, and Adam wasn't going to drive into the wilderness and do something he shouldn't. She looked up again, the brilliant blue autumn sky greeting her.

"My daddy just taught me to be vigilant," she said. "Especially when I lived in the city. I promised him I'd pay attention to what was around me and who I was with—and always know where I was going." She looked over to Adam and flashed him a small smile. He took it, but didn't return it.

"I've been back for a while, but it's still a habit." She gave a light laugh. "I did date a guy with a serial killer name once."

Adam blinked at her, clear shock running through his eyes. "Of course," he said. "I should have told you. I apologize."

Everything about him screamed professional and buttoned up, and Joey wondered what it would take to get him to relax and loosen up and show her who he really was. Since he'd opened the date with a no-games rule, she swallowed, trying to decide if she could say what she really wanted to.

They drove in silence with a quiet radio playing in the background, and just as he pulled into the parking lot at Sip and Stay, she found her courage.

"You know, you can be yourself around me," she blurted out. "You're not my band manager and I'm not your client."

He looked over to her as he came to a stop right there in

the middle of the driveway of the parking lot. "Am I treating you like a client?"

"Yes," she said simply. "A little bit."

"I didn't mean to do that," he said. He hung his head as his shoulders and hands and everything about him softened. "I guess I'm always just a little keyed up. And I just had a two-hour long meeting with the band and Harry and Bryce and then the dinner invitation." He sighed. "I don't know. I'll try to relax."

She smiled at him again as he raised his eyes to hers. "Is this something other people have told you—that you need to learn how to relax?"

"Maybe," he said.

She giggled and reached to tuck her hair behind her ear. "Oh, I don't think there's a *maybe* anywhere in that, Mister Harmon."

He chuckled too, and when Joey looked this time, he wore a smile. Oh, it was beautiful and glorious, and she wondered how much light it would beam out when he finally unleashed the full power of it on the world.

"You know what you need?"

"What?" he asked.

She reached over, feeling flirtatious and bold and so unlike herself. She brushed her hands through his hair, swooping it to the side where it already went. Pure shock coursed through his eyes, stinging through Joey as well.

"You need a cowboy hat," she said. "Every man worth his salt in Wyoming owns a cowboy hat."

"Do they?" he asked, that grin appearing again. "Well, as

it so happens, Miss Young, I was planning to buy one this weekend."

Giddiness romped through Joey like a herd of wild horses. "Oh, I want to go with you," she said. "In fact, we should go this afternoon. Then you can wear it tonight at dinner and use it to hide your face when Grams or Gramps asks you something you don't want to answer." She giggled again. "That's what cowboys do, you know. The hat has many uses."

He looked over to the coffee shop and then into the rearview mirror, and finally eased his foot off the brake. He parked several spots down and turned to look at her.

"I want to get coffee first," he said. "And then I might take you up on going cowboy hat shopping together. Maybe then I won't get taken advantage of and walk out of there looking like a fool."

Joey didn't think Adam could ever look like a fool, but she buttoned that up and simply smiled at him as she got out of the car. Adam met Joey at the front bumper, his movements so natural as he reached for her hand and secured it in his. He ducked his head again, and oh, the man definitely needed a cowboy hat.

Joey managed to keep her smile contained, though she had not dated a lot and didn't really know how to act around a man she liked as much as she did Adam.

They went into Sip and Stay, and Joey paused only two steps in, taking in the atmosphere. "You were right," she said, plenty of awe in her voice. "This place is amazing."

Shades of blue hung on the windows and in all the art

on the walls—coffee cups and mugs and traveler containers. One framed picture showed animals sitting at a table, chatting and sipping coffee, the bison, antelope, and foxes all sitting and sipping together. The tables boasted cream with hardwood chairs, which brought together an inviting atmosphere with the rugged mountains where they lived.

"I want to come here every day," she said.

Adam chuckled and took her toward the ordering counter. "We actually want our coffee to go," he said. "Is that doable?"

"Yes, sir." The woman there smiled at him. She had snowy white hair with a dark root shaved short on one side, where it hung long on the other. She glanced over to Joey and said, "Oh, hello, Joey."

"Hi, Louisa." Joey smiled at her mother's friend. "I didn't know you'd opened this place."

"Turns out coffee sells better than tea," she said. "At least in Wyoming."

"Probably helps that the place isn't full of cats," Joey said, and thankfully, Louisa laughed.

"I honestly don't know what I was thinking." She smiled over to Adam. "What'll you two have?"

She didn't seem to think it was weird that Joey was there with Adam at all, but part of Joey rioted that her parents might find out about this date before she told them. Of course she'd said nothing, and she'd reasoned it away, because she wouldn't have told them about a first date with anyone, not just Adam.

"I want the extra-large Americano, please," Adam said, and he turned to Joey, his eyebrows raised.

Joey glanced up to the menu, which seemed pretty standard for coffee fare. "I'll have a mocha latte," she said. "With a drip of mint."

"Mint mocha latte," Louisa repeated. "Extra-large Americano. Can I interest you guys in any pastries?" She moved down a step and indicated the case there. "We have cherry focaccia today, as well as a pistachio croissant, and it looks like we only have one of our orange scones left."

Joey's mouth watered, and she said, "I would love the croissant, please."

"Nothing for me," Adam said, already pulling his wallet out of his back pocket. He wore black slacks and a polo the color of a pale tangerine whip that Joey had once made to go with a duck breast in one of her classes. The polo had four buttons, and he had three of them done up. He wore black loafers with the pants, and he seriously could have been an alien who'd crashed here in the Teton Mountains while on the way to LA.

The thought made Joey smile as Adam paid and Louisa set about making their orders. She collected napkins while Adam went to get the raw sugar packet he wanted.

"Do you really want to go cowboy hat shopping?" he asked.

"There is nothing I want more," Joey said, glancing over to him.

"You know her?" he asked next.

"I grew up here," Joey said. "I left for a year to go to

Wyoming State, and then I went to New York City to the Culinary Institute for a year. So yes, I know her—and probably every other person in town."

She smiled, though that wasn't quite true. "My stepmother owns a bookshop on Main Street." She raised her eyebrows, clearly asking him if he knew that.

Adam nodded. "Yes. I've been in there and bought some books for my nieces for Christmas."

"She knows a lot of people who own shops, which is how I know them," Joey said. "Plus, I work for Pork and Beans, and we do a lot of catering, and that puts me in contact with a lot of people as well."

"And do you like people?" Adam asked.

"Yeah," Joey said, genuinely. "I actually do. I know I might seem quiet, but—"

"I wasn't saying you were quiet," Adam said.

Joey blinked and tried to figure out what he *was* saying. Her family was so large that if she wasn't doing the worm on stage during a country music concert, she could be considered quiet.

"You like cooking?" he asked next, and Joey nodded.

"I love cooking. I love reading. I love soaking up the sunshine. I'm basically an indoor cat." She laughed and glanced over to him. "You seem like more the outdoor type."

Near the end of October, he'd have spent all summer outside, and his forearms did bear a tan to indicate as much. "When I have time, I can admit I like to go for a hike," he said. "This part of the country is so beautiful, and I wasn't sure how long I would be here."

"Do you know how long you'll be here now?" Joey asked.

Adam lifted his gaze to meet hers. "I think I reckon I'll be here for a while now," he said. "My contract with Country Quad is three years, and then we'll renegotiate after that."

Joey nodded, her chest suddenly tight with the mention of her father's band. "And...." She let the word hang there, glancing over her shoulder to see where Louisa was in their coffee prep. One cup sat on the counter ready to go, and it looked too big to be her mint mocha latte.

"How do you feel about...?" She couldn't seem to string more than two or three words together. She finally exhaled, boxed her shoulders, and looked him straight in the face. "I'm not saying we're going to start dating or anything, but let's say we do. What are we going to do about my dad?"

Adam blinked at her, his eyes widening a little bit. Then he leaned forward, and with his lips practically brushing against her cheek, he murmured, "I'll follow your lead on that, Joey. We'll do whatever you want."

"Joey," Louisa called, and Adam stepped back and turned away in one fluid movement. Joey had no idea what she wanted when it came to Adam Harmon, but it definitely involved buying a cowboy hat, going out with him again, getting to know him better, and telling her father about them...eventually.

6

The moment Adam walked into the hat shop, he
knew he was completely out of his league. He
already held Joey's hand, and now he squeezed it.
"Good thing you came with me," he said. "Look at all of
these hats."

She gave a light laugh, the sound of which would torture
Adam in his quiet moments, make him smile, and long to see
Joey again.

"How can I help you?" a man asked as he approached,
and he seemed to be wearing the just-right hat for his face,
shape, head, body, walk, and everything. The man looked
from Adam to Joey, and his smile bloomed bigger. "Oh,
howdy, Joelle."

"Hi, Randall," she said, and Adam would have to get
used to the fact that she knew everyone—at least the shop
owners.

"This man is going to be staying in town for a few years," she said. "And he thought he needed to get himself a cowboy hat." Joey grinned over to him, clearly enjoying herself. "I told him I'd come along for moral support."

"Oh, is that what this was?" Adam smiled at her and stepped forward to shake Randall's hand. "I'm Adam Harmon."

"Oh, sure. You're the new manager for Country Quad." Randall grinned like this was great news. Surprise shot through Adam, and he'd really need to get used to how things worked in a small town. He'd been working with celebrities in cities for a long time now, running errands and managing personal affairs, so that they could stay home without getting mobbed. He'd grown up in small-town Tennessee, but it had been a long time since he'd been there —a lifetime, really.

"Well, what style are you looking for?" Randall asked, and he turned to face his shop. It was more like an alley, only about twenty feet wide, with hats stacked from floor to ceiling along both sides.

"He's a band manager," Joey said, thankfully, because Adam had no idea what he was looking for. "He needs a celebrity cowboy hat, Randall—something sophisticated and high-end." She glanced over to Adam, her eyebrows raised. "Might cost him a little bit more, but people will notice."

Adam gave her a slight nod, because, yes, he could afford something that cost a little bit more. He went with Randall toward the back of the shop, and about two-thirds of the way there, Randall stopped and indicated the hats at eye level.

"What color are you thinking?"

Adam looked at Joey again, but she simply gazed back at him. "It's your hat, cowboy," she said, and oh, Adam liked that flirtatious tone of her voice. He'd only interacted with Joey on a couple of previous occasions, and neither one of them was lighthearted or all that fun. This new side of her made him feel sparkly and alive in a way that Adam hadn't felt in a while.

"I think black's a little too dark for me," he mused, taking in the array of cowboy hats again. "Maybe brown." He looked at a cream hat and kind of reached toward it before pulling his hand back. "Do real people wear these?"

"Oh, sure," Randall said, picking up the ivory-colored hat. "These are really popular for rodeos and what I call 'cowboy wannabes'."

Joey stifled a giggle and took a step away, feigning interest—Adam was sure—in a hat a few feet away. He could admit he was a cowboy wannabe, and he smiled broadly at Randall. "Well, that sounds like just what I need. I'm certainly no cowboy."

"There are plenty of things around here that'll cure that," Randall said good-naturedly. "Guitar lessons, horseback riding. Heck, I know several ranchers who are looking for hired help." He raised his eyebrows at Adam, and then shook his head. "Not that you're looking for a job."

"No, sir," Adam said in his crisp manager voice. "But I definitely think I want a brown cowboy hat."

"Well, we've got an array of browns." Randall led him over another foot or two, and sure enough, brown was the most common color on Planet Earth, and Adam cataloged at least ten different shades in the few seconds it took him to look left and right and survey the cowboy hats.

He'd never felt so lost in his life. "How do you know which one is the right one?" he asked.

"Well, I don't think you want a flat brim," Randall said. "You're not really wearing it to keep the sun off your shoulders. You're trying to make a fashion statement."

"That's right," Adam said, and in his mind, all he could think was *cowboy wannabe fashion statement*. What in the world was he doing here?

"I think this one," Joey said, easing back to his side, lifting a deep brown hat from the rack. It wasn't the darkest brown there was before the hats melded into blacks, but it definitely looked like good rich earth had been mixed with water, and this hat had been dipped in it for a while.

"That's a nice one," Randall said. "That's our Cowboy Gentleman line, and it's definitely on the higher end. It's good, pliable beaver pelt. And this one—" He flipped it over and examined something on the inside. "Yep, it's got a 50X. This is a real nice hat." He grinned and turned it back over, and Adam tried to figure out if he liked it or not.

"It's got the classic dented crown," Joey said, and Adam had no idea what that meant. She grinned at him and picked up another hat. "This one is more pinched in the front. See? It makes a triangle."

"Yeah, that's a V-shaped crown," Randall said. "This one is just your traditional dent, curled brim."

To his great relief, Adam could see the difference. He looked down the row and found one that looked square, and that was different still.

"We've got some curled brims with our standard dented crown," Randall said. "We've got some square brims as well." He moved down to another rack and picked up a different hat. Adam didn't like it nearly as much as the one in his hand. Could he really buy the first hat that was presented to him?

Adam had spent years choosing the things he liked most, and he rarely went with the first thing. He was very good at research and comparison, but he kept coming back to the Cowboy Gentleman hat in the color that Joey had chosen.

He took it from Randall and stepped over to a mirror. He told himself he'd worn hats before, and he settled it on his head. He transformed right before his own eyes, and Adam smiled.

"I think I just like this one," he said, moving it ever-so-slightly on his head, and met Joey's bright blue eyes in the mirror. If he wore plaid, he could definitely pull off the cowboy vibe, and maybe he'd finally fit in somewhere.

He checked out, saying goodbye to almost two thousand dollars for this single article of clothing. He told himself he'd spent that much before on something he wore to make himself into something he wanted to be, and he did want to be a cowboy.

He and Joey exited the small-town hattery to Main Street, and he looked across the road and found Beck's

Books sitting there. Something hammered through his body, and he suddenly understood why Joey had asked him what they were going to tell her dad.

"You didn't tell your folks about this date, did you?" he asked.

"Absolutely not," Joey said.

"Why?" he asked.

Joey flicked a look over to him, and then headed around the car to the passenger side. She got in while Adam put his hat in the back seat, and then he joined her up front.

"How old do you think I am?" she asked.

Adam wasn't into playing guessing games, but he said, "Mid-twenties."

She gave a half snort, half scoff. "I'm twenty-two, Adam. I'll be twenty-three in February."

"Great," he said. "I just turned thirty-one."

"And that right there is why I didn't tell my daddy about us," she said. "I wouldn't have anyway, to be clear. I usually wait until I've been out with someone several times and we decide that he's my boyfriend before I tell anyone."

"Oh, what does that take?" Adam asked, suddenly interested.

Joey gave him a severe look. "A lot more than a to-go coffee and a cowboy hat shopping spree," she said dryly.

She may only be twenty-two, but she could definitely hold her own, and Adam really liked that. He pulled away from the curb and drove past the bookstore. Joey didn't even look at it.

He gripped the wheel, the things he wanted to ask her storming through him. "I would like to take guitar lessons," he said. "Do you know anyone who does that?"

"Yeah," she said. "My dad."

"Besides him," Adam said with a laugh.

"Bryce," Joey said.

That actually sat really well with Adam, and he nodded. "I'll ask him if maybe he can teach me, but I fear he's going to be real busy with his ranch and his baby."

"That's true," Joey said. "But I would ask him for a reference. I never learned."

"Weren't interested in following your daddy's footsteps?" he asked.

Joey shook her head. "I'm not really the kind of person who likes the spotlight."

Adam looked over to her, the connection between them real and strong and fiery. "Me either."

She blinked at him, another scoff falling out of her mouth. "Are you kidding? You work with celebrities."

"As a *behind-the-scenes* assistant," he said. "Never the one out front." He turned his glare back out to the windshield so it wouldn't be aimed at her. "I grew up around celebrity, and I didn't want it."

"I think that might be the first thing we have in common," Joey said.

Adam scoffed now, but he realized quickly that Joey hadn't made a joke. "You really think we don't have anything in common?"

"Name something," she challenged.

"We both like coffee," he said without missing a beat. "We both like staying out of the spotlight. We both like living in a small town. We both like cooking." His grin appeared instantly on his face. "Okay, I can't tell a lie. That last one is totally false. I hate cooking."

Joey burst out laughing, and that had been Adam's goal. He wanted to make her laugh like that every day for the rest of her life, and then maybe she wouldn't look so sad standing in the shadows at her own family party, and he wouldn't find her crying around the corner of any more houses.

He made a turn and started back to her grandparents' place. "We're nearing the end here, Joey," he said. "You've got to tell me what you want."

She reached over and took his hand into hers. She covered it with her other one, and all ten of her fingers stroked along his, tracing his fingernails and running down the sides of his fingers, between them, and along the lines on his palm. Adam fought against the shivers threatening to shake his whole body with every touch of her skin against his.

"I think," she said, as he came to a stop at a red light. "I mean—if you asked me out again, I would say yes."

"So you want me to come to dinner?"

"If you're comfortable with it," she said.

"No," he almost barked. "That's not what we agreed. You said you would tell me if you wanted me there or not."

He looked over to her, not sure how long this particular light would hold them at a stop. She glared back, and oh, he could see the same stubbornness and headstrong qualities inside her that he possessed. Another thing they had in common.

"All right, cowboy," she said. "You can come to dinner— if you wear the hat."

7

Joey's ribs tap danced against her heart as she led Adam down the sidewalk to her grandparents' condo. She'd been living there for a while now, but she still couldn't call it her house. Adam hadn't asked her why she lived there, but something compelled her to tell him.

"When I dropped out of culinary school," she said. "I felt like a real loser. I couldn't do anything for more than a year at a time, and I didn't really know what I wanted to do with my life."

He looked over to her, that serious expression on his face. "I know that feeling," he said.

"Did you ever go to college?" she asked.

He shook his head. "No, and I literally just spent the last couple of years of my life getting paid to go to Walmart for your cousin." He cracked a rare smile, but he didn't let it get to megawatt status.

"When I moved home," Joey said, feeling safer and more comfortable with him now. "I didn't want to move back into my mom and dad's place. My biological mother lives up in Dog Valley with my grandmother, and she's been sick for a long time. I didn't want to move there either."

"I didn't know your mother lived up there," he said.

"Yeah, Dog Valley is nice."

"I need to buy my own place," he said. "And I'm gonna look everywhere. Dog Valley, Rusk, Coral Canyon."

Joey made a face and shook her head.

"What?" he asked with a slight laugh.

"Rusk?" She shook her head again. "Do you know how far away Rusk is?"

"It came up within the radius I put on the real estate website," he said. "Within an hour, I think." He glanced over to her, and she liked the way he seemed to ask her without words.

"Yeah, it's a good, solid hour," Joey said. "I don't think my uncles are going to be driving up to your place for meetings an hour away."

"You're probably right." He turned thoughtful and faced forward again.

"You're just renting right now?" Joey asked.

"Sure am," he said.

"I'm not even doing that." She sighed and looked up into the autumn evening sky. The sun had already started to set, and since the Tetons stood to the west, shadows fell over Coral Canyon early in the evening.

"My grandpa had just had surgery, and he needed help.

Gramps loves having me here, because I cook for them, so I'm helping her—and him. And they decorated my room and welcomed me into their condo."

"That's great," Adam said. "It's nice to have family."

"Do you have family?" she asked.

"In Tennessee," he said. "I've got a sister and a brother—twins—a couple years younger than me. They're both married, and they both have a daughter. Ellie's is three, and Ian's is two."

"Your nieces," Joey supplied, because he'd mentioned buying a book for them.

"Yes." Adam smiled over to her. "My mom still lives there too, but when my parents got divorced, my dad moved to Minnesota."

Joey wrinkled her nose. "Ew. Why would someone move north if they don't have to?"

Adam chuckled again, the sound deep and rich to match his voice. "I don't know," he said. "But that's where he is. Saint Paul." He nudged her, and since he stood several inches taller than her and had to outweigh her two to one, she stumbled slightly. He looped his arm around her and hauled her back into his side. "Sorry, baby doll, but I just wanted to point out that we live somewhere really cold." He reached up and pressed his palm to his cowboy hat. "For me, the biggest shock is the wind. My *word*, the wind never stops here."

Joey smiled, feeling like she had been plugged in and turned all the way to high. "The wind *is* murder," she said.

They reached the door a moment later, and Joey twisted

the knob, not expecting to find it locked. It wasn't, and in she went, relieved at the warmth that fought against the deepening chill outside—and yes, the wind. Adam tumbled into the condo after her and then pressed the door closed.

Both Grams and Gramps sat in the living room, each in their own recliner. The TV played with an old western, though neither of them watched it. Grams had her embroidery in front of her, and Gramps had curled back the front cover of his puzzle book. He looked up at her over the tops of his glasses and said, "Hey, you're back," in a voice rough as gravel. That was his happy voice, and Joey smiled at both of them as she unlooped her scarf from around her neck.

"Adam got something new," she said, and she smiled at him quickly before she turned her back on her grandparents and went into the kitchen. Her hands shook slightly as Adam told them about his new hat. "It's a Country Gentleman. I figured, since I'm going to be living here for a while, I should look the part."

"*Hoo-whee*," Gramps said, whistling. "That is a nice cowboy hat."

Joey knew her grandparents didn't have much money. She kept her head ducked and her hands busy as she lifted the lid on the crockpot to find the chicken finished and ready to shred. She collected a couple of forks and got that done while Grams entered the kitchen.

"I'll get the cream cheese out," she said.

"And that bottle of Italian dressing," Joey reminded her. She mixed up the chicken and added blocks of cream cheese before resetting the lid and turning the heat to low. She flipped on the sink and let it start running, as it took several seconds for her grandparents' water to turn hot. When it finally did, she filled a pot and set it on the stove.

Adam had taken a seat in the living room, and he seemed to be able to converse with Gramps just fine, though Joey had seen her own father come over and sit there in silence with his daddy. Adam may like to be out of the spotlight, but he was definitely a people person—just like her.

Twelve minutes later, she and Grams had the table set, a salad made, and the noodles perfectly al dente. "It's time to eat," she called into the living room, and she set a potholder on the table so Grams could bring the crock over.

She continued into the living room to help her grandfather out of his chair. He'd had some trouble with his kidneys in the last couple of years, and he'd slowed way down physically. She balanced him while he stood, and he grinned at her with all the love a grandfather could.

"How was your coffee date?" he asked.

"Gramps, Adam is sitting right there."

"So you can't say how it was?" Gramps raised his eyebrows and shuffled past Joey. "That might be a red flag, Roo."

Joey sighed, wiped her hands down the front of her apron, and turned to face Adam.

"Roo?" he asked, something playful dancing in his expression.

"It was really great, Gramps," she said, half-turning her back on Adam. "If it wasn't, I wouldn't have brought Adam back for dinner."

Gramps huffed, as if Joey's answer had come too late and wasn't good enough. She was used to him, so she turned her attention back to Adam.

"Yeah, Roo is my nickname," she said. "You know, like a joey is a baby kangaroo."

"Is Joey your full name?" Adam stood from the couch, and in any other circumstance, Joey felt certain that he would have drawn her into his arms in that moment. As it was, his normally graceful, elegant movement stuttered, and he sidestepped her instead of touching her.

"My name is Joelle," she said.

"So you have two nicknames," he said, as he went past her to help Gramps sit. While Joey marveled at the attention to detail Adam had, he brought over salt and pepper shakers, and then asked Grams if she needed anything else.

"Just the crock, dear," she said, practically beaming light out of every pore. "It's too heavy for me." She looked to the living room, where Joey still stood as if watching a movie of her life play out in front of her.

That crock was *not* too heavy for Grams. She'd gotten it out of the lower cupboard that morning, so that Joey could even make tonight's dinner. Grams smiled and gestured quietly for Joey to come join them.

She did, pausing at Gramps' side and asking, "You got everything, Gramps?"

"Yes," he whispered, and Joey sat down.

Adam put the crock on the table, surveyed everyone, and frowned. "What else?"

"Nothing," Joey said, giving him a quick smile. "Sit down."

He did, flashing her a quick look before he smiled at her grandparents. "Thank you so much for having me," he said. "I can't remember the last time I ate something homemade." He laughed and added, "Probably when I was out at Rising Sun, and Codi fed me."

Joey smiled too, because Adam sure seemed to know how to break the ice and make things less tense. He could play the part of relaxed, easygoing dinner attendee, but Joey thought he just absorbed all the tension and held it in his own body to be released later—or not at all.

"Was that recently?" Grams asked, and she picked up the tongs and started putting salad on her plate.

"Oh no," Adam said. "This was a few months ago. Bryce said she doesn't get around nearly as easily these days as she used to."

Gramps looked over to Grams. "We need to get out there, Jerry."

"And do what?" he asked. "We can't move around and do farm work either."

"I most certainly can do something," Cecily said. "And you can keep Bryce company in the stables while he feeds the horses." She nodded like that was set. "We'll go tomorrow."

Joey watched Gramps, who certainly didn't want to go up to Dog Valley and Bryce's ranch tomorrow, but he'd do whatever Grandma told him to do, Joey knew that.

Grams put down the salad bowl and looked at Joey. "Let's say grace."

Joey had not made a move toward any food, and neither had anyone besides Grams, so she simply smiled and reached for her grandfather's hand on her left, and then Adam's on her right. He looked like he didn't quite know what to do, but he managed. The last thing Joey saw before she bowed her head was him dropping his.

"Dear Lord," Grams said in her sweet, elderly voice. "We're so grateful for another good harvest season. We're grateful for mountains and the wide open sky and a good crisp air to breathe. We're grateful for our family and that we have enough to eat and that we have a warm place to sleep as this upcoming winter approaches. Bless those who stand in need that they will receive Thy bounty. Amen."

"Amen," Joey whispered, and she quickly pulled her hands back to herself. Then, she half-stood and picked up Gramps' plate to get him some noodles. She dished them up for everyone, even Adam, while he took charge of dishing out the Italian chicken Alfredo, which went over the top of the noodles.

Joey had made this multiple times in her life, and it was nothing special. It was easy and fast, and everyone loved it because it was creamy and salty and came with pasta.

"I've never had anything like this before," Adam said as he lifted his first forkful to his mouth. He took the bite, and his eyes widened and then rolled back in his head. He moaned in the most unprofessional way Joey had ever heard, which caused her to laugh.

"Holy cow," he said around his mouthful of creamy and salty chicken and noodles. "This is the best thing I've ever eaten." He scooped up another bite, a big one, and put the whole thing in his mouth.

Joey couldn't help feeling like a million bucks because of his praise, and her face heated as she watched him enjoy her food. Then she looked over to her grandmother.

Oh, no. Grams had seen something there, for she now wore a smile that looked like the cat had eaten the canary.

"So," she said, her voice higher-pitched than usual. "What's going on with you two?"

Adam choked on his enormous bite of chicken and pasta while Joey's face doubled in temperature. "Grams," she muttered. She shook her head. "What is with you and Gramps asking embarrassing questions right in front of Adam?"

Gramps continued to eat as if he'd done nothing wrong and had no interest in the conversation, but Joey knew he heard every word. He hung on them, actually, and he would definitely have an opinion.

She looked over to Adam, who now had a napkin covering his mouth as he continued to cough. When he finally quieted, Joey said, "We're nothing right now, Grams. Adam asked me to get coffee with him, so that he could explain something to me, which—come to think of it, he never did—" She shot him a look, then swung her attention right back to her grandmother.

"And then we went and bought him his first cowboy hat."

He ducked his head then, effectively using said hat to conceal his expression.

"So you're friends," Grams said, looking between Joey and Adam and back.

"Sure," Joey said. "We're friends."

"So it wasn't a coffee *date*," Gramps grumped.

"Gramps, did I tell you it was a coffee date?" Joey asked. "No, I did not. Maybe you two should just mind your own business. Have you ever thought of that, you Nosy Nellies?" She looked between Grams and Gramps, and neither of them seemed to care about her ire.

Grams squinted at her and then started to laugh. "All right, Joey, we won't ask any more embarrassing questions."

"Good," she said. "And you don't need to be saying anything to my daddy either. Remember how I'm an adult and can make my own decisions?"

"If we can't tell your dad, then there must be something going on," Gramps said.

"No, that's not what that means," Joey said. "And don't you think that *I* would like to be the one to tell everyone if Adam and I do date? I certainly don't need one of you to do it for me."

"She's right, dear," Grams said, as if Gramps had been the one who had brought this up in the first place. She reached across the table and patted Joey's hand. "Don't worry, dear, your secret is safe with us."

She looked over to Adam and nodded, and when Joey looked at him, her face once again flaming like hot lava bursting out of a volcano, she found the most adorable look of confusion on his face. If she didn't feel like dying of embarrassment, she may have started laughing.

Thankfully, Gramps said, "Oh, your grandmother called. She wanted to know if you were going to be up there on Halloween to hand out candy."

Joey had forgotten that her mother had asked her to come do that. "I'll call them," she said.

"That's what I told her," Gramps said.

Joey finally forked up a bite of her own dinner and put it in her mouth. She may make this faux chicken Alfredo and pasta a lot, but it was actually extremely delicious, and she found herself moaning the same way Adam had.

"See?" he said. "It's that good."

She grinned at him, hoping that she would have the opportunity to cook for him in the future. He didn't like it, and she did, and everyone deserved a home-cooked meal.

Didn't they?

Now she just had to figure out how to get him to ask her out again.

8

Adam set a kettle of water on the stove and lit the burner. Though Halloween still sat a couple of days away, it had started to get cold in Wyoming, and they were even predicting the first snowfall for next week. He'd been told that it had snowed much earlier in previous years, and he supposed he'd better count his blessings that this year, Mother Nature had decided to wait until November.

Adam could admit he did not possess very much patience, and it was something he was working on. He had two meetings today, one with a catering company that Morris wanted to hire for the first two concerts in December —one they would turn into OJ's birthday party, and the other Bryce's.

Adam checked his watch and then the clock on the microwave, noting that the representative he was meeting with from Pork and Beans was late. Irritation fired through him instantly, because Adam had very little tolerance for tardiness. He ran fifteen million details of his own life—and other people's lives—and yes, sometimes he had run a little bit late. Not very often, though.

He had a very narrow window to meet with the catering company, finalize the contracts, and go over the menus before he needed to meet with a woman named Diane Dodd. She was a realtor in town, and he wanted to get her going on the kind of property he wanted to buy.

Now that Adam knew he would be in Coral Canyon for at least three years, he wanted somewhere to call home. He wanted a big office right off the front door of his house, so that people could walk in and do business, and he wouldn't have to worry about having dishes in the sink. Perhaps with an all-cash offer, he could make the move before deep winter set in.

He wanted to live a more normal life, and in the few days since he'd taken Joey for coffee and eaten dinner with her grandparents, it had become apparent all of the things that "regular people" had that he didn't. He smiled just thinking about Joey, and he picked up his phone, remembering that she had texted about a half-hour ago.

Leaving the other night had been filled with awkwardness, as Adam had wanted to ask her out again, but didn't want to do it in front of her grandmother and grandfather. He hadn't known if he could hug her or touch her, and he'd ended up literally patting her arm and walking out like a fool.

They'd been talking since, but Adam had been busy with Morris as they laid the groundwork for the five-concert series that Country Quad had agreed to do. Yes, even Luke, who'd texted Adam early the next morning with a few simple words that Adam could only imagine him grunting: *Fine, I'll do the concert series.*

He'd prepared contracts for each member of Country Quad to sign, but they hadn't done that yet. He'd met with Bryce, who'd said that he would find at least one more horse rescue operation to donate the charity funds to, and Adam had asked for a reference for a guitar teacher.

He'd been to Jackson Hole, where he'd bought a guitar, a stand, and the book that the teacher had instructed him to get. He'd been busy in a whole new way—the way someone was when they got a new job and were trying to figure out how to do it.

Adam also wanted to figure out how to live like a person who belonged at the family dinner table with Joey and her grandparents. He wanted art on his walls that represented him, towels he picked out because he liked them, and yes, he'd even considered taking a cooking class. Because normal people made their own meals, right?

He looked down at his phone, his thoughts all over the place today. Joey had texted a little bit ago with something funny about her family. *My momma loves animals, and we've had at least two dozen over the years. OJ has picked up on that, and he's always begging for a new cat or dog.*

She'd included a couple of emojis of cats, dogs, and even

a snake. Adam remembered why he hadn't responded. He didn't know how.

Was he supposed to ask her if she liked dogs or cats? He already knew she didn't have any pets, and Adam looked up as realization streamed through him. Now that he'd be living in Coral Canyon, semi-long term, he could get a pet.

His mind whirred with what kind of pet he might want to get. Something that required him to come take care of it at night, he knew that. At the same time, if he got an animal, especially a baby one, he might be chained more to the house than he would like.

Indecision rained through Adam, and he hated how he knew exactly what to do for his clients, but when it came to himself, he was always second-guessing.

"Where is this person?" he grumbled, realizing that the caterer was now ten minutes late. How long did he have to wait? He didn't need to meet with Diane for another fifty minutes, but anxiousness streamed through him that it wouldn't be enough time to finalize contracts, go over the needs of the band and crew for the concert, and choose a menu.

He swiped away from Joey's text to Shawn Avery's. He'd said he would not be able to make the meeting, but he would send someone who could handle everything Adam needed. He'd just tapped to call the man when his doorbell rang. Relief flooded through him, and he told himself to chill out. This was not high-stakes-LA or country-music-star-Nashville. This was small-town Coral Canyon catering, and who cared if he had to reschedule or couldn't get everything done in one meeting?

He didn't have anything else on his calendar, and no one from Country Quad would be texting him to find out details of the meeting within moments of it finishing.

Adam simply had a very hard time relaxing—and no, Joey was not the first person who had told him that. His mom, his dad, his sister, and literally every girlfriend he'd ever had had said the same thing.

He left his phone sitting on the dining room table, along with his notes for the catering company and the real estate agent. He opened the door and started to say, "I thought you'd never—" when he realized the person standing on his front step was none other than Joelle Young.

"Joey," he said, his attitude and mood morphing immediately. She wore a bright pink parka that looked like it had sprinkles covering it. No, not sprinkles—glitter. She wore skinny jeans that disappeared into a white pair of puffy boots that she'd obviously never worn outside before. That, or she bleached them every time she did, because they were so blindingly white that they made Adam smile.

His eyes zoomed back to her. "What are you doing here?"

"This is your house?" she asked, seemingly as surprised to see him as he was her.

"Yes," he said. "My rental, at least."

She lifted a navy blue binder. "I'm here for Pork and Beans. Shawn said it was for catering?"

Adam blinked, the pieces finally lining up together.

"Yeah, you're in the right place." He backed up. "Come on in."

Nerves ran through him that she would see where he lived. She would know how impersonal it was—how bland and boring—and she might attribute those same characteristics to him.

He cleared his throat as she went by, the scent of her hair or her perfume fruity and fun—and reminding Adam that she was almost a decade younger than him. The bright pink glittery coat probably should've done that as well. He smiled as he closed the door behind her and turned to follow her.

"Let me guess what your favorite color is," he said, a laugh following it.

Joey had gone down the hallway to the back of the house, and she turned to face him. "Are you making fun of my coat?" Her smile appeared, and Adam could not look away from her mouth.

"It's pink, isn't it?" He reached for her hand and realized how icy cold it was when she let him hold it. "Did you ride your bike over here?"

"No," she said. "But not all of us have heated steering wheels in our cars." She unzipped her coat, and Adam hastened to take it from her.

"I like the coat, Joey," he said, in all seriousness. "And listen, I've been meaning to text you."

Joey looked around his living room with its standard beige couch, a stand with the TV, and no window coverings.

She met his eyes for a moment, then continued her visual inspection of his space by looking into the kitchen.

"You have?" she asked. "And what were you planning on texting me?" She brought her gaze back to his, and oh, Adam found the challenge there that had also resided in her voice.

"Well," he said, and he ducked his head, his eyes landing on those boots. "I really like these boots. Where do you get something like this?"

"New York City," she said. "They were a splurge buy, but they're actually really useful in Wyoming."

He looked up at her again. "Normally, I would have asked you out at the end of our last date, but *that* was pretty awkward. And then I've been kind of busy getting this concert series going."

"Yes, I didn't know Country Quad was doing a concert series." Her tone carried an icy coolness that made Adam's pulse skip over itself.

"Joey." He grinned at her. "Are you upset your daddy didn't tell you about the concert series?"

She folded her arms over the rustic orange sweater she wore, and he took that for a *yes*. He chuckled. "So you're mad when he doesn't tell you something, but you didn't tell him about our coffee date—oh, wait."

Adam chuckled and backed up. He moved down the table and pulled out a chair for Joey. "That wasn't a coffee date—at least that's what you told your grandpa."

Joey eyed him as she moved to take the seat. "You have

to admit, it wasn't very date-ish." She held her head high as she sat down.

"I bought you coffee and a croissant," Adam said.

"And then you ate dinner at my grandparents' house."

"We went cowboy hat shopping." Adam rounded the table to take the seat opposite kitty-corner to her.

"And you're not even wearing it."

Adam grinned because he liked this banter between them. He liked that Joey could come back at him, as it showed she had a quick mind and a good sense of humor.

"I've been wearin' it to all my meetings with your uncle," he said.

"And now you're dropping G's." She grinned at him. "*Wearin'* it." She set her arms on the table and opened the binder. "Shawn said you didn't have much time."

Panic ran through Adam. "I was asking you out," he said. "Do you want to skip past that?"

Joey looked up from the binder with only her eyes, her head not moving at all. "Go on then."

"If what we did the other afternoon wasn't a date, fine," Adam said. "I'll plan something really amazing for our first date. Are you free on Friday night?"

It was only Monday, and Adam kicked himself for suggesting the weekend. Joey shook her head anyway. "No," she said. "I'm catering an event that night."

"What about Thursday?" he asked.

"It's Book Club at the bookstore," she said. "And I already told my momma I'd work it."

Familiar frustration started to build within Adam. "Wednesday?"

"Halloween," she said. "I'll be up in Dog Valley."

He sighed and looked away. "Sounds like you're making things difficult on purpose." He looked over to her, and she simply grinned at him.

"This week, I'm not working Saturday at all."

"Saturday it is," he said, seizing onto the idea. "Do you want a day date or an evening date?"

She reached over and touched his hand, which sent a sizzling sparkle through his whole body. "You decide," she said. "And text me. I'm sure it will be great."

She looked down at the binder. "Now I'm pretty sure you were irritated when I got here, because I was late, which I can assure you, is not my fault. Sean told me about the appointment at two o'clock."

"We were supposed to meet at two," he said.

"Which is why I was late," Joey said. "I ran out the moment he gave me the binder and the address, and I got here as quickly as I could."

"All right," Adam said. "I may have been a little irritated, but I'm not anymore." He reached over and took her hand in both of his. "It's good to see you, Joey."

She nodded to the left. "I see a guitar over there. Did you find a teacher already?"

"Yes," he said. "We've had one lesson on Saturday."

"And you didn't text and tell me about it?" Her eyes landed on his, and Adam felt properly chastened.

"I...." He trailed off, not quite sure what to admit. "I

thought maybe you didn't care," he said. "About the mundane intricacies of my life."

"Well, if we're going to start dating," Joey said. "Then that's what you share—the mundane intricacies of your life. If you can't share those with me, who can you share them with?" She lifted her eyebrows, and Adam conceded the point.

"So Saturday," he said. "I want to go out to breakfast, because Harry's been telling me about this really great place." Secretly, he thought a breakfast date could turn into a lunch date, which could turn into a dinner date. It could be an all-day date with Joey, and he wanted to spend as much time with her as possible.

"What's this really great place?" Joey asked.

"Brunch House," he said. "Have you been?"

She shook her head. "No, but I've heard it's good."

"Great," he said. "Is nine too early?"

She belted out a laugh and said, "Oh, honey, I get up every day at three-thirty to make it to the bakery by four. Nine is practically lunchtime."

He laughed with her, and he felt more normal than ever now that he had a date on the calendar with the beautiful Joelle Young.

9

*C*ousin movie night sometime next week?

 Joey looked at Harry's text, already feeling a bit overwhelmed with her schedule. She wasn't sure why; she'd been working the two jobs, helping her grandparents, and hanging out with her cousins for months now.

She passed the sign welcoming her to Dog Valley, and Joey suddenly knew why she felt overwhelmed.

She hated coming to Dog Valley. She didn't enjoy her time with her mother that much, but her sense of duty would not allow her to simply stop visiting.

She had no set schedule for when she needed to be here, other than before the trick-or-treaters came. So Joey pulled over and picked up her phone. It would be far easier if she could have a dynamic conversation with Harry, so she tapped to call him.

"Hey, Joey," he said jovially, and why shouldn't he be? He had an amazing fiancée, millions of dollars in the bank, celebrity status, and a brand-new house. Yes, everything seemed to be coming up roses for Harry and Belle.

Joey bit back on the bitterness, knowing that Harry had worked incredibly hard to be where he was, and Joey truly did not resent any of his success. He just seemed to have so many things figured out that Joey didn't.

"Hey," she said. "I just thought it would be faster if I could call."

"You're the busiest of us," he said. "That's why I asked you first."

She nodded, feeling a bit guilty. "I usually work every evening except Wednesdays," she said.

"That works for us." He paused, and then hissed, "I'm not going to ask her that," clearly not talking to her.

Joey's heartbeat tensed inside her body.

"You ask her."

Scuffling came through the line, and then Belle said, "Hey, Joey," in her sweetest, kindest voice.

"Hey, Belle," Joey said, smiling because she liked Harry's fiancée a lot. "What do you want to ask me?"

Belle hesitated, and then said, "Um," in such a way that Joey already knew what would come out of her mouth. She waited anyway, because if they wanted to know what was going on with her and Adam, they *did* have to say it out loud.

"Harry said he saw you and Adam last week when

Morris and Leigh were moving, and...and I guess we're just wondering what's going on there."

Joey sighed. "Yeah, I guess I'm wondering that too."

"So you're *not* seeing him?" Harry asked.

"Am I on speaker?"

Harry only chuckled, and Joey laughed too. "You're supposed to tell someone when they're on speaker, Harry."

"You're on speaker," Belle said.

Joey looked out her side window and then through the windshield again. "I don't really know if I'm seeing Adam or not," she said. "I definitely wouldn't say we're dating, though...."

"Oh, boy." Harry chuckled. "There's a *though?*"

She smiled at the incredulity in his voice. "We got coffee last week. He said he was going to explain about how he came to be the band manager, but he never really did, and then Grams got her hooks into him and invited him for dinner."

"Oh, Grams will do that," Harry said with a chuckle. "That's not really a date."

"That's what *I* said," Joey said, feeling vindicated. "He did ask me out for brunch on Saturday. And I said yes, but I obviously haven't gone yet. So seeing him? Dating? I would have to say no to both of those."

"But you have a date with the man," Harry said, and he sounded pretty happy about it.

"I have a date," Joey said.

"Do you like him?" Belle asked.

"Would I go out with him if I didn't like him?"

"She's not like that," Harry said. "That's exciting, Joey."

"Is it?" she asked. "Are you okay with me going out with him?"

Harry full-on belly laughed, and the longer it went on, the more foolishness Joey felt. "Why are you laughing like that?" she asked.

"Adam's a grown man," Harry said. "He can do whatever he wants. He doesn't need my permission to go on a date."

"Even if it's with me?" Joey asked.

"Even if it's with you," he said. "You're my cousin, not my sister."

She smiled and ducked her head. "How many dates have I told you about?"

Silence answered, and Belle finally giggled. "I'm guessing none," she said.

"Zero," Joey said. "I have told Harry exactly *zero times* about the men I go out with. I just want you to know that that tradition is going to continue."

Harry huffed, clearly not happy with that answer. "Okay, fine," he said. "But cousin movie night on Wednesday?"

"Cousin movie night on Wednesday," Joey confirmed. "Thanks for asking me first, Harry. I really do like coming."

"I know," he said. "I like having them."

"We'll talk to you later," Belle said, and she and Harry started a mini-argument about whether they should have asked Joey about Adam at all before they managed to hang up.

Joey giggled to herself, looked out the windshield, and with a much lighter heart, continued to her mother's. She'd recently turned fifty, which wasn't that old, and yet she'd been chronically ill since Joey was eight years old. She didn't leave the house, and her own mother had moved in to help care for her about a decade ago now.

Heaviness settled over Joey's shoulders as she got out of the car and walked up to the front door. The sky had turned a menacing shade of gray, and Joey wished she was home in her pinkified room with a good book. Then Adam would text about the houses he'd seen that day, and she'd be warm and safe and flirting with him.

She didn't know why her mom couldn't simply put a big bowl of candy on the doorstep, and call it good. Apparently, she'd done that last year, and the candy and the bowl had all been stolen.

Joey didn't know why she cared. She could just turn out all the lights and not answer the door. How many people would really come trick-or-treating anyway?

The truth, which neither of them ever really spoke, was that Joey's momma knew she didn't like visiting. So she came up with reasons to get Joey to the house—something that would keep her busy, something where they didn't have to talk the whole time, something with a time constraint on it.

Joey could admit that she'd done similar things in the past, agreeing to come for the duration of a movie, or the Fourth of July concert broadcast on TV. She'd come to bring her mother dinner and cake for her birthday, but she had another appointment she needed to get to a couple of hours later. Their unspoken agreement had become two or three hours together, and not much more.

Handing out Halloween candy satisfied all of that, and Joey hitched a smile in place as she pushed into her mother's house.

"Hey, Momma," she called. "It's just me."

"Oh, Joey's here," Mom said fondly from the kitchen. Joey closed the door behind her, unsurprised to be greeted by a cat brigade. Her mother owned *five* felines, and they acted like her bodyguards whenever anyone came over, which, of course, no one but Joey ever did.

She crouched down to say hello to all the kitties, which gave her mother time to shuffle out of the kitchen. Joey straightened, shock running through her. "Wow," she said. "You cut your hair."

Her mother had resisted getting her hair cut for years now. She reached up and brushed her hand self-consciously down the back of her head. "Yeah," she said. "It was time, and I actually don't hate it."

"I love it," Joey said, with every sincere bone in her body. She took the two steps to her mom and took her face in her hands. "It looks so good. Did she color it too?"

She got all of her white-blonde, blue-eyed genes from her mother, who nodded. "You don't think it's too brassy?" she asked.

Joey shook her head, still marveling that her mother had made this change. "No," she said. "I think it looks great." She hugged her mother tight. "You look so good, Mom. It's *so* good to see you." And she meant it, when sometimes in the past she hadn't.

She stepped back, feeling sparkly and springy, and asked, "What did Grandma make for dinner?"

She had inherited her love of cooking from her grandmother, and growing up, she had enjoyed coming here because she always got to make something new and learn family recipes.

"She made your favorite, of course," Mom said. "Chicken pot pie with no carrots."

Joey grinned as she moved into the kitchen, where she found her grandmother tenting the tops of the individual chicken pot pies she'd made. "They're almost done," she said. "They're just getting a little bit too brown."

"They smell amazing," Joey said. "You didn't have to take the carrots out."

"You don't like the carrots," she said.

Joey couldn't deny that. "Who *does* like cooked carrots?" she asked, because she didn't think anyone did.

Grandma smiled and scanned Joey down to her puffy boots. "You're not wearing a costume."

"I brought it with me," Joey said. "I just need to change real quick."

"About fifteen minutes on the pies," her grandmother said, who also wasn't wearing a costume. "We've got the candy here, but your mother says you like to sort it."

Joey grinned, because she so did. Sorting things brought her far too much happiness, but she'd decided to embrace it. She hurried down the hall to the bedroom that was still made up for her, though she hadn't stayed here in a few years. She stripped out of her leggings and sweater, which she'd worn to work this morning at Cake Bites, and stepped into the black cotton dress that had angry, triangular fringes along the arms and hem. With a witch's hat and a little dab of black eyeliner to simulate a mole, Joey was ready to answer the door and hand out candy for the next couple of hours.

Back in the kitchen, she cut open the bags of mini Kit Kats, Snickers, and peanut butter cups. Her mother had bought good candy, and no wonder there would be kids at her doorstep.

Joey loved a Kit Kat as much as almost anything, and she got out a long rectangular serving tray with three compartments. She'd used this at Thanksgivings and Christmases past for cheese and crackers or veggie plates. Tonight, the Kit Kats went on the left, with the peanut butter cups on the right, as they both had orange packaging, and the Snickers went in the middle.

Satisfied with her arrangement of mini candy bars, she smiled over to her mother. "So what's new with you?" her mom asked.

Joey's first thought was Adam, but just like Harry, she'd never told her mother much about her love life. "Same old, same old," she said. "Though I'm catering Kimberly's wedding this weekend. On Friday."

Her mom shook her head sadly. "Can you imagine?"

"What?" Joey asked, her smile dissipating. "Getting married?"

"She's twenty-two years old," her mom said. "She's far too young."

Joey smiled. "Mom, you weren't that much older when you married Dad."

"No, I know," she said. "I just can't even imagine *you* getting married."

"No?" Joey asked, something defensive rising up inside her. "Because I'm so immature?"

"No, of course not," her mom said, suddenly backtracking. "That's not what I meant."

Joey certainly wasn't going to tell her about Adam now. No one had been happy when she'd dated Tim at Wyoming State, and she couldn't blame them. There was a known serial killer at large with that name at the time, though Joey hadn't realized that her mom thought she was too young to date and get married at all.

Thankfully, the doorbell rang, and then smaller hands knocked on it. Joey swept the platter of candy bars into her arms and said, "That's my cue," before she went to answer the door. Hopefully, this would be the start of a steady stream of trick-or-treaters, and she'd barely have time to enjoy her chicken pot pie with only peas before she had to leave.

After all, she didn't want to talk about how Kimberly was too young to get married, though she'd literally graduated from college a few months ago. Joey hadn't managed to do that, and she wondered if her mom thought she was as big of a loser as Joey thought she was.

Then a hissing, whispering thought in her mind

reminded her that Adam had not graduated from college either, and he certainly wasn't a loser. Warmth filled her even as the icy early evening air hit her in the face when she opened the door.

College was overrated, and so was waiting to get married when you found the love of your life. She wasn't sure if Adam could be that person. They hadn't even had their first date yet, but as she let the kids take as many candy bars as they wanted, Joey decided that dreaming had always been good for her soul, and Adam made her dreams that much better.

10

Adam pulled up to the fourth house in as many hours, ready for this day of looking at real estate to be over. At the same time, he'd seen and learned a lot of good things today. Number one, real estate in Dog Valley was far cheaper than Coral Canyon, and he got way more for his money. No wonder Morris had purchased land and built a house here, and Adam had since learned that his twin also lived in Dog Valley, and that Tex lived on the northwest side of town, closer to Dog Valley than the house where Adam lived now.

Luke had also moved to Dog Valley, which meant only Trace and Otis would have to make the drive for meetings, and Adam did not anticipate having very many of those anyway. Yes, Dog Valley had become a serious contender for his new home.

"This one looks great," he said to himself as he peered out the windshield at the house.

Diane, a woman in her sixties, had been trucking along beside him for the past several hours, going over listings, leading him through houses, sending off texts to real estate agents to get answers to any questions he had.

From the outside, this house definitely looked the nicest. It was two stories and done in a dark brick with black shutters. The front door was also black, and Adam didn't hate it.

The yard had turned the color of straw, and it ran back along one side of the house, while the other had an enormous cement parking bay for boats, toys, or an RV. Not that Adam had any of those things, but Diane said the owner of this house had built it specifically for all of the outdoor items he had. The three-car garage sat extra deep, as the current owner ran a construction firm and a handyman business, and he'd installed a workbench and a woodshop in his garage.

He'd seen pictures of the backyard, and to be honest, this house was far too much for Adam. It checked all of his boxes, though, and he got out of his SUV and joined Diane on the front sidewalk. "First impressions?" she chirped, something she'd asked him three previous times.

"I really like this place," he said. "It puts off a very...." He paused and looked back to the house. "It feels sophisticated, far more than the last couple of houses we've seen."

"Yes," Diane said. "I agree. *Sophisticated* is a great word for this house. You'll see those touches all throughout as well." She continued to talk about the interior finishes, from the soft-touch cabinets that had been painted a pale green—custom, apparently—to the hardwood floors, the quartz countertops, and the classic subway tiles in the kitchen, all bathrooms, and laundry room.

Adam had worked for celebrities in the past, and he understood what luxurious accommodations looked like and felt like. The moment he stepped foot inside the house, he knew he'd just entered a space like that.

Diane had told him in the office that sometimes places built by their owners, as handymen or construction workers, were the most jerry-rigged of all. But this place seemed immaculate. Every corner perfectly square, the rugs precisely placed and beautifully chosen to fit the decor. It was a mountain house with wood beams in the ceiling and one wall in the office made completely of blonde pine wood, but also modern, with cream paint on the walls and gray trim around the doors and ceiling.

"This would be the office," Diane said, and Adam stood in the middle of the room and turned in a slow circle.

"This is perfect," he said.

Diane shone like all the stars in the sky, as if she herself had built this house for Adam. She led him through the kitchen, the dining room, the living room, and the full bath that sat only steps down the hall. The master suite was as big as his entire floor in the house he rented now, and he could see himself retreating here with a cat—his pet of choice—and a recliner, a television, and his bookcase full of his beloved mystery novels.

The second floor held bedrooms, another great room,

and bathrooms, and they all seemed to have the exact same attention to detail, high-end finishes, and sophistication running through them.

"There's a basement as well," Diane said. "It's unfinished right now. The previous owner used it to store construction materials." She opened the door and showed the bare wood steps going down.

"Oh, I don't think I need to see the basement," Adam said. "I'm not even going to use the upstairs."

"It's an additional two-thousand square feet," she said, without taking a step down. "Completely open. You can design and finish it however you want."

Adam nodded, though he seriously did not see himself doing that. This house had everything else he could possibly want.

"Let's talk in here," Diane said, turning back toward the kitchen. "A storm has rolled in."

Adam nodded and went with her. The family that had owned this house had already moved out, and thus there was nowhere to sit—no bar stools, no dining room table, no couch.

"We can definitely pull more listings for you," she said. "It's a great time to be in the upper market where you are, as things have slowed down there quite a bit, and prices have fallen."

He nodded, because he'd heard all of this at their meeting on Monday.

"I still think you'd be happy in the lakeside community," she said.

Adam shook his head. "I don't want to be behind a gate," he said. "I've lived my whole life behind gates."

Diane pursed her lips but nodded. She had short blonde hair that had started to turn white, and sharp eyes that missed nothing. She made a check mark on her clipboard. "Well, there's definitely more houses here in Dog Valley, but I have to admit, this is probably the nicest one. Now, we could go up several hundred thousand dollars, and there are two or three homes here that are real showpieces."

Adam shook his head yet again, starting to feel a bit robotic "I can't imagine I'm going to need more house than this." He swept his arms wide. "*This* is too big."

She frowned and tilted her head. "It is everything you wanted, though. Big garage, front office, roomy spaces. You wanted mountains combined with contemporary charm. This is it."

"Yes," he said. "I did like the first house we looked at as well."

She looked back at her list. "That one seemed very 'neighborhoody' for you."

"Yes," he agreed. The neighbors were quite close, and he didn't mind, but he also wanted to have plenty of parking for when the Young brothers came for their meetings, and Adam really enjoyed his privacy. He wanted to sit on a back deck and sip coffee in his boxer shorts if he wanted to, and put in a hot tub that he sat in all winter long—and maybe he wouldn't wear a swimming suit at all.

He grinned at his scandalous thoughts, and then smiled at Diane too. "I think this is it."

"You want to put an offer in on this place?" she asked. "Now they've got it priced...." She flipped a page. "It's actually really reasonable—right at market value. I'm not sure I could get them down anymore, though it has been empty for three months."

Adam put his palm over her clipboard. "Diane, all cash. I want to move in as fast as possible."

She blinked at him, surprised. "You don't want to wait for an inspection even?"

"How long will an inspection take?" he asked. The window above the sink rattled, and both Adam and Diane looked at it. Yes, a storm had blown into town. He'd known it was coming as they'd been out and about, and he'd watched the sky darken and foam with every passing minute.

"I can usually get an inspector to come the very next day," she said. "I could probably have someone here tomorrow. I don't think you should buy a house without an inspection. Things can look really good on this side of the walls."

"Okay," he said. "I still want to put in an all-cash offer so I can move in as fast as possible. So if that means we speed along some aspects, then that's what it means."

"Well, they're not living here," she said. "So I can't imagine that they'll care when you move in. And you won't need a bank loan, so as soon as we can get things underwritten, you should be done."

"How long, do you think?" he asked.

Diane sighed and shook her head. "It's impossible to

know, Adam. Some people aren't as motivated to get deals done, but I'd like to say...two weeks."

"Two weeks," Adam said, his impatience already rearing inside him. "I suppose I can wait two weeks."

"I'll get the offer in," she said. "Right at asking...." She glanced at him, her eyebrows raised.

"Do you think that they would be more motivated to take an all-cash offer?" he asked. "Perhaps we could go lower because it's cash."

"Let me text Jonathan," she said, turning half away from him to do that, and Adam turned to survey the house again. It had beautiful bones and a pretty face, and Adam could already feel it seeping into his soul. He wasn't sure what that meant, because he'd made very few decisions with his heart in the past. He did trust his feelings, and he'd followed his gut a lot.

He once again thought of dinner with Joey's grandparents. He wasn't sure why that single experience had made such an impact on him, but it felt tattooed in his heart. Adam had not given much thought to prayer or religion or church in a great many years, though his mother was devout and attended services every week. He'd been brought up reading the Bible and serving others, but he'd given all that up the moment he'd left home.

A yawning, yearning hole opened up inside him, and Adam had no idea what it meant. He wouldn't know the first thing about going to church, and yet, something inside him pointed him in that direction.

"Jonathan thinks we can knock fifteen thousand dollars

off if we go in with all cash," Diane said, and Adam turned away from his thoughts, glad for the distraction.

"Let's do it, then," he said. "I don't want to be moving while it's snowing."

Diane nodded, wrote a few things on her clipboard, and said, "Well, we better get going, so we don't get stuck up here."

Adam startled and blinked. "Is that a possibility?"

"This is Wyoming," Diane said with a smile. "The weather is unpredictable, and anything is possible."

She led the way out of the house, and Adam followed her, his footsteps as crisp as hers as they exited to big, fluffy snowflakes falling straight down. For once, there was no wind, and Adam had no idea what to make of it.

"I'll be in touch," Diane called through the storm, and then she got behind the wheel of her pickup truck and practically screeched away from the curb. Adam lifted his hand in goodbye just as a gust of wind kicked up and blasted snow in his face. He muttered an obscenity under his breath and yanked open the car door.

It did not open.

Adam always locked his car from years of living with celebrities in cities, and he cursed himself again as he fished in his jacket pocket for the keys. He had not lived through a Wyoming winter yet, and thus he didn't own anything more than the lightweight jacket he currently wore—and which did not produce his keys.

"Come on," he muttered, looking up. The snow had started falling at some point while they were in the house, and already his whole car was covered, and now he could not find his keys.

He checked all of his pockets once and then twice, panic building within him. Could he get back in the house? Had he dropped them somewhere? And if so, how had he not noticed?

He moved to the front of the car and looked back down the sidewalk, a prayer in the front of his mind. *Help me find those keys.*

The thought ran on a loop as he moved back down the sidewalk. The snow had already covered his and Diane's prints, and Adam's thoughts blitzed from one thing to another as he searched.

Are there hotels in Dog Valley? If so, perhaps he could get a room.

You have no idea how to drive in the snow. He'd lived in Tennessee his whole life.

But how hard can it be? People here did it all the time.

The wind assaulted his face, and he shielded his eyes with his hand as he scanned left and right, his prayer for a miracle still going strong. He went back up the steps and onto the porch, which did offer a little bit of protection, but he had not found the keys, and this house had a lockbox on it. Only Diane had the code.

Then frustration, annoyance, and irritation mixed together inside of him in a deadly Molotov cocktail. He looked up and ran his hands through his hair, dislodging plenty of snow and slicking his hair back.

Then he exhaled and looked down, where the faintest

glimmer of silver rested in the dark bark of the flower bed lining the porch. Adrenaline drove through him, and Adam rushed back out into the snowstorm to see if that odd-shaped lump nearly buried in snow was his keys.

It was, and Adam grabbed them, along with a couple pieces of bark that he flung away. He hurried back to his car, clicking it open as he went, and starting it from several paces away so that it would start to warm up.

Safely inside, he opened his glove box and pulled out some fast-food napkins that he used to wipe his face and dry his hair the best he could. His seat heater had already started working, but he shivered nonetheless as he buckled his seatbelt. Nerves ran through him that he would have to make this unfamiliar drive in the dark...and the snow.

Before he could put the car in drive, his phone made a horrible screeching sound—an all-access alert. Adam snatched it up, because the sooner he looked at it, the sooner the sound would stop.

"Weather Advisory," he read out loud. Yeah, no kidding.

Ten inches of heavy, dense, wet snow expected in the next ten hours, the advisory read. *Shelter in place. Do not attempt to go outside or travel. Coral Canyon police are working in conjunction with Dog Valley Police, and all roads will be closed after six p.m.*

Adam's eyes darted up to the top of his screen, where he found the time to be 5:43. There was no way he would make it back to Coral Canyon in fifteen minutes. He wasn't even sure he could drive to the end of this block in fifteen minutes.

A shelter-in-place mandate would be great if he was home with a working furnace or a fireplace, but he didn't think the police department meant stay in your car without food, water, or heat.

He glanced to his gas gauge, and his tank was half-full. He quickly tapped on his browser button to find out if there was a hotel where he could go. Every passing moment brought more desperation to the back of his throat, so much so that his lungs felt like someone had filled them with cement by the time he looked up five minutes later and said, "There are no hotels in Dog Valley."

But you know people who live here, his mind whispered, and Adam launched back into his phone. He did know people who lived here—Luke, Morris, Gabe, for three. And Bryce's ranch sat on the cusp of Coral Canyon and Dog Valley.

But he didn't text any of them.

It was Halloween, and that meant *Joey* would be at her mother's right here in Dog Valley, and if they just closed all the roads, she'd have to stay overnight too.

Adam suspected she'd be upset by that, and as he tapped to call her, he hoped he could find shelter at her mother's place...and offer her comfort at the same time.

11

J oey sat with her back pressed into the puffy pink headboard of the bed where she'd be sleeping that night. Yes, she'd cried when the alert had gone out about fifteen minutes ago, because it meant she would not be able to get back to Grams and Gramps until tomorrow.

Trick-or-treaters had dried right on up, and it wasn't even six p.m. yet. She sniffled, determined not to let her mother or grandmother know that staying here had caused her to cry.

Her phone rang, startling her, and Joey dropped it to her lap and then picked it right back up, for she had seen Adam's name on the screen. She swallowed back her emotions as she swiped on the call.

"Hey," she said as brightly and as bravely as she could. "What's up?"

"Are you at your mom's?" he asked in his no-nonsense managerial voice.

"Yes," she said. "They closed all the roads, as I'm sure you've heard. They send out an alert to everyone within a fifty-mile radius."

"I got the alert," he said.

Her nose ran, and Joey had to sniff to pull it back.

"I'm actually really glad you're there," he said. "Because—"

Joey sat up straighter, her heart pounding a little bit harder. "Because why?"

"I came up to Dog Valley to look at houses this afternoon," he said. "And now I'm stuck here, sitting outside a locked house that has no furniture inside, even if I could get in. There are no hotels in Dog Valley. Did you know that?"

Joey smiled because for someone like Adam, the fact that no hotels existed in a place boggled his mind. "Yes," she said. "I did know that."

"Maybe your mom has an extra bed I can sleep in tonight," he said.

All of the air left Joey's lungs in one horrible rasping sound. "You want to come stay here?"

"Yes," Adam said. "It's pretty much my only option, which is shrinking by the minute, by the way, as I'm pretty sure my car is almost buried in snow, and I'll be lucky to make it off this curb as it is. So I'm gonna need an answer pretty much right now."

Joey jumped off her bed, her pulse pounding through

her whole body. "Let me go talk to my mom." She muted the call and hurried down the hall.

"Mom," she called. "I have a friend who's stuck up here in Dog Valley. Can he stay here?"

"Of course," her mom said. "I mean, we don't have another bedroom, but he can sleep on the couch."

The thought of Adam with his long legs and dignified personality sleeping on her mom's ratty, lumpy couch somehow made Joey's soul sing. "All right," she said. "I'll tell him." She tapped to unmute the call and turned her back on her mother and grandmother. "She says you can stay here, but there's no bed, Adam. It's a couch."

"A couch is better than my car that doesn't have heat," he clipped out. "Can you text me the address, like, right now?"

"Yes," she said, her fingers flying to do that. "I'm doing it right now," she yelled into the phone. "How far away do you think you are?"

"I don't know," he growled. "I don't know where your mom's house is."

She sent the text with the address and watched as the circle moved around and around and around. It finally went through, and she shouted, "It sent."

She tapped back over to the call and lifted the phone back to her ear. "I just sent it," she said.

"I see it," he said. "It looks like—" He trailed off, and Joey didn't like the urgency in his voice. It sounded a lot like panic, and Adam didn't live his life from that place. Joey didn't know him very well, but she knew that much.

"I'm eight minutes away," he said. "On a dry road. On these roads—I gotta be real honest, baby doll, I've never driven in the snow before."

Joey's breath left her lungs for the second time, but for an entirely different reason now. "You've never driven in the snow?" she asked. "Do you even have snow tires?"

"Are snow tires a real thing?" he asked.

"Yes," Joey said. "They are a real thing."

Adam chuckled and asked, "Will you just stay on the line with me until I get there?"

"Which way are you?" she asked. "Seven minutes up, or seven minutes straight across, or seven minutes down?"

"I'm flipping a U-turn," he said. "It looks like I stay on this same road for a little bit, and then I'm going to turn left."

"That's up," she said. "You're probably going to have to come up a couple of streets."

"Yes," he said. "Looks like it."

"That's uphill. Adam, can your car go uphill?"

"I don't know," he said. "I'm moving down the street right now. If I have to, I'll walk."

"You cannot go out in this weather," she said. "Do you have a coat with you? A blanket?"

Adam didn't answer, which Joey took as a no to both. She'd have to tell him what winter living was like in Wyoming, and that included a tote with food, water, hand warmers, body warmers, emergency supplies, a blanket, and a coat in his car at all times.

Knowing Adam, once he knew what he needed to put into a kit, he'd have it all, and he'd rotate it every week. But since he didn't know, his car was probably spotless. He was totally the type who would dust his car and spray protectant onto his plastic so it wouldn't crack in the sun.

She smiled at the thought, though nothing about this phone call and situation should be funny.

"I'm making the turn," he said. "It looks like it's actually three blocks up, and then I have to turn right again."

"If you can make it up those three blocks," she said. "When you turn right, it will be flat again, and then it's just straight down the street."

"Okay," he said. "I'm making the turn. It's really creepy out here."

Joey moved to the front window and looked outside. "Everyone will be on their way home, or they're already there," she said. "We watch the weather pretty religiously in Wyoming."

"We checked it too," Adam said. "It said the storm wasn't going to be here until nine o'clock tonight. I didn't think it would be a problem."

"Me either," Joey murmured. She'd seen the weather report, and she had planned to be gone by seven so that she could be home by 7:45. "Sometimes Mother Nature can be so cruel," she told him.

"Bright side," Adam said, his voice pitching up. "You won't have to stay at your mother's alone. I'll be there in three minutes."

Joey scoffed. "You think that's a bright side?"

"Yeah," he said slowly. "You won't have to be there by yourself."

"And who am I supposed to say you are?" she whispered. "My boyfriend? This guy I know? Someone I'm going out with on Saturday?"

"What did you tell her when you asked if I could stay there?" he asked.

Joey's memory fired at her. "I told her you were a friend," she muttered.

"I mean, I don't really like that label," he said. "But I'll take it for now, because you're right. We haven't really been out on our first date yet."

"This is no time for teasing," she said.

"This is the perfect time for teasing," he shot back. "Otherwise, I'm gonna start panicking, and that's the last thing I need to do."

Joey drew in a deep breath and held it for a moment before releasing it. "I think I'll just tell her that you're my dad's band manager."

"Sure," Adam said. "That works too."

He didn't sound super happy about it, but Joey didn't know what this in-between place was, or how to categorize it. They *weren't* dating. Adam was *not* her boyfriend. They'd flirted with each other a little bit, and he'd taken her for coffee. Kind of.

"Where are you?" she asked, her heart suddenly warming at the idea of not having to be alone at her mother's that night.

"One more block," he said. "I'm almost there, baby doll."

She liked how he called her *baby doll*, and she wanted to

keep him distracted so he wouldn't panic while he drove. "Did you find a house you like?" she asked.

"Yes," he said. "This one here in Dog Valley, actually. My realtor is going to put an offer on it, and I'm hoping to move in only a couple of weeks."

"Wow," she said. "A couple of weeks?"

"I'm paying all cash," he said, and Joey felt certain he would not have disclosed that had they been hunkered down in a warm, homey booth about to order dinner. "We're going in under asking," he added. "It's a really great place. I mean, way too big for me, but I mean, I think it'd be great for a family."

He finally stopped talking, and Joey could not stop grinning. She'd found one of Adam's weaknesses—he said too much when he was nervous.

"I'm making the turn," he said next. "Oh, boy, my wheels are spinning." She heard the engine of his luxury SUV grunt and groan and growl, and then he yelled, "Oh my heck, I'm going. Oh boy, now I'm going *too* fast."

Joey certainly wasn't a driving instructor, nor that great in the snow herself. So she simply said, "You've got this, baby. Turn into the slide." She knew that much, because her father had told her that.

"Okay, I'm okay," he said, and he panted a little bit. "I'm all right. It looks like it's just down here."

A few moments later, headlights cut across the front lawn as Adam turned into the driveway and parked behind her pathetic tan sedan.

"I think I'm here," he said. "Two cars in the driveway?"

"Yes, I see you. I'm hanging up now. I'll have the door open."

"Thank you," he said. "I'll be right in."

Joey ended the call so that he could handle whatever he needed to with his car. "He's here," she called, and then moved to unlock the door and open it. She pushed open the screen door as well, letting in the iciness of the Wyoming storm.

Adam hustled down the sidewalk and up the stairs, hunkered down in only a thin jacket. He kept his head ducked low against the wind pushing the snow sideways, and he hurried straight into the house and past her.

"Holy horses and cows," he said, as she closed the door and locked it behind him. He turned to face her and brushed his hands through his hair to dislodge the snow.

And just like that, Joey had never seen a sexier man in her whole life.

As Adam stood there in his black slacks, the wet jacket, wearing such an intense look in his blue eyes, and his hair all messed up and wet....

"That was touch and go," he said, no smile in sight.

Joey was so happy to see him, and the tension inside her demanded to be released. She stepped over to him and brushed her hands across his shoulders, sending water droplets flying. "I'm so glad you made it," she said.

He hooked one arm around her waist and pulled her close. "Me too."

She tipped her head back, and Adam looked down at her. "I left my cowboy hat in the car," he murmured.

Nothing else seemed to exist except for the two of them.

"That's okay," Joey said. "Because now you won't have to take it off when you...." She trailed off, but Adam tilted his head.

"When I what?"

Joey couldn't get herself to say the words, but she let her eyes drift closed, and Adam seemed to get the hint, because the next thing she knew, his lips had touched hers.

Her whole body caught fire, the hottest part where his mouth touched hers. He pulled away a moment later, growled, and then kissed her again, this movement stronger and deeper and absolutely filled with tension. It released with every stroke of his mouth against hers, and Joey forgot completely that she stood in a living room where her mother and her grandmother could come around the corner at any moment.

She was kissing Adam, and that was all that mattered right now.

12

Adam could not believe where he stood and what he was doing. Joey wore a black, witchy dress that felt soft under his hands. He moved them into her hair, which felt like silk gliding along his fingers, and his whole body sighed as he finally relaxed in a way that he never had before.

He couldn't believe he'd kissed her, and now he couldn't stop. He'd been pulled under, and yet somehow, he could still breathe.

A noise sounded behind him—it could have been a mug breaking or a chair squeaking—and Adam became aware of it. That got him to pull away. He dropped his hands back to his side and backed up a step, his chest impossibly tight.

He drew in a breath and then another, trying to find the center of himself again—the man who didn't panic in a snowstorm, who hadn't walked into his non-girlfriend's mother's house and kissed her within the first ten seconds.

Joey reached up and touched her fingertips to her lips gently. Then, someone said, "Joey," from behind her.

Adam turned toward the woman's voice, hoping with everything he had that Joey hadn't been wearing lip gloss. If she had, he certainly would be. He met a similar pair of blue eyes as hers, instant recognition flashing through him.

"You must be Joey's mother," he said, striding toward her. In a small space, it only took two steps, and he reached out and grabbed her hand. "Thank you so much for letting me stay here. It is *crazy* out there."

Joey moved to his side. "Momma, this is Adam Harmon," she said. "He's Daddy's band manager." She looked up at Adam, and he glanced down at her super-ficially.

"Oh, sure," her mother said. "I heard your daddy was getting a new manager." She smiled at Adam and gestured at him to follow her into the kitchen. "Do you want something to drink? Coffee, tea, hot chocolate?"

"Yes, ma'am," Adam said. "It's freezing out there." He followed her into the kitchen, putting more distance between him and Joey, somehow needing it.

"Lauren, come sit down," another woman said.

"This is my mother," Lauren said. She sighed as she sank into a recliner in the dining room. "I'm afraid I have worn myself to the bone today, but you can make yourself anything you want in the kitchen." She indicated the kettle sitting on the stovetop, as well as the coffee pot, which had brew in it.

"I'll help Joey make up the couch," her mother said, and she flashed a smile at Adam as she left the kitchen. He watched Joey go down the hall after her grandmother, and part of him really wanted her to come back. He felt somewhat thrown to the wolves, and he didn't even know why. He'd walked away from her only a moment ago.

"I'll just have coffee." He started opening cupboards to find the mugs, thankfully locating them on the third try.

"Sugar is in the cupboard next to the microwave," Lauren said. "And there's cream in the fridge."

"Thank you." Adam calmed as he spooned in two tablespoons of sugar and stirred everything together. The dining room table only held two chairs, and the remnants of dinner sat on the stovetop, and he took a sip of his coffee and smiled over to Lauren. "How long have you lived here?"

"I moved here right after Otis and I got divorced," she said thoughtfully. "So about fifteen years now."

Adam nodded, a lump in his throat that the half coffee did not push down. "I can clean this up," he said, and he turned around to start putting aluminum foil over the chicken pot pies on the stove.

"Oh, Joey will do it," Lauren said, and that only made Adam press his teeth together tighter.

"What about you?" she asked. "Where do you live?"

"I've got a place in Coral Canyon right now." He ripped off a piece of aluminum foil. "But I'm looking for new houses. That's why I was up here in Dog Valley."

"I imagine you'll be in town for a while, then," Lauren said. "Now that you're managing Country Quad."

"Yes," Adam said. "At least a few years."

And if he bought the house he wanted, he'd only live a few blocks away from Joey's mother. He wondered if that would be a strike against him, and his face flushed as he remembered the kissing incident from only moments ago.

He heard Joey and her grandmother talking in quiet voices in the other room, so when he finished up with putting away their dinner, he took his mug and went to see what he could do to help.

"This will have to do," Joey said when she saw him. He took in the twin sheet she'd fitted around the couch cushions, the four pillows, and the enormously puffy blanket.

"This looks like plenty," he said. "I'm probably gonna sweat to death out here."

"Oh, you won't." She patted his arm as she moved past him to take a pillow back down the hall. "My mom keeps the house really cold."

"We'll be lucky if we keep the power for much longer," her grandmother said.

"I'm Adam," he said. "I didn't catch your name."

"Oh, I'm Gloria," she said, and she gave him a firm handshake. "In fact, I'm gonna go turn the furnace up right now while it's still on." She bustled halfway down the hall to do that, and Joey snuck past her and came back into the living room.

"Have you eaten?" Joey asked, and Adam whipped his attention back to her.

"No." He gestured toward the kitchen. "But I just put all the food away."

She grinned at him, a ray of sunshine in Adam's life during this awful storm. "Why'd you do that, silly?" She squeezed his hand, and then ducked around him to re-enter the kitchen. "You like chicken pot pie, don't you? Being from the South, I would think so."

"I like chicken pot pie," Adam said. "But really—" He cut off when Joey threw him a severe look. He blinked and put a smile on his face, all in the same second. "Will you heat it up for me, please?"

A small smile touched her face before she ducked into the fridge, and Adam moved to the edge of the kitchen. He threw a look over to her mother and found that Lauren had closed her eyes and seemed to be asleep.

Joey didn't try to be quiet at all, but after she'd slammed the microwave and slid his pot pie into a bowl, she came toward him. "You can eat dinner in your bed." She handed him the bowl, and the scent of creamy sauce and roasted chicken rose to meet his nose.

Then he stepped over to the couch and sat down on the bedsheet-covered cushion. Joey joined him, and he cast a look down the hall where her grandmother had gone. He didn't see Gloria anywhere, and he figured that hallway held a couple of bedrooms and bathrooms.

He dug into the pot pie with his spoon, the crackling of the crust music to his ears. "Did you learn to cook from your grandmother?" he asked.

Joey nodded and looped her arm through his. She didn't

seem to want to talk, and Adam took the steamy bite of food as her nerves pranced through him again. He didn't have to stuff the silence with sound either, and he ate his whole dinner before Joey asked, "Good? You liked it?"

"Yes." He reached across her and set the bowl on the end table. "I'm fed, I'm warm, and I have somewhere to sleep." Adam grinned at her and lifted his arm around her shoulders. "Thank you so much for letting me come here."

Joey searched his face, something vulnerable swimming across hers. "We really might lose power, but my mom has a generator that should kick on within a couple of minutes."

He nodded and reached up to tuck her hair behind her ear, a soft smile accompanying the gesture. Everything about her made him want to be softer, kinder, better. "Okay."

"My mom goes to bed really early," she said next. "We can put a movie on after they do."

"All right," he said. "Whatever is fine with me. I have headphones in my car, and I can listen to a podcast or an audiobook without disturbing anyone."

She smiled and shook her head, sending her silky hair swinging. "You can't go get anything out of your car."

He frowned. "Why not?"

"I bet the doors are frozen shut."

"You're kidding."

Joey giggled and shook her head. "I'll go get your coffee."

"You don't have to," he said, but she'd already pushed to her feet. Adam watched her go, his throat tight. When she returned, he took the mug and tracked her as she sat down again.

"What?" she asked.

"You don't have to take care of me," he said. "I'm capable of heating up food and getting my own coffee."

Joey blinked at him, and it looked like she might fire back at him. Then her chin dipped, and her shoulders sunk in. "Okay," she said. "I'm just used to helping while I'm here."

"You don't have to do that for me." He threaded his fingers through hers. "In fact, if you want anything tonight, you let me know, and *I'll* get it for *you*." He leaned over and pressed his lips to her temple.

"Are we going to talk about...us?" she asked.

"What about us?"

"You kissed me before our first date."

He drew in a deep breath. "First, you closed your eyes, so yeah, I kissed you."

"So you just lock lips with every woman who closes her eyes?" she teased.

"When they do it the way you did, yes," he said back without missing a beat. He could still feel the ghosts of her hands on the sides of his face, see the needful way she'd gazed at him, picture the way her eyes had drifted closed and her mouth had opened slightly.

Yes, she'd been begging him to kiss her, and Adam had wanted to. So he had.

She smiled at him. "I've never been kissed before the first date."

"We can count the coffee and cowboy hat as a date, if that makes things better for you." He smiled at her.

"Because I don't feel bad about kissing you. I'd do it again and again in the same situation."

Her blue eyes sparkled. "Again and again?"

"Yes," Adam said simply. "I haven't had a girlfriend in a while. Maybe the kissing was bad? If so, I can accept that. We don't have to get brunch this weekend."

"I want to get brunch this weekend."

"So the kissing wasn't bad," he stated.

Joey grinned at him. "I mean, it wasn't *that* bad." She nudged him with her shoulder and gave a light laugh. Adam thought it sounded like soft spring rain, and he let his feeling flow through him freely.

And he liked this woman a whole lot.

"You know what would be amazing?" he asked. Joey raised her eyebrows at him. "Popcorn. A movie and popcorn, while the storm rages around us."

The moment he said that, something popped in the house. Joey yelped; the lights went out; Adam pulled in a breath and held it.

Someone else yelled from somewhere in the house, but for some reason, Adam couldn't tell where the sound had come from.

"I'm right here, Mom," Joey said. She moved beside him, and the flashlight on her phone illuminated the room in the next moment. "The generator will come on in a minute." She got up and went into the kitchen.

Adam followed her, mostly because he wanted to be near her—and he wanted to be helpful too.

"Let's get you to bed," Joey said. "Then you can plug in your phone and watch a show and not have to navigate the house in the dark." She helped her mother stand from the recliner, and Adam moved to her other side.

"I'm okay," Lauren said, and Adam stayed out of the way. He told himself not to overstep, that helping Joey wasn't exactly the same as helping her mother. He let Joey shuffle out of the kitchen, and to help, he cleaned up his dishes and the pot pies for a second time.

He'd just set his bowl in the dishwasher when the lights flared back on, the generator kicking in the way Joey said it would. He turned off all the lights he could and still see, because he saw no reason to use more energy than necessary.

He returned to the couch, and while it wasn't the most comfortable item of furniture he'd ever sat on, it would be fine for a single evening. He leaned back and sighed as his eyes closed, the exhaustion of the day weighing on his shoulders.

A yawn stretched through him, but he knew it wasn't anywhere near late enough for him to actually lie down and go to sleep. It took Joey several more long minutes before she rejoined him on the couch, a sigh slipping through her lips as she did.

"They're both settled in their rooms," she said, leaning back against the couch beside him.

"Is it time for bed then?" Adam grinned and turned his head to look at her. The dim light he'd left on over the stove in the kitchen barely haloed her, and he found her incredibly beautiful.

"It's not even seven o'clock."

"It feels later," he said. "It got dark so early."

"And it's not even really winter yet." Joey flashed him a smile, and Adam lifted his arm and drew her into his chest.

"Maybe we can just sit in the dark and tell each other secrets," he murmured.

"Secrets?" Joey kept her voice low too. "I don't think I have too many of those."

"I've got a few."

She snuggled closer. "Go on, then, if you're so keen to spill secrets in the dark."

Adam stroked one hand down the length of her hair. "I don't know how to truly relax."

"Not a secret," she said.

"If you let me be your boyfriend, this'll be the first relationship I've had in six years."

"You alluded to that already."

Adam exhaled heavily on purpose. "You don't like any of my secrets. Tell me one of your own."

"I—I feel like a loser," Joey said. "I can't seem to do anything for more than a year or so."

"That doesn't make you a loser," Adam said. "And you've been living and working here for about a year, haven't you?"

"A little longer," she said. "I've been thinking about getting my own place."

"Is that a secret?"

"Yes." Joey squeezed his hand. "It's scary for me to live alone—and I haven't told anyone that I've been saving so I can get my own place."

"I love living alone." Adam chuckled. "I mean, it's better than roommates, but mine were never my grandparents." He leaned down and took a deep breath of her hair. "I won't tell anyone, okay? Your secrets are safe with me."

"Tell me another one of yours," she whispered.

Adam's heart throbbed at him, and the words piled up in his throat. "I think...I think I need to go back to church, but I don't even know where to start."

Joey lifted her head off his chest, and his eyes had adjusted to the dimmer light well enough for him to see her. "I can help you with that."

"Yeah? You go?"

"Yes," she said. "Almost every week, with Grams and Gramps." She grinned at him, her teeth practically gleaming in the available light. "They'll be *thrilled* to have you sit with us."

Adam chuckled and shook his head. "I don't think I'm ready for that, but I'd love it if you could text me the address of the church where you go."

"I can do that." She reached up and swept her fingers through his hair.

"Here's another secret," he whispered. "I desperately want to kiss you again."

"Then do it." This time, Joey didn't let her eyes drift

closed, and Adam held her gaze for one, two, three breaths, his need and desire for her blowing up with every moment.

Then he let his eyes fall closed as he moved to touch his lips to hers. The entire world tilted for the second time that evening, and Adam was totally here for the ride.

13

J oey greased the dough ball she'd just put back in the bowl and then lifted the plastic wrap to go over it. She made sure it was still loose so that the dough could push against it as it rose, and she turned back to Aunt Faith.

"All right, that one's rising," she said. "What do we need to do next?"

They'd been making doughnuts for the past couple of hours, and Joey loved baking with her aunt. She had just had a baby about six weeks ago, and little Harmony had fallen back asleep almost an hour ago. Uncle Blaze had gotten up with the other kids—Grace, Celeste, and Tyrone— and he'd taken them out to walk around the lake until breakfast was ready.

"Let's do the sausage next," she said, and she opened the fridge and pulled out two enormous packages of sausage links. "I can man the grill if you want to put two pans on that left side," she indicated the stove top with the biggest burners, and Joey reached for the pans hanging from the rack above the island. Her aunt and uncle lived in a luxurious mountain home in the lakeside community, with a gate, and Joey could only hope to live somewhere half as nice as this place one day.

She loved babysitting for her aunts and uncles, but her two jobs rarely allowed her to do it, and most of those jobs went to Rosie, Liesl, and Corinne anyway.

"I wanted to ask you something," Joey said, taking her thoughts away from where she lived and who she was meeting after she finished having breakfast with the Blaze-Young-branch of her family.

"Sure," Faith said good-naturedly.

"I remember a long time ago, you did holiday orders for doughnuts. Remember that—when you still owned your trucks?"

"Of course," Faith said. "I did it because one of my trucks kept breaking down, and I needed to stay in business."

Joey nodded. "Grams and I like to make Thanksgiving pies," she said. "And I was thinking that I could take holiday orders the way you did...using social media."

Faith glanced over to her, her kind smile growing by the moment. "That's a great idea, Joey."

"Do you have any advice for me?" Joey asked.

Faith thought about it for a moment, and she ran a knife down the end of one of the sausage packages. "Have a set menu," she said. "So say...offer five pies and nothing more. That way, you won't be making one lemon chiffon, and fifteen pumpkin, and then a pecan, and an apple, and this and that."

"That's a good idea," Joey said. "Grams is really good at pecan, and I love pumpkin and apple."

"Then just do those three," she said. "Pumpkin, pecan—very classic for Thanksgiving."

Joey nodded and swallowed. "I just want to earn a little extra money to maybe get my own apartment."

"I thought you liked living with Cecily and Jerry."

"I do," Joey said quickly. "I do. Of course, I do." She exhaled as she started layering sausage into her pans too. "It's just, I'm getting older, and it feels like the adult thing to do."

"I still have my house," Faith said. "It's really small, kind of like one and a half bedrooms." She grinned at Joey. "Blaze and I rent it."

"I didn't know that," Joey said.

Faith nodded. "We have someone there now, but I don't know what their plans are. If they move out, I'd be more than happy for you to move in there."

"I could pay rent," Joey said, though she currently wasn't paying any. She did put a few hundred dollars into her savings account as if she did every month, because she knew she would need a first month's rent, last month's rent, and a security deposit, and it could cost thousands to get into a new place.

She thought of Adam and how he'd put in an offer—all

cash—on a house in Dog Valley that cost over eight hundred thousand dollars.

The sellers had accepted his offer, of course, and he was actually trying to move by next weekend. She hadn't seen him since Thursday morning, when they'd gotten up to almost a foot of fresh snow. She'd made breakfast for her family and him, and they'd waited a couple of hours until the snowplows had been out to clear the roads before they'd left.

Joey had not worked at Cake Bites that day, but it didn't matter. When snow came to town, everyone shut down to stay safe.

"It might be helpful if you had a website too," Faith said. "I can help you get a really simple one set up. I'm sure you have pictures of you at culinary school and making pies." She raised her eyebrows as a question.

Joey nodded as she had been bringing holiday pies to their family gatherings for a couple of years. "Yes," she said. "I have all of those things. Would it take very long and cost very much?"

"Not at all," Faith said. "We can get hosting for ten dollars a month, and I can help you build it. In fact, I would *love* to build it for you." She grinned over to Joey. "I love my kids, but I've been feeling more and more like I need something more to keep my mind sharp. The girls are in school, so it's just Tyrone and me and the baby."

"And Blaze doesn't even have a job," Joey said, which caused them both to giggle.

"He's very helpful with the kids," Faith said. "I could easily put a website together for you in a couple of hours."

"What do you think I should call it?" Joey asked.

"That's a good question," Faith said. "We can do a little bit of research and see what other websites are out there. Though, if you're just offering for Coral Canyon and Dog Valley, it won't matter much."

Joey nodded, her mind now buzzing with possibilities. She and Faith fried sausage, and when that finished, she tonged the cooked links onto paper towels to drain. Then Faith pulled her glazed doughnut dough closer to her and started to roll it out.

"They should be back soon, and these don't take long to fry."

Joey looked at her batter, and she had done a denser batter for bars. "This isn't quite ready yet," she said.

"Those always take longer." Faith peered at the dough too. "Yeah, that needs another half-hour at least."

Joey agreed, and she glanced at the clock on the stove. She would need to leave in another hour to meet Adam for brunch. He'd forgotten that he'd signed up for guitar lessons on Saturday mornings, and since it was only his second one, he hadn't wanted to cancel. Joey had agreed to simply push their brunch date back to a more appropriate brunch time, and they were meeting at eleven now, instead of nine.

The back door slid open, and in walked Celeste and Grace. Blaze waited while Tyrone toddled up and entered the house too, nearly toppling as he lifted his foot to go over the lip of the door.

"Careful there, bud," Uncle Blaze said, and Joey smiled at her cousins.

"Momma's making the doughnuts right now," Celeste said.

"Can we have the pink frosting with sprinkles?" Grace asked. They both slid onto a bar stool and watched Faith and Joey roll out the dough and cut it into rounds.

"Up, up," Tyrone whined, and Uncle Blaze swept him up into his arms.

He babbled something else to which Faith said, "We're doing pink frosting and chocolate." She smiled at her son. "You can have the chocolate one, buddy." He flapped his arms, causing Uncle Blaze to lean away.

"I might not be able to stay long enough to do the bars," she told Aunt Faith.

"Oh, it's fine," Faith said. "The girls and I will finish them up. They want to take them around to their cousins and grandparents." She smiled at her girls. "And they should have to do some of the work if they're going to get all that gratitude."

"What do you have going on?" Uncle Blaze asked, and Joey's heartbeat froze in her veins. She had not introduced Adam to her momma as her boyfriend, and either her momma wasn't very observant, or Joey and Adam had hidden the way they'd been kissing and holding hands well enough to not be detected.

She glanced over to Aunt Faith, who lifted another ring's doughnut out of the dough and set it on a tray to rise.

"I—" Joey said. "Well, truth be told, I have a date."

"A date?" Uncle Blaze's eyebrows went up.

"I haven't told anybody about him yet," she said, giving her grouchiest uncle a smile. "Not my momma or my daddy —so I'm certainly not going to tell you."

Rosie would have cocked her skinny hip and demanded to know who Joey was going out with. Harry and Belle had already asked, but Uncle Blaze simply held up one hand and said, "All right, I'm not going to make you tell me if you don't want to."

She didn't want to, but Aunt Faith bumped her with her hip.

"Looks like you like him," Faith said.

"Does it?" Joey asked. "What makes you say that?"

"You're wearing a special smile," Faith teased.

She thought about the kissing her and Adam had done earlier that week, and her face heated.

"Oh, she likes him all right," Blaze said, his smile growing. "Is this your first date?"

Her uncles were known for asking a lot of nosy and difficult questions, but Uncle Blaze wasn't usually one of them. Of course, he couldn't know that this question was actually difficult when it shouldn't have been.

"I'm not actually sure," she said, and he chuckled.

"That's kind of weird, don't you think? Wouldn't you know if you'd been out with him before?"

"Well, I guess what you could call our first date was... kind of not really a date. So, yeah, I don't know." She also didn't want to have kissed Adam before they'd even gone out, which made Uncle Blaze's question far more complicated than he even knew.

Thankfully, Blaze and Faith didn't ask a bunch more questions, which was why they were one of the safer couples for Joey to tell about her date. Blaze didn't like his business being splashed all through the family and around town, which meant he would never do that to her.

Joey made a traditional glaze and a pink frosting and a chocolate frosting, while Faith manned the fryers. There was nothing in the world as good as a freshly fried doughnut, hot from the oil and dunked in traditional glaze, and Joey bit into the sweet and crispy treat, a moan coming out of her mouth.

"You can take some for your date," Faith said. "If you want."

They'd let some of the other doughnuts cool, so that the frosting wouldn't melt, and Uncle Blaze currently strapped Tyrone into his high chair while the girls put the plates of sausage and utensils on their table.

Joey looked at the pink and chocolate doughnuts, her heart expanding a couple of sizes. "I'd love that."

Aunt Faith handed her a paper plate, and Joey took a chocolate, a pink-frosted and sprinkled, and a regularly glazed doughnut and put them on the plate for Adam. She sat down and ate a couple of sausage links, and then said, "I don't want to eat too much because we're going to brunch."

As she stood, she took in the floury, doughy, glazy mess that had become the kitchen, and she turned back to her aunt. "I'm so sorry I'm leaving. I forgot I always stay and help you clean up."

"It's fine," Faith said. "We're used to a little chaos around here." Uncle Blaze laughed just as their new baby started to cry.

Joey went over to get her out of the swing, lifting the tiny infant in her arms. Harmony quieted quickly, and Joey gazed down at her softly, so much love filling her. She took her over to Faith, who cradled her in her arm and continued eating as if such a thing were simply easy. Joey could barely feed herself, so holding a baby *and* dealing with three other kids *and* eating had to be a skill that Faith had learned at some point.

She went around and hugged and tickled all of her cousins, swept a kiss along her uncle's cheek, and hugged Faith before she left.

Adam's guitar lesson was in Jackson Hole, so he drove almost an hour to attend it. They'd agreed to meet at Brunch House, and Joey made the drive there quickly and found the parking lot almost overflowing.

She couldn't find anywhere to park, and ended up going up and down the street, looking for somewhere to put her car. Her phone chimed a couple of times, and Joey cursed herself that she was now late. Adam did not like it when people ran late, but Joey could hardly help the crowd at brunch time, could she?

She finally went around to the other side of the block and found a parking spot behind a dance studio that was not open. She lifted her phone and found that Adam had texted.

Wow, there's a lot of people here today. I'm still looking for somewhere to park.

I just found somewhere in the back lot, she said. *If you go all the way around the block, you'll find it.*

Adam didn't answer, and Joey quickly stashed her phone in her purse and left the car. She'd only taken two steps when Adam climbed out of his luxury SUV as well.

"I was just about to text you the same thing," he said, holding up his phone. "And then I saw you drive by in front of me." He grinned at her, and then looked over to her car.

Embarrassment drove through Joey, and she didn't dare look at her pathetic sedan.

"Now I know what kind of car you drive," he said good-naturedly, and Joey died a little bit inside.

She joined him, enjoying the woodsy, calming, cottony scent as he leaned in and kissed her cheek. "It's the same car I got when I turned sixteen," she said. "My daddy made me buy half of it, and I don't know, we've been through a lot together."

He pulled back and looked at her, something curious moving through his expression. "There's nothing wrong with your car."

"Well, it's not like yours."

Adam sighed in a semi-frustrated way, which made Joey's pulse blip strangely through her chest. "I don't care what kind of car you drive, Joey," he said.

"Okay," she said.

"I don't need you to compare yourself to me."

She swallowed, because Joey had been comparing

herself to everyone for most of her life. "It's a special skill I have," she said. "Comparing myself to others."

"Well, I wish you wouldn't," Adam said. He pulled her close, his lips brushing her earlobe as he said, "Remember, we don't play games with each other. A car is just a car. It doesn't say anything about the person driving it."

Joey wasn't sure she agreed, but she sure liked standing in the warmth of Adam's arms. She pulled back and looked up to him. "How was your guitar lesson?"

"I'll tell you about it once we have food." He grinned at her and leaned closer. "Right now, I just want to kiss you hello."

Joey smiled, because she would like that too, and she let him hold her and kiss her in the back parking lot, feeling a little reckless and dangerous, because literally anyone in town could walk by and see them, and hardly anyone had the discreetness of Uncle Blaze and Aunt Faith. Because of that, she didn't let him carry on too long.

She ducked her head and said, "I'm starving. Let's go in."

Adam chuckled and took her hand so they could walk around the buildings to the entrance.

"Don't think I don't know you've just eaten something," he said. "You taste like frosting."

She grinned at him. "I went and made doughnuts with my aunt this morning. I've got some for you in the car."

"Hmm, I can't wait for that," he said, and Joey found that she couldn't wait for a lot of things when it came to Adam. She wanted to help him move into his new place.

She wanted to see what he would do for Country Quad. She wanted to show him things about herself that she'd kept hidden from everyone else. She wanted to share her hopes and dreams about moving into her own place and maybe having her own pie bakery someday.

But for now, she enjoyed the way he held her hand, the way he made her feel strong, and the way he said, "Oh, by the way, I got your text about offering pies for the holidays. I think it's a great idea."

14

Adam regretted suggesting the Brunch House the moment he opened the door. Loud laughter, tons of talking, and blasting music greeted him, and he hadn't even stepped inside yet. Joey did, as if the wall of noise didn't bother her. It did bother Adam, and he'd already driven back from Jackson with the radio off. He liked having quiet time in his life where he didn't have to have something coming at him all the time.

Life seemed to come hard at him constantly, and Adam often simply needed some silence to help him make the many decisions he needed to, even if they weren't for him. Adam had learned early on that his attention to details and the way he handled events and schedules and people meant that he needed a way to cope with the stress that brought.

Sometimes, his favorite classical music and a really big order of French fries did the trick, but he'd found that

145

leaving his headphones home and getting on his bike and going for a forty-mile ride worked better.

Adam had not found the best way to work out in Coral Canyon, as he'd been dealing with Harry, and then this new job, and then buying a house, and now starting something with Joey. He hadn't even had time to locate a gym and decide if he should join it. Adam didn't love working out indoors or with other people, and he'd found himself more often than not hiking the trails around Coral Canyon by himself. With winter closing in on them, though, he knew he wouldn't be able to continue doing that for very long.

Your new house is plenty big enough for a home gym, he told himself as he followed Joey down the hallway that had been erected by a wall on one side and a chest-high barrier on the other.

She turned back to him and said, "This place is really loud."

Relieved that she'd realized it too, all of his muscles practically sagged off his bones. "We can go somewhere else," he said. "Heck, lunch places are open by now."

Joey turned and looked at the several people standing in line in front of them who hadn't even been seated yet, and then faced him again. "Would you hate me if I said I wanted to go somewhere else?"

"Of course not," Adam said. He had literally just suggested it.

"We can come here another time when it's not so busy—maybe a weekday," Joey said.

Adam turned and went back toward the entrance, squeezing out past another couple trying to come in.

"I'm not as familiar with Coral Canyon as you are," he said. "What do you suggest?"

Joey gave him a playful look as they started down the sidewalk to go back around the buildings to where they'd parked. "How adventurous are you feeling?" she asked.

Adam chuckled. "Oh, boy, that's a loaded question."

"Are you a very adventurous person?" she asked.

Adam sobered and finally shook his head. "I think I would say no to that if I'm being honest."

"Yeah, I didn't think so either." She bumped him with her shoulder. "The way you wear slacks everywhere is a dead giveaway."

"Hey, I like my slacks," he said, looking down at them.

"I like them too," Joey shot back. "I'm just saying, you live in Wyoming now, and you manage a country music band. *They* don't even wear slacks."

Adam blinked and looked down the sidewalk. "Well, I don't think I own jeans."

"Another thing we can go shopping for," Joey said.

He scoffed immediately, rejecting the idea. "There is no way I'm taking you jean shopping with me."

"No?" Joey asked. "Why not?"

He glared over to her. "Because you're not my mother."

Joey grinned back at him, full of light and playfulness. "I think it would be fun."

"I think we should eat," he said.

"Right." Joey cleared her throat and shook her hair over

her shoulders. She adjusted the scarf around her neck, and while she didn't wear the pink puffy coat, today's outerwear was more of a buckskin-rawhide-leather color she'd paired with a scarf in bright pink, blue, and white.

"So I was thinking," she said. "I would go by the grocery store and get everything that we need for biscuits and gravy, and then I can meet you at your house, and I could cook for you."

Adam paused at the corner of the parking lot. "Didn't you spend the morning cooking already?"

"That was *baking*," she said.

"Biscuits are also baking," he shot back.

Joey grinned at him and leaned into his chest with both palms. He still hadn't had time to find a proper coat, but she gripped the lapels of his windbreaker as he balanced her with both hands on her hips.

"It'll be quiet at your house," she said. "Which means we can talk, and I can show you that I'm a good cook."

"I already know you're a good cook," he said. "I want this date to be easy and fun for both of us."

"Cooking is easy and fun for me," she said. "And I'll be with you." She raised her eyebrows, those pretty blue eyes filled with such hope.

He swallowed and looked away, indecision raging through him. "All right," he said, making up his mind. "But then tonight, you have to let me take you somewhere nice and pamper you."

Joey's eyebrows went up.

"You said you weren't working," Adam said, and maybe,

if he played his cards right, he could get her to stay all after-noon. They could watch movies on his boring couch, and he could send out for ice cream so that they could have mid-afternoon sundaes.

"I also don't want you to buy the ingredients," he said. "Let's go to the grocery store together."

"Oh, no," she said, laughing, but not with any humor. "There is no way I'm letting you in my car."

"Great," he said without missing a beat. "Then I'll drive."

She threw him a glare but didn't say anything, and when they reached their cars, she went to his passenger door without another word.

Adam smiled to himself and managed to erase the grin before he got in the driver's seat. He'd never taken a woman to the grocery store for a date before, but he navigated them there, and even managed to get around to Joey's side to open her door before she got out.

Of course, that was because he had child safety locks on his car and forgotten, and she couldn't actually open her door.

"You locked me in," she said.

Adam laughed and reached for her hand. "I forgot about the safety locks, is all."

They went inside where Joey pushed around a half-cart and gathered cream, a tube of sausage, and a pound of butter before she turned to look at him. "Tell me what pantry ingredients I'm working with."

He blinked at her. "Pantry ingredients?"

Joey grinned. "I knew this was going to be fun."

"Hey, you don't have to make fun of me," he said. "I have sugar and stuff."

"Does your 'and stuff' include baking powder?"

Adam shook his head.

"Flour?"

Again, no.

"I'll get everything I need for the biscuits," Joey said, and she led him down the baking aisle, where she expertly plucked ingredients in boxes and bags and put them in his cart. He had no idea how someone made bread or a biscuit from the things she'd selected, but by the time they checked out, they had five bags of groceries that Adam was sure would make more than one meal.

"If you don't want to keep them at your place," she said. "I can take them home with me. Grams and I do a lot of baking."

"Yes, tell me about the pies," he said.

Joey lit up as she pulled her seat belt across her body. She faced him again and said, "I'm actually really excited about the pies. Grams and I have been talking about doing it for a couple of years, but last year, I was still pretty new to town, and before that, I was off at college."

"What kinds will you be making?" Adam asked.

"I think we're gonna do pecan and pumpkin," Joey mused. "Those are our two specialties."

"Are you the pumpkin or the pecan?" he asked.

"Pumpkin." She smiled at him. "I *love* pumpkin pie."

"Of course you do." He smiled too, glad she had something as simple as pie to make her happy.

"You don't like pumpkin pie?" she asked.

"Not really," Adam said.

"How very un-American of you," she teased.

Adam grinned, too. "I like pecan, though, and apple. Apple is as American as they come."

"You're right," she said. "I think I might do apple. I talked to my Aunt Faith about it, and she said not to offer too many varieties."

"That's probably smart," Adam said.

"So I was thinking pumpkin, pecan, and apple, but then I don't have a citrus option."

"Apples are kind of citrusy," he said.

"No, like key lime or lemon chiffon or coconut cream," she said. "Ooh, coconut cream." She seemed to disappear inside her own mind for a moment, and Adam let her go.

He pulled up to his house, and Joey glanced over to him. "Oh, we're here already," she said.

"Yes, we're here already." He grinned at her, and then carried in all the groceries, and he unpacked them while Joey examined his stove and stovetop. She opened drawers and pulled out the things she would need, muttering about the "lack of measuring cups" and how she would have to make do. When she met his eyes again, he simply chuckled.

"I thought you knew I didn't cook," he said. "Did you think I was lying or was a closet baker?"

She laughed. "No one's a closet baker."

"They're not?" he asked.

"No," she said, in an almost scoff. "There are people who dedicate entire social media accounts to their baking. People are *proud* of it."

He grinned at her. "Do you have a social media account for your baking?"

Joey's mouth tightened, and she shook her head.

"Well, maybe you should start one," he said. He genuinely believed she could start a social media account for her baking, and she lifted her head and met his eye. She searched and searched his face, and Adam could practically hear her comparing herself to every other baker out there.

Then that fierceness he loved about her drew through her shoulders and blazed in her eyes. "Maybe I will— starting with these biscuits."

She put them together quickly, and because they didn't have to rise, she got them in the oven and then started browning the sausage on the stove. Adam simply watched her, enthralled by the way she moved around the kitchen. His kitchen.

Her presence in his house was absolutely powerful.

By the time she served him an open-faced biscuit with plenty of creamy, peppery sausage gravy over the top and two fried eggs on the side, Adam was pretty sure he'd fallen in love with her.

He forked off a bite, made a big show of smelling it, and then carefully slid the biscuit and gravy into his mouth. Pure perfection exploded through him—and he felt the same way whenever he kissed Joey.

Or looked at Joey.

Or heard her laugh, which she did right now. "Sounds like you like it," she said, giving him a coy smile.

He swallowed, the amount of pepper absolutely right. "It's amazing." He cut into his egg and let the yolk run out. "You're incredible." He beamed at her, really liking the way her face pinked up and she ducked her head over her own plate of biscuits and gravy.

Adam was definitely falling for Joey, and he reminded himself that they were still new. This was technically their first date, and he'd always been cautious when it came to the big things in his life.

But Joey made him want to jump on the nearest horse and spur it into a gallop. Full-steam ahead. All the way. So he let himself slip and slide and get a little more comfortable with the idea of having Joey in his life long-term.

And that felt like pure perfection too...though it did cause a slip of fear to settle in the back of his throat that he couldn't quite swallow down.

Long-term with Joey meant long-term in Coral Canyon, and while Adam was here for now, he certainly didn't know if he could commit to more than the three years of his contract with Country Quad.

He pushed the troubling thoughts away. Three years was a long time, and Joey had already proven she could leave Coral Canyon to try different parts of the world, to experiment with doing different things with her life.

He simply had to figure out how to be the man that she loved more than this small town where she'd grown up...and all of her family.

15

Harry Young finished writing down the last title of tonight's movie. With so many different personalities in the Young family, and all of them somewhat opinionated, he'd learned early on to have a system where one person's preferences were not put above another's.

In the days leading up to cousin movie night, he would take any suggestions for movies, write them on little slips of paper, and put them in his cowboy hat. A different person got to pick every month, and Harry tapped on his phone to get to the list to see whose turn it was tonight.

"Liesl," he muttered. Then he got up from the desk, collected the slips of paper, and went out into the main living area of his house. Belle had already arrived because they spent most of their days together, and Harry couldn't wait until they woke up in the same house, in the same bed, and truly merge their lives together.

In the New Year, when she would become his wife—and Harry's mind blanked there. He'd never been married, and he actually had no idea what life would be like after January eleventh.

He had told her Belle could move her cats in at any time, as they would be living in his house once they got married.

"Popcorn," she said, turning from the small counter next to the microwave.

"Smells great," Harry said. "Salty and sugary at the same time." Belle loved white chocolate popcorn and had been making it for cousin movie nights for the past couple of months. "They should start arriving any minute."

"Did you put in the order for the burgers?" she asked.

He shook his head and sank onto a bar stool to do that.

"Did you invite Adam?"

He looked up, his eyes locking onto his fiancée's. "I couldn't make myself do it."

"Bryce and Codi come, right?"

"But Bryce and Codi are married," Harry said. "We don't even know if Joey is dating Adam, and I've never invited him before."

Harry had no problem with his cousins bringing their significant others, but only he and Bryce had them—that he knew of. Cash lived in Jackson Hole and would not be attending, though Joey, Beth, and Boston had all confirmed. Cole and Rosie would be there with Corinne, Eric, and Liesl.

All of the other cousins were under the age of twelve, and Harry didn't invite them. Of course, at this point, he could have invited Melissa and almost OJ, who would turn eleven next month.

At the same time, Harry wasn't sure he would ever invite those cousins. He loved them, and they loved him. He enjoyed his time with them, but in reality, he'd been inviting the older kids who'd come from their daddy's first marriages, and that did not include Melissa or OJ or Lars, who had just turned twelve very recently.

"Do you think I should start inviting OJ?" he asked.

Belle turned back to the fridge with a sigh. She started pulling out twelve-packs of soda and bottles of lemonade and sweet tea. "I don't know," she said, a bit of grumpiness in her tone. She started making coffee and kept her back to him, which was her way of telling him she didn't want to talk about this. Her family lived far away, and Belle still struggled to spend a lot of time with a large group of people at all. In the end, Harry liked it best when it was just her and him, and he knew Belle did too.

She sighed again and faced him. "I don't see how you can invite OJ and not invite Melissa. Her feelings will be incredibly hurt."

"I know." Harry looked back at his phone to finish up the burger orders. "I'm getting a ton of fries," he said. "I'm sure they'll get eaten."

Belle rounded the island and sat down next to him. "Harry, baby?" she asked in a gentle voice. "It's not your job to unite them."

"I *know* that," he said. "But I still *feel* like it is. And Melissa doesn't feel left out of the family the way the group of people coming here tonight do. And I just think OJ probably has some of those feelings. He's adopted, you know."

"We all know that." Belle looped her arm through his and gently took his phone from him. "Let me get this order in before you forget to do it completely." She grinned at him, and Harry let her take the device and finish up.

Then the doorbell rang, the front door opened, and people entered his house. Someone, probably Rosie or Boston, kept ringing the doorbell over and over until Harry turned away from the island and yelled, "All right, enough with the doorbell!"

Sure enough, Rosie cackled like she was the funniest person alive, and she entered the house last and closed the door. Harry opened his arms to his younger cousins, Liesl and Corinne. They both lived up in Dog Valley and often drove together. They'd brought Eric with them this time, as Morris had just relocated his family to the border of Coral Canyon and Dog Valley.

He didn't see Bryce or Codi, but he moved on to hugging Cole and Rosie and Beth next.

"I told her not to ring the doorbell," Beth said in a very practical voice. She'd been raised by a very proper mother in Jackson Hole, though she'd split her time between there and Uncle Mav's house.

"Oh, it's fine," Harry said. "I knew it would be Rosie or Boston."

"Hey," Boston protested good-naturedly. He stepped

over to Harry and gave him a hug, complete with pounding on the back.

"How you doin', brother?" Harry asked.

"Good. Well, good enough." Boston smiled as he stepped back.

"Have you found a job yet?" Harry asked.

"Not yet," Boston said. "I'm actually going to talk to Adam this weekend about being a reference. You're still okay to do it?"

"Absolutely," Harry said. "Any place in town would be lucky to have you."

Boston had worked with Harry on his online concert series, and he had proven to be a good manager of details. He learned quickly, and he took direction well.

"Looks like we're just missing Joey, Bryce, and Codi," he said, and just as he turned away from the front door, it opened again.

"Howdy-ho," Bryce called, and Harry turned back to watch him twist to help his very pregnant wife up the step into the house. Joey followed, and she carried an enormous tray of cinnamon rolls.

"Howdy, guys." Harry hurried forward to relieve Joey of the heavy tray. "You are a goddess," he said. "Look at these things."

"I only did the frosting," Joey said. "Grams made the rolls while I was at work this morning."

"Then they'll be doubly good." Harry grinned at her, hoping he could simply see how her date with Adam had gone over the weekend. He couldn't, and he turned away before Joey caught him staring.

"I ordered the burgers," he yelled to everyone as he entered the kitchen. He slid the tray onto the counter and faced them all.

"They should be here in about fifteen minutes," Belle said.

"Which is just enough time for us to go around and get caught up on things." Harry's eyes locked onto Joey, but not a single muscle in her face moved, though he was at least expecting an eye twitch or a blink. She was a solid rock, and Harry found himself chuckling.

"We'll pick the movie too," he said, sweeping the papers up off the counter, plucking his hat from his head, and dropping them inside. "Who wants to go first?"

The Youngs weren't well known for their ability to let one person talk at a time, and when they all got together, the noise could awaken the dead. But of all the people that Harry invited to cousin movie night, they were definitely the quieter ones, the ones on the fringes, the ones left behind, the ones left out.

The ones left over.

He knew they each felt like that in some regard, though some had said it out loud and some hadn't.

"I'll go first," Beth said. "I'm applying for a graduate program at a college in Maryland for my MBA." She beamed around at everyone. "So I'd appreciate your prayers that I'll be able to get in and get a scholarship."

Harry knew full well that Mav would pay for anything

Beth wanted to do, but he simply nodded and said, "I'll pray for you, Beth," along with several others.

"I'm looking for a new job," Boston said. "In event management, hospitality, or customer service. If you hear of anything, let me know, would you?"

Winter wasn't the greatest time to be looking for such a job, but Harry knew Boston didn't want to go back to college, and he was fine to stay in small-town Coral Canyon if he could earn enough money to move out of his parents' house and have his own life. Of them all, only Boston was not a Young, and Harry knew it plagued him in ways he wished it wouldn't.

"They're going to induce Codi on Monday next week," Bryce said. "Apparently, the baby's getting really big, and they're worried she won't be able to deliver him if we don't take him a week early."

"Oh, that's great news," Joey said, grinning at Codi. "A week early—you must be thrilled."

"I can't wait," Codi said, and she rested both hands on her pregnant belly. "I feel like a one-humped camel, and I can't move."

Bryce grinned at her and put his arm around her as they looked around at the group.

"I'm auditioning for a cello solo in the orchestra for the spring concert," Corinne said.

"Oh, that's great," Bryce said. "I'm sure you'll get it."

Corinne shook her head, her dark curls bobbing. "I'm sure I won't, but it's just part of my New Year's resolution to do something every month that makes me uncomfortable."

Harry grinned at her because he didn't like doing things that made him uncomfortable either.

"My daddy thinks I'm going to kill us all when I get my driver's license." Liesl grinned out at everyone. "He makes Momma go driving with me because he said it just makes him too nervous."

Harry chuckled, though he knew the reason Uncle Gabe didn't like driving with Liesl was because it reminded him of how grown-up his daughter had become.

"My daddy says I'm never, never allowed to learn how to drive," Rosie said, and she rolled her eyes. "But I started working with a new horse a couple of weeks ago, and Gypsy is amazing. I think we're going to win everything next rodeo season."

Harry had no doubt that she would, because all of Rosie's fire and sass melted away whenever she got on a horse. It transferred to them, and they performed well for her in barrel racing.

Eric raised his hand halfway. "I'm going to apply to be the FFA president at school."

"Oh, you'll be perfect for that," Liesl said kindly. Harry nodded along with several others, though he thought Eric might accidentally light the agriculture wing of the high school on fire just as easily. The boy seemed to bring a windstorm with him everywhere he went, in everything he did.

"That just leaves you, Cole," he said.

"And us too," Belle said.

Harry turned to her. "Do we have news?"

"Well, we sold a couple of songs last week."

He grinned at her and took her hand in his. He lifted it to his lips and said, "Yeah, we did sell a couple of songs last week. That's how we're paying for your burgers." He laughed, because everyone in the room knew he had plenty of money. He'd made three professional albums with a major country music studio in Nashville, and done two huge world tours and then a third online.

"How's Adam doing with Country Quad?" Bryce asked, and Harry's gaze flew to him.

"He's doing great," he said. "And Cole, don't think we've forgotten about you, but I wanted to ask you guys about Adam."

He cleared his throat and looked over to Joey. "He's my best friend who doesn't have the last name Young, and I've thought about inviting him to these movie nights several times. I've never done it, though, because until very recently, I was also his boss. But now that I'm not...." He let the words drip there and end, and Joey simply folded her arms and looked at him.

"I mean, if there were any other announcements...." He didn't look away from her either, and that brought several other people's eyes to her.

"Yeah, Joey, we haven't heard from you," Rosie said, picking up on all of the things Harry put down.

"I don't have much news," Joey said. "I got stuck at my mother's on Halloween during that big snowstorm. And while I love Grams and Gramps, it reminded me that I want to get my own place, so I'm going to be doing Thanksgiving pies to earn some extra money for my security deposit."

"Oh, that's awesome," Harry said. "I can share on social media."

"Would you?" Joey's whole face lit up. "I'd really appreciate that, Harry."

"I can too," Bryce said. "Just let me know all the details."

"Aunt Faith is finishing up with my website today," Joey said. "And she's going to text Joe about posting on the Hole in One page as well."

"Is your mom going to post on the bookstore page?" Belle asked.

Joey nodded. "And Hilde said she'd put flyers at all the registers in the furniture store."

Harry's family did have an amazing network of people, especially because his daddy, along with all of his uncles, had married small business owners in Coral Canyon. Aunt Sterling could post about the pies on her massage studio's social media, and Aunt Ev could also put flyers at the dance studio. Aunt Dani worked at a florist shop, and Harry was sure that Joey had asked every person possible to help her.

"I didn't see that on the family text," he said casually.

"That's because I didn't put it there," Joey said. "I've just been texting the aunts to see what they could do to help —and Adam said he would talk to the band members to see if they could put it on Country Quad's social media as well."

Her voice gave nothing away about any relationship with Adam, though Harry knew they had been out on Saturday. He wished he didn't feel like dying such a slow death by not knowing. Joey would not appreciate him asking, so he simply swallowed all his questions and looked over to Cole.

"You're up, bud."

"I think I just need prayers to make it through the last five months of school," he said.

"Six," Rosie corrected him. "There are *six* months of school left."

He looked at his sister, while Corinne chuckled. "I actually think there are seven, Cole," she said.

He rolled his eyes and said, "I don't get why it matters at all, but I promised my daddy I'd graduate. He said he'd fillet me alive and never allow me to go into the rodeo if I didn't."

Harry grinned and grinned, because that so sounded like Uncle Jem. He totally understood not wanting to go to college, as well as the senioritis, because Harry had had quite the bad case of it himself.

The doorbell rang, stealing their attention, and Harry let Boston, Rosie, and Cole go to get the food. He managed to get himself next to Joey and he leaned in even closer. "Really? You're not going to give me a single thing about Adam?"

She looked at him and said, "I could invite him to movie night next time you have it."

He grinned and grinned. "Are you saying what I think you're saying?"

Joey ducked her head and tucked her hair. "Yeah, we had a great date, and we're going out again."

Harry whooped and reached to toss up his cowboy hat, only realizing at the last moment that he had already put the movie titles in it and set it on the counter. Still, plenty of attention came to him, and he bustled over to the counter and picked up his hat.

"Let's pick a movie. Liesl, it's your turn to draw."

She moved over to the hat, reached inside, and fished around. She pulled out a slip of paper and opened it. "Twilight," she said, and half the crowd groaned, and the other half cheered.

Harry didn't much care what they watched that night, and he stood a pace away as everyone crowded around the burgers being set on the counter by Boston and Rosie. He loved cousin movie night, and he loved his cousins, and he quickly pulled out his phone to send a text to Adam to let him know that he was well loved too.

16

Boston Simpson climbed the steps at the nondescript house and rang the doorbell. "I hope this is it," he muttered to himself, because this place didn't look at all like where he imagined someone as charismatic and powerful and capable as Adam Harmon to live.

"Come in," a man yelled, and it sounded very much like Adam.

Boston didn't see any other vehicles parked in the driveway, but he found the door unlocked and the heat welcome as he stepped inside. "It's me—Boston," he called, and he moved through the tiny foyer and hallway into the back of the house. Adam had piled boxes on the dining room table, and he stepped around from a tower of them, confusion ripe on his face.

"Boston, what are you doing here?"

"I came to help you move." He tucked his hands in his leather jacket, also confused. "Where is everyone else?"

Adam wore a frown between his eyebrows as well, and he approached and shook Boston's hand. "I don't know what the others are waiting for."

"Joey texted us all and asked us to come help you move," Boston said.

Recognition and surprise marched across Adam's face as he lifted his eyebrows. "So that's who she got to help me move."

Boston grinned at him. "Pretty sure Harry will be here, as well as Cole and Rosie and Eric. Corrine had a cello lesson, and Liesl is on the driving range today, so I don't think they'll be here."

The front door opened again, and both he and Adam looked that way to see Joey entering. "Boston, you found it," she said.

"I found it, all right." He raised his eyebrows at his cousin. "You didn't tell him we were coming?"

She grinned with all the radiance of the sun. "I wanted it to be a surprise."

"I'm pretty sure he was surprised," Boston said, and he looked between Adam and Joey, trying to put the pieces of them together. She had said nothing about him at cousin movie night only a few days ago. But they definitely had a vibe going on.

"Howdy, ma'am," Adam said.

And Boston narrowed his eyes. "Why are you coordinating his move, anyway?"

"Why, indeed," Adam asked, and then he zeroed in on Boston again. "You said you had something you wanted to talk to me about."

"Oh, sure." Sudden nerves ran through Boston. He wasn't sure why. He'd worked with Adam on the summer concert series, and he knew him quite well. "I'm applying for a bunch of jobs around town," he said. "Mostly event centers, like wedding venues and high-end lodges, where they do parties and conferences and have concierges—stuff like that. I kind of feel like it goes along with some of the coordination and details that I learned during the concert series, and I was hoping that I could put you down as a reference."

Adam, in his business-like way, simply nodded. "Yes, of course. That would be fine."

Boston nodded too, hoping he wouldn't have to be as serious as Adam to work at a cowboy lodge in the Teton Mountains. At the same time, he knew plenty of rich people came to Wyoming to escape the bigger cities and the pressures of their busy lives, and they probably did want a concierge wearing a suit and tie, who could give them all the luxuries of country living.

"I'm just looking right now," Boston said. "I haven't seen anything come up yet, but I just wanted to make sure it was okay."

"Yep, it's okay," Adam said, his eyes glued to Joey as she moved into his kitchen and opened his fridge. That felt like such a personal thing to do, and Boston volleyed his gaze between her and him, finally stepping closer to Adam. "What's going on with you two?"

"Nothing," Adam said quickly. "What makes you think there's something going on with us?"

Boston grinned at him. "Your high-pitched question to my question makes me think there's something going on," he said. "Is there?"

Tension radiated off Adam while Joey bent to slide a tray into his oven, and he was saved by the doorbell ringing. Instead of yelling, "Come in," again, he glared at Boston and walked away.

Cole and Rosie had arrived with Eric, and Adam welcomed them to his house. When they'd all arrived back in the great room, Joey looked up from her phone. "Harry says he's five minutes away with the truck. You have every-thing packed?"

Adam folded his arms. "Do you think I would not be ready for a nine a.m. moving time?"

Joey tipped her head back and trilled out a laugh unlike anything Boston had ever heard before. Oh, this was flirting at its finest, and though Boston hadn't had a girlfriend since high school, he suddenly knew exactly what kind of vibe was going on between Adam and Joey.

They *liked* each other.

"Can I have one of these kolaches?" Rosie asked, and Boston whipped his attention to a tray that now sat on Adam's kitchen counter that had not been there before.

"Where did those come from?" he asked.

"I just heated them up," Joey said. "You didn't seriously think I'd ask you to come move someone without feeding you, did you?"

Rosie picked one up and handed it to Boston. "Ooh, they're just a little bit warm."

"They won't be all the way hot," Joey said. "I only put them in the oven for five minutes."

Kolaches went around, and then Harry came in through the garage entrance. "Truck's here and the wind's picking up, so let's get this done."

Adam moved to stand next to Harry, and he raised both hands to get everyone's attention. "Thank you all so much for coming. I don't actually own any of the furniture here, so we don't need to take any couches, tables and chairs, or the bed. I have boxes and one trunk that belonged to my grandfather in the bedroom. I marked it."

Joey moved to his side and added, "We'll get everything loaded up here, and then we'll drive to Dog Valley and unload there." She looked up to Adam, her expression so... open and full of something Boston could only identify as adoration.

"You've got furniture we need to move and put together, right, baby?" she asked.

"Baby?" Rosie screeched, and all activity, conversation, and eating of kolaches came to a sudden halt. Adam's face reddened, but Joey simply ducked her head, looking sheepish.

Harry started to laugh, and Boston knew why. He

grinned, because he liked Adam a lot, and maybe if he started dating Joey, she would finally realize how amazing she was. Boston knew she suffered with self-esteem issues—because he did too, and they talked about it.

"Yes, I ordered furniture," Adam growled at the group. He glared over to Harry. "What is so funny?"

"I think you two better start comin' clean," Harry said. "There are a whole bunch of us here." He scanned the crowd, grinning and grinning and *grinning*. "And some of us can't keep a secret."

Joey cleared her throat. "I don't expect anyone to keep a secret. Adam and I are dating, and I'm going to put it on the family text after we get him moved into his new house, where he has new furniture that might need to be placed, as I believe Aunt Hilde was delivering it last night and this morning."

"That's right," Adam said, practically clipping the words out in a yell. "All the boxes are labeled as well."

Boston wouldn't expect anything less. Joey laced her fingers through Adam's and squeezed. He visibly relaxed, and Boston found the two of them just so cute. He also wanted someone in his life who could hold his hand, say nothing, and calm him down.

"Adam was able to get into his house last night," Joey said. "And he stocked the freezer full of pizza, so we'll feed you guys before you leave as well."

"There are a couple of pieces of furniture I bought online," he said. "Bookcases and a nightstand and TV stand. I'll need help putting those together."

"I brought the power tools," Harry said.

"If you have to leave early, that's fine," Joey said. "But we'll take as much help for as long as we can get it."

Boston had nothing else to do, and he certainly wasn't going to return home to his parents' house earlier than he had to. He really needed to find a job, because he really needed to get out of his parents' basement, and he closed his eyes in a long blink and said a quick prayer.

Please, God, I just need something to open up for me.

"Harry, someone saved you some kolaches," Joey said.

"Oh, thanks." He moved over to get the last couple, and Boston figured now was as good as any time to pick up the first box and get this moving day started. He did, and that spurred others to do the same.

Since they didn't have to move any furniture out of Adam's house, it took less than a half an hour to load the truck. It would take forty-five minutes to drive to Dog Valley from his rental, and though Boston had just eaten a kolache, he couldn't wait for the pizza buffet feast.

"What about you?" Cole asked as Boston climbed in the truck with him and Rosie. "Are you seeing anyone secret we should know about?"

Boston laughed and shook his head. "Absolutely not. You?"

"Sure, I need my daddy riding me about finishing school *and* having a girlfriend," Cole said, and that made Boston laugh all over again.

"Rosie, what about you?"

His cousin turned beet red, and even her brother turned to look at her.

"Rosie," he said, shock and scandal in his voice. "You are *fourteen years old*." He leaned closer as if her age were a massive national secret.

"I'm not dating anyone," she bit out. "There's just this boy in my French class that I like, and he seems to like me too. Shocking, I know."

"Why is that shocking?" Boston asked at the same time Cole said, "Of course, he would like you."

She rolled her eyes and folded her arms. "Oh, come on, everyone knows I'm not the type of girl that boys like."

"What does that mean?" Cole asked.

"I'm mouthy," she said. "And smart." Her face turned bright red again. "And I look like a boy."

"You do not," Cole said. He looked in the rearview mirror and met Boston's eyes.

His heart hurt for Rosie, and he said, "Yeah, I never seen a boy look like you, Rosie."

She twisted and looked at him. "Really, Boston?"

"You got real pretty hair," Boston said. "And those freckles across your nose are super cute. And Rosie, boys like smart girls. Don't ever feel bad about that."

"Why do they act like they don't like me, then?" Rosie asked. She sounded small and vulnerable, which were two words that Boston would never, ever use to describe her.

"They're just scared," he said. "I know, because I was really intimidated by girls when I was younger. Heck, I still am. It's not that boys don't like you, Rosie, it's that they *do*, and they're afraid that you'll think *they're* the idiots."

Cole nodded, and he pulled away from the curb once Harry had driven the moving truck past them. "I know Spencer liked you."

"Oh, Spencer's an idiot," Rosie said with a scoff.

Boston tipped his head back and laughed again. "That's exactly why boys are afraid of you, Rosie. They know you're going to see right through them to who they truly are. It's going to take someone special to capture your heart."

"Is that who this guy is?" Cole asked, looking at his sister out of the side of his eye. "What's his name, anyway?"

"I am not telling you," Rosie said. "The last boy I told you about, you marched up to him the very next day and scared him off."

"So has something started between you two?" he asked.

"Well, I'm going to be fifteen before Valentine's Day," Rosie said. "And Daddy and Momma said I could go to the dance this year. So yeah, we've already talked about him taking me."

Cole nodded, his jaw tight, but Boston beamed at Rosie. "That's great," he said. "You should go out with a lot of boys, Rosie—as many as you can. Then you'll get to know what kind of guy you like."

She twisted to look at him again, and Boston simply gave her his best smile. "Don't worry about your momma and daddy either," he said. "You're a good girl, and they know it."

To his utter surprise, she sniffled and turned around, and Rosie had never been known to be quiet, but Boston could barely hear her as she said, "Thank you, Boston."

He looked out the window, feeling like he finally belonged in this family. It might only last for a moment, but for right now, Boston sure liked being a Young.

17

"Thank you so much," Joey said as she leaned in to hug Rosie. "Really, thank you." She'd said it fifteen hundred times in the last five minutes as her cousins had all prepared to leave Adam's new house.

All of his furniture had been put together and positioned in the places he wanted. Some of his boxes had been unpacked, mostly in the kitchen and bathrooms, and he could do his clothes to fill his master closet and his linens and his shoes by himself.

"Thanks for having us," Rosie said. "We're headed to Bryce's now to help feed the horses. I can't wait to meet their new baby when she comes." She grinned from ear to ear, turned, and left the house. Joey watched her jog after her brother, and then she brought Adam's front door closed and twisted the deadbolt, locking herself inside with him.

She sighed, because it had been a very busy day already,

and the clock had barely struck one. Her legs ached, and while Joey worked two pretty physical jobs in the kitchen, she somehow felt more tired now than she did after working both of those.

Adam had thanked everyone as a group and retreated to the couch while Joey continued individual conversations with her cousins. Now she sank down next to him, a hefty sigh pulling out of her mouth. "It's done," she said, and she actually laid down with her head in his lap.

He stroked her hair back, his touch gentle and soft and wonderful. "Thank you so much for arranging for them to come help."

She turned and looked up at him. "Of course, and I didn't even have to tell any of the uncles."

It'd been a few hours since she'd been caught calling Adam "baby," and her stomach vibrated as if the garlic knots she'd eaten for lunch had taken up arms and were about to revolt.

"You're going to have to tell them, though," Adam said, raising his eyebrows. "When are you going to do that?"

Joey groaned as she sat up and moved back to his side. "Have I told you about our family text?" she asked, knowing full well that she hadn't.

"No, ma'am," he murmured.

"Well, it's a beast of its own," she said. "It's hard to describe until you're actually on it. So let me show you."

She tapped and swiped to get her phone open, and then she moved to the group messaging app, where she actually did have plenty of multi-person conversations. For example, she'd made a group chat with the people she'd asked to come help Adam move that morning.

On her phone, she'd named the whole Young family group chat "The Big Shebang," and she tilted her phone toward Adam. "Every aunt, every uncle, every person over the age of fourteen," she said. "That's the rule we came up with. There's like sixty of us."

"Sixty?" Adam's eyebrows went up. "That can't be true."

"Oh, it's true," Joey said with a chuckle. "Leigh's brother and his wife are on here, and so are Ev's brothers and their wives, even though they're not Youngs. It's definitely over sixty. In fact, I think Liesl added it up once and it was sixty-one, and that doesn't include Denzel and Michelle, Kassie and Reggie, or Shawn and Enid. Oh, and let's not forget Abby's brother and his wife—Wade and Cheryl. You should see us when we get together for a party."

Joey sucked in a breath and turned toward him. "In fact, Uncle Tex is hosting Thanksgiving at his ranch."

She cleared her throat, knowing she could ask Adam to come eat dinner with her that day, and Aunt Abby wouldn't care at all. There would be plenty of food. Wade and Cheryl and their kids would be there as well, and so would her parents. Sometimes Georgia's parents joined the big Young family as well, and sometimes so did Aunt Faith's sister and her family.

"Would you want to come with me?" she asked. "What are you doing for Thanksgiving?"

Adam blinked as if he hadn't even realized Thanksgiving was so soon.

"They're actually having it on Sunday," she said. "Instead of on Thanksgiving Day, because everybody seems to have their own core family things, and then they can come to the big family thing if they want."

"What are you doing for Thanksgiving?" he asked.

"Well, I was going to go...." She trailed off and then reached way down deep for her well of bravery. "To my parents' house. Grams and Gramps are going with Uncle Jem and Aunt Sunny this year, because Cole and Rosie are going to be in Las Vegas with their mom."

She swallowed. "You could come to that too, if you want. I think this year it's me and my two younger siblings, my momma and daddy, and they invited Graham and Laney Whittaker, because they're technically OJ's biological grandparents, and we do a lot with them."

Adam looked away out the big windows to his right that showed his backyard. "What are you going to tell your parents?"

"I'm not going to tell them anything different than I tell everyone else," Joey said, deciding on the spot. "My daddy's going to call. I know that."

"Do you think he'll be upset?" Adam asked.

Joey thought for a moment, this question not new in her mind. "I don't know," she said thoughtfully. "I can't imagine he would be. He knows you; he respects you. If he didn't, there's no way he would have signed on with you being the band manager for Country Quad."

"Having someone be a band manager is totally different than thinking they'd be a good boyfriend for your daughter."

"Well, it doesn't really matter what he thinks, does it?" Joey asked.

Adam swung his attention back to her.

"I think you're a good boyfriend for me, so it doesn't really matter what he thinks."

Adam cradled her face in one hand, and Joey loved it when he did that. She felt cherished and seen, as Adam never let his attention wander somewhere else when talking with her. He didn't overlook her, and he wasn't biding his time with her while he waited for something better to walk by.

"So I'm just gonna tell him," Joey said, tapping in the message box at the bottom of the family text. She grinned. "And it might as well be fun, right?"

"I don't think any of this is fun," Adam growled, and that made Joey laugh. Her thumbs flew over the screen and she typed out whatever came into her mind.

Hey, everyone, since the holidays are coming up and we'll be spending time together as a big group, I just wanted to let everyone know that I started seeing someone, and I'd like to invite him to the big Thanksgiving dinner at Uncle Tex's.

She sent that and held her phone out so Adam could see it.

"Ten seconds," she said. "My young adult cousins and I tease how no one can put anything on the family text and not get a response within ten seconds."

"That can't be true," Adam said.

Sure enough, a message popped up from Aunt Hilde.

Oh, that's great, Joey, I'm sure it's okay if he comes.

It's absolutely okay, Aunt Abby said. *I can't wait to meet him.*

You're seeing someone new? Georgia asked, and Joey pointed to the text. "That's my momma."

Have you told your mother? Georgia asked.

The real question is, if she's told her father, Luke sent.

Does this boy live in Coral Canyon? Uncle Gabe asked. *Or Dog Valley?*

She pointed to that one, even though it blipped up as more messages came in. "He's asking that because he knows I'm in Dog Valley a lot to see my momma."

"Hmm," Adam said, humming somewhere deep in his chest.

I'm sure it's not a boy, Uncle Gabe, Bryce said. *Joey's twenty-two, so I'm sure she's dating a man.*

It's definitely a man, Harry said, with a laughing emoji.

She tilted her phone toward Adam so he could see Harry's text. "He and Belle asked about us. I told them we went out last weekend."

Adam grunted. "He's texted me a couple of times too."

"What did you tell him?"

"Nothing." Adam pulled her closer, keeping her warm and safe under the protection of his arm. "I ignored him."

Well, I'd like to know who it is, Mav said. *Unless you're not telling.*

She'll tell when she's ready, Aunt Faith said.

She has to tell, Uncle Tex said. *She's bringing him to dinner in a week. A FULL FAMILY dinner.*

Besides, she wouldn't have texted on here if she didn't want to tell, Boston said.

MORE AND MORE MESSAGES POURED IN, AND JOEY giggled with each one. Adam scoffed and said, "Look how many there are."

"Oh, and here comes Grams," she said, as the first message from her grandmother came in. *If it's who I think it is, I'm thrilled,* she said.

She looked over to Adam. "She's saying that, so my daddy won't be upset."

"He hasn't answered yet at all," he said. "Do you think he hasn't seen it?"

"Oh, he's seen it," Joey said. "He's probably talking to Georgia about it, and she's probably calming him down, and he's going to be dying." She trailed off, trying to decide if she should give her father five minutes or one.

"Are you going to tell him privately?" he asked.

"I bet Daddy's waiting to say anything until I do," she said. "He grew up here, and he knows a lot of people here. He's been raising his family here for a long time. He'll definitely want to know who it is."

"So does everyone else," Adam said, gesturing to the phone. "Even your cousins who saw us are asking."

"That's because they're trying to thread the needle," Joey said. "That's what we do for each other in the Young family." She looked over to him, suddenly insecure. She lowered her phone. "My family is huge, Adam, and you're used to being by yourself."

He searched her face, and she wondered what he saw. "I'm a people person," he said softly. "I can handle your family, because at other times it's just me and you like this."

She softened into his side and kissed him gently. That gave her the strength she needed to say, "Okay, I'm gonna tell them."

She leaned her head closer to his and said, "With picture evidence. Are you willing to be on my family text?"

She prayed with everything inside her that he would say yes, and she tapped on her camera app, and held her phone out to take a selfie.

Adam pressed his temple to hers and smiled. Joey snapped the picture and could not stop grinning at it. "We're so cute," she said. "Look at us."

"Well, one of us is," he said.

Joey nudged him with her shoulder, and then navigated back to the family text string so that she could upload the picture. Below that, she captioned it. *This is him.* In parentheses, she added, (*It's Adam Harmon, by the way, for any of you who don't know him.*)

Her thumb hovered over the arrow that would send the text to the sixty-five-plus people on the string.

"My daddy will call within thirty seconds," she said.

"It's fine," Adam said. "You can put him on speaker, and we can both talk to him." He swallowed, the only sign of nerves Joey saw in him. Her heartbeat stampeded through her veins, and she wished she could be calmer, more confident.

"You know what you want," Adam said. "You're a grown adult, and you're one of the strongest women I've ever met." He gently put his thumb over hers, and they pressed the send button together.

Messages streamed in, even faster now, some of them only emojis of the mind-blown smiley face or a heart. Only seconds later, her phone rang, and *Daddy Dearest* sat there.

"Told you," she said, and she jumped to her feet, because she couldn't have this conversation sitting down. She swiped on the call, and then tapped the speaker button. Then she drew a breath as she waited for the call to connect, and then she said, "Hey, Daddy, you're on speaker with me and Adam."

18

O tis Young turned and faced the closed door of his office. His wife called it his music studio, and Otis could be found plucking through chords on his guitar from time to time.

Sometimes a song would come into his head fully formed, and he could barely keep up with his fingers to get it out. Sometimes he knew exactly what to say to his children, and sometimes, no matter what he did, he felt blank, hollow, and empty. Without words. Silent.

He hated it the most when he didn't have lyrics and music in his life, and sitting on the phone with his oldest daughter and finding only silence terrified him.

"Daddy?" Joey asked, and Otis cleared his throat.

"Yeah, I'm here." He blinked, and he could see the picture of Adam and Joey, their heads tipped together, their smiles wide. OJ had been in the middle of his song, and Otis had interrupted him and sent him out to the kitchen for a snack.

"Just a minute," he said. "Your mother is knocking on the door."

"You've barricaded yourself in your office, haven't you?" Joey teased, and somehow the fact that she wasn't nervous helped Otis feel more comfortable.

His wife had not knocked on the door, and Otis prayed for forgiveness for the little white lie. As he crossed the room and opened the door, he heard voices down the hall—Georgia's and OJ's—and then Georgia stepped past the dining room table and looked down the hall.

Even from twenty feet away, Otis could see the concern in her eyes, and somehow that soothed him too. He lifted his phone away from his ear and said, "It's Joey."

She nodded, though they both knew that he had called her and not the other way around. Georgia gave him a soft smile, which reminded Otis to bury anything that would drive Joey further from them.

He'd been worried about his daughter for a great many months now, though she was a good person and a hard worker. She took care of his mother and father, and they both adored having her in their condo. Otis simply wanted her to realize how integral to the family she was and how much joy she brought into all of their lives. He wanted her to feel loved and valued, and he knew she didn't.

He stepped back into his office. "Sorry, we have something with OJ."

"Yeah? What's he doing?" Joey asked.

"He wants Bailey to come for the holidays," Otis said, reaching up to rub his eyes. His mother had told him that every child came with their own set of wants, needs, and problems, and boy, was she ever right.

"Is she not coming?" Joey asked.

"I think for Christmas," Otis said, as he sank into his office chair. "But not Thanksgiving, and you know how OJ can get."

"Oh, I know how OJ can get," Joey said with a light laugh. "I know how *you* can get too, Daddy, and you didn't interrupt something with OJ to call me and talk about him."

"No, I didn't." Otis blew out his breath. "So you like Adam, huh?"

"Yes, I like Adam," Joey said, and her tone carried sunshine and sparkles. Otis remembered he was on speaker with the two of them, and he could only imagine them making goo-goo eyes at each other.

"What's your objection?" she asked.

"Who says I have an objection?" Otis said. "You just haven't dated in a while, and maybe I'm a little surprised."

"Yeah, you're a little surprised because *it's Adam*," Joey said. "I know you, Daddy. Just tell me what it is, so that I can talk you out of it."

He smiled. "I used to be the one talking you out of the things you were worried about," he said.

"Oh, you still do," she said. "So, what is it?"

Otis pressed his eyes closed and tried to listen to the Lord. He'd always aimed to be as honest as possible with his children, though he didn't believe in telling them everything before they were mature enough to handle it. Joey would be twenty-three in February, and every cell in Otis's body told him that she could handle this.

"I think he's too old for you," he said. "There, that's it. I think he's too old for you."

On the other end of the line, Adam cleared his throat, but he said nothing.

"Yeah, he thinks that too," Joey said.

Relief rushed through Otis. "So I'm not being completely unreasonable."

"I mean, I think it's silly," Joey said. "One of your favorite country music stars is fifty-six and his wife is twenty-six."

"Yeah, and I think he's too old for her too," Otis said. "I just don't have to deal with them in my daily life."

"Well, Adam's not thirty years older than me," Joey said.

"How much older?" Otis challenged.

"It's like...eight years...." Joey said, her voice trailing off. "And some change."

Eight years felt like a lot, but Otis ground his teeth together to stay silent. What else was he supposed to say? He only had the one complaint about the meticulously detailed band manager that Country Quad had just hired. Adam was clean-cut and professional, well-spoken, and excellent at his job. Otis happened to know the man's salary, and Joey would be well taken care of.

So what's eight years? The words slithered through his

mind like a snake that had found the warmest, sunniest rock and could finally stretch out and relax.

"All right," he said. "What about his job?"

"He has a good job."

"Yes, he does." Otis glared at the wall opposite of him, where he'd hung all the covers for Country Quad's albums. "And what happens if it doesn't work out between you two?" Otis was really asking if she'd leave town then, because Joey tended to go into avoidance mode rather than deal with contention and confrontation.

Joey remained silent, and Adam cleared his throat again. "Sir, if I may...."

"I know what he's really asking," Joey said into the resulting silence. "Coral Canyon is small, but it's not like I'm involved in the band at all. I'm sure I can handle seeing an ex-boyfriend from time to time."

"Mm." Otis wasn't sure he believed that, but he didn't feel like perpetuating the issue right in front of the person who could *be* the issue. "All right," he said. "Sounds like you have it worked out."

"Wait—you're not going to forbid me from seeing him?" Joey asked, and Otis wasn't quite sure, but he thought she was teasing him.

"Have I ever *forbid* you from seeing someone?" he asked. "How dare you?" He laughed, glad when Joey joined in with him. His concern remained, but ultimately, he couldn't control the situation. He could only offer love and support.

"We'd love to have you over for dinner," Otis said. "Is he coming for Thanksgiving?"

A pause came through the line, and Otis could practically hear them talking silently to one another, using only their eyes, the way he could do with Georgia sometimes.

"Yeah," Joey said. "He'd love to come for Thanksgiving dinner."

"Well, it's just us and the Whittakers," he said, "I guess maybe Bailey, if OJ gets his way."

"I'm sure it will be wonderful, sir," Adam said, and Otis almost rolled his eyes.

"You don't have to call me sir," he said.

"Yeah, he doesn't like that," Joey said with a giggle. "Makes him feel old."

"I *am* old," Otis shot back.

"Daddy, you're only fifty," Joey said. "It's not that old."

"All right, well, I love you, Roo," he said.

"I love you too, Daddy."

The call ended, and Otis slid his phone onto the top of his desk just as OJ rapped lightly on the slightly ajar door.

"Can I come in, Daddy?" he asked, and Otis gestured for him to come in. Georgia followed with a cup of coffee and a square of peanut butter bar.

"How'd it go?" she asked.

"Oh, just fine," Otis said.

"You think he's too old for her, don't you?"

"Yes." Otis accepted the coffee and then drew Georgia onto his lap. "He *is* too old for her, but they're both adults. And did you see that picture?"

Georgia smiled at him and ran her fingers through his

hair. "I saw it," she said. Over on the stool, OJ started to strum lightly, moving through a C-major scale on his strings. "They were adorable."

"Yeah, I know," Otis said with a sigh.

"Don't sound so happy that your daughter is dating someone she likes," Georgia said.

"I am happy about it," Otis said. "It's just—it feels kind of messy, you know?"

"Because he manages Country Quad?"

"Yes," Otis said. "I mean, what if they break up? Adam can't just leave town, which means Joey will."

"I don't think Joey wants to leave town," Georgia said.

"Whether she wants to or not won't matter," Otis said. "She's a runner, and Coral Canyon is small, and Adam is intimately connected to our family now—for the next three years. So either it works out and everything's fine and great."

Otis pressed his eyes closed and tried to imagine that future, but nothing would come forward. "Or things end between them, and Joey packs her bags, and we won't see her again for a year. She'll become even more distant, more disconnected than she already feels."

Georgia watched him soberly for several long moments, then she leaned down and pressed her lips to his in a chaste kiss. "I don't think you're giving your daughter enough credit," she said as she stood from his lap. She faced their son, her smile beautiful and bright. "OJ played his song, and he sounded real good. Didn't you, baby?"

She walked over to OJ and ruffled his hair. "We have

that movie at three o'clock, so you'll need to be done in here pretty soon."

Otis nodded to acknowledge her, and then she left them alone in the music room. He didn't feel like continuing the lesson, but he found such hope on his son's face.

"You want to play it for me, bud?" he asked.

OJ nodded and started into the song. The boy did have talent, even as a ten-year-old, and if he wanted to go into country music, Otis would do anything and everything he could to make it happen.

He wished he knew what he was doing, that there was some manual on how to be a good dad with checklists and questions to ask children of both genders at any age. Since he didn't have that manual, he simply did the best he could.

He consulted with his brothers and his parents and most of all, his wife. He prayed every morning and every night that he wouldn't do anything too badly to mess his children up too much or drive them away from him and Georgia.

OJ finished the song, and Otis had barely heard a note of it. But he clapped and said, "That is sounding real good, buddy."

OJ set his guitar aside and came closer to the desk. Otis already knew what he wanted, and he nodded to his phone, "You can text her," he said. "But buddy, Thanksgiving is in four days, and we don't really know what she's doing."

"I know," OJ said.

"You don't think her parents have invited her?"

"No," he said. "Grandpa Graham said they did."

"What else did Grandpa Graham tell you?" Otis asked.

"He said she hadn't decided," OJ said, something earnest on his face. "And I just think that I could invite her too, and maybe she'll feel comfortable coming down. We've got those adopted ducks right now, and one of 'em needs his wing looked at."

Otis gave his son a small smile. "Maybe she won't want to work when she's not at her own clinic, bud."

"Yeah, I know," OJ said. "But it doesn't hurt to ask, right?" He raised his chin, something hard glinting in his eyes. "That's what Momma says. Momma says it doesn't hurt to ask, and so every night, when I get down and pray, I just figure it doesn't hurt to ask God for what I want. And He's been helping me be a real good guitar player and a good older brother. And I am *so* good with those ducks, Daddy, so I just think I could text her, and maybe—"

"Okay, okay," Otis said before OJ really got started. The boy *loved* to ramble, and once he got on a roll, it could be difficult to slow him down. "I told you to text her, so go text her."

OJ grinned and took the phone over to the couch. He started typing, a look of great concentration on his face. A few minutes later, he brought the phone back and handed it to Otis.

He read the message, because that was their rule. OJ got to type the message and Otis would help him refine it, hopefully teaching him a little bit about texting as well as how to deal with a delicate situation.

Hey, Bailey, OJ had said. *It's OJ, and I talked to your daddy, and he said that he invited you for Thanksgiving, but that he didn't know if you were coming or not. They're coming to our house, and we're gonna have a giant turkey and a big candied ham, and I'd love to see you.*

"Wow," Otis said, chuckling. "You put in a turkey emoji."

"Yeah, but not like the turkey that's the animal," he said. "But like the turkey you eat."

Otis lifted one eyebrow as he looked at his son. "They're the same thing, bud."

"No, but the emojis aren't the same," OJ said. "Look, I put the ducks down below."

An overwhelming wave of love crashed over Otis as he continued reading. *We've also got a pair of adopted ducks right now. They're living with our chickens, and one of them has a sore wing, and I know that you could help him get better. The vet here doesn't seem to know what he's doing at all.*

Sure enough, after that, he'd included two duck emojis.

Anyway, no pressure. I just thought I'd ask.

Otis looked up, his heart bursting with pride. "This is a great text, bud." He handed the phone back. "You can send it."

"Really?" OJ asked. "You didn't change nothing?"

"I didn't change *anything*," Otis corrected. He nodded to the device. "Go ahead and send it."

OJ took a deep breath and then sent the text. He practically dropped the phone as if it had caught on fire. "I'm not going to get my hopes up, okay, Daddy? If she can't come, she can't come."

"That's right, son," Otis said. "It would be nice to see her, but if she can't come, she can't come, and we don't get to decide what's best for her."

"No," OJ said. "She gets to decide what's best for her."

"Yep," Otis said. "And sometimes people want to do things, OJ, and they simply can't, because they're sick, or they can't afford the gas, or whatever."

He looked down at the phone for a moment, and pure, childlike innocence filled his eyes as they widened. He looked back at Otis. "We could pay her gas."

Otis grinned and shook his head. "That's not the point, buddy. Bailey's a vet. I'm sure she can afford the gas. I'm just saying—more often than not, we don't know the reason *why* someone can't come. It *could* be something like they can't afford it, or they're too ill, but it could also just be something emotional that we don't understand, and we don't *have* to understand. You know what I mean?"

OJ tilted his head and said, "I don't know if I get it, Daddy."

"It's like that boy...Travis," he said, surprised that the name of one of OJ's classmates had arrived in his head. "He invited you to his birthday party and you didn't want to go. Remember?"

OJ's features darkened. "Yes," he said. "He's not very nice."

"Right? But you had no reason that you couldn't go. We were free that Saturday. We have plenty of money to buy a present. Me or your mother would have driven you. So why didn't you go?"

"Because I don't want to be his friend," he said. "He's not nice to anyone, even his friends."

"I'm sure that's not why Bailey wouldn't come," Otis said. "But she has a lot of complex feelings, and she's allowed to have those feelings. All we can do is invite."

"I know," OJ said.

The phone buzzed, and they both looked at it. OJ looked at Otis again, and he nodded. "Pick it up; see what she said."

OJ did, and he read out loud, "Thanks so much for this invite, OJ! I don't know if I'm going to be able to make it, but I should know by Monday, and I'll let you know. Okay?"

He looked up, and Otis saw all the hope and apprehension in his son's eyes. He gently took the phone from him, as OJ said, "So we'll know by Monday, yeah? Then we'll know if we need to go buy more food."

Otis chuckled. "Buddy, it's one person. We're not gonna need more food."

"Yeah, but Bailey really likes those brown sugar carrots," he said. "I could make them for her."

"Sure," Otis said, because this was not a hill he was willing to die on. "Why don't you go ask your mother to see if that was part of her menu, and if it's not, and Bailey comes, I'm sure she'll let you make them."

"All right," OJ said, and he skipped out of the office. Otis watched him go, and then looked down at his phone as it started buzzing again. This time it was a smaller group message with just him, Luke, Trace, and Tex in it. Trace had started it, and he'd asked, *How are you feeling about Joey and*

Adam? Do you think this is going to be a problem for Country Quad?

Otis thought about the question for a moment, feeling a gentle chastening move through him. Either he trusted Joey...or he didn't.

Then let his thumbs fly as he typed out his response.

Not at all.

19

Joey sat next to Grams, who wore her Sunday finest—complete with a hat. It wasn't a showy piece like what women wore to the Kentucky Derby, but a beautiful, petite cap in pale blue nonetheless. Joey tried to pay attention as the pastor spoke about gratitude, which went right along with the Thanksgiving season, but her attention kept wandering to her email.

Aunt Faith had gotten her website up and running last week. Joey had named her pie bakery Rooelle Pies, and at the same time she'd coordinated Adam's move from Coral Canyon to Dog Valley, she'd cleared with Shawn to use the industrial kitchen at Pork and Beans on Tuesday and Wednesday to bake her pies.

She'd been talking about the pie orders on social media, and all of her aunts had helped spread the word through the bookstore, the furniture store, Ev's dance studio, everywhere.

Adam had reposted her post to the Country Quad page, and the traitorous hope built up in her as she tapped over to her email again. She pressed her eyes closed, imagining dozens and dozens of emails, all pie orders that had come in in the ten minutes since she'd last checked.

Joey wasn't sure if she wanted to run a pie bakery full-time, but she'd set a goal of making an additional one thousand dollars this holiday season. That would be enough for a security deposit on any of the one-bedroom, one-bath apartments she'd seen online. That too had consumed all of her free time this week.

She almost scoffed at the thought of having free time, as she seemed to run from sunup to sundown and well into the night. Her heart took courage when she saw a single email sitting there, an order for the chocolate silk toffee pie.

A smile spread across her face, and she tapped over to the spreadsheet where she kept track of the orders. That chocolate silk pie brought her total to twenty. She looked up, an awful mix of hope and desperation in the back of her throat. Twenty pies equaled a two hundred dollar profit, and that only comprised twenty percent of Joey's goal.

She told herself the pie bakery website had been talked about for three and a half days, and she couldn't expect hundreds of orders within the first hour. Thanksgiving had come early this year, as the first had been on a Thursday, and she had five weeks to keep selling for holiday parties and Christmas.

She glanced over to Grams, who bent her hatted head down. "What is it, dear?" she whispered, and Joey appreciated that her grandmother didn't scold her for not paying attention to the sermon. She somehow sensed that Joey needed her, and she would set aside anything to be there.

"Do you think I should post again about the pies?" she whispered. She tilted her phone so that Grams could see the extra pie order.

"Couldn't hurt," Grams said, and she patted Joey's knee as she straightened again. Gramps had not been feeling well this morning, and they'd left him at home on the couch with a football game playing, his glasses perched on his nose and his Bible open in front of him.

Joey glanced up toward Pastor Michaels as he talked about what God expected of them. "A broken heart and a contrite spirit," he said. "And hands willing to do the Lord's work."

An idea struck Joey's mind, and while it wasn't exactly religious and had everything to do with her earning more money, she quickly navigated over to her social media.

She found the picture of her in a professional culinary institute uniform of a chef's jacket and a tall toque. She uploaded it and typed in: *Let my hands do your Thanksgiving pie work! Hi, my name is Joelle Young, and I'm the owner of Rooelle Pies, and this holiday season, I'm offering full-size pies and mini pies for any occasion, including Thanksgiving, Sunday family dinners, birthday parties, holiday parties. Whatever you can imagine, I will bring the pie.*

Thanksgiving orders must be in by Monday at 4 p.m. and I'm offering four flavors: spiced pumpkin, classic apple streusel, my granny's famous pecan, and a decadent chocolate silk toffee that will have everyone skipping the turkey and reaching for dessert first.

Check RooellePies.com to order!

She added as many relevant hashtags as she could think of and posted the picture. She wasn't sure why, but a weight felt like it had been lifted from her chest, and she turned her phone over face down on the bench next to her.

Then finally, she was able to tune in to the pastor's sermon about showing and expressing gratitude year-round. She could definitely do a better job of that, and while she'd heard of people doing gratitude journals for the month of November, she'd never done anything like that.

There's nothing stopping you from doing it in December, she thought, and she knew Georgia would have leftover gratitude journals at the bookstore.

An hour later, she parked in the condo parking lot and looked over to Grams with a sigh. "I was thinking something fast and easy for lunch today," she said. "Or are you and Gramps going out to Bryce's to help with the nursery?"

"Tex and Abby are there to help them with last-minute things in the nursery," Grams said. "I don't think we're going to go."

"Can we have grilled cheese and chicken noodle soup?" Joey grinned at her grandmother, who nodded. Growing up, Grams had made this meal for Joey plenty of times, always opening a can and pouring out the condensed soup with the star-shaped noodles Joey had loved as a little girl.

But Joey hadn't eaten canned soup in a long time now, and the moment she walked in the door, she set a pot of water to boil for broth and got out carrots, onions, and celery to make the holy trinity of mirepoix to start the soup.

Joey forgot her cares while in the kitchen, and she told herself that twenty pies would keep her plenty busy, and certainly was something to be grateful for. Her phone chimed with Adam's assigned ringtone, and Joey wiped her hands on her apron and moved to pick up her phone.

Saw your post. You're the cutest chef I've ever seen. Adam never sent emojis, but Joey would have added a smiley face and a person wearing a chef's hat right there. *I reposted it again. How many orders are you up to?*

Her heartbeat skipped a couple of times as she went back to her social media to see if there had been any questions or comments left on her post. When she saw it had over one hundred likes, she leaned back against the counter as if her legs couldn't hold her body weight.

"What is going on?" she murmured. Joey had never gotten over one hundred likes on anything, and she tapped on the button that told her how many times her post had been shared.

Seventeen.

Joey didn't even know seventeen people outside of her own family, and her blood raced with excitement through her body.

She tapped there, and she saw Adam's repost from

Country Quad, as well as one from her momma, one from Bryce, one from Kassie, and—"Oh," she said as realizations fell into place.

Pork and Beans had reposted her post with a caption that said, *Joey is one of our fantastic chefs at Pork and Beans. She's offering pies in her own company this year. And trust us, you won't be disappointed if you get one. It'll be the crowning jewel of your holiday meal!*

Their post had been reposted a couple of times, including by the Daily Grind, which Michelle owned. She had not posted for Joey a couple of days ago.

A new warmth filled her from the soles of her feet to the tips of her hair. "Cake Bites reposted," she said, her heartbeat doing funny things in her chest. She hadn't exactly spoken to her boss about doing the pies—and Cake Bites didn't offer pie anyway, so she didn't think it would be a conflict of interest. She *had* asked for Tuesday and Wednesday off at the bakery, and now her boss would know why.

She hadn't gotten any texts or reprimands, and her pulse picked up the pace as she tapped over to her email to see if she had gotten any more orders. Almost ninety minutes had passed since she had posted from the pews at church, and she pulled in a breath and held it as her email brightened on her phone.

She had seventeen new messages, and she whooped right out loud.

"What in tarnation?" Gramps asked. "Are you trying to give me a heart attack, girl?"

"I got seventeen more pie orders!" She rushed out of the kitchen and into the living room, where Grams had settled next to Gramps and had her knitting out. "From that post I made in church. Grams, look!" She thrust the device at her grandmother, who surely couldn't see it before Joey pulled it back. "Oh, perfect pumpkin pie. Two more just came in. Nineteen orders!"

Giddiness galloped through her, and she tapped back over to Adam's text. *Almost twenty new orders today!* she said. *I think it's because Uncle Shawn reposted from Pork and Beans and then Cake Bites picked up on that and posted too.*

That's so exciting, he sent back. *I miss you. What are you doing this afternoon?*

The scent of chicken broth suddenly filled her nose, and she whipped her attention back to the kitchen. She quickly stirred the celery, onions, and carrots, which she had been sautéing, and then poured them into the boiling broth. She'd give them a couple of minutes just to make sure the carrots would be nice and soft, and then she'd put in the noodles.

I'm going to have chicken noodle soup and grilled cheese sandwiches ready in twenty minutes, she said. *You should come eat.*

I have a surprise for you, he said. *Do you want it now or when I get there?*

An *I miss you* and a surprise? Joey's anxiety couldn't handle this. Plus, all those pie orders....

My heartbeat is already doing gymnastics, she said. *From all the pie orders. Just tell me.*

I booked us a horseback riding date on Friday.

She grinned and grinned. *Are we going out to Uncle Tex's or Bryce's?*

Bryce's, Adam said. *Your Uncle Jem said we could ride his horses and he'd meet us there.*

That sounds amazing, Joey said. *You checked the weather?*

No snow in the ten-day forecast, Adam said, and Joey added that to her list of things to be grateful for. Standing in the kitchen, she pressed her eyes closed and murmured, "Thank you, Lord."

I'm headed out, Adam said. *I'll see you in about thirty-five minutes.*

Can't wait, she sent back, and then she tapped back over to her email just to see if she'd gotten any more orders in the past five minutes.

One, for a full-size pumpkin and a half-bite apple, and Joey felt like the goals she'd set for herself were finally achievable.

Now she just needed to get this soup finished and her grandparents fed before Adam arrived, because she wanted to talk him through their upcoming Thanksgiving dinner with her family, find out more about what his family did for the holidays—and oh right, she needed to somehow convince him to be her pie-baking wingman on both Tuesday and Wednesday....

20

Bryce paced the length of the small hospital room, his cowboy boots making soft scuffing sounds against the linoleum floor. Codi lay in the bed, her face serene despite the steadily increasing contractions. The waning afternoon light filtered through the blinds, casting stripes across her face.

They'd been here forever.

His stomach ached and growled all at the same time, and he just wanted this baby to be born.

Bryce had been in this situation before, but this birth was nothing like the one he'd experienced when OJ had come into this world.

Codi groaned, and Bryce spun back to her. "Okay?" he asked, using that word for probably the hundredth time that day. They'd had to check in at six o'clock that morning, when Codi had been put on a Pitocin drip. She had dilated pretty steadily and then stalled, and Bryce felt like they might be in the hospital until Thanksgiving.

"I'm okay," she said, forcing a smile to her face. "Come lay with me. Your pacing is making me nervous."

He couldn't fit in the bed with her, so he took the chair beside her bed and took her hand in both of his. "I'm just...." He swallowed hard. "Lord, please bless this baby to come fast." He closed his eyes and tilted his head back, as if petitioning heaven. "Codi's real tired, and everyone's been waiting for him for so long. Keep them safe, but could we speed this up a little bit?"

"I'll say amen to that," Codi said.

Bryce opened his eyes and found her smiling at him. That gesture fell away quickly as pain whipped across her face. A contraction gripped her, and her hand tightened against his. Bryce's eyes flew to the monitor as the lines peaked. He'd learned about all these machines in the birthing classes they'd attended, but seeing them in action was different, more real. He'd been in such a haze when OJ was born, and every moment of this baby's birth felt amplified in both color and sound.

A nurse entered the room, checked Codi's chart, and then her vitals. "Let's see how you're doing." She checked Codi's progress and said, "Oh yes, you're ready for the epidural."

"Am I?" Codi asked, her voice filled with such hope.

"I'll call the anesthesiologist right now," she said. "You're up to a six, and that means you've progressed quite nicely in the last hour. We'll want to get the epidural now, or we might miss our window."

"I don't want to miss the window," Codi said.

Bryce didn't want that either, and the nurse nodded as she moved over to the phone on the wall and picked it up. He quickly texted his father, who'd been out in the waiting room for a couple of hours now. Bryce had tried to tell his parents not to come until he texted that the baby was here, but they were simply too excited.

He had his daddy, Otis, Georgia, and Abby in a group text, and he quickly messaged, *They're giving her the epidural. She's dilated to a six.*

Oh, that's great movement, Abby said almost instantly. *Georgia and Otis just got here with an early dinner.*

I hope that baby comes soon, Georgia said.

Tears pressed into Bryce's eyes at the kindness of his aunt. Otis and Georgia had adopted OJ all those years ago, and he knew his other biological son would be out in the waiting room waiting to meet this baby too.

"Can Abby come in?" Codi asked. "Just for a minute."

Bryce looked at her, finding a hint of panic there. "Of course she can, baby. I'll text her right now." He stood and pressed a kiss to his wife's forehead, and then texted as he walked out of the room. *Abby, Codi wants you to come back. I'm coming to let you in.*

He wasn't sure he dared go all the way into the waiting room, and he slowed as he passed the nurse's station. The double-wide doors just ahead required a code to enter or someone to come out and get a person, and he looked down at his phone as Abby said, *Of course, I'm right by the doors.*

Relief flooded Bryce, because Abby got it. He continued the last few steps and pushed the door open. Her eyes flew to his. "Is she okay?" she asked.

"I just think she's really nervous," Bryce said.

Codi's mother had died several years ago, and yes, Codi had confessed to Bryce that she wished her mother could be there, that she had someone she could talk to and ask questions of. Abby had been that person for her, and she brushed past him with kindness and determined in one expression. "Room four-seventeen, yes?"

"Yes," Bryce said, taking a moment to drink in the people in the waiting room. It seemed like half the town had arrived, but really it was just his family—Otis, Georgia, and OJ—and they'd brought along Anaya as well. Harry and Belle had claimed a corner, along with Kassie, Reggie, Joey, and Adam. Of the other uncles, only Uncle Mav had arrived, and he'd brought along Lars and no one else.

He nodded to his father and then ducked back inside, his own nerves stampeding through him. He approached the room and paused outside it. He loved his wife with everything inside him, and he knew she loved him. He also knew a woman needed her mother, and that Codi sometimes confided things in Abby that only another woman would understand. Something told him to hold back and wait, so he did.

A couple of minutes later, the door opened, and it seemed like the entire hospital staff streamed out.

"What's going on?" he asked, his pulse suddenly like a ping-pong ball ricocheting through his veins.

"Epidural is done," the nurse chirped. "She's doing great. You don't have to wait out here."

"Yeah, I know," Bryce said. He waited until the last medical professional had cleared the area, and then he stepped inside.

"You got the epidural so fast," he said as he smiled at Codi.

"I think he wanted to get it done before he went home for the day." Codi smiled too, and she definitely seemed much more relaxed. "It feels great."

Abby smoothed her hair back and held out a cup. "Have some more ice," she said. "You're going to progress really fast now, I just know it."

He looked between them, not quite sure what to ask. The monitors wailed again, signaling another contraction. Codi groaned, but she didn't cry out.

"Does it hurt?" he asked, because he'd been expecting it *not* to hurt.

"It's just a lot of pressure," she said, exhaling in a burst.

"I'm going to go back out," Abby said. "Okay? You'll be all right, Codi. You know what you're doing." Codi looked to her and nodded a couple of short, terse times.

"Thank you, Abby."

"Trust yourself," she said as she lovingly pushed Codi's hair off her face. She smiled at Bryce and then left the hospital room.

He knew that had probably taken every ounce of her

willpower, but both he and Codi had told everyone in the family that they wanted to be the only ones in the room when the baby was born.

Another contraction came, and it startled Bryce because it had been so close to the other one. Two more nurses entered the room, and when one checked Codi, she said, "Oh, you're at a nine now. I'm so glad we ordered that epidural when we did. Let's call your doctor."

Codi nodded again, and then she locked eyes with Bryce. "We're going to have a baby," she said, and her voice had almost turned into that of a cartoon character.

He moved to her side and stroked her hair back. "Yes, and it's going to be amazing."

Only a few minutes later, two more contractions had come and gone, and the room filled with people, warmers, blankets, and equipment. Finally, their doctor walked in, and Bryce didn't feel like the floor was going to vanish beneath his feet anymore.

"Let's see what we got," Dr. Azera said. She checked Codi quickly. "Oh, you're ready. This baby is ready." She smiled encouragingly. "We're going to watch this monitor, and when it starts to tick up, we're going to push."

"I feel like I'm going to pass out," Codi said.

"Your vitals are fine, honey," a nurse said. "Pulse is strong, oxygen is good."

"You've got this," Bryce said. "One hundred percent, baby."

The beeping grew closer together, and Dr. Azera said, "All right, Codi, now's your time to shine." She gripped the railings on the side of the bed and pushed. Bryce stood there helplessly, wondering how on earth women did this. He marveled at his wife's strength and capability, and several minutes later, after one more final push, the room filled with the strong cry of his son.

"It's a boy," Dr. Azera yelled, and a nurse whisked away the infant. Tears streamed down Bryce's face, and he squeezed Codi's hand and said, "I'm gonna go with him."

She lay back in the bed panting, and she nodded. He went over to where the nurses were cleaning the baby, noting how upset he was that he'd had to leave the warm embrace of Codi's womb.

"Do you have a name for him, Mister Young?" one of the nurses asked.

He couldn't look away from the perfectly pink skin and the shock of light, wispy hair. "Matthew," he said. His tiny hands had all ten fingers and his crumpled feet all ten toes. "Matthew Tex Young."

The nurse handled this tiny infant who had just been ripped away from his mother like a football, drying him and wrapping him quickly, and then she turned to him and plunked the baby in Bryce's arms. "There you go, Daddy. Go show your wife."

Matthew quieted, turning into Bryce's chest. He couldn't take his eyes off the infant, but they drifted closed as he leaned down and pressed his lips to his son's forehead.

"Bryce," Codi said, and he turned, squared his shoulders, and walked over to her.

"Look how perfect he is," he said, carefully passing the baby to Codi.

"He's one hundred percent perfect." She gazed at Matthew with pure love in her eyes. "How big was he?" Codi asked, and Bryce realized that he'd fallen down on the only job she'd given him.

He turned around and thankfully, the nurse who had given the baby to Bryce said, "Eight pounds, seven ounces. Twenty-one inches long."

"Oh, you're such a big boy," Codi cooed at the little baby.

"You can have two visitors back here at a time, Mister Young." She held up two fingers, emulating a peace sign. "*Two.*"

Bryce grinned at her. "You've met my family, right, Rhonda?"

"You can take the baby out to them too," she said. "But we'll want to give him a bath and make sure that he's warm enough before you do."

Bryce nodded, and in fact, they hadn't even left the delivery room before another nurse entered. "I'm going to take him for his blood tests and his bath. You can come, Daddy. Codi, they're moving you to four-thirty-four."

"Four-thirty-four," Codi said. "Bryce."

"Four-thirty-four," he repeated back, torn between staying with her and going with his son. In the end, he went with the nurse, because Codi did not want their baby to be alone.

The nurses who worked in labor and delivery certainly

knew how to do things efficiently, and it only took a couple of minutes to bathe Matthew and wrap him back up in clean blankets and a pale blue hat on his head.

"Is he warm enough?" Bryce asked as they passed the baby back to him.

"He's doing great," the nurse said. "Vitals all look good. We got all the blood we need for the tests. He's yours for a little while."

"Will Codi be breastfeeding?" another nurse asked. "We have a lactation specialist we can send in."

"Yes," Bryce nodded, his voice soft. "Can I take him out to meet my family first?"

"Yes," the first nurse said. "He should be fine."

Baby Matthew grunted and snuggled in closer to Bryce, who always wanted to keep the boy close to his heart. He didn't want to walk without looking at his son, but that proved to be more difficult than he'd like to admit, and he found that he couldn't carry a baby and walk at the same time—not without looking up.

He did that and pushed out into the waiting room only a few seconds later. This birth was so similar to OJ's, and yet so different. That had been a time of extreme turmoil and hurt and pain for Bryce, and yet such a celebration in their family. This time he got to enjoy the love and hope and joy a new baby brought to a family.

"He's here," Bryce said, though his father's eyes had already locked onto him. He stood first and reached for Abby's hand. They came over first, and Bryce tipped Matthew toward them slightly.

"He came really fast," he said. "Codi dilated like crazy after she got the epidural."

"It sometimes helps women to calm down," Abby said. "Look how beautiful he is."

Bryce passed the baby to his momma, suddenly feeling empty and lost and like he didn't know what to do with his hands. Daddy wept as he bent over the baby too, and when he looked up, Bryce grabbed onto him and clapped him heartily on the back.

"I'm sorry, Daddy," he said because Bryce knew that his father had suffered a lot of pain by not being able to be OJ's grandfather the way that he would have liked.

"Nothing to be sorry about," Daddy said. He stepped back and turned, gesturing for someone to come over. OJ had stood, and now he practically flew over to their huddle.

"My daddy texted all the uncles," he said. "He said Luke is gonna be *hoo-boy-mad.*"

Bryce laughed and cried at the same time, and he put his arm around OJ's skinny shoulders. "This is Matthew," he said. "He's kind of your cousin and kind of your brother."

"Yeah," OJ said. "Look at him. He's so small."

"I think you were a little bit smaller," Bryce said, though he couldn't quite remember how big OJ was. "You're gonna have to fight all the aunts to hold him, but I'm sure you'll get a chance."

He met Abby's eyes and said, "Codi has only seen him for a few minutes," his way of saying he couldn't stay out in the waiting room for very long.

Abby leaned down and gave the baby a kiss. "Well, we

can't keep him from his momma." She took the baby over to Georgia, who stroked her hand down his head with tears in her eyes. OJ sat down next to her, and Abby let him hold the baby for a couple of minutes.

Kassie and Reggie came over, along with Harry and Belle and Adam and Joey, and they all gushed over the perfect, long, straight, Young nose, and speculated over whose eyes he'd have when he finally grew into them.

Bryce hugged them all, basking in their love, their support, the easy way they'd forgiven him and welcomed him back into the family. Finally, he returned to the room where Codi waited. Her eyes fluttered open as he entered, and she sat up a little straighter.

"Oh, goodness, I fell asleep," she said. "Is he okay?"

"He's amazing," Bryce said. "I've already taken him out to everyone for right now, though, the second wave of Youngs is on the way." He passed her the baby, and this time he did crowd into the bed with her, putting his arm around her shoulders and letting her settle into his chest.

"I love you so much," he said. "You are incredible."

She leaned into his kiss, and together they gazed down at their tiny Matthew—the baby who had made them a family.

21

"I'm going to label all of these," Adam said as his *ten-minute-until-pickup* alarm sounded.

"Okay," Joey said, sounding a bit harried and breathless.

He'd spent a couple of hours with her last night, both of them pushing a cart through the grocery store as she loaded it with all of the ingredients she needed to bake sixty-one pies today and tomorrow.

It was 2:51 p.m., and the first wave of pickups were slated to begin at three. She'd allowed eight people to pick up pies every hour, between three and eight p.m. tonight, or ten and four p.m. tomorrow. It was more than enough slots, and it allowed her to work on pies in the order of which they would be picked up.

"I printed the three o'clock orders right there," she said.

"I know," Adam replied. "I have them all taped on the

counter—three, four, five, six, and seven." He nodded to the sheets she'd printed and he'd taped down.

Five hours of pickup tonight, but only twenty-one pies would leave the kitchen of Pork and Beans. Instructions had been emailed to everyone, as Adam had typed them up himself and sat with Joey as she'd sent them out this morning.

That done, she'd been baking all day, and he looked at the three pies that needed to be ready by three, the four by four, and the two by five. The other twelve pies needed to be ready by six p.m., by which time Joey said she would be working on the ten a.m. pies for the following day.

Her aunt Faith had printed the stickers for her and called in an emergency order to get the pie boxes here on time. Adam loved that Joey had so many people around her supporting her, but he could admit he wanted to be the loudest and biggest cheerleader of all.

So he picked up the apple pie, carefully placed it in the box, and closed it. The buyer's name had been printed on a sticker that he put on the back top of the box, and then he peeled off a large, four-inch round sticker that indicated this was an apple pie by Rooelle Pies. He smiled at the logo of a kangaroo with a joey poking out of the pouch and holding a pie. Both cartoon animals grinned for all they were worth, and Adam hoped that through all the chaos and craziness that this pie-baking adventure made Joey happy.

He wanted nothing more than for her to be happy, and he'd almost gone onto her website yesterday afternoon and bought all of the remaining pies himself. He could put a note in the comment section that said, *You don't need to really bake these. I just want you to have your own place.*

He didn't mind going to her grandparents' place, as Cecily and Jerry were exceedingly kind to him, but Adam knew Joey wanted her own apartment, and therefore he wanted that for her as well.

He labeled the second apple pie, and then the pumpkin, and continued to box and sticker all the pies that were ready. Joey worked on chocolate custard, and when a timer went off, she moved like flowing water over to the industrial ovens and pulled out three trays of two pie crusts each. She slid them effortlessly into the cooling racks and moved down to the fridge, where she loaded three more trays with weighted pie crusts. She put those in the oven and went back to her custard.

"Can you come help me with the Oreos?" she asked, and Adam abandoned his labeling station to do that. "Two whole packages, baby," she said. "And a whole stick of butter. It should do four crusts, and that's all we need for the chocolate."

"Okay," he said, and he looked at the food processor that she had already taught him how to use. He felt like a walrus with flippers instead of hands as he opened the packages of cookies and poured them into the food processor.

"Pulse," he muttered to himself, and he pushed the pulse button a couple of times to get the cookies to break up before he simply jammed his thumb down on the button and let the processor whir.

He'd tried to multitask before, and that had ended badly

for him, with dark cookie crumbs everywhere and Joey blinking at him like she'd just happened onto a horrible baking crime scene. So this time, he stayed with the food processor until the cookies were finely ground, then he moved to the fridge to get the cube of butter. He unwrapped it, dropped it in a bowl, and stuck it in the microwave.

"I'm here to pick up a pie," someone said, and Adam spun, his heart in the back of his throat.

"Yes," Joey said pleasantly. "How are you, Miss Myers?" She moved over and hugged the woman lightly around the shoulders. "I think you have the pumpkin."

"Yes," she said, glancing down the table of boxed and labeled pies. "And I'm getting my sister's, but she's not supposed to pick up until five. Is that okay?"

"Yes," Joey said. "We've got the five o'clock orders right here." She handed her the two pies and checked her off on the clipboard. When they were alone again in the kitchen, Adam met her eye and grinned at her.

"Two pies," he said.

She ducked her head, but her smile was the absolute biggest Adam had ever seen. Abandoning his cookie crumbs for now, he moved over to Joey and wrapped her up in a hug from behind.

"You're incredible," he said. "You have this dream, this vision, and and you're doing it."

"A lot of people do that," she said.

"No," he said. "They actually don't. You've got to give yourself credit for this."

She stood stiffly in his arms, gently moving the cream

around in the pan as she waited for it to bubble. She had ingredients lined up on the counter beside her, including the eggs that she would temper, the chopped chocolate, and the finishing butter and vanilla.

"Hey," he said. "Take ten seconds with me." He turned her in his arms, and she sighed in a way that told him she didn't want to take ten seconds with him.

"Why can't you admit that you've done a great thing and take pride and joy in it?"

"I am," she said. "Did you see me smile?"

"Yeah. But then you're right back to work."

Her eyebrows lifted. "You're going to lecture me about going right back to work?"

"No," he said. "That's not...." He exhaled heavily, tamping down the annoyance rising through him. "I just think you're incredible, and you don't believe me."

"Yes, I do," she whispered.

"Then say it," he said.

She glared at him, her eyes filled with blazing blue fire now. "Adam, I don't have time for this."

"It'll take five seconds," he said, taming his smile. "Just say it. *I'm incredible. I made delicious pies that people are going to be so happy to eat because I am a fantastic chef.*"

He nodded to her. "Your turn. Say it."

"I can't even remember what you said," she griped. "It was too long."

"Then just say two words." His fight-reflex hovered at an all-time high, and he didn't want to walk away from this.

"It's okay to admit you're good at something. It doesn't make you proud or sinful."

"I've never said that," she said.

Adam shook his head, because now was not the time to talk to her about her faith or beliefs. "I think you're incredible," he said, his eyebrows going up with the corners of his mouth. He waited, and Joey exhaled impatiently.

"Fine," she said. "I'm a good pie baker."

"You're an *incredible* pie baker."

She met his eye. "I'm an incredible pie baker." A smile curved her lips, and Adam's jumped to his face and crinkled his eyes all the way.

"You're an incredible person."

"I'm an incredible person," she said, and she seemed to draw life and strength into her shoulders.

Adam nodded and leaned down and touched his lips to her cheek. "All right," he said, stepping back. "You can go back to work now."

"Gee, thanks." Joey turned back to the stove and said, "Oh, this is boiling."

That meant she had to get to work to finish the chocolate pudding, and she went through several utensils to do that, including a ladle as she tempered the eggs, a whisk as she violently stirred them into the boiling cream, a rubber spatula to get all the way down into the corners as she melted all the chocolate in, and then finally, that vanilla and the very cold butter for added taste and shine. While she did all that, Adam managed to mix together the melted butter and cookie crumbs and section it into four pie pans.

"I need those crusts that just came out of the oven," Joey said, and Adam moved down to the cooling rack to get them for her.

She poured the chocolate custard into the four chocolate cookie crumb crusts he'd already done, and he followed behind her with a roll of plastic wrap, so he could press it over the hot pudding before it formed a skin.

Industrial plastic wrap was like wrestling with a sticky feather, and he managed to get the first two pies done while Joey took the pot over to the sink and filled it with water. But when he tried to rip the third piece, somehow a corner of it got stuck to his elbow and then seemed to suction to his whole forearm.

He shook his arm as he tried to get it off, and it wouldn't go. He finally peeled it off in a long strip of stuck-together plastic wrap, which he flung away from him with disgust. He tried again, and this time he ripped a too-long piece, and it folded on itself before he could float it over the top of the pie.

He growled as the fold touched the pudding before he could pull it back. Joey giggled at the same time he said, "I need help here."

She stepped to his side. "It's just plastic wrap, cowboy."

Yes, Adam wore his hat in the kitchen that day, and he glowered at her from underneath the brim of it. "This stuff is like super sticky paper that's attracted to itself," he said. "I don't know how anyone uses this."

Joey ripped off a piece effortlessly and floated it over the pie the way she'd shown him, easily pressing it down onto the pudding all the way around to the edge of the cookie crumb. She repeated the task as easy as breathing for her, while Adam stood there, still holding the folded piece of plastic wrap with the line of chocolate pudding on it and wondering what to do with it.

The timer went off, and Joey went to get the pie crusts out. "I need those cookie ones," she said. "Can you handle it?"

"Yes," he barked at her. "I've already done eight."

He pressed the cookie crumbs into the tins while she put the baked crusts on the cooling rack and went to get a couple of more regular pie crusts. She helped him finish up the last two, and then she slid those into the oven.

"These chocolate pies go in the fridge."

"Why is your smile so big?" he asked, picking up one of the pies. He didn't dare carry two, in case he suddenly couldn't walk and hold something in his hand, and he dropped them both.

"I just think it's funny how inept you are in the kitchen," she said.

"We all can't be baking superheroes," he grumbled. He opened the fridge and slid his pie in and then turned to take the ones she brought over to him. That done, he closed the fridge and looked at her, still grinning like the Cheshire Cat.

"Thank you for being here to help me," Joey said, her smile morphing from teasing and playful to beautiful and genuine. "It really means a lot to me, Adam."

"I wouldn't be anywhere else," he said, and he meant every word.

Joey nodded, and Adam thought he saw the slightest wobble of her chin. Then someone said, "Howdy-hey, I've got a pie pickup."

He automatically stepped in front of her to shield her from whoever had arrived. "Yes," he said. "Welcome to Rooelle Pies. I'm Adam. What did you have?"

He went to take care of the customer, who left smiling with his apple streusel pie. By the time Adam turned back to the kitchen, Joey was bent over her list, consulting it to see what she needed to make next. He watched her for a moment, and when she looked up at him, beautiful, unspoken things were said—so many that Adam ducked his cowboy hat to break their connection.

Joey giggled. "That's what you use a cowboy hat for, all right."

He grinned, feeling happier with himself than he had in a while. This new version of Adam Harmon was part country boy, part band manager, and falling all the way in love with Joey Young.

He wasn't sure who he'd be on the other side of everything, but he knew the Young family and Joey were changing him in the best ways possible.

22

Joey set the lid over the pot of potatoes on the stove, and then turned her attention to filling the pressure cooker with the remaining cubes. Yes, Thanksgiving dinner was really coming together now, and she stepped out of the way as Georgia reached to open the oven.

"I think this turkey is done," she said. "Yep, look, it's popped."

Joey turned to the island to put down some potholders for her. Georgia slid the turkey out of the oven and onto the counter.

"I'll go check the rolls," Joey said, already moving toward the dining room table, where she'd put the dough to rise earlier. "Once we bake these," she said, finding them properly proofed and ready to bake. "We'll be able to set the table."

"OJ and Anaya can do that," Georgia said. Joey's

younger brother poked his head up over the top of the couch.

"I have to do what?" he asked.

"Come set the table, baby," Georgia said. "Ana, you too. People are going to start arriving soon."

She moved down to the mouth of the hallway, and called, "Otis, I need you to come look at this ham."

They'd bought a candied ham this year from one of the pig farmers out in Rusk, and personally, Joey couldn't wait to taste it. She loved pork candy more than almost anything in the world.

She glanced at the clock, because while dinner wasn't for another forty-five minutes, she expected Adam to ring the doorbell very, very soon.

"I think your momma put the plates out in the garage," Laney Whittaker said to OJ.

"Oh, right," OJ said, and the two of them went out there to get the things they needed to set the table.

Graham, Laney's husband, who had been entertaining the kids in the living room as well, stood. "What can I do?" he asked.

Joey slid both trays of rolls into the oven and closed it.

"Oh, nothing," Georgia said.

"Georgia, he can make the punch." Joey nodded to the folding table that she'd staged on the other side of the island. "The kids like to have a rainbow of drinks for Thanksgiving," she said. "Well, really just red, orange, yellow, and brown." She grinned. "All the autumn colors."

Graham came around the end of the couch and moved

over to the table. "So we've got lemonade, wild cherry, orange Tang." He lifted the container and grinned for all he was worth. "I love this stuff. My momma used to serve it hot, and it's almost like wassail at that point."

Joey smiled because she enjoyed warm orange Tang as well.

"Any word on Bailey?" Georgia asked, and Graham set down the canister of Tang.

"She's gonna make it only moments before dinner time," he said. "We won't have to wait for her. Apparently, there were a bunch of bison who didn't get the memo that it's Thanksgiving Day and they should just be resting in the fields." He smiled. "She's on the way, though."

He glanced over to the garage door just as OJ and Laney came back inside.

"Graham," Laney said. "If you could come get the rest of this stuff, we'll work on the table."

"Yes, ma'am," he said, and he went to do as his wife asked.

Joey took stock of everything in the kitchen. She'd helped OJ peel and cut the carrots into rounds. They'd blanched them, and then Joey had set them to cook slowly with butter. Once they were fully cooked, she'd shown OJ how to put the brown sugar over them and set them aside.

The pot of creamed corn sat on the back corner of the stove, and Joey reached to turn on the flame underneath it. It only took about fifteen minutes, but corn stayed hot for a long time. She realized then that she had forgotten to set the timer on the rolls, so she quickly did that. The sound of the beeping nearly covered the chiming of the doorbell. When her brain caught up to the noises, she sucked in her breath and turned around.

"I'll get it," Georgia said.

"Georgia," Joey started, but she didn't know what else to say. Not only that, but her daddy had finally made an appearance in the kitchen. He'd obviously heard the doorbell too, and he cast a look at both Georgia and Joey, and then turned to go toward the front door.

"Georgia," Joey hissed, now a clear warning in her tone.

"I'm going," Georgia said. "Don't worry."

Oh, but Joey worried. She reminded herself that she'd given Adam a complete synopsis of what would happen at dinner today. He'd also met her parents before, and she turned her attention back to the green bean casserole, reminding herself that Adam was a people person.

He'd have every member of their holiday party eating out of the palm of his hand before the first course was even served. Not that they did courses in Joey's family. She'd have everything laid out on the island to be served buffet style, and they'd sit down at the table and eat.

She'd been working in the kitchen for hours, and she always lamented the fact that the meal only took fifteen or twenty minutes. But watching other people enjoy the food that she had created brought so much joy to Joey's heart that it didn't matter that it only lasted a few minutes.

She heard voices coming from the front of the house, and she turned to set out more potholders. She moved the green bean casserole from the stovetop to the counter and set the fried onions next to it. She'd remove the aluminum foil and sprinkle those on top at the last minute, so they didn't get soggy.

Footsteps came down the hall from the front door, and Joey braced herself. For what, she wasn't exactly sure. On her right, OJ and Anaya chatted with Laney and Graham as they set the table, but Joey could barely hear them.

Georgia came around the corner first, looking over her shoulder with a wide smile on her face. Perhaps Adam had charmed her already. He came next, and Joey's breath caught at the handsome sight of his chiseled face, those pretty blue eyes, and his sandy hair—which he had allowed to grow a little bit longer—coming out the bottom of his cowboy hat. He wore a festive brown button-up shirt with what looked like little embroidered turkeys all over it.

An instant smile sprang to Joey's face before she looked to her father.

"It hasn't been bad this year," Daddy said as he brought up the rear.

"It just means it'll snow more in December, January, and February," Georgia said. "Maybe all the way to May."

"Harry's warned me a lot about the Wyoming winters," Adam said good-naturedly, his eyes landing on Joey as she moved toward him. "Joey's given me a few warnings as well. I now have a winter storm kit in my car because of her."

"Is that right?" Daddy raised his eyebrows and looked at Joey as she approached too.

"Hey," she said, feeling awkward inside her own skin.

She reached Adam and tipped up onto her toes to sweep a kiss across his cheek. "You found the house."

"He's been here before," Daddy growled.

Joey stepped back, her anxiety buzzing through her like a live electrical wire. "Oh, well, I didn't know that."

"They met here when they were discussing terms for the Country Quad contract," Georgia said.

Joey nodded and swallowed, because Adam had also not told her that. She couldn't believe she felt left out in her own childhood home, with her own family and her own boyfriend. Her gaze quickly slipped past all of them, and then she turned to go back into the kitchen.

"The potatoes will be done soon," she said, making her voice bright. "And then we just have to do the gravy."

"I need you on this ham, Otis," Georgia said, and everyone flowed into the kitchen with Joey. She didn't need to start the gravy right away, because it only took a few minutes and was best served hot. She checked the time. They still had thirty-five minutes until two o'clock, when they'd planned to eat.

"Do you need any help?" Adam asked.

Joey faced him again. "Yeah, you know what? You can take this butter over to the table to OJ and Anaya. We've got extra salt and pepper shakers here too." Joey indicated the items on the corner of the island.

Adam picked up the plate with the butter that had been molded into the shape of a turkey. "Well, I'll be," he said, really sounding like a true-blooded cowboy. "I've never seen butter shaped like a turkey." He looked up and grinned at Joey.

She smiled back, sure her parents were taking a thousand mental pictures of what kind of smile it was. "Really?" she asked. "With all the celebrities you've eaten dinner with, there's never been turkey-shaped butter?"

Adam let loose a genuine laugh, which made Joey giggle too. He turned toward the table as he continued to chuckle, and he said over his shoulder, "Believe it or not, there's been no turkey-shaped butter at the charity dinners that I've organized."

"Such a shame," Joey teased, and she turned to her daddy as he cleared his throat. Both he and Georgia watched her, and she glared back at them.

"What?" she hissed.

Laughter erupted over at the table too, and Joey felt whipped between the two places in the house. She looked over to Graham and Laney and found them all laughing, even OJ and Anaya, who had climbed up on a chair. She somehow had a drawing that she'd done and was showing it to Adam. He glowed like he'd swallowed moonlight, and Joey couldn't look away from him.

"You like him too much." Daddy's words, low and deep, hit her eardrums and made her flinch.

"I do not," she hissed back. "Come with me." She grabbed onto his hand and towed him out of the kitchen and down the hall.

"Joey," Georgia said.

"You too," Joey practically yelled over her shoulder. "Right now."

She had no idea who else was looking at her, and in that moment, she didn't care. She marched into Daddy's music studio and let go of his hand in a huff. Thankfully, Georgia had followed her, and she closed the door behind her. Joey stomped all the way over to the window before she turned back to face them.

"I am not doing anything wrong by dating him," she said, folding his arms. "Yes, I like him. *Of course* I do, or we wouldn't be dating."

"We know that, Roo," Daddy said.

"Don't *Roo* me," Joey said. "If this is how you're going to act when I bring him over, then I just won't bring him over."

"That's not what we want." Georgia exchanged a glance with Otis and quickly moved toward Joey and put both hands on her shoulders.

Joey loved her stepmother, and all the cells in her body quivered with emotion.

Georgia smiled and reached up and pushed Joey's hair back behind her ear. "You are just so beautiful," she said. "You have worked so hard to put this meal together for everyone. You're amazing and smart and wonderful. And we worry that you don't know it."

Joey thought of a very similar situation where she'd found Adam standing in front of her, demanding that she tell him how amazing she was.

"I'm working on it," she said.

"We worry," Daddy said, as he joined them with a much

slower step. "That because he's older than you, and you're not quite ready for a serious relationship, that this is going to end badly."

Joey switched her attention to him. "You think I'm not ready for a serious relationship?"

"Baby," he said in the kindest voice Joey had ever heard him use. "I think you're the most amazing person in the world, but I don't think *you* believe that, and until you love yourself completely, I don't think you can love another person the way they deserve to be loved."

Joey nodded and looked away, because her father was most likely correct. "Like you and Momma," she said with a sniffle.

Daddy stepped in front of Georgia and drew Joey into his chest. "If I had been ready for a serious relationship, your mother and I would still be together," Daddy said. "I just don't want to see you have to go through any of that same pain."

"I know, Daddy." She clung to him, glad when Georgia joined them and made it a three-way hug.

"We just barely started dating." She stepped back and wiped her eyes. "Like, a month ago. He's not going to be proposing anytime soon."

"We know a lot of good counselors," Georgia said, but Joey shook her head.

"They're not going to do anything that you haven't already done for me," she said. "And you know what? Adam tells me how great I am, too. And I think if I keep working on it, I'll definitely start to believe it myself."

Georgia stepped back a little bit and glanced over her shoulder. "I really don't think we can leave the food alone like this. You guys finish up quickly." She gave Joey a knowing look. "Adam's out there alone." She crossed the room and opened the door.

The office sat too far from the living room for Joey to hear any talking, and Georgia didn't close the door again. She looked at her daddy. "If this was going to be too weird for you, you should have said something."

"It's not too weird for me," Daddy said. "It's *new*, and I'm sorry I teased you."

Joey nodded. "I am an incredible chef," she said with a smile, the words moving all the way down through her, ringing with truth. "And Georgia's right, I can't really leave the food. That's not what a good chef does."

Daddy grinned and chuckled and hauled her in for another hug. "You are my favorite person on the whole planet," he whispered. "And I want you to know it, and I want him to know it. Okay?"

Joey nodded, and together, she and her father went back into the kitchen. The table had been set, and Adam now sat on the couch with OJ on his right and Anaya pressed in on his left, while he held OJ's tablet. He looked up and met Joey's eyes, plenty of questions in his. Joey smiled at him, the gesture feeling somewhat timid on her face. She glanced into the kitchen, where she found Georgia stirring the creamed corn and only a few minutes left on the rolls.

"The potatoes in the pressure cooker are done," Georgia said over her shoulder.

"All right," Joey said, but she didn't join her. A couple of days ago, Adam had told her to take ten seconds to be with him, and she walked around the huge sectional couch that separated the living room from the kitchen and dining room. She leaned over his shoulder and looked at the tablet. "What are you guys doing here?"

"I'm just showing him a gallery of all of our animals," OJ said. "He didn't believe that we had a parrot, but I have picture proof."

Joey laughed. "You sure do, bud."

"And when Bailey gets here, she's gonna check on the ducks," OJ said. "She called on Monday and said she would."

"Right," Joey said. "But we're going to eat first, OJ. Remember?"

"Yeah, I remember." He reached up and swiped on the tablet. "This here was a dog Momma brought home once."

Joey pressed her cheek to Adam's, glad when he leaned into her touch, then she straightened and faced the kitchen again.

"All right," she said, a new sense of purpose streaming through her. "I think we have to whip the potatoes, make the gravy, brush butter on the rolls when they come out, and finish up that creamed corn." She surveyed the food already on the counter. "Daddy, you're totally in charge of this candied ham. It needs to be sliced and arranged on a platter. Graham, can you come carve the turkey?"

"Yes, ma'am," he said, and he got off the couch where he'd been sitting with his wife.

"Table is ready," Joey said, as she turned to look at it. "We got the drinks made." She took in the Tang, lemonade, wild cherry punch, and huge vat of root beer—the brown offering for this autumnal feast—and then she met Georgia's eyes. "What else?"

The doorbell rang before anyone could say anything, and Laney popped to her feet at the same time OJ started to squawk, "That's her. That's her." He ran around the back of the couch and toward the front door.

"Let the circus begin," Daddy mumbled, but at least he had started carving the ham.

23

Adam made the turn onto Rising Sun Ranch, his heart filled with gratitude this Thanksgiving season for the golden sunshine that bathed the land. Mother Nature had been kind, except for that one snowstorm that had left him snowed in at Joey's momma's place on Halloween. There had been a few dribbles of rain this month, but no more snow. So far.

He'd been told to turn down the lane just before the house, and when it came into view, he found Codi's big white dog-washing bus parked alongside the garage, along with a couple of other vehicles.

She and Bryce and their new baby had come home from the hospital on Thanksgiving morning, only a day ago. Adam did not expect to see Bryce out near the stables at all. He had coordinated this horseback riding morning with Jem

Young, who boarded three of his horses here at Rising Sun Ranch.

As he rumbled past the bus and the garage, the ranch came into view with its stables and barns. He also realized that there were multiple pick-up trucks here. He'd expected two, as Joey was catching a ride with her uncle Mav and Boston, who had caught wind of the horseback riding this morning and had wanted to come. Jem had texted Adam yesterday and asked if that would be okay, and Adam certainly didn't mind.

He hadn't been on a horse in at least fifteen years, and he figured the more people around to help, the better. But there wasn't just Jem's truck and there wasn't just Mav's.

Two other pickups that looked like they belonged to men who had plenty of money sat parked in the neat line too. Of course, everyone in the Young family fit that bill, and Adam had no way to predict who else had been invited.

Joey had told him that the big family Thanksgiving party would be on Sunday at Tex's house on the eastern edge of town. Adam had been there several times, as that was where the recording studio sat, and as the band had started practicing in the past three weeks, he'd attended a couple of their sessions.

He pulled in next to a truck he'd seen at Tex's before. He'd seen Otis's truck only yesterday parked in front of his house, and it wasn't his. "So it has to be Trace or Luke."

Adam killed the engine, realizing that *both* Luke and Trace were here, and with Mav and Jem, that would be *four* of Joey's uncles, and then her cousin—and then him and Joey.

"So it's a family riding event," he muttered to himself, not sure if he was happy about it or not. He got out, also not sure where to go, and thankfully, only a moment later, Jem exited from one of the stables a handful of yards away.

"Howdy-ho," he yelled, waving his hand above his head.

He wore a wide smile, and he had a perfect cowboy gait as he walked toward Adam. More people spilled out of the stable behind him, including Trace and Luke, as Adam had deduced. But Blaze also came forward, and Adam's pulse hopped around the back of his throat for a moment.

"Howdy," he said to Jem, who had arrived in front of him. They shook hands, and Jem said, "I didn't text you about everyone coming, because I figured you'd run for the hills." He chuckled and indicated the other broad-shouldered, dark-haired men in the Young family. "This is my brother, Blaze. He and I rode in the rodeo together."

"Howdy," Adam said, reaching to shake the man's hand. "You're Faith's husband."

"That's right," Blaze said.

"Joey was so amazing with those pies," Adam said. "And she was *so* grateful that your wife helped so much to get the boxes here in time and all those stickers printed."

Surprise entered Blaze's expression, and he nodded. "Yeah. Faith was real excited about that. How many pies did Joey end up selling?"

"Sixty-one," Adam said, beaming with pride. "It was a

lot, especially that second day. And I know she's already got a handful of orders for next month."

"I'm real glad," Blaze said.

They looked to Trace, but of course, Adam didn't need to be introduced to anyone in Country Quad. "I didn't know you guys were coming." He quickly shook Trace's hand and then Luke's, and neither one of them smiled.

"Oh, come on," Jem said. "This is a *family* horseback riding event on the day after Thanksgiving. You can't smile at the man?"

"Yeah, you're not doing a concert," Blaze said. "My word." He muttered more under his breath as he turned away.

"Mav and Boston aren't here yet then," Adam said, turning to Jem so he didn't wilt under the combined gazes of Luke and Trace.

"Harry and Belle are on their way too," Trace said. "I hope that's okay."

"It's fine," Adam said, flicking a look over to him. "Joey and I have just talked about horseback riding together. It's something that neither one of us do very often, and I'm trying to become more of a cowboy." He chuckled and looked at Luke. "How am I doing?"

He wore a blue plaid shirt with a brown leather jacket over it, his blue jeans, cowboy boots, and cowboy hat. If he had dark hair, he could be a twin to the members of Country Quad, but his lighter looks definitely stood out.

Luke let his gaze drip down at him all the way to his boots. "You sure look the part."

"Yeah, you look good, brother," Trace said. "Perfect for a country band manager."

He finally cracked a smile, and Jem said, "And...there it is," with a laugh following.

"Your son didn't want to come?" Adam asked, switching his attention back to Jem.

Jem's eyes blazed for a moment, but Adam couldn't tell if it was angry or if he just possessed a lot of charisma. "The kids got together this morning to start planning a little bit for Gabe and Morris's birthday party," Jem said.

"Oh, that sounds fun."

Adam wouldn't even know how to start making sure that they celebrated every birthday in the Young family, and thankfully that wasn't part of his job description.

Behind him, the crunching of tires on gravel sounded, and everyone looked that way as Mav drove down the road and parked next to Adam. He, Boston, and Joey got out, but Adam only had eyes for the white-blonde woman walking toward him.

"Hey," he said, going to meet her.

He'd lived many days without Joey in them, and he honestly had no idea how. He slid one hand along her waist and leaned down and kissed her quickly. "You made it."

"How long have you been here?" she asked.

"Oh, only a few minutes," he said. "Did you know that all of your uncles were coming?"

Joey peered past him and then looked up at him again. "That is not all of my uncles." She grinned. "But it's a lot of them. Come on, I heard we're riding over to Kassie's and she's going to have scones with raspberry butter for us."

"Oh, that sounds fancy," Adam said. "And very Southern."

"Well, it should. Kassie is from Louisville."

"Oh, that's right," Adam said. "I had just been hired by Harry before she and Reggie got married."

"So you must've been at their wedding." Joey raised her eyebrows at him.

"Yeah," Adam said.

"I didn't go," Joey said. "I think only Harry's parents went—and Bryce's, since she's his best friend." She hooked her arm through his, and they turned back to her uncles.

"All right," Jem said. "This is our first test, and if you don't pass it, you can't ride." He sounded serious, but he wore a smile in his eyes. "I need everyone who's a beginner to raise their hand."

Adam glanced around at the group of men and then raised his hand. "I haven't ridden a horse in about fifteen years," he said. He looked over to Joey, who also had her hand up.

"I mean, I rode a little sooner than fifteen years ago," she said. "But it's been a while."

No one else had their hand up, and Jem clapped Adam on the back and said, "All right, everyone passes. You guys come with me. I'm going to put you on a couple of Bryce's super tame rescues."

"Blaze, you're going to grab Cisco, Pebbles, and Little Sister for me and you and Mav," Jem said. "And we can use any of the horses in the green stable, so Boston, Trace, and Luke—go pick whoever you want."

"Sounds good," Mav said. "We'll meet you out there."

Jem led Adam and Joey to a stable that didn't seem to have a color on it. "Are these the permanent residents of Rising Sun Ranch?" Adam asked.

"Yep," Jem said. "They're horses that are too old to go back out onto ranches or into service, and Bryce just keeps them here. He says they're all real tame and used to people and riding, so it shouldn't be a problem."

"Who's in the green stable then?" Joey asked.

"Those are the horses Bryce isn't going to keep," Jem said. "He uses some of them to train the others in the yellow and red stables, and then he sells them."

"Oh, I see," Adam said. "Red must be his worst candidates."

"Yep, the most abused," Jem said. "The skinniest, the ones who need the most vet care, the most skittish. He keeps them there until they're healthy and strong and able to work with him and Codi, and honestly, usually me or Blaze, and then we move them into the yellow stable."

"I didn't know you worked out here, Uncle Jem," Joey said.

"A couple times a week," Jem said. "I've been helping a lot since Codi's been pregnant, and now that they have the baby."

Joey looked over her shoulder toward the house. "I still haven't held that baby."

"They just got home yesterday," Jem said. "From what I

understand, Tex and Abby brought a bunch of food over, and they just kept to themselves."

"Probably the best with a newborn," Adam said.

"Right." Jem led them through saddling the horses, and Adam knew about four steps in that he would never be able to do this by himself, not even in an emergency. Maybe if he came to do it every single day, but that was what it would take for him to remember what all the pieces were and where they went. Thankfully, Jem got both horses saddled quickly, and he brought out a stool.

"All right, Roo," he said. "Up you go."

She stepped up onto the stool and then put her foot in the stirrup and swung her leg over, landing easily in the saddle, everything she did so fluid and graceful and easy. Adam weighed twice as much as her and suddenly felt like the biggest oaf on the planet.

"You want the stool?" Jem asked, looking at him.

"I mean...." A slip of embarrassment pulled through him as he looked over to Joey, who looked so regal sitting in the saddle. She'd worn a deep purple coat that day with her trademark splashy scarf and hat. His ears tingled with the cold, and he said, "Yeah, you better let me use the stool," in a quick clip of a bark.

Jem grinned at him. "There's no shame in using the stool, brother. Put your hand here." He indicated the saddle horn. "You step up here, left foot in the stirrup, right leg over, and you're in."

Adam still had not found time to work out, but he had

filled his house with things that required him to unbox, put together, move around, and he'd counted that as his exercise.

Please, dear God, he thought as he stepped up onto the stool. *Don't let me make a fool of myself in front of Joey.*

He put his left foot in the stirrup as instructed, and pushed with his leg and pulled with his hands, and the next thing he knew, he sat in the saddle. He grunted, and Jem chuckled.

"Nice job, cowboy," he said. He moved the stool out of the way and then walked in front of the horses to collect their reins. "You guys come on over here with me, and once we're all saddled and ready, the horses will just all stick together."

"Okay," Adam said dubiously, but as the magnificent creature beneath him walked along with Jem, he looked over to Joey, a new glow starting inside him. "I'm riding a horse," he said.

She grinned at him. "You're riding a horse, cowboy."

"You need a cowgirl hat," he said.

"I used to have one when I was growing up." She looked forward again, thoughtfully studying the horizon. "I'm not really an outdoor person. I like stargazing and watching the sunrise and sunset, but otherwise, give me a good book and a heated blanket and a bean bag and I won't bother you for days." She laughed, and Adam simply enjoyed the sound of it.

They joined the others who had their horses saddled already, with Boston and Mav waiting atop their horses, and

Blaze, Trace, and Luke swinging up. The moment Jem arrived, he handed the reins to Joey and then to Adam. "You don't really need to do anything. Just kind of hold 'em loosely."

"Okay, all right," Adam said, and he watched as Jem catapulted himself onto his horse.

"We're just following the trail over to Kassie's," he said. "She said she'd feed us breakfast, and Reggie's got a horse he has to bring back to the ranch, so he'll ride back with us."

"Sounds good," Blaze said. "Lead us out, Trace."

Trace did so without complaint, and Luke moved his horse up by his brother as well. Adam wanted to fall to the back so that nobody could watch him, but Jem and Blaze refused to go after Mav and Boston, and Jem raised his eyebrows at Adam.

"How do I get it to move?" Adam asked.

"You get *her* to move," Jem said, grinning. "By giving her a little nudge with your foot, and tellin' her, 'Come on. Let's go.'"

Adam looked at Joey, and she looked at him, and they somehow had an unspoken pact to do it together. He looked forward, hoping and praying with all he had that he could get this animal to move.

He moved his right foot back, barely feeling the horse's belly before he pulled his leg forward again, and said, "Come on. Let's go." The horse started to move in a slow, plodding way, but Adam had never felt such pride fill his chest.

"What's her name?" he asked Jem.

"You're on Cinnamon Toast," Jem said from behind him. "Joey, you're on Rainbow Bright."

"Of course I am," Joey said. "Rainbow is my favorite color."

Adam tipped his head back and laughed. "Rainbow is not a color, Roo," he said, and then the breath froze in his lungs.

He had never called Joey "Roo" before, and he could barely believe the nickname had come out of his mouth now. But it definitely had. She looked over to him too, her eyes blazing with something Adam couldn't decipher.

He cleared his throat. "I thought your favorite color was pink."

"Pink is part of any good rainbow," she said.

"There's actually not pink in a rainbow at all."

Joey held his gaze for one more beat, and then rolled her eyes and looked at the horizon. "That's why rainbow is a color," she said. "Because it's full of pink and purple and teal and gold."

All the colors of her scarf, and Adam smiled and faced the horizon as well. He did like being outside, even if it was a little bit chilly. He drew in a deep breath of the good country air, and he felt everything in his life slow down and soften. He needed that more than anything, and he sighed, letting the breath take with it any stress or worries or cares that he carried with him.

He didn't need them today. He wasn't working. There

was no email to answer, no event to coordinate, no band practice to sit in on—just him and the big Teton Mountains in the distance, and the yawning sky above, and God.

He looked over to Joey and found her watching him. "What?" he asked.

"That was just a big sigh," she said.

"I think I finally relaxed." He smiled at her. "I'm not quite sure, because it's such a foreign feeling."

She grinned back. "For you, I bet it is."

"It feels good." He drew in another breath and released it without nearly as much tension or pressure. Out here, he could hear better and think clearer. He liked the gentle movement of the horse beneath him, this connection to another living thing. He felt more connected to *himself* than ever, and he reached over to Joey.

She reached for him too, and her horse edged a little bit closer to his. He caught her fingers and squeezed. "We should do this every week."

"We can," Joey said. "The horses are always here, and Bryce won't care."

"I cannot saddle a horse," Adam muttered out of the corner of his mouth.

Joey giggled. "Me either. Maybe Uncle Jem would meet us to make sure we don't die."

He lifted her hand to his lips and kissed the backs of her knuckles quickly, because he had to lean over to do it, and he felt like he might fall out of the saddle. A pinprick of panic moved through him, and then he straightened and everything righted.

Yes, today was about him learning how to relax, and the big Teton Mountains in the distance, and the wide sky overhead, and God.

And, as he ducked his cowboy hat to hide his smile, he thought: *And Joey.*

Today was definitely about Adam being with Joey.

24

Bailey McAllister knew where to park at Bryce's ranch. She'd been here a few times before, and she eyed the row of pickup trucks warily as she parked way down on the end of them.

Thankfully, she was the closest to Bryce's house, and she half expected to see him coming down the back steps and jogging across the lawn to greet her. He'd done that before, but today, the ranch sat silent and still, with the noonday sun shining down on all of it.

Winter had definitely arrived in Wyoming, the same way it had in Montana. All the trees had been stripped bare of their leaves, leaving only the pale brown branches reaching up into the winter sky. The fields had gone dormant, the grass had turned yellow, and yet Bailey found such beauty in the absence of color. Soon, snow would come and blanket everything in white, and Bailey didn't mind that either.

She got out of her SUV and went around to the front of the house. Someone had taped a sign there that said, *don't ring the doorbell, just come in,* and she hoped it hadn't been placed there just for her. She felt uneasy simply walking into someone's house, but Codi and Bryce had just brought their new baby home yesterday, and Bailey wanted to be respectful.

She hadn't wanted to come see the baby at all, though it wasn't the worst thing that could have happened to her. After Thanksgiving dinner yesterday, she looked at the duck that OJ had talked to her about and diagnosed it with a wing sprain. She told him just to watch it and not let him fly for a few weeks, and then the duck would probably be fine.

From there, OJ had started showing her pictures of Matthew, and he said they were coming out to Bryce's ranch for lunch today, and she should come too.

Bailey had a very hard time telling OJ no, and so she'd made the drive from her family ranch up the canyon from town all the way up the Apple Highway to Rising Sun Ranch.

She leaned in close to the door, hoping to hear a loud party environment beyond, then she could disappear into the sidelines, and it wouldn't be a big deal that she'd come. She didn't have to hold the baby. She could smile and coo at him from afar and then get her favorite soda on the way home.

She opened the door, and while she could hear some

talking coming from the back of the house, where Bryce had a big living room, a dining table and chairs, and a kitchen, she didn't hear the rowdiness she normally did when the Youngs got together.

He'd told her that they were expecting a lot of people that day. Apparently, Joey's new boyfriend, Adam, had arranged for horseback riding for him and Joey, and several of Bryce's uncles had attached themselves to that party. They'd gone over to Kassie's, but Bryce said they'd be back for lunch, and they all wanted to see the baby too. He said his parents would be there, as well as Otis and Georgia, Harry and Belle, and Kassie and Reggie.

She stepped up into the house and found Kassie sitting on the couch. "Oh, hey, Bailey," Kassie said. She'd balanced a plate with a slice of pizza on her very pregnant belly, and Bailey blinked.

Her vision changed from Kassie on the couch to herself in that same position. So, so pregnant, barely able to get on and off the couch, and so miserable. She'd lived in her parents' basement for the last few months of her pregnancy, the weight of so many lives and so many decisions and so many consequences on her shoulders.

"Hey, Kassie," she managed to rasp out.

"Baby, you want a cola?" Reggie asked as he poked his head into the living room. "Or lemonade?"

Kassie made a face and shook her head. "Neither. Both of those will give me heartburn; just water is fine."

Bailey smiled at her. "Everything I ate or drank in the last trimester gave me heartburn."

Kassie's face brightened. "Really?"

"Totally."

"Codi never got heartburn," Kassie said. "I swear she's kind of like a robot." She laughed, and Bailey smiled.

Harry and Belle came around the corner with their pizza, and Harry said, "Oh, Bailey's here," and moved right over to her and hugged her as if they were old friends. She clung to him for a moment, because Harry Young had been instrumental in a huge part of Bailey's healing. He hadn't known it at the time, but he'd taken one of the most significant pictures of Bailey's life, and she loved him for it.

"How are you?" she asked. "Done with your concert series?"

"Done with everything," Harry said. "Belle and I are getting married in a month or so, and we're writing songs for Nashville."

"Of course you are."

Bailey glanced over to Belle. "I'm not sure we met at Bryce's wedding."

"I don't think we did," Belle said, casting a quick glance to Harry. "It's great to meet you."

"You too."

"There's pizza and salad in the kitchen," Harry said. "They've got heaters out on the deck, but I guess I'm more of a diva than I thought, because that's too cold for me." He chuckled and moved over to the couch in front of the window that faced Kassie.

Bailey nodded and continued her solo journey into the kitchen, where she found the dining room table full of uncles eating pizza. "Bryce," Otis said when he saw her. "Bailey's here."

She found Bryce in the kitchen with Joey, Adam, and Anaya. He handed the plate to the little girl, and then lifted his eyes to Bailey. "Hey, you made it." He moved over to her and gave her a quick one-arm tug. "Codi is feeding Matthew right now and then she'll bring him out. Come eat."

He made it seem so natural that she was there, though she wasn't part of this family.

"Hey, buddy," she said to OJ, and he grinned at her, pure glee radiating from him.

"Momma thinks that she might have to go pick up another cat."

Bailey smiled and shook her head as Georgia called, "I told you that was a maybe," from somewhere behind her.

OJ picked up a piece of cheese pizza. "I know, but I can still be excited about it."

She loved that he loved animals and that he'd been given a mother who did too. She collected a piece of pizza and turned to face the rest of the house, wondering where in the world she should sit.

"Over here, Bailey," Joey called, and she and Adam had gone into the living room and sat on two-thirds of the couch. She nodded to the place next to her. "I saved you a spot."

Relief and gratitude filled her as she went past everyone at the table and said, "Hello, hey, hi," until she managed to sink into the couch next to Joey. She'd only taken one bite of pizza when Codi came down the hall with the baby.

Joey sucked in her breath, shoved her plate at her

boyfriend, and jumped to her feet. "Oh, baby raccoons, there he is," she said. "Can I have him first?"

Codi grinned and passed the little boy to her. Joey glowed with a soft white light as she gazed down at a tiny bundle in her arms. She moved back over to the couch and sat down, sinking into Adam's side carefully. He put his arm around her and balanced both of their plates on his lap.

"Look at him," Joey said, her voice soft. "He is so beautiful."

She looked up at Adam, and Bailey had no idea how long they'd been dating, but they sure seemed close. Her heart ached for that kind of closeness, for someone who knew her so well and wanted to take care of her, who knew what was important to her and made it important to him too.

Joey ran the back of her finger down the side of Matthew's face, and the baby simply gazed up at her with eyes made mostly of pupil. Bailey had had very little experience with newborns, at least of the human variety, but she blinked and her reality glitched again.

This wasn't her baby that she had just delivered and gazed down on before she gave him away, but she remembered OJ's newborn eyes all the same.

She expected the pain to crash over her like a tidal wave, pinch through her heart, and make her breath come in gasps, but it didn't. She finished her piece of pizza and dusted her hands together while conversations and laughter surrounded her. Then, seeing as how she was the only other woman in the room besides Georgia and Codi, she looked at Joey and said, "Can I hold him just for a minute, and then I'll go."

"Of course," Joey said, as if this were the most natural thing in the world.

Bailey knew it wasn't, and she knew that God had given every member of the Young family a heart made of gold and marshmallow. Joey transferred the tiny baby into Bailey's arms, and she gazed down at him as well. He squirmed and grunted, and she smiled and shushed him as if it was the most natural thing in the world.

She wasn't sure if all the conversations around her had stopped, or if everything in her mind had simply silenced to be in the pureness of this moment. "You are a beautiful baby," she said, and she could see the same sloped nose in Bryce's son that she saw in OJ.

Matthew had wispy white hair across the top of his head while remaining bald on the sides, and Bailey smiled at it as she whisked her fingers through it gently.

"You got a lot of hair here, bud. What are you going to do with all that hair?"

The baby blinked in a slow way, as if he were the robot. Bailey leaned down and pressed her lips to his delicate forehead. She'd been stitching together pieces of her life for a while now, and she felt like she'd done a good enough job to live her daily life without the massive and crushing regret, guilt, and shame she'd once carried.

She looked up and found both Codi and Bryce sitting on the love seat kitty-corner to her. Their eyes locked on her and Matthew. "He is wonderful," she said, her voice tightening and pitching up at the same time. Tears flooded her eyes, and she suddenly remembered the card that she'd brought.

She stood and passed the baby to Bryce. "I have something for you, and then I need to go."

"You don't need to go, Bay," he said.

Codi, who'd surely put up with the irritation of having Bailey in Bryce's life, looked at her as well. "You really don't," she said. "You're welcome to stay as long as you want."

Bailey nodded and fished the card out of her purse. "I'll just leave it here for you," she said. "For when you're not so busy." She set it on the entertainment center across the room from them and turned back to face the love seat.

"I do have to go. I'm picking up some meat for my mother from the smoke shop up here, and they close soon."

"All right," Bryce said, and he transferred Matthew back to Codi's arms.

"I'll take him," Georgia said, and she she squeezed herself into the end of the love seat where Bryce and Codi sat.

Bailey went to get her paper plate, so as to not leave any mess behind for Codi, but Bryce took it from her and tossed it on the table. "Let's go out the back."

"I don't need you to walk me out," she said.

"It's fine." He opened the door and went in front of her.

"Your whole family is here," she said as she joined him on the back deck, and she pulled the door closed behind her. "He really is beautiful, Bryce. I'm really happy for you and Codi."

"Thank you." Bryce smiled at her as she joined him at his side. "I know it's hard for you to come, Bailey. You don't have to feel like you need to."

"OJ invited me," Bailey said with a sigh. "And you know I can't tell him no." She gave a light laugh. "Heck, I diagnosed a *duck* for him yesterday, and every injured and abandoned animal that comes into my clinic, I think first of telling him about them. I know he would take them all, and nurture them back to health, and love them."

Bryce chuckled. "He sure would. That kid loves animals."

Bailey's throat tightened, and she watched the branches sway in the wind. "It was good for me to see Matthew," she said to the sky. "I'm getting better, Bryce, I really am."

"I can tell." He looked over to her. "How long are you here?"

"I leave tomorrow," she said. "It's a long drive, and I stay overnight in West Yellowstone."

"Sure," Bryce said, his gaze stuck on the mountains in the distance too. "You ever think about coming back to Coral Canyon?"

Bailey hugged herself, though the afternoon sunshine lent warmth to the cold air. "All the time," she admitted. "All the time."

25

Tex Young stood on his heated back deck, a mug of coffee warming his hands as he watched his brother-in-law open the barn doors. Several teens and kids hovered around Wade, who knew all of them though he'd never asked to be part of the enormous Young clan.

He wore his prosthetics today, and Luke, Jem, and Blaze had gone downstairs to the yard to help with the horses too. Tex sipped his coffee, enjoying his birds-eye view of the people he loved best.

The late November air held a bite, but that hadn't stopped him from suggesting they get the horses out and give them the exercise they needed. Blaze's girls loved to ride, and all of Jem's kids did too.

Wade and Cheryl's kids could always be persuaded to ride a pony as well, and he looked over as Trace eased up to the railing next to him. "Hey-o," Tex said. "I can't believe I have room for this coffee, but it's going down." He chuckled, because he'd definitely gorged himself on the Thanksgiving meal Abby, her mother, and his had put together.

They'd had people sitting in every available seat, as the ranch house here where Tex had grown up wasn't exactly huge. He had pushed out the back a bit and then added on this big deck. He and Abby had installed heaters a couple of years ago, and it provided enough space for all of them to sit down and eat.

"There's pie," someone called from inside, and Tex groaned.

"I'm with you on that one, brother," Trace said, chuckling. "I can't stay away from that Cajun chicken that Cheryl makes."

"It's so good, right?" Tex had eaten plenty of that—along with the smoked turkey and then a couple of sweet and sour meatballs too. All of his brothers had brought sides, and Tex didn't want to be rude by not sampling everything.

"You two aren't riding?"

Tex turned toward Otis as he stepped outside and brought the sliding door closed behind him. The chatter from the house dimmed, leaving Tex with the cold country air and only the sound of those squabbling over who would get to ride first down by the barn.

"Nope," Tex said. "I'm afraid everything I just ate will come up if I try to get on a horse."

Otis chuckled and moved to stand on Tex's other side. "I sent OJ and Ana down with Joey."

Sure enough, Joey appeared at the corner of the house, leading the way toward the barn. Adam strode at her side, tall and strong and quite handsome in his dark brown cowboy hat. Joey held Ana's hand, and OJ—ever the life of the party—skipped ahead, then turned back to say something to everyone.

Tex's heart warmed at the sight of them, because the four of them looked an awful lot like...a family. He cut a look over to Otis, who likewise watched his children and Adam.

Tex held his tongue, because in situations like this, Otis had to be the one to start the conversation. So he took another sip of his coffee, enjoying the heat in his hands and his throat.

"My fingers needed this break," he said.

Trace grunted in agreement, though he didn't say anything. Tex knew his brother still played his guitar daily, but Tex hadn't been doing that. Being out in the studio again had definitely brought some aches to his old joints, though he did love playing and singing and being with his brothers.

He watched as Grace, Bennett, and Carver got to ride his horses first. Blaze and Jem stayed with the kids who had to wait their turn, and Wade led a few more over to his ranch, where he opened his stable and started getting out his horses.

"Would you look at that?" Trace said from beside him, and Tex glanced over to him. Trace nodded toward the stable, where Joey helped Grace to the ground, and Adam swept Pippa into his arms.

Tex's youngest daughter squealed in delight, and she

grinned at Adam as he set her in the saddle. "Our new manager's got a way with kids."

"And with Joey," Otis added quietly, his tone carrying a hint of fatherly concern.

Tex understood his brother's worry. As the oldest of the nine brothers, he'd watched the family dynamics shift and grow over the decades. Joey had always been one of the gentler souls among their crew, and Adam Harmon definitely had a way with Tex's quieter niece.

"He's a good man," Tex said, knowing Otis needed to hear it. "Harry and Bryce love him, and I've never seen a man work as hard as him."

"All things I know," Otis said. "I just worry about what might happen if they don't work out."

Down below, the second round of kids started on their horse rides, and Adam swept his arm around Joey's waist, tucked her into his side, and pressed a kiss to her temple. She looked up at him, her smile wide enough for Tex to see from the side.

"Don't look like they won't work out to me," Trace said in his quiet monotone.

"It's the honeymoon phase," Otis said. "They've only been together about a month."

"Yeah, and you were in love with Georgia after that long." Trace leaned forward and grinned at Otis, who only scoffed.

"She's looking for apartments," Otis said next.

"That's good news," Tex said. "Right?" He looked at

Trace and then Otis. "I mean, I know Momma and Daddy like her living there, but it's not necessary."

"No, it's not," Otis said. "And yes, it's good." He paused and then turned his back on them, leaning against the railing and facing the house instead. "He just seems so much older than her."

"Does he?" Tex asked, looking down at them again. Joey now held Tyrone in her arms, while Adam held Clay's hand while they waited for the horses to come back. "He seems just like Harry or Bryce to me."

"And Joey's five years younger than Harry," Otis said.

"Only three," Trace said.

"They feel the same to me," Tex said. "Girls are more mature than boys." He waved to Pip as she came around the corner of the barn, pure joy on her face. He smiled too, and the sound of the sliding glass door caused him to turn.

Abby stepped out, carrying a fresh pot of coffee. His wife's presence always settled something in his soul, even after all these years.

"You cowboys solving all the world's problems out here?" she asked, and she took Tex's mug to refill it.

"Just watching the kids." Tex wrapped an arm around her waist, drawing her close against the chill. "And maybe doing a little observation of the newest person to come into the family."

Abby followed their gazes to where Adam now lifted Clay into the saddle. He took the lead rope this time, and he and Joey walked with the horses while Blaze stayed back with the kids.

"They do look sweet together," Abby said. "And Joey sure seems to like him."

Joey laughed at something Adam had said, her blue eyes shining with happiness Tex could see from all the way up on the deck. They reminded Tex of how Everly had drawn Trace out of his shell years ago.

"Speaking of sweet," Trace said. "Harry and Belle are writing a new song for their wedding."

"That's fantastic," Tex said.

"Is it?" Trace asked.

Otis cleared his throat and stepped back. He took a couple of slow, measured steps away from the railing, and then he practically ran for the house.

"You better hurry," Trace called after him.

"What's goin' on?" Tex asked.

"They're workin' on it with him," Trace growled. "I even asked nicely, and I was told no, they would not share it with me until the wedding."

"Oh, that's sweet," Abby said, then she too wisely headed back inside.

"It's *not* sweet," Trace said. "He's my son, and I want to help him with the wedding song."

"And he wants it to be a surprise for you and Ev," Tex said, somehow just knowing that was true. "My guess is, it's his gift to you, for being such an amazing dad."

"Oh, please." Trace rolled his whole head. "It's fine, but I'm gonna tell you the same thing I've told everyone else."

Tex turned toward him. "Go on, then."

"It's okay that I'm upset about this." Trace's jaw

jumped. "I don't have to just lie down and be happy about everything."

Tex gazed at his brother, feeling his genuine hurt. "I'm sorry, Trace." He stepped into his brother and wrapped him in a hug while Trace stood there, stiff and unyielding. After a moment, he finally softened, and he sagged into Tex's chest.

Tex held him until Trace stepped back, and they both settled at the railing again. "You know, for the longest time, I thought I just needed to get Bryce to eighteen." Tex chuckled softly. "But I think he needs me now more than ever." He looked over to Trace. "Harry will always need you, in a new and different way."

"Yep." Trace nodded. "I just wish...I don't know what I wish."

"And wishing doesn't change anything anyway," Tex said.

"No, it doesn't."

"Dad!" Carver's voice carried across the yard as he ran down the sidewalk and closer to Tex. "Daddy, can I show Adam how to do the new guitar chord you taught me? He's takin' lessons, and he said he wants to hear me play."

His nine-year-old son's enthusiasm for music warmed his heart. The boy had been practicing religiously since getting his first guitar, and Tex could admit he enjoyed their lessons together.

He glanced over to Adam, who smiled up to Tex. "Sure, bud. Whenever you guys come back in."

Carver whooped and ran back toward the stable just as

Cash joined them. Tex nodded down there with the brim of his hat. "What are we thinkin' about Cash?"

"You're thinkin' something about Cash?" Trace asked. "I don't feel comfortable talking about this without Blaze." He grinned and shook his head. "For real, though. I think Blaze thinks enough about his own son for all of us."

"He came home for the holidays," Tex said. "That's all I'm saying."

"He comes home all the time," Trace said dryly. "And it's Thanksgiving."

"He didn't bring anyone with him."

"Can you imagine?" Trace laughed then. "It'll take someone as headstrong as Cash to tame his wild heart."

"Oh, I don't know about that," Tex said. "I just think someone like Faith." He grinned at his brother. "Or Ev—you know, someone who can put up with your black mood."

"*My* black mood?"

Tex laughed and watched as Adam started to come into the house with Carver, leaving Joey with Blaze and Jem and the other littles. "Besides," he said. "Cash doesn't have a black mood. He just lives life at a hundred miles an hour."

"So maybe he'll meet a race car driver," Trace said.

"Yeah, maybe."

The sliding door opened again, and this time, Carver poked his head out. "Daddy, I'm ready to play, and Momma says you need to get in here and get your chocolate banana cream pie 'afore it's all gone."

Tex immediately pushed away from the railing. "The chocolate banana cream pie is almost gone?" He entered the house and drank in the sight of at least a dozen people eating various flavors of pie—and he spied at least three people eating his beloved pie with the inch of chocolate custard on the bottom and then a layer of sliced bananas, all topped by banana pudding and whipped cream.

"I invite you-all to my house, and you eat all my favorite pie?"

"Calm down, Daddy," Carver said. He giggled and galloped into the kitchen. "Me and Momma saved you a whole half pie."

Tex grinned at him, and the others he walked by. "A whole-half?"

Carver tipped it up, his eyes wide and innocent. "Yeah, lookit."

"I see it, bud." Tex picked up a fork and then the pie tin. He saw no reason to use a plate if he didn't need to. "Go get your guitar," he said, shooting a look over to Adam. He'd gotten himself a piece of pecan pie, and he smiled as Carver stopped in front of him and said he'd be right back.

Carver skipped off toward the door that led downstairs, and Adam lifted his eyes to Tex's. Tex grinned at him, because hey, he wasn't dating Tex's daughter, and Tex happened to like Adam a whole heckuva lot.

"You okay over here?" Tex asked, stepping over to him.

"Absolutely." Adam lifted his pie. "I'm eating your mother's pie, and I have to admit...." He looked past Tex to the rest of the kitchen, where the crowd spilled into the living room around the corner too.

His eyes came back to Tex's bright and filled with

earnestness. "It's been a while since I've been part of a family like this."

Tex nodded, though he didn't know every aspect of Adam's life. "Well, you're always welcome here."

"Thank you, sir."

"Where is your family?"

"Tennessee," Adam said, turning as Joey came up beside him. He smiled at her and handed her the plate of pie. She took the fork and then a bite, her eyes rolling back in her head as she moaned. "The twins still live there."

"Twins?" Tex asked.

"Mm, yeah." Adam nodded. "I've got two younger siblings—a brother and a sister. They're twins. Both married. Both with one little girl."

"Wow," Tex said, his eyebrows going up. He glanced over to Joey, who swallowed.

"Grams's pecan pie is the best food in the whole world."

Tex grinned at her. "How you doin', Roo?"

"Peachy, Uncle Tex." She moved into him and gave him a quick hug. "Thank you so much for having us today."

"Of course." He stepped back and watched her fit herself right back against Adam's side. He slid his arm around her, and Tex would never, ever tell his brother he thought they were a super-cute couple. "Are you two going to Tennessee for Christmas or anything?"

Adam blinked and shook his head. "No, we have the Country Quad concert series."

"Oh, duh." Tex chuckled as his son yelled from the basement. He nodded that way. "If you really will indulge my boy in listening to his song...."

"There's nothing I want more," Adam said, and he dropped his hand to Joey's as they both turned to head out of the galley kitchen and around the corner to the stairs that led down.

Tex watched them for a moment, then met his wife's eye as Abby joined him in the kitchen. "They're really cute," he said. "I don't get why Otis and Georgia don't like them together."

"I think they like them together just fine," Abby said, also watching as Adam disappeared around the corner after Joey. "I think they're worried about what happens if they're *not* together."

"Daddy!" Carver stomped up the last of the steps and came skidding around the corner. "What are you doin'? Bring that pie down with you so I can play."

Abby grinned at their son. "You better get going."

"Yep." Tex swiped a plastic fork from the counter as he went, because he actually loved listening to his son play the guitar—and he could keep an eye on Adam and Joey at the same time.

26

Joey pulled up to the light blue house, finding big wooden numbers that were almost the ones she had been given. A quick look to the right, and she found the basement entrance to the apartment with the address on it that could become hers. A quiet excitement built within her as she put her car in park.

"It looks nice," Belle said from the passenger seat, and Joey blinked over to her.

"It does, right?" she said. "The pictures online looked really good, too. They've remodeled it, so even though it's a basement, it looked nice."

Joey had been looking at apartments for rent for the past month, and since she'd been saving since she moved back to Coral Canyon a year and a half ago, she hoped that even though she hadn't made her one thousand dollars from

Rooelle Pies, she'd still be able to get into a place starting in the New Year.

"Let's go," Harry said from the back seat, and his seat belt clanged against the plastic of the door, because the retractor in that one didn't work. He didn't comment on it and got out, and Joey's pulse hammered at her as she did the same thing.

The sky around and above her held only gray, and it felt ominous and dangerous as she rounded the hood of the car and joined Belle and Harry on the sidewalk. "It's going to snow," she said.

"Supposed to," Harry said, as he led the way down the sidewalk with the pale brown grass bordering it on both sides. "This is nice, Joey," he said. "Easy access to the street."

"Yeah," Joey said.

She wasn't sure why she hadn't wanted to look at apartments alone, but she hadn't. She could have asked Boston to come with her, but he'd gone to Jackson Hole this week, as he'd expanded his radius for jobs and had applied to a few places there and gotten interviews.

Harry paused at the top of the stairs and let Joey go past him. He grinned at her and said, "Lead us in, Roo."

She flashed him a tight smile that felt like it choked her, and then she went down the steps. The door had a lock box on it, and Joey quickly whipped her phone out of her purse. She'd taken a screenshot of the code, and she navigated to that quickly, and then moved the numbers on the combination lock to the correct position, and pressed her thumb up against the compartment.

It didn't budge.

She frowned and looked at her phone again. "It's three-eight-one-two," she said, knowing she'd put it in right. She looked at the combination, and sure enough, it was right. The metal burned her hand with cold, and she stepped back.

"Will you try it, Harry? Maybe I'm not strong enough to move it."

Harry edged in, checked the combination, and then jammed his thumb against it as well.

"You have to press the side there," Belle said, pointing. "Look how there's a button."

"Oh." Harry did that, pushed again, and sure enough, the compartment slid open. He reached inside and pulled out a pair of keys. He handed them to Joey, who retook her place in front of the door, fitted the key into the knob, and unlocked it.

She pushed the door open and paused before she stepped over the threshold and into the apartment. A gray, flat light echoed throughout the space the same way it did outside, and Joey could only imagine how much sunlight she'd have in the spring and summer. She peered inside and found the living room on her left.

"The carpet is new," she said, taking that first step inside. Her foot landed on beige tile, which ran straight in front of her, down a hallway, and expanded to the left into the kitchen. The carpet only sat in the living room, and Joey knew from the pictures that it was in the bedroom as well.

"This is just a one-bedroom place?" Harry asked, entering after her.

"Yes," she said. "One bedroom, one bath. Big laundry room, though. They said their last tenant used it as a miniature office."

Joey swallowed because this apartment was unfurnished, and she did not currently own a couch, a dining room table or chairs, any lamps, a TV, a TV stand, or a real adult-sized bed.

Doubt started to swirl through her, because she had no idea how she could possibly afford to purchase all of those things *and* pay the security deposit *and* the first and last month's rent.

"This is nice," Belle said. She'd branched off into the kitchen, and Joey turned around while Harry closed the door.

"Really big," Belle said. "This will be perfect for your cooking."

The fridge stood at the corner of the wall, and the kitchen wrapped around with plenty of counter space, a sink, a dishwasher, and the stove. The window sat on the back wall with plenty of room for a big dining room table. The island was shaped like a trapezoid, and everything had been done in gray and white, including the granite in the countertops.

"This is almost too nice for me," Joey said, running her fingertip along the cold slab of stone.

It didn't take long to go down the hall and peek into the bathroom, which had matching tile and a full tub and shower combo. The laundry room sat in the very corner with the washer and dryer included, and a folding table across from the appliances with plenty of space between.

"Yeah, this is nice," Harry said.

Joey moved into the bedroom next, which would have plenty of room for anything she owned, including a bean bag that she could make into a reading corner.

"It's the first place I've looked at," Joey said as she returned to the main area of the apartment.

"That doesn't mean you shouldn't get it," Belle said. "Do you like it?"

"Yeah, I love it," Joey said.

"Everything is brand new in here," Harry said. "Paint, flooring, everything."

Everything inside Joey felt tight, and she nodded. "I don't know if I can afford this," she said.

"I thought we were looking at it because you could afford it." Harry's frowning gaze came back to hers. "How much is it?"

"Eight-fifty," Joey said. "Plus first and last month's rent, and a security deposit."

Joey needed *two thousand dollars* to move into this place, and she thought of her bank account and sighed. "I have the money," she said. "To get into the apartment, but how am I supposed to live here? I don't have any furniture."

She wasn't like Adam, who could simply call up Aunt Hilde and rattle off a list of all the things he needed and have them show up—paid for—by the weekend.

"It's a nice place," Harry said.

"Didn't you have a couple of others we were going to go look at today too?" Belle asked.

"Yes." Joey headed for the door, though they'd only been there maybe ten minutes. The pictures had spoken a thousand words, and seeing it in person only solidified for her that she liked it.

"There's one that's furnished, so maybe it will be better."

She led the way back out to the car, and she, Harry, and Belle went to see two more apartments. Then she dropped off Belle and Harry at his house with only twenty minutes until she had to get to work at Pork and Beans.

She connected her phone to Bluetooth, so she could call Adam hands-free, and she dialed him before she pulled out of Harry's driveway.

"Hey, baby doll," Adam said. "How were the apartments?"

Joey sighed heavily and looked out the side window.

"That doesn't sound good." Adam's voice slowed and lowered, and she could almost see him looking up from his work or settling down from whatever he was walking away from. "What's going on?"

"One of them was really nice," Joey said. "The first one we went and saw? I sent you those links."

"Yeah," Adam said. "I looked at them."

"The second one was okay," Joey said. "But it's in a big complex, and I don't really like that."

"Right."

"The third one was furnished," Joey said. She wasn't sure why such a keen thread of unhappiness moved through her. She didn't want to be ungrateful, and perhaps she didn't deserve any better. "But it wasn't nice, Adam," she said. "I feel stupid saying that, like I'm just some dumb twenty-two-year-old, and—"

"No." Adam's bark cut her off. "You are *not* some dumb twenty-two-year-old. You work two jobs; you take care of your grandparents. You deserve somewhere nice to live, and if it wasn't nice, then it wasn't nice."

Joey swallowed, tears pressing so close to the surface. "It wasn't very nice," she said, her voice coming out nasally and tinged with tears.

"So you'll get the first one," Adam said. "You deserve somewhere really nice to live, baby doll. I want that for you."

"I can't afford it," Joey said, her frustration thankfully covering up her emotion. "Well, I mean, I can, but I don't have any furniture."

"Oh, well, furniture is easy," Adam said, as if he was talking about how the sky just shone blue every day or the grass grew in green.

"It's easy for *you*," Joey said, a bit of bite in her tone now.

"What, uh—?" Adam cut off and didn't continue. Sudden tension threaded through the air, so thick Joey could almost taste it on her tongue.

"I can help you get some furniture," Adam finally said, his voice as neutral as Joey had ever heard it.

"I don't—"

"We can go shopping together," he said. "The way you came with me when I got my cowboy hat. We'll just go to your aunt's place, and we'll walk around, and you'll pick out all the things that you like."

Joey ground her teeth together. "There is no way I can let you do that."

"Why not?" he asked.

"Because we've been dating for one month," she said.

"Six weeks," he corrected.

"I'm still not going to let my *boyfriend of six weeks* buy me an entire apartment's worth of furniture." Joey gripped the steering wheel like she was trying to strangle the life out of it.

"Even if I want to?" Adam asked. "I'm an adult; I know what I'm doing."

"I know that." Joey sighed again. "I just...I can't." The differences between her and Adam felt so stark in that moment. She didn't want them to be so apparent, but she worked two jobs according to someone else's schedule, and he worked from home according to his own.

"I'm going to think about it," she said. "I'll look at my finances again when I get home tonight."

The twin bed she slept in now was from her childhood, and she could take it with her. Joey felt selfish and greedy as she thought, but she didn't want a twin bed in her new apartment. She wanted to feel like an adult, and adults had big beds.

"Okay," Adam said. "I'll call you later tonight, and we can talk some more about it."

Joey wasn't sure she wanted that, either, but she didn't argue.

"I just want you to be happy," he said.

"I know," she said. "It's not that I'm *un*happy with Grams and Gramps. I've always loved them, and they've been so good to me."

"That's not really what this is about," Adam said quietly, and Joey hated that he understood her so completely. She should be happy about that, and in most cases, she was. Right now, she told herself that he simply didn't get it.

Adam had had money in his life for a long time now, and he'd merely forgotten what it was like not to be able to buy anything he wanted.

Joey wanted to make her own way in the world. She didn't want to have to go to her parents or grandparents or anyone else to get help, even as unfeasible as that was at this stage in her life.

"I'm baking tomorrow," she said. "Are you still planning to come?"

"Yes," Adam said. "If that's okay."

He'd been making the drive to Coral Canyon every day for lunch, as Joey got off from Cake Bites by eleven and didn't have to be at Pork and Beans until four.

"Yeah, of course it's okay," she said. "I can't wait to see you."

"I could have come apartment hunting with you today."

He made his voice light, but Joey still heard the hurt inside it.

"I know," she said. "But you had all those phone calls to make. Did you get everything sorted with the sound and light company?"

"Yes, finally," he said, his tone turning a bit darker, because it had taken him a long time to find the proper equipment he needed for the concert series. "We'll have everything we need for the concerts."

"Oh, that's great," Joey said. "They're coming up fast."

"Yeah, just a few more weeks," Adam said.

Joey made the last turn to the big historic church where Pork and Beans had their catering office in the back. "All right," she said. "I'm at work. I have to go."

"All right, Roo," Adam said. "Seriously, call me tonight."

"Okay," she said, though she wasn't sure she'd call him. Knowing Adam, even though they'd only been dating for a couple of months, she knew he'd call her if she didn't. "Talk to you later."

"Bye, baby," he said. He ended the call, and Joey sat in her car, still a few minutes early for her shift. She stared out the windshield, a single question running through her mind: *What is he doing with me?*

Everyone, from her Uncle Tex to her daddy to Adam himself, had been trying to get Joey to see how awesome she was, but as she sat in the driver's seat, alone, thinking of how much it would cost her to furnish an apartment and move into it, Joey had never felt so low.

She closed her eyes against the burning tears, determined not to let them fall. "Dear God," she prayed. "I am trying to see myself as Thy daughter, worthy of good things in my life, like a nice apartment and my sweet boyfriend, Adam. Will You please help me see it? Help me see in myself what he sees. Help me see and understand what my daddy sees and what Georgia sees and what Grams sees, because right now, I just feel like a problem."

And to Joey, there was no worse feeling.

She waited, the gentle air of the heater blowing through the car, and her own mind blissfully quiet. She opened her eyes and found the snow had finally arrived, big, fat flakes drifting down and melting when they touched her windshield.

She smiled, because Joey had always liked living in Wyoming. She didn't mind the winter or the snow, because it meant she could plug in her blanket, make a cup of hot chocolate, and collapse into her bean bag and read for the day.

Not that her life allowed her to do that very often anymore, but the thought that she *could* brought her comfort.

You are precious to me, the words entered her mind in the same near-silent way that the snow fell, and Joey let the tears burning in her eyes streak down her face, for she knew God had just spoken to her and confirmed to her that she was His daughter and she did have worth.

Though she couldn't quite see how or why He loved her, she could feel absolutely that He did.

She knew He had not abandoned her, and that if she

continued to try to see herself the way those who loved her did, He would eventually open her eyes and provide that sight for her.

"I won't give up," she promised Him, and then she hurried through the falling snow to the back door of Pork and Beans, wondering with every step if she should just take a leap of faith and get that apartment before it was leased to someone else.

27

Joey had not called Adam last night after her shift at the catering company, and he'd called her instead. She'd said she was going over her finances one more time, and then she was going to talk to Grams about perhaps asking the family if they could help her furnish an apartment with a simple couch and a folding table.

Maybe, she'd said. *I don't know.*

Adam knew that wasn't what she wanted at all, but he'd listened to her, everything he wanted to say getting stuffed way down deep in his throat.

"You're going to have to come clean," he told himself as he walked down the icy sidewalk toward her grandparents' condo. The scent of apples and cinnamon met his nose a good ten feet away, and he didn't bother knocking and then waiting.

Instead, he knocked and opened the door at the same

time, calling, "It's just me," as he hurried in, out of the wind, and shut it out behind him.

"Oh, hello, Adam," Cecily said. She wore an apron with elves all over it as she stirred something in a bowl. "Joey just went to help Jerry for a moment."

"Okay," Adam said. He'd come to sit with her grandfather while Joey and Cecily baked, and he wondered how he could get Joey away from them to tell her what he'd done. *Maybe you should tell her in front of them*, he thought. *Maybe then she won't break up with you.*

Adam swallowed and glanced toward the mouth of the hall as Jerry and Joey came shuffling down it.

"Oh, you're here," Joey said. "Can you help Gramps back to his recliner? I'm pretty sure the pie crust needs to come out."

"Does it?" Grams asked, turning toward her granddaughter. "I didn't hear a timer."

"It's on my phone," Joey said, and Adam hurried to her side to relieve her of helping Jerry, whose hips and back ached in bad weather. Adam helped him over to his recliner, where he sat down with a sigh. The scent of browned pie crust filled the condo, and Adam turned back to the kitchen.

"It looks good," he said.

"It's too dark," Joey complained, and she seemed irritated and rushed already. He wished he would have left earlier, but they'd requested soups and salads from a diner that didn't open until eleven, and then they'd been extremely busy. "I brought lunch," he said. "Whenever you guys are ready."

"Oh, thank you," Cecily said, though Joey had just thrown him a dirty look.

"I didn't say you had to eat it right now," he said. "I literally said whenever you're ready."

She nodded and turned back to the stove. "I just feel off-kilter today," she said.

"Already?" He moved into the small kitchen, knowing he'd get shooed out soon enough.

"Oh, she burned a few cakes at work," Cecily said, smiling at him.

"Not a few." Joey threw her a look. "I burned *one* batch of cupcakes, which I guess is a few cakes. It just...sort of set me off kilter."

"I'm sorry, baby doll," he said, running his hand along her waist. "What can I do to help?" He took in the disaster of flour and butter, spices, sliced apples, and chopped chocolate, and knew he should not stay anywhere near that kitchen.

Joey turned toward him and planted her hands on her hips. "I do not need any help from you, mister," she said, and at least she smiled.

"Well, that's rude," he said, with a grin. "I seem to remember me totally killing those Oreo chocolate crusts."

"Those are already done," Joey said, and she moved into him.

He received her into his arms and leaned down to kiss her. "You seem stressed already, baby doll," he said. "Seriously, what can I do?"

She kissed him, and that was plenty to calm Adam

down. Then she sighed and said, "Nothing. Just help Gramps today, okay? That will help a lot."

"All right," Adam said. "I mean, I can be a taste tester too."

Joey laughed and gave him a little shove away. He moved into the living room and sat down on the couch, her giggles making everything in his life better. Jerry had picked up a book and he didn't even look over to Adam, which was about how Jerry was.

Adam looked at his phone and found several more texts from the members of Country Quad. He automatically turned it more into himself, as if Joey would come look over his shoulder and see it.

She's going to find out, he told himself, and he decided he definitely better tell her in mixed company if he wanted to keep his life.

"Hey, so what happened with that apartment?" he asked over his shoulder.

She sighed at the same time that Jerry growled, "Don't ask," under his breath.

"Don't ask?" Adam asked, and he twisted to look at Joey in the small condo kitchen. "Did something happen?"

"They rented it to someone else," she said. "I knew it would go fast. It's really nice and it's not very expensive."

His heart twisted strangely in his chest. "Oh, I thought they were going to wait for you."

"I guess they've had a lot of interest in it," Joey said, almost matter-of-factly. "It would have been a really nice place."

"She's quite upset about it," Grams said, though Adam didn't think she was acting that way.

He glanced over to Jerry, who mimed crying. Alarmed, Adam turned back to Joey. He had not detected any trace of tears, but he didn't spend twenty-four hours a day with her, either. He got to his feet, suddenly unable to keep sitting.

"So funny thing," he said, his pulse booming against the back of his tongue as he paced toward the end of the couch and looked into the kitchen. Joey had her back to him as she stirred something on the stove.

"I texted your uncles," he said. "And your daddy—just the guys in Country Quad. And I asked them if there was any way that they could put together a move-in...furniture... kit for you."

By the time he finished speaking, he wasn't even sure if he'd gotten the words in the right order.

Joey turned from where she worked at the stove, her face a mixture of surprise and horror. "You did what?"

"Oh, that's a great idea," Grams said, and she looked at Joey meaningfully. "I told Joey we should ask on the family text if anybody had extra furniture they weren't using. Among all of us, surely there's a couch or a table not being used."

"Surely," Adam said.

"*Surely?*" Joey demanded, "What have you done?"

Adam swallowed and looked to Jerry for help. The older man glared back at him, and Adam didn't think he'd be getting any assistance there.

"They didn't rent that apartment to someone else," he said. "They're holding it for you."

"What?" Joey's confusion really was cute, what with that little frown between her eyes.

"I told them it was a surprise," Adam said. "Until I could talk to you, and well, now is the first time I found to be able to talk to you about this."

"And you think *now's* a good time?" She indicated the unfilled pie crusts and the pounds of butter waiting on the counter. Then she faced him again and folded her arms. "I'm in the middle of baking my weekly orders on my only day off."

"I know," he said, swallowing. "Maybe it's not the best time, but it's the only time we've got."

"Just listen to him, dear," Grams said.

Joey looked at the stove, and then her grandmother. "Adam and I are going to go for a walk," she said. "I'm going to give him exactly *ten minutes* to tell me *exactly* what's going on. By that time, these pie crusts will come out, and I'll be back to finish this pumpkin custard."

"Sounds great," Grams chirped as if nothing was happening out of the ordinary.

"Good luck," Gramps muttered, and Joey picked up her coat and put it on right over her apron. "You're coming with me," she said, and Adam wasn't sure if he was scared or excited.

He quickly put his jacket back on and stepped with her outside.

"You better start talking," she said. "And don't stop until you get all the way to the end."

"All right." He drew a deep breath. "After I heard you on the phone call yesterday and how excited you were about that apartment—"

"I wasn't excited," she said. "I was upset I didn't have enough money for it."

"Yeah, and that indicated your excitement," he said, sending her a glare of his own. "I called and asked them to please hold it through tomorrow morning."

"Did you have to pay them?" she asked.

"You told me to go all the way to the end."

"Fine," she huffed. "Go all the way to the end."

"I told them I would give them a couple hundred extra dollars if they would please just hold it for me for one day, so that I could see if we could make it a reality for you. And then I texted Country Quad. Your daddy and uncles have been talking with everyone privately about any furniture they might have that they'd be willing to donate—or sell for very little."

Adam tapped on his phone and moved to the list that Tex had sent less than an hour ago.

"This is what they came up with. Sterling has a couch in her massage studio that she doesn't want anymore. It's full-size, for three people." He glanced over to her, but Joey walked along like an animated statue.

"I guess Cheryl and Wade have a dining room table that they've outgrown. Cheryl wants a new one, but the one she has is her mother's, and she wasn't sure how to get rid of it. This way, she can give it to you and feel good about it."

Joey said nothing. She hugged herself tightly, her arms folded across her chest in a definitely-angry way.

"Mav and Dani have several queen-size beds in their basement that no one is using. They're sending one to Jackson Hole with Boston and—"

"Wait." Joey reached over and grabbed his arm. "Boston's moving to Jackson Hole?"

Adam glanced over to her and found alarm running across her face. "I guess he got a job at the Elk River Lodge there," he said. "He's going to be moving in with Cash, but Cash doesn't have a bed for him, and Beth's going to Maryland, whether she gets into school or not."

The Youngs definitely overshared, but in this case, Adam hadn't minded. "So Mav and Dani have some extra beds, and they're happy to just give one to you."

Joey's jaw hardened, and he thought the best thing to do was to go back to his list. Get it all out. Go all the way to the end.

"Michelle has a TV from Daily Grind that she wants to get rid of. She says the coffee shop isn't a sports bar, and she's doing some remodeling and doesn't want it."

He glanced over to her as they neared the end of the sidewalk that led to the parking lot.

"Your Aunt Hilde said she would donate any bedding you didn't have, as well as towels and other linens, and your momma and daddy apparently have a credenza that came from the bookstore that's just taking up space in their garage."

Adam closed his phone and shoved it away. "From what I can tell, that only leaves maybe a nightstand and a desk in your bedroom, maybe some drapes or something, and maybe a loveseat or a recliner, so that you have more seating. But it should be plenty to get you started." He stopped and reached out to touch her elbow. "Will you please look at me and tell me why you're so angry?"

She didn't look at him, but she did stop and face him. "I told you I didn't want you to help me with this."

"Not true," he said. "You said I couldn't buy the furniture for you, and I didn't." He let her eyes flit all over the place, and then Adam slid his hand along her jaw and into her hair.

Her eyes locked on his then, and he leaned closer, hoping to drive his point home. "Joelle, I am falling in love with you, and if I can make your life easier, I want to do it."

He enjoyed the way she closed her eyes and breathed out as she calmed down. He rested his forehead against hers. "I just need you to *allow* me to help you. This is what I'm really good at—putting together all these pieces, finding all these details." He lowered his head and pressed his cheek to hers. "Please, just let me do this for you. It's not costing me anything. I'm not giving you a single dime."

"No, you've just done all this work," she said, her voice broken. "And it is going to cost you money—two hundred dollars to hold the apartment."

He pulled away and looked into her gorgeous blue eyes filled with such worry. "You are worth two hundred dollars," he said. "And besides, Blaze said he would pay that." Adam gave her a smile and watched her chin wobble. "Please, baby doll."

One tear splashed her cheek, and she wiped it away quickly. "I just don't know if I'm good enough for you," she said.

"Funny," he shot back. "I spent last night wondering the same thing."

"What?" The word exploded out of her body in mostly air, and he realized how that had sounded.

"No, no. I meant—I spent all last night wondering if *I* was good enough for *you*."

"Well, that's just silly," she said.

"That's how I feel about what you just said." He dropped his hand and pocketed it. "All it takes is one text to get all those items," he said. "And one phone call to get that apartment. We can have you moved into that apartment before Christmas."

"Really?" Joey asked. "I wasn't planning on moving until January first."

"Just imagine baking all your pies in that new kitchen," he said.

"I don't want to cut Grams out of it."

Adam smiled and pulled Joey into his arms. This time, she relaxed into his embrace and hugged him back.

"Joey, you are so good to everyone around you. When are you going to put yourself first?"

"I don't know," she murmured. "I was kind of taught *not* to put myself first."

"Right," Adam said, his mind flowing through the things he'd been taught too. "We can serve others. We *should* serve others, help them, but we can't do that if we're in dire need of care ourselves. God doesn't expect that of us."

"No," she said. "He doesn't."

"If you don't want to move in until January, that's fine," Adam said.

Joey pulled back and looked up at him with wide eyes filled with hope and wonder. "Can you imagine me having Christmas in my own place?"

He grinned at her. "So am I going to send the text and make the phone call? I bet I can do it before we even get back to the condo."

She took his face in her hands and gazed at him in a way no one had ever looked at Adam before. "You're fast becoming my favorite person."

"Good," he said. The thought of her having anyone else she liked more than him made him a little jealous.

She closed her eyes and leaned her head against his chest. "I'm a little scared," she said.

"Of living by yourself?"

"No," she said. "Of falling in love with you."

Adam had been battling his own army of fear against such a thing, and he didn't know how to reassure Joey. He took her hand, and they started back to the condo, and he simply let the quietness of the winter seep into him.

Just outside the condo, he asked, "So you're not breaking up with me, right?"

"No," Joey said.

"And you want me to make sure that you get this apartment and coordinate your move." He leaned closer, hoping she could see the parallels between them. "Like you coordinated mine."

Joey grinned. "I did coordinate your move, didn't I?"

"Yes, you did, and see? You do a lot of good for other people, and it's okay for you to accept help too."

She nodded, something still storming in her eyes. "Okay, I want the apartment."

"Your wish is my command," Adam said, nodding toward the condo as a particularly nasty gust of wind came and tried to steal his cowboy hat.

Joey turned to the condo and pushed open the door, squealing. "Grams, I can't wait for you to see this kitchen," she called, suddenly all laughter and giggles.

Adam entered the condo too, and he whispered, "Thank you, Lord," —his first uttered prayer in a long time.

28

J oey used the weight of the to-go bags she carried to push down on Adam's door handle, then she opened the door with her foot and entered his house. She'd known he had meetings this morning, but she hadn't realized that they wouldn't be over by the time she arrived with lunch.

Now, she stood framed in the double-wide archway that led into Adam's office, six grown men staring at her.

"Howdy, Roo," Daddy said. "What are you doing here?" He cut a quick look over to Adam.

Joey didn't think she needed to answer, what with all the food she carried. She still said, "I brought lunch, and I'm about to drop it."

Uncle Tex and Uncle Luke stood the closest to her, and they lunged at her and took the food.

"Did you bring some for all of us?" Uncle Tex asked.

"No," Joey said. "I didn't know you'd be here." She looked at Uncle Morris and Uncle Trace.

As the scent of the Italian food drifted away from her, she added, "But I did order a couple of family-size pans of pasta for Adam, so there's probably plenty—if he doesn't mind giving up his dinner for the weekend."

"He doesn't mind," Daddy said, and he clapped Joey on the shoulder as he exited the office.

"We're not done here," Adam called after him, but Uncle Trace and Uncle Morris got up as well. Uncle Morris hugged Joey and said, "Sure is good to see you, Roo," before he continued past. Uncle Trace did the same, adding, "I'll keep them back here in the kitchen for as long as I can, but I wouldn't dawdle." He grinned at Joey and headed down the hallway that led into the rest of Adam's mansion.

She faced her boyfriend and smiled. "And you didn't think you needed those pans of pasta."

He rolled his eyes as he shuffled some papers on his desk. "We're really not done."

"I didn't mean to interrupt," she said. "I told you I'd be here at twelve-thirty."

"It's not your fault," he said. "We're having trouble... staying on task today."

"Oh, you hate that," she teased.

He got to his feet and came toward her. "I don't hate seeing you." He took her into his arms and kissed her quickly. "You can bring me some more pasta tomorrow, right?"

Joey grinned at him, enjoying the feel of his strong body

in her arms. "Yeah, I'll bring you pasta any day you want." She nodded toward the arched doorway. "What are they having trouble with today?"

He took her hand, and they left the office together. "Believe it or not, clothing."

"Oh, I believe it," Joey said. "Have you met Uncle Luke?" She giggled. "You should watch some of the old Country Quad videos."

"Oh, I've seen them," Adam said. "He really is good at putting on a show."

"He's the one who organizes every detail of things like that," Joey said. "It's extremely important to him."

"Which is why they were so popular," Adam said. "But it's wintertime, and I keep telling him they're going to be performing outside. They're already going to be dealing with instruments in varying temperatures, and we don't need to be dealing with wardrobe issues too."

"Why can't he just wear one of his puffy vests?" Joey asked. "He gets a billion comments on posts where he wears the puffy vest," she said, the last part as she entered the kitchen.

Uncle Trace waved his hand toward her. "There you go, Luke. The younger generation has spoken."

"I told you we should wear those puffy vests," Uncle Tex said.

"Really, the puffy vest?" Luke glared at Joey and then turned back and lifted an enormous tong-full of spaghetti onto his plate.

"Save some food for Adam, would you?" Joey said. "And me, seeing how I paid for it."

"I can send you some money," Daddy said.

"Oh, it's fine," Joey said, but had she known she was going to feed her father and four of her uncles, she would have expected them to pay her. "Are you guys really hung up on clothes?"

"Just a little," Uncle Tex said.

"What else?"

"Otis needs to finalize the set list," Uncle Luke said.

"The first concert is in two weeks," Joey said, swinging her gaze to her father, who'd wasted no time loading his plate with garlic bread and spaghetti. "You don't have the set list finalized?"

"We do," Daddy said.

"Not in writing," Luke said.

"We play the songs in the same order every time we practice," Uncle Trace said. "I know the set list."

"It needs to be in writing," Luke insisted.

"He's right," Adam chimed in as he joined the line. He picked up two plates, and Joey smiled at his thoughtfulness. "I need to publish it online."

"Well, you've been at practice," Daddy said.

"Give the man a set list," Trace growled as he took an Italian sausage with his penne pasta. "I saved one of these for you, Roo." He turned and put it on one of the plates that Adam held. "She loves these."

"She does?" Adam asked. "Huh. You learn something new every day."

"Yeah, especially when you've only been dating for a couple of months," Daddy said dryly.

"Yeah, we haven't eaten at every restaurant in town yet," Joey threw at him. "So of course, Adam wouldn't know every single favorite of mine."

"Oh, boy," Trace said, glancing at Joey. "I didn't mean to start anything. I just thought Joey liked the sausages."

"I do, Uncle Trace," she said. "Thank you."

"Go sit," Adam said, smiling at her. He sure seemed to know how to deal with her uncles—and her daddy. "I know what else you like."

She wasn't quite sure what to do with herself in a situation like this, but she did like being pampered and taken care of, so she went and sat down next to Uncle Luke. "The puffy vest really is still cool," she said. "You guys could get new ones in matching colors—or an array of colors. Either way, it would be awesome."

"You really think so?" Uncle Luke asked.

"Yeah," Joey said. "It's probably too late to get your logo on the chest, but you could call Mike and ask him."

"I already called Mike," Adam called from the kitchen. "We literally have to tell him *today* if we want the vests done or not."

"I think we should do it," Uncle Tex said. "Then I can still wear that long sleeve shirt I want and I won't look like a sixty-year-old."

"Brother, you're sixty," Trace said. "You look sixty."

"Yeah, but a *hot* sixty," Joey said. "With the vest." She grinned at her uncle, who grinned right back.

"When are you moving into your new place, Roo?" Uncle Tex asked.

Joey sighed. "Not for another week and a half."

"It was going to be this weekend," Daddy said. "But then they had a leak upstairs, and the water went into the basement, and they're fixing some stuff."

"That's right," Joey said. "But I really appreciate all you guys helping me get furniture and stuff." She smiled around at everyone, glad that they seemed to be enjoying the food too.

"Oh, yeah, sure," Uncle Tex said. "My whole basement is full of furniture we don't use."

"That's not true, Uncle Tex." Joey rolled her eyes and smiled at him. "Did anybody hear from Boston today?" She looked around, though Uncle Mav wasn't there.

"Nothing yet," Trace said.

"Nothing on the family text either," Daddy said.

"Well, he's done two interviews now," Joey said. "Surely he'll get the job."

"He's moving to Jackson no matter what," Uncle Luke said. "Mav told me that last night."

"Really?" Uncle Morris asked. "I hadn't heard that."

"That's because Mav just told me last night," Luke said, twirling up another fork full of spaghetti and putting it in his mouth. "Him and Blaze are moving Boston to Jackson Hole this weekend."

"Wow," Uncle Morris said. "I'm surprised we haven't heard that."

"They're not gonna need any help?" Uncle Tex asked.

No one said anything, and Joey looked around at the uncles. "I imagine it'll be a lot like me," she said. "I can fit everything I own in my car, so how much help could Boston possibly need?"

Luke pointed his fork at her. "That. Mav is taking a bed, and they're getting everything else in Jackson."

"I'm not super happy about it." Adam put a plate of fettuccine Alfredo with Joey's Italian sausage and a bread-stick in front of her and pulled out the chair beside her to sit down.

Surprised, she looked over to him. "You're not happy about Boston moving to Jackson Hole? Why not?"

"Because I wanted him to help me run the concert series," he said.

"You've got Uncle Morris to help you with the concert series," she looked over to her uncle. "Right?"

"I just thought it would give him something to do," Adam said. "He was real good at it with Harry."

"Well, if he doesn't get this job at the lodge," Uncle Trace said. "I bet you could entice him to come back for a couple of months." He looked around at the other members of the band, and they all nodded, which meant they had just agreed to pay Boston if he didn't get a job at the lodge.

"I got four new pie orders for next week," Joey said, feeling her chest balloon with pride. "And you guys are the first to know that I only need *one* more order to hit my goal of one hundred pie orders to make an extra thousand dollars to move into my own place."

"That's incredible, Joey," Uncle Tex said, smiling widely.

"Yeah, way to go, Roo." Daddy reached out and patted her hand. "And you've still got two weeks till Christmas."

"I'm not doing any orders next week," Joey said. "I'm going to push everybody off until Christmas, and I'm hoping I'll get a bunch of orders then, like I did for Thanksgiving."

"I know Ev wants pies," Uncle Trace said. "I'll tell her to get on your website." He gave her a warm smile too, and Joey liked this feeling of doing something good with her life.

"It really helped that Uncle Shawn posted it from Pork and Beans," she said, watching Uncle Trace. "I didn't ask him to do it last time, but do you think I should this time?"

"Yeah," Uncle Trace said. "Why wouldn't you?"

"I don't know," Joey said, ducking her head as a round of foolishness moved through her.

"She doesn't like asking for help," Adam said.

Irritation blitzed through Joey, and she glared at him out of the corner of her eye.

Daddy started to chuckle. "No, she does not. You're right about that."

"I am sitting at the table," Joey said, lifting her eyes to her father's. "Don't talk about me as if I'm not here."

"Hey, I didn't mean to do that," Adam said. "I wasn't making fun of you." He looked at her earnestly as if they were the only two people in the room. "Okay?" He slid his hand over hers and squeezed.

With his touch, she did feel like they were the only two people in the room, and she worked to remind herself that she absolutely could not lean toward him and kiss him in front of the other five members of her family. Instead, she nodded and dropped her head as part of that motion. "Okay," she said.

She hadn't been planning to talk about any of this during today's lunch. She'd wanted to talk to Adam about coming to church with her. She went and he didn't, but he'd told her last week he had grown up religious and that his momma still went to church every week and that he had started praying.

She didn't want to rush him along his own journey, and they hadn't really had time to talk in depth about their religion. There had been a few texts before he'd said, *You have to get up in six hours. I'll talk to you tomorrow, baby doll.*

Joey cleared her throat as her uncles talked around her, and they continued their band meeting as if she'd simply brought catering for them. She finished first and took her plate into the kitchen, where she rinsed it and put it in the dishwasher. She started cleaning up the food and covering it with the aluminum foil lids and putting it in the fridge.

"We've gotta wrap this up," Adam said. "I only get to see Joey a couple of hours a day, and she's gotta go to work in a little bit." He herded everyone back into the office, and fifteen minutes later, he managed to get them out of his house.

He sighed, ran his hand through his hair, and reseated his cowboy hat on his head as he sank onto the couch with her. She glanced at him and smiled. "They can be a lot."

"You're not kiddin'," he said, and Joey liked how he dropped the G and sounded like a real cowboy.

"Thanks for lunch, Roo." He reached for her and gathered her close and pulled her down with him as he lay on the couch. She tucked her back against his chest, the weight of his arm along her waist heavy and comforting. "I could get really used to you walking in the house with lunch every day," he said. "Sure was nice."

"You just like spaghetti and meatballs," she said, not daring to raise her voice louder than he'd spoken.

He chuckled. "I think it's more than that."

Joey definitely felt like there was more to them as well, and she laced her fingers through his and held their hands close to her stomach. "I wanted to follow up with you on your conversation about prayer," she said.

"Hm," Adam hummed.

"Do you think you might want to come to church with me?" she asked. "Once I move out, I'm going to have to go by myself, and I think you know I'm not very good at doing things by myself."

"You're great at doing things by yourself," he said. "You just don't like doing it for the first few times."

She had never told him that, and somehow, he knew it anyway. "Right," she said. "So this week I'll go with Grams, but the week before Christmas, it'll just be up to me to walk in by myself, and I just thought if you wanted to come—then we could walk in together."

"I'll think about it," Adam said. "Though I have really been considering my faith and where it is and what I need to do with it." He tightened his arms around her, and let a few moments of silence pass.

"What if I don't want to go to church?" he asked. "What if I'm just not super religious like you are? Do you think that would be a problem if we got married?"

Joey pulled in a breath through her nose. She had not started thinking about marriage with Adam yet, though as she lay there in his warm embrace, she realized that she really probably should

"I don't know," she whispered. "I've never had a relationship as serious as this."

"We'll just keep talking about it," Adam said. "I want us to be able to talk about anything, because in the relationships I've had in my life, the best are the ones where we have open communication, even if we don't agree."

"Okay," Joey said. "We'll just keep talking about it."

"All right," he murmured. "For right now, I just want to hold you and maybe take a nap."

She giggled as he buried his face in her hair because she knew the mighty Adam Harmon did not nap. Just getting him to slow down long enough to relax on the couch with her was a major feat, and Joey congratulated herself for that.

She knew there would be no napping when he asked, "So what book are you reading right now?" as if he really cared—and Joey knew that he did.

Her heart warmed and her blood blazed through her veins as she turned in his arms and whispered, "I'll tell you about it later," just before she pressed her lips to his.

29

Adam glanced at his phone when it rang. So much of his life was conducted through a text that when his phone rang, he really paid attention. *Momma* sat on the screen, and Adam looked away from his spreadsheet to swipe on the call.

He tried to talk to his mother every week, no matter what he had going on, and he realized that today was Friday and he hadn't called yet.

"Hey Momma," he said, leaning back in his executive desk chair. "I'm sorry I haven't called yet. Been real busy this week."

"We've been keeping busy down here too," she said.

"Yeah, what have you got going on?" he asked, because the more his mother talked and the less he did, the better the call would go for Adam. He loved his mother, and it had actually been his dad who'd told him to call her once a week and keep her updated with everything in his life. It had been good advice, because Adam knew he could always go to his mom for anything he needed.

"Ellie's going to have another baby," Momma said. "Her and Paxman are so excited."

"Oh, that's great news," Adam said, smiling at the same time he realized that his mother would want to know about his love life as well. That she'd likely called to tell him about his sister's pregnancy—and to give him her standard lecture on his single status.

"Before you ask," he said, as she started to say something. "I've started seeing someone."

"You have?" Momma asked. "Oh Adam, this is great news."

"Momma, don't act like that," he said.

"Don't act like what? You never tell me when you're dating until it's really serious."

"Name the last person I told you I was dating."

"Exactly," she said without missing a beat. "You haven't dated anyone seriously in years. So this is huge."

"Or maybe you just called me on a Friday afternoon with news about Ellie, and I knew you were going to ask me if I was seeing anyone." He grinned, because he had his mother pegged. "Because you want to have grandbabies, one right after the other."

"Well, you can't fault me for that," she said.

"Actually, I can, Momma. You had your three babies."

"And it was very hard to get all of you," she said. "Your father and I had to work really hard."

Adam reached up and ran his hand over his eyes. He'd been going over logistics for an hour to make sure that all the lighting, the stage setup, the heating elements they needed, the instrument changes, and everything could be handled by him and Morris.

Country Quad said they had a whole team of people that they traveled with or worked with at stadiums, but this was no stadium tour.

They needed a few instruments and stools, lights and multiple cameras, as Harry had promised to livestream each of the performances to his own social media. He had subscribers that paid a monthly fee for exclusive content, and he was going to be live for them.

"Her name's Joey," Adam said. "She's got a couple pictures of us that I can send you."

"How long have you been seeing her?" Momma asked.

"A couple of months," Adam said. "One of the guys in Country Quad; she's his daughter."

"Oh, Adam." Momma let his name hang there, filled with disappointment.

"It's fine," Adam said.

"Until it isn't," Momma said.

"Yeah, but right now it is," he said. "Listen, I wanted to ask you something."

"Okay," she said. "Is it about Joey?"

"No," Adam said, he pressed his eyes closed. "I mean, maybe a little bit." He blew out his breath and got to his feet. He needed more coffee to have this conversation.

"She asked me to go to church with her in a couple of

weeks. She's moving out. She doesn't like to do things by herself." That alone had prompted Adam to want to go to church, but he wasn't sure if it was for the right reason or not.

"You used to love going to church," Momma said. "When you were a little boy, you'd get up before all of us and start making pancakes, so we wouldn't be late."

Adam smiled to himself as he started making a new pot of coffee. "Did I really? I don't remember that."

"You really did," Momma said, chuckling. "You used to get so mad at the twins, even when they were tiny babies, because it took me so long to get them ready to go."

"Well, that's because the twins are slow," Adam said.

"Ellie had a lot of hair," Momma said. "It would take me a while to get it done, that's for sure." She sighed a happy little sigh. "And you'd bring me a blueberry pancake that was barely cooked all the way through. I ate it anyway, because I wanted you to think I liked them."

"Momma," he said. "This is proof that I've always been a terrible cook. No wonder you kept chasing me out of the kitchen."

"Oh, so you remember *that*?" Momma asked.

Adam laughed. "Yeah, that I remember." He got out the sugar bowl and his favorite mug. "Joey is a real good cook," he said, pride moving through him for absolutely no reason whatsoever. "She works at a bakery in the morning and a catering place at night, and she went to a year of culinary school in New York."

"Mm, hm," Momma said, and Adam knew she wasn't listening.

"Yeah," he said. "And then she got abducted by aliens and disappeared off the face of the planet for a couple of years."

Silence for a beat. Then two.

"Oh, Adam, she's *pretty*," Momma said.

His heartbeat spiked, punching the back of his throat. "What do you mean? How would you know she's pretty?"

"You said she was one of Country Quad's daughters."

"You *Googled* her?" he asked.

"She comes up with her daddy...though she looks pretty young in this photo."

Adam had no idea what picture his mother had found, but his throat had turned tight, the words right there on the tip of his tongue, unable to be ignored. "Yeah, well, that's because she's pretty young," he said.

"What do you mean?" she asked.

"I'm sure she doesn't have a Wikipedia page," Adam griped. "She's younger than me, Momma, by quite a lot."

"How much younger?"

"Why does it matter?" he asked. "She's an adult."

"Is she like, an adult last week, or like, an adult a year ago?"

"Momma, she'll be twenty-three in February," he said. "She's been an adult for almost five years. She's lived in New York City, for crying out loud."

"Oh, okay," Momma said, and that was that.

Adam wished things could be as simple for Otis and

Georgia, but he also understood why they weren't. He'd signed a three-year contract with Country Quad, and he wouldn't be going anywhere. He'd have to see the Youngs for all of those days, even if he broke up with Joey.

Be real, he thought to himself. *If this relationship ends, it'll be because she doesn't want to see you anymore.*

How would that go when she had to see him just to show up to her own family's events?

As the coffee started to percolate, he reminded himself that he was not her daddy's personal assistant. He was the band manager, and Joey could choose to be as involved with the band as much or as little as she wanted to be.

So if they broke up, he wouldn't have to see her. He still would, and it would be painful, because Adam could not imagine his life without Joey in it.

He suddenly wanted to ask his mother about love, but he figured he better stick to one topic at a time.

"So what about church?" he asked. "Should I go with her?"

"Oh, honey, you're thirty years old," Momma said. "You can decide for yourself if you want to go to church or not."

"I'm actually thirty-one."

"Right, so make your decision."

If only Adam didn't have to make so many, perhaps this one would be easier. "I want to go with her," he said. "Simply because it would be easier for her, but I also want to go for the right reasons."

"And what would the right reasons be, son?" Momma asked.

"I don't know," Adam said, feeling flustered. "A desire to feel the spirit, to hear the word of the Lord in my life?"

"Do you want either of those things?" Momma asked.

Adam thought for a moment, finding it very easy to say, "You know what, Momma? I do."

"Great," she said as if she didn't care at all if he went to church or not, but Adam knew his mother had been down on her knees morning and night praying for him since the day he had been born. "Then you should go. And even if you're just going for her, God still might have something to say to you while you're there."

Adam had never quite heard the voice of the Lord the way his mother did, but he didn't want to argue with her either. He never had, and she'd always given him the grace and space to learn for himself.

"All right," he said. "I think I'll go with her then."

"Well, that sounds wonderful," Momma said. "And if I don't have a picture of her in the next thirty seconds, I may just buy an airplane ticket and come up there so I can meet her in person."

Adam laughed. "Momma, don't do that," he said. "You'll be throwing a hip out on the airplane."

"That happened *one time*," Momma said, and Adam laughed again.

"She's taken all the pictures on her phone," he said. "So let me text her and get one. Can you give me ten minutes?" He glanced at the clock. "Might actually be longer, Momma; she just got to her second job."

"She has *two* jobs? Adam Lewis Harmon, why are you letting your girlfriend work *two* jobs?"

Adam smiled and said, "Momma, if I could just have you tell Joey to let me take care of her, the world's problems will be solved."

"Does she not want you to take care of her?" Momma asked, the incredulity in her voice off the charts, like such a thing was so foreign she couldn't even comprehend it.

"Momma, we've been dating for *two* months," he said. "I don't think she's quite ready to take every dime I can give her."

"Oh, well, I guess I can see that," she said.

"You guess you can?" Adam teased. "The last woman I dated for *eight months*, mind you, and I offered to pay her cell phone bill *once*, and you lectured me for twenty minutes about not letting women take advantage of me."

"Oh, it wasn't twenty minutes," Momma said, though it had definitely been twenty minutes—maybe more.

"All right, Momma," Adam said, chuckling. "I gotta go. I'll send you a picture real soon."

"All right," she said. "I love you, son."

"Love you too, Momma."

Adam let her end the call, and he poured himself a cup of coffee before he texted Joey to get a selfie.

I decided I want to come to church with you on Sunday. Is that invitation still open? I know you're working right now. Just text me when you get a minute.

He took his coffee to the back window that overlooked the yard. Darkness had started to fall already, as it was the second week of December, and winter had definitely come to Wyoming. Adam found he didn't mind it, but he pretended to be put out for Harry's sake. Joey loved winter, and that had only made him like her more.

His phone chimed, but he'd left it in the kitchen, and it took him an extra minute to feel like checking it. When he did, he found Joey had texted him back.

Yes, I can text you the address. They're doing a Christmas service on Sunday, so we'll probably want to get there early if we want to get a seat. It starts at ten.

That would be a long drive for Adam, but he got up early in the morning, and he didn't anticipate it being a problem. The next text that had come in was the smiling selfie that Joey had taken the day she'd told her family that they were dating.

Adam grinned at the two of them, and he quickly downloaded the picture and sent it to his mother. He'd focused on church in the phone call, but now he typed out the second question that he'd been thinking about.

Do not freak out, he started. *And don't call me again. But how do you know when you're in love?*

30

Boston climbed up into the bed of his truck and then grabbed onto the bungee cords he and his dad had put around the mattress. He pulled with all of his strength, and with Daddy pushing, the mattress slid right on top of the box springs.

He hated moving, but it felt necessary. He hadn't been able to find a job in Coral Canyon, despite the fact that there were several event centers and luxury lodges here. They seemed full-up with staff—and Jackson Hole was the biggest tourist town in Wyoming.

He'd started applying there and gotten interviews instantly. He'd slept on Cash's couch for the past week and a half, and his back ached as he jumped down to the frozen ground.

"At least it stopped snowing," he said.

His daddy grinned at him and turned to go back in the house. "You got everything?"

"Did you grab that duffel bag?" Boston asked.

"Yep." Daddy led the way down the snow-cleared path and up the steps into the house.

Boston didn't want to live here, but he didn't want to move either. The warring emotions felt like tearing himself right in half, but he put a smile on his face for his mother.

"All set?" she asked, her eyes bright with what Boston hoped was excitement, though he knew his mother worried about him moving to Jackson Hole. His grandparents had come too, and he stepped in to hug his mother before moving over to them.

"I'm all ready," he said.

She indicated two big brown grocery sacks. "Grandma bought some food for you and Cash," she said.

Boston kept his smile in place. "Thank you so much. We'll really appreciate this."

Daddy looked up from his phone. "Uncle Blaze has left," he said. He turned the device toward everyone. "And Uncle Gabe just sent this."

Boston looked closer and found a smiling picture of Liesl behind the wheel with Gabe in the passenger seat. They both gave a double thumbs up, and Boston grinned. "Oh boy," he said. "I hope that goes okay."

"She's a good driver," Momma said. "They'll be fine."

"It's one of their first long trips on the highway," Daddy said.

Boston sent up a silent prayer for his cousin, because he

knew driving made Liesl nervous, especially with her daddy beside her. Uncle Gabe was the buttoned-up type, who wore a suit everywhere he went, spoke properly, and had been educated as a lawyer. He'd been the youngest lawyer in Wyoming, in fact, having graduated law school by the time he was Boston's age.

He'd done one year of college before coming home and trying to figure out what to do with his life. He'd really enjoyed working for Harry on the concert series, and he'd been really good at handling details, scheduling things, and working with people.

He'd thought about returning to school to do hospitality management or something of that sort. But no matter what, he needed a job to be able to move out of his parents' basement. He picked up the bags of groceries—and probably some of his grandmother's famous fire-roasted corn chowder —and headed for the door.

"You leavin' Boston?" Lars asked as he gained the stairs.

"Hey, buddy," Boston said, and he quickly passed the bags of groceries to his dad. "I'm gonna text Momma and Daddy all about my new place, okay?" he said. "And my first day on the job, so you'll get to see it."

Boston's younger sister, Emilia, came upstairs too, and he knelt down and hugged them both. "You guys be real good for Momma and Daddy, okay?"

"Okay," Emilia said, and Lars looked to their daddy.

"Can't I come?"

"No, buddy," Mav said, and he ruffled the boy's hair.

"Momma needs you here to do that de-icing on the driveway. Remember?"

"Yeah, I 'member," Lars said, and he semi-stomped back into the kitchen toward their mother.

Boston took one bag of groceries from his daddy, and they left the house. They didn't say much on the way to Jackson, with Boston driving his truck with his daddy in the passenger seat. He'd get a ride back to Coral Canyon with Uncle Blaze, who'd taken the opportunity to come see his son.

They drove through the National Park, and Boston did love the majestic mountains, wide open fields, and glistening lakes. "Big herd of buffalo here," he said, approaching a slowdown in traffic. Tourists and wildlife photographers alike always pulled over whenever there were animals in Teton National Park.

Part of Boston's new job would be to keep track of those animal sightings, so that he could tell guests at the Elk Ridge Lodge about them.

"The traffic in this town is incredible," Daddy said when they reached the outskirts of Jackson and ran into a throng of cars. Once they made the turn, it would open up a little bit, but this area was definitely congested all the time.

He drove through Jackson Hole to the west side, and then turned to go back up around the other side of Teton National Park, toward the lodge where he would work.

The Elk Ridge Lodge was an exclusive lodge with custom rooms that cost over one thousand dollars per night. The guests who chose to stay there usually found out about the place from other high-end customers who had been there before—celebrities, country music stars, actors, and others looking for an escape to the Wyoming wilderness, where privacy and confidentiality was king.

Boston had been hired as the outdoor adventure liaison, and he didn't start until January third. He'd been talking to Cash for a couple of months, the frequency of their chats increasing once Boston had decided to look for jobs in Jackson Hole.

Cash had a two-bedroom apartment that he normally shared with another rodeo cowboy, but Slate had moved to Butte to continue his training in Montana. Cash could afford the rent on his own, and he hadn't bothered to find another roommate.

Boston felt like God had been opening doors for him left and right, and he pulled in to the single duplex unit just off the main road. It would still take him twenty minutes to get to work, but he and Cash were only about fifteen from the grocery stores, convenience stores, and nightlife in Jackson Hole—not that Boston planned on living a raging after-work life.

He had no idea what his cousin's training schedule was in the winter, but they had indoor facilities, and he assumed Cash would work as much as he did.

"Uncle Blaze is here," he said as he pulled up, nearly touching his front bumper to his uncle's back one. Then he backed into a space in front of the apartment, glad this spot had been left for him.

"I don't see Gabe and Liesl," Daddy said.

"They're coming all the way from Dog Valley," Boston said. He'd lived on the western highway leading into Coral Canyon since he'd moved to Wyoming a good fifteen or sixteen years now. "We had to be in front of them."

He looked over to his daddy, who nodded. "I don't think we really need Uncle Gabe to get started," he said. "Do you?"

Boston shook his head. "I think he used the trip as a chance to get Liesl to drive—and to talk to Cash. He told me he wanted him to come so they could talk about something."

"Oh, interesting," Daddy said. He got out of the truck and Boston followed him. He collected the groceries from the back seat first, and went to knock on the door, surprised his uncle hadn't already gone in.

Daddy and Blaze chatted at the tailgate while Boston knocked on Cash's door. The duplex stood two stories tall, with a living room, kitchen, and bathroom on the first floor, and two bedrooms and a bathroom upstairs. It would be plenty big for both Boston and Cash.

Cash opened the door wearing blue jeans, a black long-sleeved button-up shirt, and a black cowboy hat.

"Hey," he said, with a laugh. "You made it." He stepped in to Boston and hugged him with the groceries between them and everything. Then he took a bag and said, "Come on in. It's cold out there."

"It shouldn't take long to get all my stuff in." Boston followed Cash into the kitchen, which definitely looked like a single man lived there. Dishes sat in the sink, and the lid on the trash can stood propped up by the amount of garbage in it. It didn't stink, though, and it had a back door that led to a little grassy area now covered in snow, with a swing set and more parking.

Relief ran through Boston simply because he was ready to live on his own again. So ready.

"Hey, Daddy." Cash ran toward the front door and right into his father's arms. Uncle Blaze said something to him in a low voice, and Boston simply watched, marveling at the tall, strong, successful Cash as he seemed to wilt in front of his father.

He stepped back and wiped his eyes and nodded. "Yeah, I know," he said. "I'm going to talk to him today. That's why he's coming."

Uncle Blaze wiped his hand along Boston's cheek too. "All right, let's get this truck unloaded." Then he nodded to Boston, and they all went outside again to start bringing in his bed, clothes, his record player, his boots and coats and other winter gear, and a dresser. He'd told his father he didn't need a desk, but once everything was set up upstairs, the room could certainly use one.

"Maybe a nightstand," he said to his daddy. "Somewhere to put my phone and a lamp?"

"We can get one at the store," he said. "And we'll fill the house with food as well."

He led the way downstairs, where Cash and Blaze sat on the couch. There was a loveseat too, and a TV in a big entertainment center.

Boston loved it all. New life and breath entered his chest, which lifted his mouth into a smile. "We're gonna head over to the Walmart," he said. "And get everything we need."

"You need anything?" Daddy asked. "We want to make sure Boston's not a problem here."

"Oh, he couldn't be a problem if he tried," Cash said. "I'd come with you, but Uncle Gabe texted and said they're almost here."

Uncle Blaze grinned. "I guess Liesl missed the turn and had to come back."

"Oh, boy," Boston said.

"Hey, learnin' to drive isn't easy," Cash said. "She's doin' great."

Boston agreed, because Liesl was doing great. In fact, the door opened in the next moment, and Uncle Gabe held it for Liesl to walk in.

"We made it," she called, pumping both fists up into the air.

"And no one died," Uncle Gabe said, and he grinned at his daughter.

"We're just heading out," Mav said. "We'll grab lunch on the way back; I'll text you to get orders."

"Sounds good," Gabe said.

Liesl lifted up a big, embroidered bag. "I brought curtains," she said. "I'll work on getting them set up while you're gone."

Boston moved over and drew her into a hug. "Thank you so much," he said.

"They're nothing special," Liesl said. "I just used some leftover fabric I had, so it's almost like a patchwork quilt."

"I can't wait," Cash said. "Maybe this place will look like someone actually lives here." He chuckled, and Boston realized for the first time that he hadn't hung art or pictures anywhere—not that he would have hung any up either.

Liesl and Gabe moved further into the apartment while Boston and his daddy went out. This time, he handed the keys to his father and said, "Will you drive?"

"Sure." Daddy watched him as he got in the passenger seat, and then he climbed behind the wheel. "How are you feeling?"

Boston drew in a deep breath, wanting to feel and experience everything authentically. "You know what?" He looked over at his father, a genuine smile curving his mouth. "I feel really good. I don't know if this is the exact thing that I need to do or how long this job will last, but right now, it feels really good to be here with Cash."

Daddy pulled out of the parking space and paused before he turned onto the highway that led back to town. "I've had a feeling that you being here might be more for him...than you." He cut a glance at Boston out of the corner of his eye.

"Really?" Boston asked. "He seems so confident."

"Looks can be deceiving," Daddy said, and Boston thought of the job he'd been hired to do.

Boy, that sure was true, and he hoped he would be able to learn his new role and settle into it quickly once he started at Elk Ridge Lodge.

31

Cash Young stayed on the couch as his daddy groaned and pushed himself up. "I'm coming, girly," he said to Liesl, who'd just asked for his help to put up the curtain rods in Boston's room.

Cash already had blackout curtains in his bedroom, because he didn't have to be at the training facility until ten a.m., and he saw no reason to get up sooner than he needed to. It wouldn't take long to get a curtain rod up, but Daddy would stay upstairs and help Liesl hang the curtains as well, giving Cash as much time alone with Uncle Gabe as he possibly could.

He glanced over to his uncle as he came out of the kitchen and paused on the threshold of tile and carpet that marked the entrance to the living room. "You want to come in here?" Uncle Gabe asked. He held two cans of root beer, and Cash got off the couch with a groan of his own.

He reminded himself he'd already done the hard work; he'd already made the awful phone calls; he'd already confessed that things had gone wrong.

"Hey, I really appreciate you coming," he said as he joined his uncle at the small dining room table that only had three chairs. The fourth was set up in the living room at a desk that held Cash's computer. He could have put that in his bedroom, but he'd learned at a young age to keep his computer out in a public area, and that habit had come with him to Jackson Hole.

He sat down at the table, honestly not sure what to expect.

"Did you get your bank statements?" Uncle Gabe asked.

"Oh, right," Cash said, and he hurried back to the desk to get them. "I wasn't exactly sure what you needed, so I just printed out the regular statements."

Uncle Gabe took them and set them inside a blue folder. "You've contested the withdrawals with the bank?"

"Yes," Cash said. "They said it could take up to ninety days to make a decision."

"Yeah, that's what they always say," he said. "Did you report Linus to the police?"

Cash nodded, his throat tight. "He'd already left town. They said they'd do what they could."

Uncle Gabe nodded again, as serious as ever. Cash couldn't seem to look at him, and he relied only on his peripheral vision to get the cues he needed.

"Hey, I just want you to know that none of this is your fault," Uncle Gabe said, ducking his head. He wore a cowboy hat today too, and with his head down, he created a smaller pocket for Cash to exist in.

Cash sure didn't feel like he wasn't to blame, but he nodded anyway, his throat tight and his anger at himself skyrocketing again. He hated feeling stupid, and he honestly thought he'd left a lot of that behind when he joined the rodeo and didn't have to take math classes anymore.

"I just feel dumb," he told Uncle Gabe.

"Which is perfectly reasonable, but I don't think things are as bad as you think they are."

Cash finally looked up at him. "You don't think so?"

"Well, you still have quite a bit of money in the bank," Uncle Gabe said, tapping the folder. "So he took some money, and he split town."

"Yes," Cash said.

"How much do you think?"

"Well, I originally told you twenty thousand," he said. "But I think it's closer to fifty."

"That's quite the hit," Uncle Gabe said. "I'm not gonna lie. I would be upset too." He put his hand on Cash's forearm, which drew Cash's gaze up to his. "But it's okay. We can get you back on track. And it's a great lesson to learn this young in life."

Cash swallowed and nodded. "I really appreciate your help, Uncle Gabe."

"Of course. Now that I've got your bank account number, I can set up some withdrawals for investments, as well as create a personal account for you, where we'll start to pay you as an employee of your business."

Cash nodded. "That should help with the taxes, right?"

"Not this year," Uncle Gabe said. "But we'll get your business set up and registered with the state of Wyoming. We'll get the bank accounts cleaned up, and we'll get payroll started in January. So I think that's what we need to go over the most—how much money you need to live every month."

Cash swallowed once again, finding himself coming up short and fighting the feelings of inadequacy. He managed to pay his bills every month just fine. "I did a little budget," he said. "Daddy sent me a sheet."

"Yep, he said he would."

Cash texted on his phone. "I did it digitally. Can I just show it to you?"

It took Cash a minute or two to get over to the budget sheet he'd done a few weeks ago when he'd first learned of his money manager's theft. He'd kept it to himself for a couple of days, and then he'd called his father and told him everything. Daddy had given him good advice, like what to document, how to call the police in a non-emergency situation, and then he'd said that Cash should work with Gabe to manage his money. He should invest now because he wouldn't be able to be a bull rider forever.

Cash had seen his own father go through multiple surgeries and literally put his life on the line for his career. He loved the rodeo, but he knew he wouldn't be able to do it forever, so he'd swallowed his pride and made another phone call to the police and then another to the Teton County Sheriff's Department.

He'd talked to Belle about what the detectives might do,

so Harry and Belle knew about the theft as well. Harry, too, had recommended Uncle Gabe for money and wealth management, and Gabe had been on the phone with Cash almost daily in the past ten days, outlining the things that Cash should do to live a financially stress-free life.

He hated being beholden to thinking and worrying about money. He made far too much to have to do that. Setting up a business that would be able to be used for investments, shelter him from certain taxes, and pay him like an employee had been an excellent solution for Cash. He couldn't say he really understood all of it, but he trusted Uncle Gabe would not lead him astray.

They chatted through the details Uncle Gabe needed to know, and since his uncle was a no-nonsense lawyer with plenty on his plate already, the meeting finished before Cash heard his father's footsteps coming downstairs.

"Thank you so much, Uncle Gabe," he said. He got to his feet at the same time his uncle did and clapped him on the back, his gratitude overflowing. "Thank you so, so much."

"It's my pleasure, son," Gabe said. He stepped back and held onto Cash's shoulders, looking him straight in the face. "Listen, don't let this derail you, okay? We all make mistakes, and there's no reason to beat yourself up over them for very long."

"I told him the same thing," Daddy said, appearing around the corner.

"You're a good boy, Cash. Don't let one little mistake define you."

"I'm working through it." Cash really was, but things weren't always as easy as he'd like them to be.

"Where should we send Uncle Mav for lunch?" Daddy asked.

Cash appreciated that Daddy wouldn't harp him to death on this, and relief filled him when Uncle Gabe said, "I really want some steak."

"I'm always in the mood for steak," Daddy said, glancing at Cash.

"Me too," he said. "But I have one more piece of news."

"Oh, my aging heart," Daddy said, and he brought his nearly black-eyed gaze to Cash's. "Is this rodeo news, personal news, financial news...?"

"Why do you need a category?" Uncle Gabe asked. "Just let him tell you."

Cash grinned at the chastisement from his uncle. "Daddy likes to prepare himself."

"How does knowing what kind of news it is help you prepare?" Gabe asked.

Daddy simply glared at Uncle Gabe, and then looked back at Cash. He said nothing, which was code for *Hurry up and say the news.*

"Okay, okay," Cash said. "This is good news, Daddy. Try not to look like you're about to commit murder."

"That's just his resting face," Uncle Gabe said dryly, and Cash laughed. He'd grown up for the first twelve years of his life in Utah, with his mother. He had a complicated relationship with her, though he spoke to her often. His father had always made sure that Cash understood the sacri-

340

fices his mother had made for him and how much she cared for him and loved him.

"It kind of has to do with Mom," he said.

And Daddy's eyebrows went up. "Oh?"

"Yeah," Cash said. "I told her a while back that I was trying to find a good church to go to up here, and she did some investigating for me and found a congregation she thought I'd like."

His father and his uncle said nothing, so Cash forged onward. "I went just before Thanksgiving, and I really liked it. So that's the news. I thought you might like to know that I'm going to church here."

"That's great news," Daddy said.

"Grams will be really happy about that," Uncle Gabe said, his smile wide.

"Yeah," Cash said. "It helps that the pastor's daughter is really pretty and stands at the door and greets everybody. Her momma died a few years ago." Cash grinned as his father's expression continued to darken. "So she comes and sits by anyone who doesn't have someone else to sit with. She sat by me last week, and it was real nice."

"Are you telling me this is church news *combined* with personal, dating news?" Daddy asked.

Cash chuckled and shook his head. "If I ever work up the nerve to ask her out, you'll be the first to know."

32

Trace's ringtone shrilled into the night, startling him out of a sound sleep. He sat up and quickly started pawing at the nightstand, where he kept his phone. He finally found it and lifted it to see who would be calling him at two-blasted-fifteen in the morning.

He squinted at the brightness as it shrilled out another ring. Beside him in the bed, Ev groaned as he finally got his eyes to work.

"It's your brother," he said.

"Which one?" Ev asked groggily as Trace said, "Hey, Reg, what's up?" He tapped to put the man on speaker, so Ev could hear.

"I think Kassie's water broke," Reggie said, and he'd always been a cool cat, slow to show emotion or get excited—but right now, his voice held plenty of panic.

"Well, then you gotta get her to the hospital," Trace said without missing a beat.

That got Ev to sit right up and snap on her lamp. "They're on the way to the hospital?" she asked.

This was Kassie and Reggie's first baby, and Trace was pretty sure his wife was more excited about it than they were.

"I'm getting dressed right now," she said. "Tell them I'll meet them there."

"It's snowing," Reggie said. "And I didn't have time to plow the driveway or road last night. I don't even know if we'll be able to get out."

That brought Ev to a complete stop, and she met Trace's eyes. "Call Bryce," she said. She lunged back around the bed. "I'll call Bryce right now; maybe see if he can come plow you out."

In the background, Trace heard Kassie say something, but he couldn't make out what.

"Her water definitely broke," Reggie said, and Trace remembered this place inside his mind where nothing really seemed to work. Reggie was a smart guy and pro baseball player. He should have no problem getting his wife to the hospital.

"It's forty-five minutes on a good day," Reggie said, and he'd clearly gone into panic mode. "She'll kill me if we have this baby at home."

Trace almost smiled, but he knew what it was like to be in the position Reggie found himself in, and he would not have wanted to have his baby at home either.

"I'm sure the plows have been out," he said. "If you can make it to the highway, you can get down to the hospital."

"I'm calling Luke," Ev said. "Bryce is on his way.

"Call Morris too," Trace said. "He'll have an ATV with a plow on it." Ev nodded, and Trace turned his attention back to Reggie.

"We're sending people to help you get out, okay?" he said.

"I'm gonna go start the car and get Kassie in it."

"All right," Trace said. "Do you want to stay on the line with me?"

Reggie panted through the line, said something to Kassie that sounded like, "I'm going to go start the car. Wait right here." Then he said, "Yeah. Could I? Just in case I have any questions?"

"Sure thing," he said. "Have you guys been timing her contractions?"

"She just woke up in the middle of the night," Reggie said. "She said she went to the bathroom, and it felt weird. I asked her if her water had broken, and she said she wasn't sure."

More panting, and then the roar of a truck engine filled the line. "But the moment she laid down, she had a contraction, and we're pretty sure it broke. I called you, but I had to call three times before you picked up."

"Yeah, my phone's on midnight notice," Trace said. "Sorry about that. I should have turned it off."

"Ev said she wouldn't hear a phone call, and to call you."

"It's fine," Trace said. Reggie and Kassie weren't due for

another week, and Trace was a little surprised that her water had broken already. First babies usually tended to take longer, not come sooner.

"She's had another contraction," Reggie said. "But I don't know how far apart they were."

"All right, Reg," Trace said. "I need you to take a deep breath for me."

"I'm going to get Kassie now."

"Stop right there," Trace said. "Wherever you are, you got to listen to me for one minute, okay? Nothing bad's going to happen to her in one minute."

"Okay," Reg said, his voice on the edge of panic.

"She is counting on you to be the rock," Trace said. "She's scared and in a lot of pain. You can't be scared too."

Reggie blew out his breath. "Well...."

"I know you're scared," Trace said. "Of course you are, but *she* can't know that. You want her to think that you know exactly what to do, and that you're in charge, and that *you* are going to take care of her. I mean, isn't that what you told her in Seattle when you guys first started dating?"

"Yes," Reggie said, and he sounded calmer already.

"All right," Trace said. "So take ten seconds; take a breath; calm yourself down. You know what to do. You're going to take your wife to the hospital. The plows have surely been out. It started snowing last night, and they didn't even call a road closure. Bryce will be there to plow you out, and you'll go."

"Okay," Reggie said. "You're right. Okay."

Ev came out of the master bathroom fully dressed, and

she raised her eyebrows at Trace. "Ev's called everyone," he said. "They're on their way. There's nothing for you to worry about."

"Okay," Reggie said. "Thank you, Trace."

"She's going to wait until she hears from Bryce that you're leaving, and she'll meet you at the hospital."

"Okay," Reggie said. "Thank you." Scuffling came through the line, and then he said, "All right, Kass, come on. We're gonna get to the car. Let me take the bag."

Trace stayed on the line as Reggie lovingly and kindly encouraged his wife into the car.

"Oh, Bryce is here," Reggie said, his voice filled with relief. A car door slammed, and then he said, "He's plowing the driveway right now. Hey, Bryce," he called. "Thank you so much for coming."

"Luke's working on the section closer to the road," Bryce yelled, and Trace closed his eyes and thanked God for the best family in the world.

EVERLY YOUNG PACED IN THE LABOR AND DELIVERY room waiting room. Her brother and his wife had been there for *seven hours* now, and Ev was really ready to see her new niece. Reggie had texted a half-hour ago that the baby had been born—finally—with no complications.

They'd named her Savannah Susannah Avery, and Ev turned back to the big double doors that her brother would bring the baby through...any moment now.

When he didn't appear, she huffed out a frustrated sigh and turned around to go back the way she'd come. Her husband had gotten the kids to school and then come to join her at the hospital, bringing breakfast and her favorite energy drink. Now, the caffeine ran through her like a rabid animal, while Trace sat in the chair and looked at something on his phone.

"Come sit down, sweetheart," he told her, and Ev managed to drop into the seat beside him.

"I just don't get what's taking so long," she said.

"Well, they've got to give 'er a bath," Trace said. "Take her blood. Maybe Kassie is trying to feed her."

"Yeah, maybe." Ev's leg bounced as she watched the door.

"Gabe and Morris went over this morning and made sure everything's clear—the road all the way back to the house, the driveway, the sidewalk up to the steps, the front porch." Trace smiled at her. "They'll be good to go home when it's time."

"It'll probably snow again," Ev said.

"Well, then they'll go out again," Trace said, as if nothing bad ever happened in the world.

Ev did appreciate his steadiness and the way he loved unconditionally and served endlessly and could call on anyone to come do something—even in the middle of the night.

"There's the baby," Trace said, and Ev whipped her head over to the door. She jumped to her feet. She couldn't believe she hadn't been watching.

Reggie came out, and her beautiful, easygoing brother had been crying. He grinned as he walked toward Ev, the perfect little pink bundle in his arms, and Everly wrapped them both in a tight hug.

"Oh, congratulations, Daddy," she whispered, and Reggie sniffled as he stepped back, tears streaming down his face as he settled the precious newborn into Ev's arms.

Then he wiped his face and said, "She's a little bruised on the one cheek right there. I guess she wasn't turned all the way, and that's why it took a little longer in delivery."

"Not too bad, though," Ev said, gently running the back of her knuckle over the tiny bruise on the baby's face. "How's Kassie doing?"

"She's really tired," Reggie said. "I said I'd bring the baby out for as long as I could, so that she could sleep."

"That's good." Ev turned and moved back to the chair where Trace sat. "Come sit down and rest too," she said.

Trace stood up and grabbed on to her brother and held him tight. Neither one of them said anything, but Trace had been almost a father figure for Reggie. Her brother adored Trace and asked him for advice, and listened to him, and the fact that he'd called her husband instead of her spoke volumes.

"What do you want for lunch?" Trace asked.

"It's nine-thirty in the morning," Ev said.

"All right, breakfast."

Trace tapped on his phone and looked over to Reggie as he sat down. "They'll deliver right here to the waiting room. Ask me how I know."

Reggie laughed, and the baby in Ev's arms gurgled as she snuggled in close.

Ev always felt closer to Heaven whenever she held a baby, more so than any other time. And she leaned down and pressed her lips to little Savannah's forehead. "I love you," she whispered, feeling that same love for the baby, for her, for Trace, for Kassie and Reggie, and for everyone from God above—and oh, what a blessing that was.

33

Joey got into her car outside Cake Bites and started it to get the heater blowing. She'd gotten two calls during her morning shift, but she'd just been promoted to baking manager, and she didn't want to abuse any of her privileges. Her teeth chattered as she tapped with frozen fingers on her phone to get the message to play.

"Hi, Joey," a man said. "This is Dalton Best."

Before he even said another word, Joey's heart plummeted to the soles of her feet.

"I'm afraid I have some bad news," he said, and at least he sounded sorry about it. "The leak in the kitchen is bigger than we thought, and we have to dig up the plumbing in the front yard."

Joey stared out the windshield, wondering if she'd ever be able to move into the basement apartment she'd found.

"I'm afraid it's not going to be ready by this weekend like we thought, as we have to turn water off to the whole house and dig around to find the problem. The weather is an issue, as I'm sure you know, and I'm not even sure of the timeline of when we'll have things functioning again. Will you please call me when you get this so that we can talk? Thanks."

The message ended, and Joey's phone started to tell her when the call had happened and give her options for what to do. She tapped numbly on the seven to delete the message, and the voicemail system went immediately to the next one.

"Hi, Joey. This is Dalton again. I just got off the phone with the excavators for the plumbing company, and they said that they'll be able to come out and start digging on Monday, but then they won't be working Christmas Eve or Christmas. But they think once we find the problem, it will go fast. I'm thinking you still might be able to move in, and maybe we should set a tentative date for January fourth? Of course, we'll prorate the rent you've already paid and make sure that everything goes toward the days you're only living here. Just give me a call when you get this. I know you're probably at work."

Another beep. More options. Joey deleted the second message.

She honestly wasn't sure what to do. She felt like crying, but to her surprise, no tears came. She flipped her car in reverse and pulled out of the parking spot and then onto the road, simply driving aimlessly.

Before she knew it, she had pulled into Adam's driveway

in Dog Valley. Suddenly, she felt too hot, and she reached to adjust the air. She hadn't been playing the radio, and the silence screamed through her ears.

She hadn't called or texted Adam that she was coming, and she struggled to remember if they'd made any plans for that day.

Sometimes, Adam texted to say he would be down in Coral Canyon, and he would pick her up for lunch. Sometimes, she grabbed something and met him at his house. Sometimes, they planned to meet somewhere. Her brain didn't seem to be functioning properly, as Joey could not bring anything forward in her recollection.

Perhaps they hadn't planned anything. She frowned, because that made no sense. Of course they'd planned something. If they didn't plan to get together during the day, Joey wouldn't see him. She didn't work Wednesdays at Pork and Beans, and so they often spent all afternoon and evening together then—her baking and Adam doing whatever she asked of him.

But today was Tuesday—one more week until the first concert at Rising Sun Ranch on Christmas Eve—and Joey suddenly remembered what they'd planned to do that day.

She cursed under her breath as she dove onto her phone in the console. She hadn't even remembered putting it there, but she tapped quickly to dial Adam, praying with everything inside her that he hadn't left yet.

"Hey," he said when he answered. "I'm so sorry I'm running late."

"Where are you?" she asked. "Please tell me you're not down in Coral Canyon."

Because they'd planned to get lunch on Main Street and go Christmas shopping today.

"Not yet," he said, and something scraped on his end of the line. "In fact, I might be another forty-five minutes or so," he said. "Because the consultation with the stage setup crew just barely ended, and I haven't even left my house yet."

"Oh, good," Joey said. "Because—guess where I am?"

"Where?" he asked, and his garage started to open.

Joey turned off her car and stood halfway from the car, raising her hand as if Adam wouldn't be able to see her parked in his driveway. "I got some bad news," she said, everything inside her trembling. Of course the tears would come the moment she stood in front of Adam.

He lowered the phone as he walked toward her. "Bad news?"

"It feels like everything in the world is conspiring against me moving out." She dropped her head and looked at her phone, tapping to end the call.

"What do you mean, baby doll?"

"The owner of that house called," she said. "I can't move in until at least January fourth, because they have to dig up all the pipes in the front yard to find the leak."

"Oh no." Adam arrived in front of her, her open door still separating them. He reached for her, and she moved sideways. He closed her door and brought her flush against his chest. "I don't think it's a sign that you shouldn't move out."

"No?" She buried her face against the fuzziness of his coat. "You don't think so?" She sniffled, feeling weak and ridiculous.

"Not at all," he said. "Sometimes bad things happen, and it's completely outside of our control. You should just be glad it's not your house that has to have the front yard dug up."

She chuckled, though she wasn't feeling very happy.

"Why did you drive up here?" he asked.

"I don't know." She leaned back and looked at him. "I just started driving, and this is where I ended up."

He smiled at her and leaned down, barely touching the tip of his nose to hers. "I'm really glad my meeting ran late, then. I was pretty irritated about it."

"I can only imagine," she whispered, breathing in the scent of his cologne and the crisp cottonness of his clothing.

"I don't feel like going shopping today," she said. "Maybe we can drive down the northern highway and get some brisket and then just come back here and watch movies."

"Is that what you do when you're upset?" he asked. "Brisket and movies?"

Joey grinned at him. "Yes—or a coffee, a bean bag, and a book."

"You're going to love what I got for you then." He took her hand and led her into the garage, and then up the few steps into the house. He had a proper mudroom off his garage, and he removed his coat and hung it on a hook, then took hers from her and did the same.

"You got something for me?" she asked.

Adam was always buying her thoughtful gifts, and some of her hopelessness faded away.

"Yep, come see."

He led her through his expansive kitchen, and past the big dining room table, and through the living room. He started down the hall, and Joey's eyebrows raised.

He led her into the first bedroom on the left and said, "Ta da," as he gestured toward an enormous pink bean bag that had been stuffed into the corner of the room.

Joey blinked at it, not quite believing her eyes.

"This room has such great light," he said. "From the big front windows, and I ordered a bookcase, but it's not here yet. I thought we could put it together on Christmas Day, and this could be your book nook."

She turned away from the most glorious thing anyone had ever gotten her and looked at him. "You got me a pink bean bag?"

"Yes," he said. "And did you see the TV tray?"

He took a couple more steps into the room and indicated the solid wood tray that barely rose over the edge of the bean bag. "I thought it would hold your snacks and a drink."

Embarrassingly, Joey began to cry, and when Adam turned back to her, the pure, pure joy on his face melted into a frown.

"I'm sorry," he said. "I thought this would be nice."

"It's amazing," Joey said, and she took the few steps to

him and grabbed on to him in a hard, tight hug. "I love it. Thank you."

He stroked her hair and simply held her, and when Joey didn't feel like she might fall apart, she let go of him and looked up. She wasn't sure why he'd decided to make a book nook for her in his house. She didn't live here, and as she searched his face, she felt herself falling more and more in love with him.

He leaned down and touched his mouth to hers in a sweet, chaste, surely-meant-to-be-comforting kiss. She allowed that for a moment, and then quickly took things deeper, hoping to let him know of her quickening feelings.

They broke apart, and Adam exhaled heavily. "I know you can't move in here with me," he said. "But I wanted you to know that that's where I want you."

Joey pulled away and searched his face again. He gave her a small smile that was about as timid as Adam ever got.

"Harry sent me the list for the wedding party today," he said. "You and I are walking down the aisle together."

Joey nodded, because she'd gotten the list too. Belle had taken her size and would have her bridesmaid's dress before Christmas. She didn't know what to say into this silence, and Adam was the better communicator out of the two of them anyway.

"It'll be fun. Don't you think?" He raised his eyebrows. "Walking down the aisle together?"

"You realize that when a man and a woman get married, they don't walk down the aisle together," she said. "It's not like we'll be practicing for our own wedding or anything."

"Of course not," he said, but the smile on his face didn't go anywhere. He sobered and tucked her hair behind her ear. "I'm really sorry about your apartment. Sometimes Satan puts roadblocks in our way, because he knows we'll start to doubt ourselves, and he knows if you do what you've been planning to do, it won't be good for him."

Surprise lifted Joey's eyebrows. "Is that right?" she asked.

He nodded soberly.

"Did your momma teach you that?" she asked.

"I actually heard it in a sermon when I was a teenager." He stepped back and took her hand. "Let's go get some food. I'm starving, and then you can decide if you'd rather read in here or watch movies on the couch with me."

"I want to be with you," Joey said softly, and Adam nodded just once.

She let him take care of her from then, driving them to the barbecue stand. He went to order from the outdoor hut while she stayed warm and dry in the car. He drove them back to his house, put their food on a tray, and tucked her in with a blanket before turning on the TV. He kept their conversation light and easy, telling her about the concert series, and how his sister was pregnant again, and that he had finally told his mother that they were dating.

Joey knew most of what he said, which was why it was so comforting for her. Once she'd eaten her fill of brisket and macaroni salad, she lay down with her head in Adam's lap. He covered her with the blanket and stroked her hair. She closed her eyes and let herself float.

She'd felt lost in her life before, and she'd been physically lost in New York City. That had been a panicked, frantic feeling, with her breath coming quickly and her mind moving fast.

Feeling lost in her life felt hopeless, like she was drifting out to sea on a raft made of sticks, screaming for help with no one around to hear. Thankfully, she didn't feel like either of those things right now.

She felt safe and cared for. She was warm and comfortable, and she knew she was exactly where she needed to be. So whether she was able to move into the basement apartment or not, it didn't matter.

She was with Adam, and for the first time, she felt deserving of his love, attention, and care.

34

Adam stepped up to the mirror in his master bathroom and straightened the tie at his throat. He'd gone Christmas shopping with Joey this week, finally picking out a few things for her parents and siblings, as well as the members of Country Quad, and lastly, Harry and Belle. He'd taken all of his gifts to a woman in the neighborhood to wrap them, as his gift-wrapping skills matched his cooking ones.

As part of that shopping expedition, he'd bought himself a tie to wear to church today. He wasn't like Cecily, who wore an apron covered in elves, and his tie was a deep, beautiful red with a gold paisley pattern woven throughout it. The thread shone metallic in the light, and Adam sighed and looked into his own eyes.

"This is it," he said, though he wasn't exactly sure what "it" was.

He got himself out of the house and down the highway to Coral Canyon. Despite the fact that Joey had not moved into her apartment yesterday as planned, and would not have to walk into the service alone, he had agreed to go with her. Truth be told, *he* was the one who needed someone to walk in with him.

He pulled into the parking lot at her grandparents' condo just as it started to snow again. He hadn't minded the weather until the last couple of weeks, when it seemed to snow for a whole day, take a day off—just long enough for everyone to dig themselves out—and then Mother Nature would arrive with another dump of the white stuff.

Adam had bought a snow-blower, and then quickly realized that he could hire a pair of teenage brothers to come clear everything for him while he sipped coffee and went over notes in his office. So he'd done that instead.

He tossed his cowboy hat onto the passenger seat before he went to pick up Joey, because the wind would simply try to steal it from him anyway. He rang the doorbell at the condo and shivered inside his suit coat in the several seconds it took Joey to answer the door.

She wore a dark green dress that looked like it had been made of a thousand pleats. Silver thread sparkled throughout it, and Adam felt the same shine move through him.

"Wow," he said. "Look how pretty you are."

He forgot all about the cold and the need to get out of it, his desire to kiss Joey much stronger. He did that, noting that her grandparents were not here, and then took her hand and led her back to his car.

"What color is your suit?" Joey asked once they'd gotten in. "Is it black or blue?"

"It's midnight blue," he said. "But you can really only tell in the bright sunshine."

"Which we don't have today." Joey peered through the windshield. "But hey, your first white Christmas."

He smiled at her. "That's right—my first white Christmas."

He would be incredibly busy on Christmas Eve, as the first concert was that evening, and then Bryce had planned a birthday party for OJ at the ranch afterward. The forecast for Christmas Eve called for wind and overcast skies right now.

He could admit he had been praying with as much fervor as he had that it would not snow during the concert. *Please, Dear God*, he thought once again. *I only need two clear hours out of this whole year.*

That wasn't entirely true, because he'd like it to be clear for the December twenty-seventh concert, as well as the New Year's Eve and New Year's Day concerts, and the January sixth concert, and he once again wondered how he had allowed himself to be talked into having five outdoor concerts during a Wyoming winter.

He looked over to Joey. "Are you ready?"

"Are you?" she asked. "This is where my family goes to church, and everyone is going to see us walk in together."

"Well, they already know we're together," Adam said.

Going with Joey wasn't the reason his pulse bobbed in the back of his throat like an apple on Halloween evening. He looked toward the building, the stained glass window overlooking the parking lot bringing an odd sense of comfort to him he hadn't expected.

Joey reached across the console and took his hand. "You're nervous."

"Yes," he said. "But not because I'm with you."

All of the Youngs were religious. They attended church, and Adam simply didn't think for one moment he could stay with Joey long term should he choose not to. She didn't like contention, and every Sunday would reopen the rift between them.

Adam also didn't want to fake his belief or his desires, and he drew a deep breath and pressed his eyes closed.

"I can say a prayer before we go in," Joey whispered.

Adam nodded without opening his eyes. Joey exhaled, and Adam focused on the sound, and then switched his focus to his own breathing. He felt as the air entered his nose and filled his lungs, lifting his chest open and wide. He controlled the way it went out, feeling it release and escape.

"Dear Heavenly Father," Joey said. "We come before Thee as Thy children to ask a special blessing on our church attendance today. Bless our minds to be open, our hearts to be pure, and our intentions to be righteous. Bless us each with the message that we need to hear to progress on our path back to Thee."

She paused, and Adam had never heard anyone pray the way Joey did. Her voice sweet and angelic, praying for him, made his chest hitch and his composure collapse. His next breath did not enter his nose smoothly, but he stuttered.

Joey's hand in his tightened, and she simply added, "Amen."

"Amen," Adam whispered, sealing the prayer with his own approval. He looked over to Joey, who gazed back at him in a soft, non-intense way that Adam really needed in his life.

"I'm glad I don't have to walk in alone," he said.

"Let's go then, cowboy." She reached into the back seat and picked up his hat and handed it to him. "Remember, you can use this any time you need to." She smiled at him playfully then, and Adam settled his hat on his head as they got out of the car together.

She met him at the hood, and Adam took her hand as they made measured, even steps and walked side by side toward the little white building with the stained glass window.

Going up the steps and through the front door was easier than Adam anticipated, and inside, the scent of freshly washed laundry greeted him, along with a heavy blast of warm air that chased the cold out of his skin and nose and soul.

Adam smiled as he entered the chapel. As a kid, he'd always described feeling the Lord in his life as a warm tingle, and he felt that same way as Joey led him down a couple of rows and then stepped in far enough for just the two of them to sit on the end of the bench. A family had taken up half of the bench on the other side, and Adam ducked his head and used his cowboy hat to hide the rest of the congregation.

He didn't need to look around for her parents, or her aunts and uncles, or her cousins, or her grandparents. He didn't need the pressure of their gazes or the weight of their expectations.

In that moment, Adam knew that only *God's* expectations mattered to him. He glanced over to Joey and amended the thought, *Well, God's and Joey's.*

His mother would say she was a good influence on him, and he helped her shrug out of her coat, which she draped across her lap. He put his arm around her and lifted his head to drink in the wood in the chapel. It looked like a boat had been hollowed out with wood everywhere, and it reminded him of the forest, and the mountains, and being outside. Adam settled further into himself, relaxing in a place he thought he never would.

Someone played the piano, but Adam didn't look around for the origin of the sound. He simply closed his eyes, and in the deep brown darkness that he could see, he focused on how he felt.

It felt *right* to be at church today with Joey. It felt good that he'd gotten up, gotten himself ready, and had come to sacrifice his time to be closer to the Lord.

The service started with the pastor announcing that they would all stand and sing two Christmas hymns together before he would begin his talk. Adam had never been much for singing, but he loved *Angels We Have Heard on High* and *O Holy Night,* and he joined his voice to the other members of the congregation as they lifted praise to God.

Then the pastor stood behind the pulpit and Adam lasered his focus on him. "Brothers and sisters," he said. "It is a beautiful time of year to reflect on our Lord and Savior, Jesus Christ, and God the Father. I would like to start by asking you what I hope is a simple question, and if it is not a simple question, that the more you ponder it and try to answer it in your own life, that it will become such."

He spoke with a big voice, and he had big hands to match that he gestured with. He grinned a big smile, and Adam felt comfortable in his presence.

"What is your relationship with God and Jesus Christ?" the pastor asked. "I want to submit to you today that the closer relationship you have with Them, the happier you will be in your life.

"Just like you get to know another person, you can learn about God. You ask questions, and learn about them. We need to be doing the same thing with our Lord. It takes time to truly know another person, and it will take time for that relationship to develop with God and Jesus Christ as well. But brothers and sisters, as we celebrate the birth of our Lord and move into a new and glorious year, what better way do you have to spend your time?"

The question struck Adam straight to the core. Yes, he'd been busy living his life these past many years, and he often worked on Sunday. He felt a true sense of chastening move through him, and he ducked his head again, as if he could hide from God. He couldn't, and he knew that. But he also wanted to be able to answer the pastor's questions.

He wanted to be able to say that he'd put in the time to learn about God and Jesus Christ—and really get to know Them. He wanted to say that he had a close relationship with Them, and that he knew Them as well as They knew him.

Right now, he couldn't say those things. He also didn't know what kind of relationship he had with God and Jesus Christ.

Probably an estranged one, he thought. But the good news was—Adam knew what to do to bridge the gap between him and the Lord.

The pastor talked about reading the scriptures and spending more time in the Bible, where the life of Jesus Christ revealed not only his character, but that of God as well.

Adam could admit, it had been a long time since he'd cracked the Bible and tried to understand the words inside. He'd been slowly coming back to communicating with the Lord through prayer, but he didn't kneel down at his bedside as of yet.

As he listened, the pinpricks of guilt became action points for him.

He *would* kneel down that evening and say his prayers. He *would* download a Bible app and start reading that very day.

Change could be instant, and his, and all he had to do was try.

If there was one thing Adam was really good at, it was making a list and completing the tasks. As his shame turned to action, and then excitement, he couldn't wait to get started on rebuilding his relationship with God and Jesus Christ.

After the sermon ended, he and Joey didn't stay long. He hadn't quite found the words to articulate how he felt, and Joey let him sit with his thoughts all the way back to his house in Dog Valley. When he pulled into the garage, he looked over to her, and she looked back at him with the kindest smile on her face.

Adam had asked his mother how he would know when he was in love, and she'd given him the vaguest answer of all: *You'll just know.*

Gazing at Joey in that moment, Adam definitely felt like he was in love with her.

"So what did you think?" Joey asked.

"I really liked that sermon," Adam said. "I got some really good ideas out of it—things I need to do."

"So did I," she said.

"Oh, yeah?" he asked. "Like what?"

Joey sighed, and she looked out the windshield toward the front wall of the garage. "Well, he said that if we develop a relationship with God, He'll guide us on the path we need to be on. And I've really been feeling lost since I returned to Coral Canyon."

"Right," he said.

"But I don't feel like that anymore," Joey said. "I could do better in my relationship with God, of course, but I feel like I've been doing okay, and what I need to do is trust that I am on the path He wants me on."

She turned and looked at him, that intense earnestness in her blue eyes now that lit him up as well. "And if I'm not, He'll re-guide me to the right place. I don't think I really believed that until today, and I'm going to work on trusting in God more, that He's going to guide me where I should be."

"That's amazing, baby doll," he said. "I'm really happy for you."

"What about you?" she said.

"Oh, I'm going to start with the basics," he said. "Like a little kid—I need to pray, read my scriptures, and get to know God all over again."

He grinned at her and added, "But first, let's go eat lunch."

35

"All right, bud," Otis said as he came down the hall from his music office. "We've got to get out to Bryce's ranch."

OJ sat at the bar and turned, a spoon dripping with milk in his hand. "I'm almost done with my cereal," he said around a mouthful of food.

"You're eating right now?" Otis asked.

"He's *starving*," Georgia said over her shoulder. She too sat at the bar, but she nursed a cup of coffee instead of a bowl of Lucky Charms.

"Where's your guitar?" Otis asked. He hated feeling like he was rushing, and he certainly didn't want to deal with Luke's wrath if he showed up late. It had snowed most of the morning yesterday, but nothing since. He'd checked the weather and the road conditions, and he should be able to get to Bryce's in the regular amount of time.

But they still needed to leave in the next few minutes.

"By the door," OJ said around more marshmallows.

"You realize we're eating in three hours?" he said. "No one in this family is going to starve in three hours." He gave his son a look as he passed him, picked up his guitar, and headed out into the garage.

They'd had a celebratory birthday breakfast for OJ that morning, because tonight, he was performing in the concert with Country Quad. Then there'd be a whole-family party at Bryce's house, partly for the beginning of this winter concert series and partly for OJ.

Otis had four guitars in the back of his truck already, but he managed to squeeze in a fifth and then OJ's, along with his backpack of clothes and personal hygiene products. Adam had picked up the puffy vests that morning and would bring them to the venue.

A certain excitement Otis hadn't felt in a while streamed through him. He loved being a dad and being home with his family. Georgia still ran her bookshop, and he didn't want to be touring the world nine months out of the year the way he once had.

But at his core, Otis adored performing. Playing the guitar gave new life to his soul, and music had always existed in his blood. Some of that seemed to rub off on OJ, though none of Otis's DNA existed inside the boy.

He turned back to the house just as OJ came out.

"Did you get your extra clothes like I asked?" Otis asked. He'd never had to be in charge of anyone by himself before, and having OJ perform had brought a new layer of stress he hadn't anticipated.

"Shoot," OJ said. "It's in my bedroom." He ran back inside while Otis sighed.

He followed his son and looked at his wife. "What else is he missing?"

"I helped him pack his bag this morning," she said. "He'll have extra clothes to change into for the party, and his Polaroid so he can take pictures."

"What about his cowboy hat?" Otis asked, because he hadn't seen it on his son's head.

"It's right there by the door," Georgia said, nodding to it. She rose and came toward him as Otis took the hat off the hook. "It's going to be fine."

Otis didn't want to snap at her that this was OJ's country music debut, and that millions of people would be watching—including music executives and record producers from around the world.

The boy had turned eleven today, and he didn't need to carry that kind of pressure. Otis seemed to be carrying it for him anyway.

"He's playing two songs that he performs brilliantly," Georgia said, smiling. "And he looks just like you."

"Not without the hat," Otis griped simply because he could.

His wife ran her hands along his shoulders and down his arms. "Baby, will you promise me one thing?"

Otis would promise her the world, but he kept his head ducked and grumbled, "All right."

"Try to enjoy this," she said.

"I'm going to enjoy it."

"Really?" she asked. "Because it sure seems like you're expecting everything to go wrong."

Otis met her eyes, something sparking and challenging moving through him. "Have you met our son?" he asked. "He'd forget his own head if it wasn't attached to his body."

Georgia giggled in lieu of an argument. There wasn't one to be made anyway. OJ was no different than any other eleven-year-old boy, and they needed their daddies to make sure they had every piece in place before they showed up on a stage and performed for the world. Otis just wanted to be that dad for OJ.

"Got it," OJ said, panting as he arrived upstairs again. "Did Bailey text, Daddy? She said she was going to try to watch."

"I haven't heard from her yet," Otis said. Sometimes dealing with OJ's questions about Bailey wore Otis to the bone. He glanced at Georgia, who said she didn't mind them, but somewhere deep down inside her, Otis suspected his constant questions about his birth mom did bother her.

"Let's go, son," he said. "We don't want to be late."

"Yeah, I don't need Uncle Luke yellin' at me," OJ said, as if *he'd* been waiting for the past twenty minutes for Otis to be ready. He marched past them and out into the garage while Georgia giggled and shook her head again.

"Hey, he's got your family's DNA in him," she said. Then she leaned in and kissed him, and Otis expected her to settle back on her feet and say she'd be out at the ranch later.

Instead, she kissed him for longer and then longer, and when she finally pulled away, Otis licked his lips and tasted her there.

"What was that for?" he asked.

"I don't know," she murmured, wiping her thumb along his bottom lip. "Just hoping you'll have fun tonight." She looked up at him, her eyes wide and earnest. "I mean, isn't that why you retired? Whatever you do now should be fun, and if it's not fun, then I don't want you to do it."

Otis nodded and swallowed. "It's going to be fun." He didn't want to cause any undue stress inside his wife, and he ducked out of the house and into the pickup truck.

"All right, bud," he said, putting on the most jovial voice he could come up with. "Before a concert, we do a check."

"All right," OJ said. "What kind of check?"

"Instrument?" Otis held up one finger.

"Guitar's in the back," Otis said, picking up on the game.

"Clothes?"

"I got my blue jeans on," OJ said, clapping his hands on his thighs. "And my black long-sleeve shirt, just like you guys. My black boots, my black hat." He reached up and realized he wasn't wearing his hat. Otis held it up for him, and OJ grinned at him, grabbed it, and jammed it on his head. "Now I got my hat."

"Equipment?" Otis asked next.

OJ looked in the back. "You got the amp, right?"

"I got the amp, and Bryce has two," he said. "Uncle Luke brings all the drums and everything."

OJ held up his third finger as well. "Equipment," he said. "Check."

"We're having a party after our concert tonight," he said. "You got extra clothes?"

"Yes, sir," he said.

"Good, because we're going to need those jeans and that shirt for our next concert in two days. We won't have time to replace them."

"I got extra clothes." OJ patted his backpack.

"Water?" Otis asked.

OJ's face went blank, and Otis started to laugh. "Adam's bringing all the refreshments," he said.

"Right," OJ said. "Adam's bringing all the refreshments."

Otis quickly mentally ran through his instruments, clothing, equipment, and after-concert items, and then put the truck in reverse. "I think we got it all, bud."

And even if they didn't, Otis was pretty sure that Adam would have anything that he'd forgotten. The man didn't miss *anything*, and he'd probably thought of a dozen things that Otis hadn't troubled himself with.

He kept the country music low on the way to Rising Sun Ranch, because he never spoke more than he needed to prior to performing. He'd save his voice for the concert instead.

He pulled onto the ranch and moved to where Stockton Whittaker motioned for him to park. Morris's truck sat there, Adam's SUV parked next to it. Trace and Luke had already arrived as well, and as Otis pulled in next to the big black truck where he'd been told to park, he found Harry and Belle spilling from it.

"I don't see Tex," he muttered to himself, and he wasn't sure why, but extreme pleasure ran through him that he hadn't arrived last.

"Leave your backpack here, bud," he said. "We don't need it 'til later."

He killed the engine, got out, and started unloading his instruments. He had done a walkthrough with Adam only two days ago so that everyone knew where to park, where to stage, where the cameras would be, and what the performance would look like.

Jem and Blaze came out of the nearest barn, opening the doors wide and tying them back.

"Looks like everyone's here," Blaze called, and pure love for his brother filled Otis.

"I didn't know you guys were helping."

"Stagehand is the best job I've ever had," Jem said, grinning. "What else you got?"

"He's got a billion guitars in there," OJ said, and both Jem and Blaze laughed outright.

"Not quite a billion," Otis muttered, glad when Harry pulled back the bedcover on his truck to reveal five guitars as well. He moved over to his nephew and gave him a quick side hug. "Glad to see you have a lot of guitars too."

Harry simply blinked at him. "How do you do a concert without guitars?"

"Great question," Otis said.

Adam came outside and started issuing instructions and

herding country music stars into the barn, where he'd heated the tack room—the one closest to the stage. It was too hot for Otis, and he eyed the puffy vest that Adam gave him like it was a viper and might strangle him.

Tex arrived, and Bryce came out from the house. With the instruments warm, and Luke tapping out a nervous beat on his drum set, Trace said, "Let's play through a song just to get warmed up."

Otis wasn't going to complain about that, though he knew Trace had suggested it as a way to soothe his own nerves. They played through their opening number—one of their biggest hits in country rock—*Wild Wild West*.

By the time the song ended, Otis definitely had settled back into his country music star skin.

He glanced over to his son, who clapped, his face alight with joy and wonder, and he turned toward Tex.

"Let's do the one with all of us," he said.

"Great idea," Tex said. "Final run-through for *Journey Home*," he called. "Everyone on stage."

Pure shock coated OJ's expression, and then he jumped up from the stool where he'd been sitting. Otis moved over to the stand where his guitar stood and picked it up for him.

"Remember," he said. "You never pick up your own guitar. Someone will hand it to you, okay?"

"I got it, Daddy." He moved the strap over his shoulder while Adam set out the three stools for Bryce, Harry, and OJ. Warmth like Otis had never known moved through him with his son sitting only a few feet from him and looking at his uncle for instructions.

"I'll blather on here for a minute," Tex said, grinning widely. "I got a real good speech prepared."

"Oh, brother," Luke said from the drum set.

Tex ignored him and smiled around at everyone. "And then I'll say this is the world premiere of brand-new song from the one and only Otis Young, with Trace on lyrics, and we've brought in our sons and significant others to play it for you today. When I say the name of the song, be ready to play."

He looked at OJ and raised his eyebrows. OJ nodded, and Tex turned to stand behind his mic, lifted the neck of his guitar about six inches, and when he dropped it, everyone started to play. OJ stumbled for a moment but kept his gaze out toward where the audience would be, or in this case, the cameras, and caught up quickly.

The amount of equipment they needed for eight people to play on stage was a lot more than four, but Adam had procured it all and had it working properly, even from inside the barn.

Otis loved this song, as it had been wiggling around inside his head for months now. When Bryce had suggested the horse rescue charity concert series, Otis had known immediately that this song would be written and played.

It spoke of a person's journey home to a physical place, as well as to a religious one inside themselves. It could be adapted for a horse or a dog or anything at all, and Otis sang, "The Journey Home is, it feels like loving you," along with everyone else, to the final chord progression.

Adam was the only spectator, and when the song ended,

he whooped and cheered as he applauded. Then he checked his phone and said, "We have forty-five minutes until we go live. Harry, I'm going to assume you and Belle know what to do with your own cameras. My Country Quad fellas, stay warm. Stay loose. Bryce and I are going to go work with the stage crew to make sure the stage is ready, the sound equipment gets hooked up right, things are heated for you, and our own cameras are ready for this world broadcast." He beamed an enormous smile out at everyone, and then left the barn with Bryce.

OJ took Otis's guitar and set it in the stand for him. He put his own in its proper stand, and he stayed out of the way as the stage crew came in and out to take Luke's drum set, the instruments, and the stools out to the staging area. He followed them once the barn was clear and stood just outside the door, so that he could see what he was dealing with.

Adam had arranged for a stage to be erected in front of all the stables at Bryce's horse rescue ranch. Not only that, but Bryce had opened all the top halves of the doors, and the horses hung their heads out and watched the activity around them. It spoke of pure country, and slower times, and things worth fighting for.

Otis relaxed further, the serenity of the land out here seeping into his soul and slowing him down.

The stage had a roof, which would help keep the sound condensed and pointed toward the cameras, and Otis could see the slim pole heaters that were in all four corners, and then the four poles throughout the stage area. Someone had dug a line through the snow and painted it bright blue, and in the cleared area on the other side stood all of their equipment, the stools, the guitars—anything they wouldn't be using when they walked out on stage the first time. Under the tent blew two more heaters that warded off the Wyoming chill and would keep their instruments warm.

Daylight had started to fade, and tension returned to Otis's shoulders. Someone came outside and he looked over to Tex.

"This is going to be great," his older brother said, ever the easygoing one. "Are you excited to perform with OJ?"

Otis found himself nodding. Finally, the thing that Georgia had asked him to do settled inside him. "Yeah," he said. "This is going to be a great time."

36

Joey bounced up and down on the balls of her feet, the excitement riding in the air at Bryce's ranch sending electricity through her whole body. Adam was the most gorgeous man in attendance, though the entire Young family had shown up for this inaugural concert of the horse rescue ranch charity series. He'd been flitting here and there, taking care of last-minute preparations, and now he stood on the stage with Uncle Morris.

The main cameraman brought his hand down, and Morris grinned for all he was worth. "Welcome everyone, far and wide," he said, his huge personality suddenly coming out. "I'm Morris Young, manager of Country Quad." He chuckled. "At least for a couple more days." He glanced over to Adam. "See, it's time for me to step down, and in my place, I—and Country Quad—are thrilled to welcome Adam Harmon as the new manager of the band."

Off to the side, Boston raised a sign that said *Applause*, and everyone who had come to the ranch to see the concert broke into clapping and cheering, Joey included. She knew this was all for show, but she couldn't erase her smile nonetheless.

"We're happy to have such an amazing, detail-oriented person on staff with us now," Morris said. "And we're excited to bring you this five-concert series over the next two weeks, as we raise money and awareness for the horse rescue operations in the United States and Canada. I'm going to let Adam talk to you a little bit more about that." He handed the mic to Adam and walked right off the stage, his part of the concert done.

Adam possessed all of the same charisma and charm as her country music star uncles, and he beamed at the camera as if it were his best friend. "I'm thrilled to be working with Country Quad in this new capacity," he said. "Some of you may know me from working with Harry Young for the past several years, though it was in a completely different role. You may have also seen Bryce Young playing with Country Quad on some of their last concert tours that they've done. Now, the band is officially retired. I don't want to have any rumors about that."

He chuckled, but Adam hated rumors and gossip. Joey pressed her gloved hands to her mouth, simply enraptured with him.

"But when Bryce approached his father and his uncles about doing a charity concert series to raise money and awareness for the horse rescue operations out there, we were all on board immediately."

Joey knew that wasn't quite true, but she suppressed her giggle.

"See, Bryce himself owns this *beautiful* horse rescue ranch where we stand today. It's called the Rising Sun Ranch, because he and his partner, Kassie Avery, hoped to give the abused and neglected horses out here a new lease on life—a new day with a rising sun, where they can live and work and be the magnificent creatures that God created them to be."

Wow, Joey thought. She had no idea who had written Adam's speech, but he delivered it with absolute perfection. She couldn't look away from him, everything about him shiny and attractive to her.

"We've set up a website where we're taking your donations tonight—and throughout the next couple of weeks until our final concert on Three Kings Day, which is January sixth. All proceeds will benefit horse rescue operations like Bryce's, which is a nonprofit ranch here in Wyoming.

"Half of the money will go to his ranch to help care for some of the magnificent horses that you see behind me. The other half will go to Teton Shadow Rescue, a horse operation on the other side of Yellowstone National Park, in Montana."

A man walked onto the stage from the right, and Bryce from the left.

"You remember Bryce Young." Adam beamed at him and

shook his hand. "When he's not playing the guitar, he's now a proud new daddy who runs this horse rescue operation with his wife and best friend, with over forty-two horses here in need of care. And this is Stan Morgan," he said, indicating the other cowboy on the stage. "He's the owner of Teton Shadow Rescue, and he runs an operation of over *one hundred* horses."

Boston flipped his sign to *Awww*, and Joey added her voice to the soundtrack, saying, "Wow, ooh," along with everyone else.

"I'm sure most people don't know what it takes to feed and care for forty-two horses, or one hundred horses," Adam said. "But these two gentlemen do, and it takes a lot of time, dedication, supplies, feed, expertise, knowledge, and money. We're asking you to donate whatever you can. We're going to keep an updated piggy bank on the website, and I'm pleased to announce that we'll have *three* organizations matching any donations that come through the website in the next two weeks."

"First, Country Quad will match any donation, dollar for dollar."

Boston flipped the sign again, and Joey whooped and cheered all over again.

"Second, the Young family has a rich tradition in the rodeo, and Blaze, Jem, Cash, Cole, and Rosie Young are going to be matching your donations, dollar for dollar, on behalf of the rodeo in which they participate."

Joey bounced on her toes again as her uncles and cousins marched onto the stage and waved to the cameras, her pride swelling. "I didn't know they were doing that," she said to Georgia, who shone like a star too.

"Me either," she called back over the applause.

"And finally, the Wyoming Animal Rescue, a private nonprofit operation that has locations in Cheyenne, Laramie, and Jackson Hole, is going to be matching your donations, dollar for dollar."

Tears actually pricked Joey's eyes then. Adam had not told her about the matching donations, and for some reason, they touched her heart. She'd been to Bryce's ranch just to ride horses, and she'd seen how hard her cousin worked. She'd personally witnessed him and Codi struggling through hot summers and dry conditions, and then winters with dozens of feet of snow and that wicked Wyoming wind that never abated.

Everyone who'd come on stage waved and left, and Adam said, "And now what you've all tuned in for." He set the mic in the stand and spread both arms wide. "I'm pleased to announce Wild—Wild—West by Coun—try—Quad!"

He brought his hands together for a couple of claps, and then ran off the stage as Uncle Tex and Uncle Trace ran on from the left, with her father from the right. The crowd certainly didn't need Boston's sign to cheer and applaud then, but he dutifully did his job.

Uncle Luke always ran on last and did some sort of theatric. Joey clasped her hands together at her throat while Daddy, Uncle Trace, and Uncle Tex settled into their guitars and stood near their mics.

Only then did Uncle Luke make an appearance, and it was not where Joey expected to find him. Instead, he came running out of the stable, and he did a round-off back handspring, right there in the snow.

More applause rained through the sky, along with plenty of whooping and cheering from the younger cousins as Uncle Luke grabbed his puffy vest from Adam, who had somehow positioned himself in exactly the right spot for the hand-off.

He threw his arms through it and jogged onto stage from the back, where he picked up his drumsticks, sat down, and launched into the opening beat of *Wild Wild West*.

Joey loved her family band, and as she listened to her uncles play and sing, clapping along and joining in on the chorus when she knew all the words, she'd never been happier to share them with the world.

You're one of them, the thought ran through her mind, and it had not come from Joey herself. She'd fought against such thoughts before, and she wasn't sure why.

Of course she was one of them.

Of course she belonged, because she was a Young, and Youngs loved and accepted everyone.

37

Bailey looked up from her phone as one song in the Country Quad holiday concert ended and a new one began—with a single guitar. Her phone fell to her lap as everything calm and peaceful moved through her.

The camera followed Harry Young, who currently strummed solo on his guitar as he walked slowly across the stage and positioned himself in front of the mic, where Bryce's father had just been.

Bailey had always been a fan of country music, and Country Quad had been on her radar long before the Young brothers had started moving back to Coral Canyon and she'd met Bryce.

She still loved him with a tiny piece of her heart that she suspected would always belong to him, and she'd be forever tied to the Youngs through him—and OJ. She loved that eleven-year-old boy with everything she had, and she was so glad that she and Bryce had been able to give him a really good life.

The life he deserved.

He'd texted her multiple times about watching the concert tonight as he would be playing, and Bailey had told him she wouldn't miss it.

"Howdy, folks," Harry said easily into the microphone, his eyes trained exactly into the camera. Bailey felt like he was looking straight into her soul; he was that charismatic and that connected through a lens.

He continued to strum quietly a tune Bailey didn't recognize. "I'm Harry Young, and I'm going to be taking over this segment of the show. First, with my number one hit single from my first album, *Going Rogue*. This song speaks of loss, of overcoming loss in such a way that you realize that the thing or person or whatever it is that you thought you needed, actually doesn't have the power to make you sad anymore." He smiled and looked down at his guitar strings. As he brought his head back up, tears filled Bailey's eyes.

"It's about healing and hope, and I thought it was perfect for this holiday season. So from me to you, and my family to yours, we want to wish you a Merry Christmas and a Happy New Year."

Bailey had not heard Country Quad say any of that, and they had yet to play a holiday song, though they had a whole album of them.

"Here's to hope, health, and happiness in the New Year," Harry said, his smile absolutely devastating.

She wanted a small-town country boy like him with a

big smile and loads of charm. She needed it to make up for her more serious and sour personality.

Harry's guitar started to sing louder, and he leaned into the mic and said, "Here's *Taste of Home*." He played another riff and then started to sing.

Bailey heard the words with her ears, and she felt them drive deep into her soul. Harry sang with such a beautiful voice, and he truly seemed sad about the things that he'd lost. And then, as he moved the ballad into a chorus about love, family, and home, his voice brightened, his entire countenance lit up, and Bailey found herself doing the same. Her tears had dried up, and she smiled at the TV, which she had connected to the live broadcast to watch.

She'd been thinking about returning home for a long time now, but something always kept her in Butte—her successful veterinary practice, for one, and those were hard to build. She'd dated on and off, but no one seriously for a while. But she had friends and colleagues and contacts in the area, and she would have to redo all of that work if she chose to move now.

Still, something called to her from Coral Canyon, even from afar, and Bailey suspected she would end up there sooner rather than later. The practical side of herself wanted to make a note in her phone to start planning the move or reaching out to others and planting feelers for how she could build her business there. She absolutely would not live with her parents. She was thirty-three years old, and doing so would feel like coming home with her tail tucked between her legs—a complete failure.

Harry finished the song, every note in exactly the right place, his fingers not missing a single spot on his guitar. Bailey broke into applause right there, a one-woman standing ovation as she leapt from her couch. They definitely had a crowd at Bryce's ranch, and they whooped and cheered for Harry too.

Then he turned, and the camera switched to a wider lens, showing the whole stage, as Belle, his beautiful fiancée, walked toward him. She wore a denim skirt and a brown leather top with a horse embossed into it. She truly looked like the Wyoming wife of Harry Young, and he received her easily into his side, his arm curling around her waist as he leaned in to kiss her cheek.

"And now," he drawled into the microphone as the camera tightened in on him again. "My beautiful fiancée, Belle Graves, and I are going to play a song that we wrote together. That's what I do now—I write songs, and some of them I keep for me or Belle, a few for both of us, and some we sell to other artists." He grinned at her as the camera panned out, showing the horses behind the stage and the vastness of Wyoming beyond that, and she sickenly-sweetly smiled back at him. "But this one should finally get us in the holiday mood."

While they'd been in close on Harry, someone had set a mic up for Belle, and Harry sat on a stool to bring their heights closer together. She stood at his side, beaming like a shiny new penny. Then Harry started to play a very familiar tune—*Jingle Bells*. Belle sang through the verse in her lower, raspier voice, and Harry came in on the chorus, the two of them melding their voices together into one rich harmony that made it sound like they truly were made for each other.

Simply looking at them, Bailey knew they were. She'd been invited to Harry's wedding. She honestly wasn't sure if she would go, while at the same time, she wasn't sure how she could miss it. He'd been nothing but kind to her every moment of his life, and Bailey loved and appreciated Harry as well.

Her phone chimed, but she didn't turn back to the couch to pick it up.

"Sing along with us now," Harry said on the final chorus, and Bailey did exactly what he said, for Harry Young could not be ignored.

When that song finished, Belle leaned in and kissed his cheek and then turned to leave the stage. She passed Bryce, who gave her a high five as he sauntered onto the stage as if he was born to be there, which, of course, he was.

He'd never had a solo career the way Harry had, though he could have. He had traveled plenty with Country Quad over the years, singing duets with his daddy while the other band members got breaks. He and Harry were obviously doing that tonight for their fathers, which only made them more endearing to Bailey.

"Merry Christmas," Bryce bellowed into the microphone. Bailey clasped her hands together and held them in front of her heart for this man she'd practically fallen for at first sight. He was so charming and so sweet, so smart and so good.

Bailey had struggled for years thinking she had

corrupted him into sleeping with her before they were married, and it had taken a lot of therapy for her to move past those dangerous and damaging feelings. She'd once begged God to allow them to be made for each other, and that had taken her a long time to get over as well—the fact that they simply weren't.

He was married now, and he'd just had a baby, and Bailey felt nothing but joy and sunshine as she looked at him on the screen.

"I'm Bryce Young," he said. "And Harry and I are going to play a song from his second album." He gave no more introduction, and instead, their guitars sang together for several long moments of intricate plucking until Harry finally started singing.

The song was more upbeat, almost something Bailey would hear a fiddle and a ukulele and a guitar play together at a small-town dance on a summer evening. Bryce and Harry went together like peanut butter and jelly, their voices perfectly unique and coming together into something combined that was wonderful and gorgeous. The song talked about drinking too much and having too good a time and not caring till Sunday morning, when they'd ask for forgiveness.

Bailey loved this song, as she'd often lived her life as a Sunday-only believer, but recently, she'd been trying to take Christ's teachings into her everyday life and live them all the time—the way she knew Harry did and Bryce did.

That song ended, and both Harry and Bryce looked to the right. Bryce and Belle had come off the left side of the stage, and Bailey pulled in a breath because she suspected OJ would come out next. The camera pulled back again, and Bryce leaned in and said, "And now for the country music debut of the next generation of Youngs."

"Wait," Harry said. "I thought *we* were the next generation of Youngs." He and Bryce both chuckled. Bailey wondered if it hurt any part of Bryce to see his own son come on the stage and not call him that.

"I guess you're right," Bryce said. "He's part of our generation. I'm just so much older than him." He chuckled, but Bailey did not. She sank back onto the couch, her heart pounding now for some reason. She remembered her phone had chimed, but she still didn't reach for it, because Bryce said, "We want to welcome to the stage Otis—Judson—*Yooooooooung!*"

He held on to the last name as OJ ran out, and there was her darling little boy, the one she'd given up for adoption. OJ had the same shaped nose as Bryce, but his hair was lighter, and his eyes definitely belonged to Bailey. He'd grown up with the Youngs, so he had their mannerisms and their way of speaking, and a perfectly heighted mic stood between Bryce and Harry.

"Howdy, fellas," he said into it.

"Tell 'em who you are," Harry said, grinning for all he was worth.

OJ looked straight at the camera, and with all the enthusiasm of an eleven-year-old boy, he said, "I'm OJ Young, and I'm real excited to be here with you this holiday season."

Tears ran down Bailey's face, even as she smiled. The

scene in front of her was everything she'd ever wanted for him, and a new sense of comfort and peace washed over her.

You don't need to worry about him anymore. The thought lingered in her mind as Bryce explained that they were going to play a song that Otis had written for the three of them.

"You've been practicing, OJ?" he asked.

"Every day, Bryce," he said. "My daddy don't let up about that."

"Oh, I bet he doesn't," Harry said.

The three of them grinned at one another, and then Bryce nodded to OJ, who started to play first. Bailey wiped her tears and caught him swallowing. While watching her beautiful boy, she whispered a plea for him. "Bless him, Lord," she said. "Not to be nervous and not to make a single mistake, and help him know that I'm watching him—and that I love him."

Harry came in on the next measure, and he and OJ played beautifully together with Harry's guitar complementing OJ's and letting him stay in the lead. Bryce came in behind them both, and then Harry leaned forward and started to sing. He was definitely stronger at that than Bryce, and Bailey had seen OJ play and sing before, and his voice wouldn't be as powerful and as refined as Harry's.

She picked up her phone and found that the text that had come in had been from him. He'd said, *I'm up soon. I'm so excited and nervous.*

She quickly tapped out a message: *I am watching you*

right now, and you are brilliant and beautiful and doing such a good job!

She sent that text, and then raised her phone and took a shot of the three of them all looking at the camera just as OJ started to sing. She took a few more, his higher voice among those deeper ones of his cousins. When the song ended, she sent him that picture and a whole text full of heart emojis. OJ loved using emojis in his texts, when she hoped Otis would show him those texts the moment he could. She clapped along with the crowd and then sank back into the couch, her heart fuller than ever.

"All right, let's get everyone back out here," Harry yelled, having done four songs and given Country Quad a good fifteen-minute break.

They flooded onto the stage again, along with Belle, and with the eight of them out there, Tex said, "This will be our last song, and then we wish everyone the happiest and merriest of Christmases, no matter where you are or who you're with, may the Lord be with you."

"And now I give you," he looked down the line at everyone and back to Luke. "A brand new song written by Otis for the eight of us, because sometimes it takes quite the journey before you find a place to call home."

He looked right into the camera, all of that Young charisma shining through him. "I give you, *The Journey Home*." He moved to the neck of his guitar, and all eight of them, from the four Country Quad members to Harry and Bryce and Belle and OJ, came in together.

The song definitely reminded Bailey of the country rock

that Country Quad was known for. She couldn't believe that they did this kind of stuff for free, and she pulled her laptop closer and did a search for the website that Adam had talked about at the beginning of the broadcast. Her clinic was doing very well, and she could definitely donate to horse rescue operations, one of which was in Montana.

She did that just as the song ended, and then Adam Harmon came back on stage as everyone else ran off, and he said, "Well, folks, wasn't that the greatest thing you've ever seen?" He spread his arms wide, as if gathering the whole world together, and then brought his hands together into a loud clap.

"The website to donate should be on your screen right now." It popped up. Bailey smiled at how flawless this presentation had been. "Remember, we've got three organizations matching you dollar for dollar, and we'd really love to give as much as we can to rescue these great equines in Wyoming and Montana.

"No matter if you can't give or if you give a lot, we appreciate you being here and listening. We appreciate your donations—and as Tex said, Merry Christmas and may the Lord be with you." He grinned for the next three seconds until the screen went dark and the broadcast ended.

Bailey sat there in the new silence in her home, feeling like she lost some of her best friends with the ending of that concert.

And then the voice of the Lord whispered to her, *You could see them all if you lived in Coral Canyon.*

38

"Adam, you haven't said anything about the concert last night."

Adam looked over to Lauren and took a scoop of the cranberry sauce she'd made. "It was great," he said.

"Oh, it was more than great," Joey said as she followed him down the buffet line at her mother's peninsula. "It was amazing, Momma. You should have *seen* him on that stage."

Surprise had him turning toward her too. "Seen me on the stage? I was up there for, like, thirty seconds."

"It was a couple of minutes at least," Joey said, putting a slice of ham on her plate. She followed that with a big scoop of mashed potatoes, and he smiled to himself. She'd confessed to him last night that she liked the sides at Christmas far more than the main dish, especially when her mother was cooking.

I don't know why she insists on having ham, Joey had told him. *But she does, and it's always kind of dry.*

Adam wasn't sure why Lauren had made cranberry sauce to go with ham, but he'd taken it as a lubricant, just in case.

"And he had the greatest speech ever," she said. "I was willing to donate my entire salary to horse rescue." She trilled out a laugh. "And this morning, they crossed one hundred thousand dollars of donations in one day."

It had actually only taken sixteen hours to get to one hundred thousand dollars, which had been Harry's original goal. He and Belle had both posted on their social media, and they'd asked their fans to think about how much they would pay to attend a concert by him, by the two of them, and by Country Quad, then to donate whatever ticket price they came up with.

Harry was exceptionally good at social media, and Adam had taken that idea and run with it. He posted the same call to action for Country Quad across all of their platforms. To double down, he'd asked people to post their receipts in the comments of any Country Quad concert they'd been to over the years. That had gotten a lot of engagement and a lot of comments, which helped the algorithms push the content out to even more people.

"I can watch it online, right?" Lauren asked.

Adam nodded as Joey said, "Yes, I've watched it three times already. Momma, it is *so* good. Daddy wrote one of the songs that's brand new, and everyone plays in it—Harry, Bryce, Belle, and even OJ."

Adam watched her mother's face, and while she wore a smile, she certainly didn't seem as engaged in the conversation as Joey was. He loved watching his normally quiet, reserved girlfriend come to life.

He waited at the end of the bar, so that she could lead them to a place at the table. It was just the four of them for Christmas this year, as they had spent Thanksgiving down in Coral Canyon with her daddy and his branch of the family.

Adam had arranged to go home in January after the concert series and Harry's wedding, when Country Quad would have nothing to do but re-watch their winter performances. He would still have plenty to do, as he had to deal with the donations, as well as all the social media. Not only that, but he had already been contacted by three organizations who wanted to partner with Country Quad in some sort of mini concert series.

That would be a hard sell, and Adam had not replied to any of them, using the holidays as an excuse to set his autoresponder and get to it later.

Joey led them over to the table, and he pulled out her chair for her as she continued to gush about the concert. He took one bite of ham with mashed potatoes, realizing everything Joey had said about the protein was correct. He slathered cranberry sauce on it after that and managed to get down the two pieces he'd taken.

Joey paused in her play-by-play of the concert, and Adam put his hand on her knee under the table. He absolutely loved her enthusiasm, because Country Quad had become such a big part of his life, and it felt like she was cheering for him and not the band. But her mother's eyes had glazed over about the time Adam had taken his first bite of ham, and he said, "Why don't you ask your mother about her tomato starts?"

Joey looked at him, questions in her eyes, but she was smart, and she looked over to her mother. Adam saw the recognition as it crossed her face, because Joey could read a room. It had just taken her a little longer this time.

"Yes, we saw some tomato starts in the garage," she said. "How did you do those?"

"They're not really in the garage," her mother said. "We had Peter from down the street come and put a little green-house against the window, so I can check on them without having to go outside."

"Right," Joey said, though Adam and Joey *had* walked past them in the garage and seen them through that window.

"It was really easy," Joey's mom said. "I set out those red plastic cups and filled them with dirt, and then I sliced a tomato and put one piece on top of each one. A little water and as much sun as possible, and now I have one hundred and twenty starts."

"Wow," Adam said. "What are you going to do with all those?"

From what Joey had told him, her mother was quite ill and couldn't work—or do much of anything physically. Gardening would definitely be a lot of up and down, hauling supplies, and physical labor, and he hadn't realized that Lauren was capable of it.

"She sells them," Gloria said. "The nurseries and hardware stores around here sell a tomato plant for five dollars," she continued. "Lauren can give them the same plant from her greenhouse, and she only charges three."

"I started one hundred and twenty more a few days ago," Lauren said. "I try and space them out every couple of weeks because people are ready to plant at different times."

"That's great, Momma," Joey said. "I didn't realize you'd done that."

"I've been doing it about six or eight months now." Lauren grinned at them from across the table. "I sold a bunch of plants to the members of the greenhouse society here in town," she said. "Once they learned I had them, it seemed like everyone wanted one so that they could have fresh tomatoes out of their greenhouses this winter."

She looked the happiest Adam had ever seen her, and he found himself genuinely smiling at her too.

The meal finished, and Adam got up to clear the table while the three women continued to chat. Just because he didn't know how to cook didn't mean he didn't know how to rinse dishes and set them in the dishwasher. One glance at the leftovers told him he might be out of his league if he tried to put those away, so he left them for Joey or her grandmother to do later.

Later was really what Adam wanted to get to. Because later, after this meal, he and Joey had planned an intimate gift exchange and dessert at his place. She'd helped him set up a Christmas tree over the weekend—on the day she was supposed to move into her new apartment—and he'd gotten his wrapped gifts back from his neighbor and put them under the tree.

He felt like a real person who did normal things for the holidays, and he'd bought a smoked turkey, mac and cheese, a dozen fresh rolls, stuffing, and a broccoli kale salad for their Christmas evening dinner. It came with brown gravy and sparkling cider as well, and Adam had bought three pies from Joey for dessert.

As far as she knew, they were eating here and doing dessert at his place later, because Adam *loved* surprising her with the things she loved and watching her face light up and then soften as she kissed him. He would do anything to make her happy, and he'd acknowledged that the reason he did those things was because...he was in love with her.

A couple of hours later, Joey rose from the couch where they'd put on a silly Christmas movie. Adam had done his best to watch it, but he kept sneaking glances at his phone instead.

"We have to go, Momma," she said.

"Already?" her mom asked.

"It's going to snow in a little bit," Joey said. "I have to get Adam home and back to Grams and Gramps."

"Oh, all right." Lauren did not get off the couch to hug Joey goodbye. Joey leaned over and did it, and put off her grandmother's offer for food once and then twice, before Adam helped her into her coat and they made it out of the house.

She'd stopped to pick him up, but he walked with her all the way to the driver's door and opened it for her. When he got in beside her and slammed out the winter weather, she drew in a deep breath and sighed.

"Sorry about that," she said.

"Hey, you don't need to apologize," he said.

"Maybe she just tires *me* out," Joey said.

"You're definitely more aware of it than I am," Adam told her. "You don't need to worry about me at all." He chuckled as he pulled his seatbelt across his body. "Just wait until you meet my mother."

Joey looked over to him, something vibrant and electric in her eyes. "Is that a possibility? Me meeting your momma?"

Adam employed his cowboy head-ducking skills and reached for her hand. "I mean, I think so," he said.

"Seems real serious," she said.

"Would you have brought me home for Christmas this year?" he asked. "If I hadn't already met your mother because of that snowstorm?"

Joey studied their hands where his darker fingers ran through her paler ones. "Yes," she finally whispered. "I think I would have."

"I'm going home in about another month," he said. "Maybe you should come with me."

She lifted her eyes to his, and this time, Adam didn't shy away.

"I'm real serious about you," he said.

A smile touched her lips for a moment, and then flitted away. "Is that so?"

"Yeah, that's so." He pulled his hand back. "Come on, let's get to my place before it starts storming."

"I don't know how long I'm going to be able to stay," she said, as she peered out the windshield and up into the gray sky.

"Well, I've got lots of bedrooms if you get snowed in," he said.

Joey's mouth tightened, but she nodded and drove them over to his house. Adam used his home security app to open the garage so she could pull inside, and then he closed it before they got out. They went in together, and Adam hung their coats in the mudroom.

"Let's do presents," he said, suddenly feeling like a much younger boy on Christmas morning. She'd brought hers in when she'd picked him up, so she simply followed him into the living room, where he guided her to the couch and then knelt in front of the tree.

"First, I got your bookcase set up," he said.

"I don't know how you have time to do everything you do."

Adam chuckled and reached for the first present he wanted her to open. "Second, I've got a bunch of stuff for you to take to your family. I don't know when you're going to be seeing them." He twisted to look at her over his shoulder. "Maybe I should just take them myself."

"It's up to you," she said. "I'll probably see them tomorrow. It's cousin movie night, and Harry invited OJ, so I'm going to be stopping by the house to get him."

He nodded, and then handed her the long, slim package. "These might be lame."

"Adam," she said kindly. "You don't know yourself at all if you think you can buy a lame gift for someone."

He simply smiled and leaned back against the entertainment center while she unwrapped the box.

"Did you wrap this?" she asked, glancing up.

"Heavens no," he said. "I had a woman around the corner do it."

"It's well done," she said.

"I'll be sure to tell her thanks."

She sucked in a breath in the next moment, and Adam loved her reactions to his gifts.

"Is this what I think it is?" she asked, and she hurried to slide her finger under the flap and open it. "Oh, my *heck*, it is. It's that heating strip I wanted."

"It fits right in your pillowcase," he said. "In fact, I got you a couple of pillowcases made specially for it."

"Thank you so much," Joey said, and she propelled herself forward and off the couch to kneel in front of him. She took his face in her hands and kissed him, and Adam loved the way she touched him.

He handed her the next gift, and she stayed on the floor beside him as she opened it.

"You got a set of these mixing bowls?" She looked at him with pure wonder on her face. "They sold out in under ten minutes."

He nodded to the card. "Yeah, you got set seventy-six."

She shook her head and said, "I can't wait to find out

what the one thing is that you can't do." She grinned at him and then opened a new pair of gloves, a scarf he'd asked her grandmother to make for him to give to her, and then finally, Adam hesitated on the smallest box.

He didn't have to give her this, but he sure was thankful that she had never once said he'd spent too much money or spoiled her. Spending money and spoiling people was Adam's specialty, and he would employ his superpower for Joey any day of the week, any time.

In the end, he drew a deep breath and handed it to her. He wanted to start with a caveat, but he held it back. Joey could take the jewelry to mean whatever she wanted it to mean.

She unwrapped the little black box, glanced at him, and then lifted the lid.

"Oh Adam," she whispered. "This is incredible." She looked at him and thrust the box toward him. He thought she might say, *It's too much. I can't.*

Instead, she asked, "Will you put it on for me?"

Swallowing hard, Adam lifted the diamond tennis bracelet out of the box and gently draped it over Joey's wrist. It clasped easily, as good jewelry did, and he lifted her hand and kissed the top of her wrist and then the side and then the inside, before he looked at her again. "You make my whole life shine like diamonds," he said.

She smiled too, a pinkish hue climbing into her cheeks.

"Is it lame for me to tell you I love you on Christmas?" he asked, his voice barely more than a whisper.

Joey pulled in another breath, and Adam gathered her

into his lap and tucked her close against his chest. "Because if it is—" He cut off and swallowed, not wanting to hold back the way he felt or wait to vocalize it.

"Then I guess I'm lame," he finished. "Because I'm hopelessly in love with you." He didn't want her to feel pressured to say it back, so he quickly touched his lips to hers and sealed his declaration with a kiss.

39

"Okay," Joey said, as she led the way inside the furniture store. "I hope you're ready for this."

Adam simply grinned at her. "I survived that birthday party at Bryce's house," he said. "And that was after a concert too. I'm sure I'll be fine."

Joey was sure of it as well, because Adam was so good at coordinating details and handling dozens of moving parts that all of the concerts had gone off without a hitch. They had one more tomorrow for New Year's brunch, and then one more on Monday.

God willing, Joey would be moving into her new apartment in three days, and part of her wondered why it mattered. Why had she felt so called to get her own place and move out?

She thought of the words Adam had said to her almost a week ago now: *I'm hopelessly in love with you.*

She hadn't said it back to him, mostly because he'd taken her onto his lap and kissed her before she could, and partly because she wasn't sure she was in love with him...yet.

She did love who she was with him because he inspired her to be a more confident version of herself. She'd started to see herself as smart and capable and wonderful—all of the things he'd told her many times.

"Oh, they're line dancing," Joey said as she opened the second set of doors into the furniture store and a rousing country music song met her ears. Sure enough, a loud stomp echoed through the store, followed by a *whoop!*, carefully timed to the dance and the music.

Adam took her hand, and she led him through the high-end living room section, and then curved through the bedroom area back to the more casual living area where Aunt Hilde staged their New Year's Eve party every year.

Every year wasn't quite true, as various aunts and uncles had hosted over the years, but Aunt Hilde donated the furniture store every other year, as it definitely had the most room for everyone in the family.

This year, they obviously had a dance floor set up. Joey brought Adam right to the edge of the crowd, so that he could see the dancing. Men and women danced alike, with Rosie and Aunt Ev calling the dance from the front. Joey joined in clapping with everyone else, and a few moments later, the song ended. Cheers raised the roof, and people streamed off the dance floor.

"Hey, you made it," Jem said. "Tonight's concert was fire," he added as he bumped knuckles with Adam.

"Thanks," Adam said. "I mean, not that I played or anything."

"When are you going to play?" Uncle Tex asked, and Joey gaped at him, her look mirroring Adam's.

"I'm not going to play," Adam said.

"I heard you were taking guitar lessons." Uncle Tex lifted a cup of punch to his lips.

"Yeah, for two months," Adam said. "I'm certainly not going to get on the stage with professional musicians."

"Oh, is that what they are?" Uncle Jem teased.

"All right, all right, all right," Uncle Luke yelled, the last time into a mic. The sound positively *bellowed* through the building and it did cut through the chatter that had broken out after the line dance. "We have something pretty amazing this year," he said, his whole persona shining. "A New Year's unlike any other New Year's."

"Here we go," Uncle Blaze said as he sidled up to Jem.

"Hey, you're the one who called in a favor to Ralph," Jem said.

"Because I thought it would be fun," Uncle Blaze replied.

"Some of you may be wondering what's over here behind this drape," Uncle Luke said with plenty of gusto and drama. "Well, you don't have to wait any longer!" He brandished his arm in that direction, and Liesl and Corinne, who both stood in the middle of the curtain, grabbed one side of it and ran toward the edge, parting the curtain and revealing what sat behind it.

Children started to scream and laugh and jump up and

down, but Joey could only stare at the mechanical bull in the middle of her aunt's furniture store.

A legit *mechanical bull.*

"Can I get Uncle Blaze and Uncle Jem over here?" Luke said as he walked toward the bull. "They're going to be our mentors tonight, and anyone who wants to ride the bull has to talk to them first. Am I clear?"

He stopped in front of his own seven-year-old who said, "Yes, Daddy, I want to ride it," in the most excited voice Joey had ever heard. Ryder vibrated with energy, and he glued himself to Luke's side as he moved over to the bull.

She linked her arm through Adam's as her uncles moved away from them. "Are you going to ride that thing?" she asked.

"Are you kidding?" he hissed back. "I don't want to break my back."

Joey giggled, though she didn't really want to ride the mechanical bull either. "It's got padding," she said. "Little kids can do it. Look." She nodded as Luke helped Ryder up over the padding and toward the bull.

"Little kids can do it?" He turned and looked at her, his expression half challenging and half teasing. "Are *you* going to ride it?"

"I mean, I don't think there's time," she said. "The clock's going to strike midnight in less than an hour. And look at the line already."

He'd started smiling about halfway through her rejection speech, and he wrapped her up in his big bear arms, a full belly laugh coming out of his mouth.

"The line is too long," he said, laughing all over again. "It's an *eight-second* ride."

He backed her out of the lights that had been shining down on the dance floor and those overhead the couches where people had clearly been relaxing. Abandoned paper plates and cups sat there from the pizza that had been brought in.

Not everyone attended every concert anymore, but Joey had been to them all, and she'd waited with Adam until everything was cleaned up at the ranch before they'd driven here for tonight's party. Joey didn't normally stay up this late, but she didn't have to work tomorrow at all.

Lights started to flash over the bull, and cheering began as someone started to ride it—probably Ryder. Joey couldn't see for sure past Adam, and she decided she didn't really care, because Adam looked down at her with an expression filled with love and desire. "It's going to be an amazing year with you."

Though so much chaos reigned around them, she definitely felt like her words would only enter his ears and that they were the only two people at this party. "You know I feel the same, right?"

He nodded as he lowered his head to kiss her. Joey could definitely lose herself inside the arms of this man, while bull-riding lights flashed somewhere around her and her family cheered like they were at the NPR Finals.

"All right, you two," Belle said, and Joey ducked her head against Adam's chest. "The ball doesn't drop for another forty-five minutes."

She and Harry joined them, and Harry grabbed onto Adam and gave him a hearty hug.

"You bought me that microphone off Kickstarter," he said, laughing. "You dirty dog."

Adam laughed too as he pounded Harry on the back. "It's great though, right?"

"It's the best thing *ever*," Harry said. "The live stream tonight was twice as crisp with that microphone clipped to my phone. *Un-be-liev-a-ble*." They parted, and Joey really liked their friendship.

"How's everything going for the wedding?" she asked Belle.

"Almost there," she said with a sigh. "My parents will be here next week."

"Only ten more days." Joey smiled at her. "When are you going to tell everyone where it is?"

Belle glanced over to Harry and Adam, who had moved on to another conversation topic. "Harry's worried about an online leak, but I don't get it. Even if people know where we're getting married, they won't show up."

Joey watched her charismatic and super-popular cousin. "I don't know about that," she said. "Harry's been immensely popular since he first started playing the guitar on his stairs as a teenager."

"I suppose." Belle leaned her head closer. "Things look like they're going well for you and Adam." She smiled at Joey, and it didn't seem gossipy or teasing but simply kind. Interested, maybe.

Joey nodded, because things were going well, and she

saw no reason to hide it. After all, she'd just been caught kissing him, and anyone in her family could have seen that.

"He's amazing," Joey said.

"You're amazing, too," Belle told her.

"Yeah, I know." Joey grinned at her. "I'm excited to get to know him a lot better this year."

Joey had never had a boyfriend on New Year's Eve before, and she wasn't sure if that was why moving into this new year with Adam felt so significant. But as Adam and Harry, and then Belle and Joey, joined the party again, Joey knew it was more than just having a boyfriend.

It was because of Adam himself.

He turned and reached for her, bringing her right back to his side as they moved over to the mechanical bull.

Jem's son, Ladd, currently rode it, and he looked every bit the professional bull rider that his daddy had been, with his heels tucked back and his hand in the air as the bull bucked and bucked and bucked.

Joey found a clock ticking up toward the eight seconds directly across from her, and she joined her voice to those cheering for Ladd to make that eight-second ride.

He did, and the family went wild, Joey included. Adam's voice was as loud as any of them, as he'd easily found his place among her family. Yes, Joey knew this year would be one for the books, and it had everything to do with Adam.

You might even have your own wedding this year, she thought, and the idea made her ridiculously happy—and terribly afraid at the same time. She didn't like that feeling, and she pushed against it, because love was kind, and it didn't have room for any fear inside it whatsoever.

So maybe she wasn't all the way in love with Adam yet, but she knew this year held great possibility for her...and for the two of them.

40

"No. No, nope," Adam said right out loud as he peered at the email he just received. "This cannot be happening." He grabbed his phone and jumped to his feet.

There was only one more concert in only two more days. Today was Saturday—not even a business day—and there was *no way* Adam could replace the lighting that he'd been renting by Monday night. Industrial and commercial rentals like that weren't even *open* on the weekend.

He tapped to dial Donna, the woman who just sent him the cancellation email, and he tipped his head back toward the ceiling. "Dear God," he said. "This cannot be happening."

It had taken him forever to find the lights in the first place, and he'd had to go all the way to Jackson Hole to do it.

"I know what you're going to say," Donna said when she answered.

"We just need them for Monday night," Adam said. "We have a contract."

"Our roof caved in on the warehouse," she said. "We have to relocate today, when we're not even open. There is *no way* that I can get anyone to bring you the lights, set them up, and run them on Monday."

"Then I'll come pick them up," Adam said.

She sighed heavily while Adam's heartbeat blitzed through his body while his mind tried to find a solution that would satisfy them both. "I've seen your guys work the lights," he said. "We know what to do."

"It is against state regulations to have someone who is not a licensed electrician run our lights," she said, and she sounded exhausted and tired and stressed—all of the same things Adam was. "This is as bad for me as it is you."

"Is it?" Adam challenged, letting his temper rise. "We have two-point-*seven million* people signed up to watch Monday's concert. I can't show it to them in the dark."

She sniffled, and Adam's heart went out to her. "Just give me one guy," he said. "I will come help you move out today." He grabbed his keys and headed for the mudroom. "I can bring a whole bunch of people to help you move out today. We'll get you guys all situated, and I just need your two guys on Monday night. Four hours."

"Adam," she said, her voice full of weariness.

"Donna," he said calmly as he got behind the wheel, "I

have to have those lights. You know you're the only commercial lighting business within five hundred miles of Coral Canyon. Trust me, I have tried to get them somewhere else before I found you. I *need* them. I will do anything to get them.

"So tell me how many people you need me to bring and help you move all your stuff. I will bring your guys home with me. They can stay in my house. I've got a big place—six bedrooms—and I'm the only one here. I'll feed them and take care of them. I *need* them until Monday at midnight, as we agreed."

Pure desperation coated every word, and Adam found that he could not breathe properly. He'd forgotten to open the garage door, and he moved to do that. "Please," he begged when Donna didn't immediately shoot him down. "I'm an hour from Coral Canyon, and I can recruit other people."

His phone rang, and Otis's name sat there. "One of them is calling right now," he said, his mind singular on this one problem that absolutely must fix before Adam did anything else.

He swiped Otis's call away, because he could mobilize the entire Young family once he knew he should.

"I'm not going to say no to help," Donna said. "But it's a mess here. We have to pick through all the debris, and there's snow and ice and water everywhere. I don't even know if your lights will be functioning once I get them out of the warehouse."

Adam swallowed, this problem much larger than he'd

originally imagined. "All we can do is try," he said. "I'll bring some muscle, and we'll help."

Donna did not confirm that she would allow him to have her people and the lights. But Adam had to do what he could. "I'll be there in an hour," he said. "Don't do all the work without me."

Donna laughed bitterly and said, "See you soon," before she hung up.

Adam exhaled, tapped to turn on his Bluetooth, and pulled out of his driveway. Thankfully, it had not snowed for a couple of days, and the roads would be clear and dry all the way to Jackson.

He quickly tapped to call Tex, because the oldest brother in the Young family seemed to have the most connections and the most sway. Though he'd heard Harry tell stories about Mav and how, as the hinge brother, *he* was the one who no one wanted to let down. But Tex was in the band, and this was definitely a band issue.

He waited impatiently as the phone rang, and Tex didn't answer. He tried Trace next, surprised when a woman answered his phone with, "This is Trace Young's phone."

"It's Adam," he heard Trace gripe.

"It is Adam," he said. "Is this Everly?"

"Yes," she said. "What's going on?"

Adam didn't want to admit that he had a problem with Monday's concert, but he had called, and he saw no way around it. "Our lights for Monday's concert just got canceled," he said. "I have to go to Jackson Hole to help them dig their equipment out of a wrecked roof and the snow and ice that caved it in. Is there any way I can get people to come help? It's an hour drive and disgusting work."

After that, scuffling came through the line, along with the crying, mewling sound of a baby. Ev started to shush it, and Trace said, "Our lights got canceled?"

"In an email," Adam clipped out. "I called Donna, and she told me that the roof had been caved in by snow and ice. She's not even sure the lights will work, but she's dedicating her entire staff to cleaning the warehouse out, and she canceled our equipment."

"That's not good," Trace said.

"I told her I was on my way to help her clean up, and that I would bring as many people as I could." Adam came to a stop at a stop sign and pinched his eyes closed. "That was a stupid thing to promise her, wasn't it? I mean, it's a Saturday."

Trace said, "I don't know what people have going on." He heard someone say something on his end of the line, and then Trace exhaled heavily. "Joey's moving today, isn't she?"

Adam swore right out loud, because, yes, his beautiful girlfriend was moving today—and a quick glance at the clock told him he should've been at her grandparents' condo an hour ago.

He couldn't believe he'd forgotten about it; he'd orchestrated all of it. Pure foolishness drove through him, lanced with regret and guilt.

"I forgot she was moving today," he said.

"I'm going to pretend like you didn't say that," Trace said. "And no one but me and you ever needs to know that it came out of your mouth, or that it even happened."

Adam bashed the palm of his hand against the steering wheel. "I'll head there first," he said.

"I'm out at Reggie's," he said. "With him and Kassie and the baby, but I can put it on the family text for anyone who's willing to go to Jackson after they're done with Joey. I don't really know who Otis coordinated with to help her."

"He didn't," Adam said miserably. "I did it all."

"Oh, well, there you go," Trace said, as if Adam hadn't just made the biggest mistake of his life.

"I gotta go," Adam said.

"Yeah, I bet you do. Good luck, brother." Trace ended the call, and Adam got on the Apple Highway leading down into Coral Canyon.

He wasn't sure who to call first—Joey or her daddy—and he finally decided that Otis would probably answer over his daughter. He'd called while Adam had been on the phone with Donna, so it was easy to tap on the screen in his car and get a call connected back to Otis.

"There you are," Otis said, and Adam couldn't tell if he was upset or not.

"Where are you?"

"Over at Joey's new place already."

Adam ground his teeth together, feeling like the stupidest man alive. "I had a huge problem come up this morning," he said. "And I left late. I'm on the way now." He swallowed hard. "Trace is going to send something out on the family text for all of you guys that will explain the situation."

He held on as he took a curve in the highway a little bit too fast. "How's Joey doing?" he asked.

"I think she's had better days," Otis said almost under his breath. "Oh, here's the text from Trace." A long pause came through the line as Otis read it, and he said, "You have *got* to be kidding."

"I'm not kidding," Adam said. "And I need to get to Jackson Hole as soon as possible."

"Well, you don't need to come here, then," he said.

Adam laughed mirthlessly. "Oh, I think I need to come there," he said. "All I can do is hope that Joey won't skewer me alive when I arrive."

"I said it was fine," Joey said, but she hadn't looked at him for more than two seconds since Adam had arrived in her basement apartment. He had coordinated with her uncles Mav, Luke, and Blaze, as they had the biggest trucks and a lot of the furniture that they had donated to Joey.

By the time he'd arrived at her place, everything had been moved in, and Georgia and Aunt Abby and Aunt Dani were unpacking her kitchen. In fact, they were almost done with that.

He was supposed to bring her pink bean bag with him to put in her bedroom, and he stared at the empty corner where it should have gone.

"Maybe you can come with me," he said.

She sighed and rolled her eyes as she turned back to him. She cocked one hip and glared. "Adam, this is an emergency. You need to go now."

"I don't want you to be mad at me," he said.

"Well, I'm already mad." She threw up her hands in frustration. "And I have a right to be mad, because *you* coordinated the whole move and then you didn't show up, and everyone was asking me all these questions, like I knew what was going on—and I didn't."

"I know." Adam hung his head, though he'd left his cowboy hat at home and could not hide behind the brim. "This is one of those things I can't control," he said.

"I understand that you can't control a roof caving in," Joey said. "I understand that the lights are incredibly important to the concert. What I don't understand is how one-track your mind is, and that you let this one thing, this work thing, overcome everything else you had going on in your life."

"I know," Adam said. "In that moment, there was only that one thing, and I needed to fix it."

"Sometimes you can't fix things."

Adam had never felt so low. He couldn't believe he'd let down an angel here on earth. He moved over to Joey and reached for her hand, barely letting his fingers brush hers. "I am so sorry," he said. "The moment I am back in town, I will be here. I want you to walk me through the whole thing."

He had only seen this apartment online, and she had

been so excited to show it to him. He really had coordinated her entire move for her and not told her any of the details, and then he had left her out to dry.

He watched her as she studied the floor at their feet. "I can bring dinner back," he offered.

"And what if you can't?" she asked. "What if you're stuck in Jackson Hole for the weekend? Have you ever been in a warehouse where the roof has collapsed due to the weight of *ice* and *snow*?"

Adam pressed his teeth together, because no, he had not.

"I know a bunch of my uncles are going to go with you. You should just go." Her voice sounded tiny and afraid, and Adam hated it with every fiber of his being. "Just go take care of it, and when it's done, you can text me."

Adam didn't want to *text* her. He wanted to *call*, and he wanted to bring dinner, and he wanted to show up on her doorstep at any hour and have her answer it and be happy to see him.

"I'm sorry," he said again.

Joey nodded and said, "I know you are."

Someone knocked on her closed bedroom door, and then it opened. "Oh, you are in here." Otis glanced over to Adam and then back to his daughter. "We need you out here in the kitchen. Little bit of an emergency."

"What can it possibly be now?" Joey asked in a tired, disgusted tone.

Adam turned and watched her brush past her father. Otis watched her hurry down the hall, and then he turned back to Adam. "You guys okay?"

Adam's jaw felt wired shut; it was so tight, it ached. He shook his head. "I don't know," he said.

He went down the hall too, where four women were now cleaning up a shattered jar of spaghetti sauce. Joey wept as she worked, and Adam knew that was because she had canned that spaghetti sauce herself this past fall, and she loved it.

As he left her apartment without saying goodbye to her, he vowed to himself that he would buy every can and jar of spaghetti sauce in the entire country, if only he could make her smile.

"You'll be lucky if she takes you back," Adam muttered to himself as he got behind the wheel and entered the address for the lighting company into his GPS. She hadn't exactly broken up with him, but as Adam drove away from the blue house with the dug-up front yard, it certainly felt like she had.

41

Joey lay in bed, her back to the window with the light streaming in behind and over her. She hadn't slept great, because it had been her first night of truly living all by herself. When she'd moved to college, she'd had roommates, and she had in New York City too. Then, she'd been living with Grams and Gramps since returning to town.

A new place always unsettled her a little bit, and this house was no different. It wasn't brand new, and they had just done some plumbing repairs. The young family that lived upstairs had two children, and while Joey was used to other units' noise, she always had Grams and Gramps just across the hall.

Her eyes burned, even though she had her phone on dark mode, and she set it down and closed them, the stinging sensation somewhat welcome as tears wetted her eyes. She looked over to the empty corner of her room, a space she'd saved for a big pink, fluffy bean bag that Adam had not brought.

Her phone suddenly felt hard in her hand because he'd texted a bunch last night, giving Joey all the updates of digging out the warehouse in Jackson Hole. About ten-thirty in the evening, he'd sent her a picture of the lights he needed for Monday's concert, and he told her he'd be staying the night in Jackson Hole.

She reached up and wiped the tear as it trickled down the side of her face, and she closed her eyes again. "Which means he won't be here in Coral Canyon for church today," she told herself.

She hadn't reminded him that he'd agreed to come to church with her that morning. He was a grown man and surely remembered. "Maybe," she muttered. She admired his dedication to his responsibilities, but it still stunned her that he had *completely* forgotten about her moving day.

Her alarm went off. Joey opened her eyes and lifted her phone to silence it. Church started in an hour, and either she was going to go—or she wasn't. She didn't particularly want to walk in alone, and she would have been more comfortable with Adam at her side, but she heaved herself out of bed and into her bathroom to brush her teeth and braid her hair back.

She could call Grams and ride with them. She lived five minutes away from her parents now, and she could easily park in front of their house and ride with them.

After stepping into a denim skirt and buttoning up a

blue striped blouse, Joey padded into her kitchen and opened the fridge. She didn't want to show up and explain to Daddy or Georgia that she couldn't walk into a church building by herself.

"Because you can," she said out loud to herself.

The bright winter sunshine shone throughout the apartment, and Joey turned toward the back windows, feeling more powerful with every breath she took.

She could go to church by herself.

She had survived her first night on her own in her new place.

She lived alone now, and a newfound sense of freedom threaded its way carefully through her, reminding her of how capable and amazing she had become.

So she didn't need to call Grams, and she didn't need to drive over to her parents' place.

She made herself a cup of coffee and sat down at the table, which had once belonged to Cheryl's mother. She ran her fingertip along the maple leaf carving in the corner, thinking of the man who had lovingly poured his energy and time and love into creating this table. Cheryl's daddy had been a master woodworker, and Joey adored old things. The two combined into a sense of wonder and fulfillment in her life, and she lifted her head to look out the window again.

"What am I going to do about Adam?" she asked. She hadn't broken up with him because she didn't want to. She'd grown up watching her father have an important job that took him away from his family sometimes, and that didn't bother Joey so much.

"So what does bother you?" she asked. "What would be a deal breaker for you and Adam?"

So far, it hadn't turned out to be their age difference, or the fact that they liked different things, or that she ran late sometimes, and he absolutely didn't—

"Except for when he does," she said.

A small smile touched her face as she thought of yesterday and how he'd been over an hour late to her apartment. She ached to show him around this place, though it was five simple rooms of used furniture.

It certainly wasn't as impressive as his mansion in Dog Valley, but it was hers, and she had worked hard for it.

She took a sip of her coffee and flipped her phone over, tapping to get to Adam's string. He had not texted that morning, and she wondered if he was still in Jackson Hole, still cleaning up the mess in the warehouse.

When he'd shown up at the apartment yesterday, he'd been wearing slacks, of course, and a pale yellow polo. She had no idea if he'd packed a bag, but the man had a credit card. Jackson was a massive tourist destination.

Joey finished her breakfast of peanut butter crackers and coffee and got up to get her shoes. She was going to go to church today all by herself because she was strong and capable and wonderful and amazing.

She didn't have to have someone at her side to do the things she wanted to do—and she *wanted* to have a relationship with God and Jesus Christ. She *wanted* Them to know that she could do hard things so she could feel Their spirit.

She stepped into a pair of white heels and put on her

absolute favorite coat—the one that made her feel the brightest and shiniest: her pink, glittery, puffy coat.

She looked at the scarves hanging on the hooks that Daddy had put beside the door, and she chose the one that Adam had given her for Christmas. With that, it almost felt like he was with her.

Properly bundled against the weather, she left the basement apartment and got in her car. "You've been good to me," she said as the vehicle started. "And I don't want you to think I'm not appreciative, but my next major purchase is going to be a new vehicle."

She smiled at the thought, now knowing that if she needed some extra money, she could earn it.

Her pies had done very well, and while she wasn't sure if she would be able to continue to sell them throughout the year, she could certainly try. She'd ended up doing eighty-four for Christmas, and her forearms ached just thinking about rolling out all that pie dough. But she'd done it with Adam acting as her chocolate croissant errand boy—a fact that made her heart flop and tears press into her eyes.

She'd text him back when she parked at the church. Yes, that was what she would do.

She didn't want to break up with him, and he'd apologized twice already. She had been angry, and when the last jar of the spaghetti sauce that she had worked on that fall had been dropped and she'd lost it, Joey had cried.

She'd vowed not to cry on moving day, but it had still happened. She told herself the same thing that she told Adam yesterday—not everything could be fixed, and she didn't need to be fixed anyway. It was okay that she got mad sometimes. It was okay that she cried sometimes, just like it was okay that she went to church alone sometimes.

"But overall," she whispered to herself so as not to have her voice be so definitive. "You don't want to do everything by yourself."

She turned into the church parking lot and went up and down a couple of rows until she found a spot. She parked facing the church, the tall steeple rising above the cars blocking the lower level.

"You want a life with Adam because...you love him."

Joey didn't like that it had taken his absence yesterday for her to finally realize that she was in love with him, but it had. She knew better than most that God worked in mysterious ways, and perhaps He had caused that roof in Jackson Hole to collapse, so that Adam would have to choose something over her.

A sense of peace filled her, though she didn't expect it to. She felt like everything and everyone had been chosen over her for most of her life, but *Adam* had always put her first.

"That was why it hurt so much yesterday," she said, just now realizing it. "But you can't always come first."

The fact that Adam had stopped by her apartment and hung his head and apologized before rushing off to take care of his problem told Joey that he wanted to put her first in all things, but in that *one thing* yesterday, he hadn't been able to.

A smile lifted the corners of her mouth. "But he *wanted* to."

She needed to go inside before she would be late, and Joey finally turned off her car, because the cold would force her in the building sooner rather than later. She took a steeling breath before she got out of the car, because if she did it outside, her lungs would freeze together.

Then she stepped out and started walking toward the church with strong, sure steps, feeling more like the bold, brave, beautiful woman she'd been trying to find since she'd returned to Coral Canyon.

42

Adam's joints ached from how hard he gripped the steering wheel. He'd really pushed his car a lot the last couple of days, taking the winding roads from Coral Canyon to Jackson and back. He'd also worked in dirty water, snow, and ice for ten hours yesterday, and that certainly hadn't helped. His lack of exercise in the past several months meant his whole body hurt, despite the painkillers he'd downed with an early morning cup of coffee from a convenience store.

He finally pulled into his garage, noting he literally had twenty minutes before he had to leave again. He glanced at his phone, noting that Joey still had not returned his texts from last night, and he left his phone to charge as he ran inside to get ready for church.

She had been at his side on his first day back to church,

and he would absolutely not miss walking in with her this morning—her first day going to church alone.

"Doesn't matter if she texts you back or not," he muttered to himself as he hurried into the shower. He soaped and scrubbed the fastest he ever had, praying the whole time that he would be able to get to the church before Joey walked in.

"Bless my car to run well," he said into the shower stream. "Bless me to be aware of other drivers. Bless me to park close to her. Bless her to have a forgiving heart."

Adam needed that last one more than anything, and he hurried to redress, grab the first tie he saw, and stuff his feet into his shiny church shoes. Then he was on the road again, back to Coral Canyon this time, praying he wouldn't get behind any trucks or slow drivers, begging God to open a parking space exactly where he needed it to be, and pleading with the Lord that he would know exactly what to say and do to get Joey to take him back, because he did not like the fact that she had not texted him in return.

She had messaged him twice yesterday, and he'd sent her twenty-three texts. Every time she didn't answer, he felt like a little piece of his heart had been cut out. He wasn't sure if he was just rubbing salt in her wounds or not, but he'd hoped to keep the line of communication open between them, so that when she wasn't mad anymore, she would be able to talk to him.

"Maybe she's still mad," Adam said as he glanced over to the cowboy hat and tie he'd tossed onto the passenger seat.

He reached over and picked up the hat and settled it on

his head. The action calmed him for some reason. Wearing this garment made him feel like the world turned slower. He didn't have to rush to and fro, because he was a country boy now, not a city celebrity assistant.

It's the Sabbath, he thought, not sure why he needed that reminder. *It's okay to slow down.*

He realized then that it wasn't his voice telling him to slow down on the Sabbath, but God's. He'd created heaven and earth in six days, and rested on the seventh, and Adam could too.

The cleanup at the warehouse would continue through today and tomorrow, but since he'd shown up with five strong, capable men, they'd gotten a lot done yesterday. Most of the equipment had been moved into drier, safer conditions, including what he needed for the concert.

Donna had said she'd let him know if she could spare the personnel, and his prayers switched to that for only a moment. "I know they're just lights, Lord," he prayed. "But they sure are important to me and a whole lot of other people. If there's *any way* Donna can get the people to run those lights for tomorrow's concert, please make it happen."

After that, his thoughts immediately flowed back to Joey, where they'd been stuck for almost twenty-four hours now. Heck, for months now, if he were being honest.

Every shovelful of snow he'd moved, every time he'd stepped in murky water, she had been on his mind. He loved her, and he'd told her that. He had apologized, and he had to believe that she would take him back.

He finally arrived at the church, and he jumped from

the SUV, scanning the sidewalks and parking lot where several people were walking in. Services would start in only a couple of minutes, and he quickly reached back into the car and grabbed his tie before he slammed the door closed. He hurried to the end of the row, and light shone down from heaven on a slim woman wearing a bright pink, glittery coat about twenty yards ahead of him.

He threw his tie around his neck, yelled, "Joey!" and took off jogging. The fleeting thought that he really needed to get back into the gym ran through his mind as the white-blonde angel turned toward him. "Wait up," he said, slowing as he got closer.

Joey blinked, her face a mask of surprise. "Adam," she said. "What are you doing here?"

She watched as he came to a stop an arm's length away from her, his heartbeat racing in his mouth, suddenly blank of words.

He reached up to tie his tie, because he knew how to do that, and Joey's eyes fell to his throat. A smile touched her face, and he let his hands fall to his side when he finished. "You realize this tie doesn't match, right?" She slid her fingers underneath it without touching him and lifted the tip.

She giggled, the most beautiful sound in the world. "I've never seen you wear a tie like this." She looked up at him. "It has shamrocks on it."

Adam looked down at the tie, finding it hideous and repulsive. He quickly moved to button his jacket to cover the worst of it. "Got it from my niece last year," he said.

Joey

Joey looked toward the building, where the bells had just started to ring. He wouldn't be able to talk to her now, and it was far too cold to hover outside and have a conversation anyway.

She hadn't dismissed him immediately, so Adam reached for her hand, and together they walked toward the church. He cut a glance over to her and found her walking with her head held high and shining with radiance. They went up the steps together in the same strong stride they had when he'd come to church for the first time, using her as a crutch.

They moved through the foyer and into the chapel, which vibrated with the energy from the congregation as they chatted with each other before services began. He had to lead her down about halfway, and they had to sit on the side, but he let her go down the row first, and then he sat on the end.

He immediately put his arm around her and pulled her close. She fit in the space there when no one else ever had. When he pressed his lips to her hairline and whispered, "I have missed you so much. It's so good to see you," she didn't have a chance to respond before the choir started to sing.

Today, they came down both aisles and through the front doors, clapping and raising their voices in hallelujah. Some of the members of the congregation stood and clapped along with them, but Adam did not. Joey likewise, remained in her seat, tucked safely and securely against his side. He didn't want to wait through the sermon to talk to her, but he really had no other choice.

441

So he settled in to listen to the pastor, hoping and praying that when he could get Joey alone to talk, the Lord would have filled his mind and mouth with the exact words that he should say.

AN HOUR LATER, ADAM FOLLOWED JOEY UP THE AISLE and out of the chapel. They waited in line to talk to the pastor and shake his hand. Joey did that first, saying, "Thank you so much for that sermon today, Pastor Michaels. I need to reread that parable in the Bible."

"It's a good one," the pastor said. He smiled at Joey, and Adam gave him a tight-lipped smile too as he shook his hand, then he put his hand on Joey's lower back and guided her out of the building.

He hadn't seen her car, because it didn't wear bright pink glitter, so he led her back to his. When she was settled and he sat behind the wheel, he adjusted the heater so it would ward off the chill. Tension thickened to the air, but Adam took a deep breath of it anyway.

"I'm really sorry about yesterday," he said.

"How early did you get up this morning to get here?" she asked.

"Not that early." He glanced over to her. "I'm an early riser anyway."

She pressed her lips together and nodded. "You went home?"

"Yes," he said. "I showered and apparently grabbed the

wrong tie." He reached up and touched his cowboy hat. "But I got my hat."

She grinned at him then, and Adam's muscles started to melt.

"I can't promise you that there won't be other emergencies that come up that force me to pay attention to them instead of you," he said. "But I want you to know that every moment yesterday where I was letting you down was pure torture for me. I wanted to be here. I wanted to be with you."

She nodded. "Are you going back to Jackson today?"

He shook his head. "We found the equipment, and they have most of their stuff moved now."

He reached for her hand, noting that she wore the diamond bracelet he'd gotten her for Christmas. He smiled at it and then raised his head enough to see her past the brim of his cowboy hat. "I'm hoping you're up for an apartment tour, and then a drive to get some brisket, and then we have one more thing to move, so I'm afraid moving day isn't over."

"No?" she asked. "That's awful news, because yesterday was a pretty bad day."

He noticed the teasing glint in her eye and the playfulness in her voice. "Moving days are the worst," he said. "And I'm really sorry that I made it terrible."

"You've apologized enough," Joey said as she lifted her chin and shook her hair over her shoulders. "So you want a tour, and then you want brisket, and then you want to continue the torture and moving day—and this is all supposed to be a good thing?"

"Well, the tour is an amazing thing," he said. "And you love brisket, and I'll do all the heavy lifting, so that the bean bag gets put exactly where you want it."

He smiled at her, all of his hopes and dreams sitting a few feet away in his passenger seat. "So what do you think?" he asked. "Can I kiss you and do we have a plan for the rest of the day?"

43

J oey leaned over and pressed her lips to Adam's, feeling his smile against her mouth. His hand came up to cup her cheek, and warmth spread through her at his gentle touch.

"I love you," he murmured.

"Mm." Joey kissed him again. "I love you too." When she pulled back, his eyes shone with happiness and his smile kicked up in the corners.

"Oh, is that so?"

"Yeah." Joey ducked her head, but she wasn't embarrassed about how she felt. She looked up. "That's so."

"Well, that's great news," Adam said. He chuckled and added, "I'll come get your car once we have you fed and reading in your bean bag."

"There is no way I'm letting you drive my car," Joey said, her resistance to that sitting heavy in her gut.

"Why not?" he asked as he exited the parking lot. "It's a sedan, baby doll. I've driven one before."

She looked over to him and caught the jumping in Adam's jaw. "Okay," she said, letting go of this idea that she could hide any part of herself from him. "I warned her already that I was going to look for a new car this year."

He swung his attention to her. "Oh, yeah? How'd she take it?"

"She started right up." Joey grinned at him and reached for his hand. "I want the raspberry barbecue sauce. Can you get some of that?"

"Of course I can," Adam said, because Adam could do anything. He navigated them to the little roadside barbecue stand on the Northern Highway, and Joey once again waited in the car while he braved the winter wind to get their food.

The scent of roasted, smoked meat and tangy, sweet barbecue sauce filled the car upon his return, and Joey took the plastic bag from him so he could get back in. Her stomach growled, and Adam returned to his house.

"Stay here; I'll go grab the bean bag, and we'll head back to your place." He looked over to her, questions in his eyes. "Okay?"

"You don't want to eat?"

"At your place, I do." He flashed her a smile. "Unless you're starving, then we can eat here."

He didn't seem to want that, so Joey simply nodded. He did too, and Joey swallowed as he ducked out of the car and hurried into the house. She reached into the bag and pulled out one of the biscuits. She pinched off a corner of it and ate it, almost in disbelief that she sat in Adam's car when only a couple of hours ago, she'd been staring into an empty corner and wondering when she'd see him again.

The back of the SUV opened, and Joey twisted to see Adam shoving her fluffy pink bean bag in. "I gotta get the seats," he said, and he moved to do that, lowering them and then sliding the bean bag all the way to the backs of the front seats.

He panted as he got behind the wheel again, and she handed him the roll. "Oh, sneaking a bite early, are we?"

"I'm a little hungry," she said with a smile. Nerves bubbled in her stomach over showing him around her humble apartment, but the moment he leaned over and touched his lips to hers, all her worries melted away, the way cotton candy does with a single drop of water.

"I said we could eat here," he murmured, kissing her again, and then again. He leaned his forehead against hers, and she breathed in with him.

"I want to show you my apartment," she said. "I can wait."

"All right." He backed out of his garage and started the drive back to Coral Canyon. Joey relaxed in the heated seat and let the movement of the SUV and the gentle curves of the Apple Highway lure her to sleep.

She woke to the whip of cold air against her face, and Adam's voice saying, "We're here, baby doll."

Her eyes opened, and the world came into focus, including her gorgeous boyfriend's face. "I'm sorry," she said, not sure where the food had gone. She'd been holding it in her lap when they'd left Adam's house.

Adam smiled at her and backed up a step. He reached for Joey's hand, and she took it easily. She rose from the SUV, the cold striking all of her exposed skin.

She tucked her scarf tighter under the collar of her coat and said, "So this is the sidewalk."

Adam burst out laughing, and Joey giggled with him. She led him down the steps and into the apartment. She took a few steps inside and looked into the kitchen as Adam closed the door behind them.

He took a few steps and set the plastic bag with their barbecue on the table. "Let me get the bean bag."

"Adam—"

"I just want to get the moving done, so we can relax." He grinned at her and dashed out. Joey pulled out the Styrofoam containers with their food, and moved into the kitchen to get plates and utensils.

A pink wall moved through the door, and Adam groaned as he muscled the formless bean bag through the frame. He continued down the hall, and said, "Come tell me where to put this."

Joey left the food and moved slowly behind him, grinning as he wrestled the bean bag through the doorway into her bedroom. "Right there in the corner," she said, though Adam already knew where to put it.

He positioned the bean bag in the corner and stepped back to look at it. "Right there? Yeah?"

"It's awesome." Joey moved past him, kicked off her

heels, and flopped onto the bean bag. She grinned up at Adam, who beamed at her with the wattage of the sun. Her heartbeat fluttered as she reached for him.

"Come see how it feels."

"I thought you were going to show me the place." He took a couple of steps toward her, which was all it took in a bedroom as small as hers. "I'm not going to—"

Joey squealed as she lunged for him, grabbed one of his hands with both of hers, and pulled him onto the bean bag with her.

Adam's breath huffed out of his mouth as he tumbled beside her, and then the bean bag held him up. Joey curled into his warmth as she slid her hands under his suit coat jacket.

"You should've gotten clothes to change into," she murmured as she looked up at him.

"I'm making so many mistakes these days." He grinned down at her, his cowboy hat crooked now.

Joey reached up and straightened it for him, her eyes then dropping to his, and then lowering to his mouth. "Welcome to my home," she whispered just before she kissed him.

He kissed her back, gently pulling away a few moments later. "I love you, baby doll."

Joey accepted that, letting the words—the feeling—bury deep into her heart. "I know you do," she said, trailing her fingertips down the side of his face. "And I love you—I realized it yesterday when you weren't here. I love how hard you work, and how you take care of everyone, and how you're becoming this wonderful city-cowboy."

She smiled at him as the love she held for him grew and multiplied and filled her from top to bottom. He slid his thumb along her bottom lip. "I love you, and I can't wait to take you home to meet my momma, and to walk down the aisle with you, even if that's not what men and women do when they get married."

She giggled, and here, in this basement apartment with her secondhand furniture and her pink bean bag and the man she loved, a steady stream of belonging tingled through Joey—and she kissed Adam to remember this moment for the rest of her life.

44

Harry sat on the couch in a beautiful family room in the Silver Sage Mountain Lodge. This beautiful property sat a few miles north of Dog Valley in the foothills of the Teton Mountains, with plenty of state forest surrounding them. Harry and Belle had chosen it for their wedding as they had a gate that could close and cameras everywhere to alert them if people came onto the property.

The upscale facility boasted robust accommodations for guests doing events there, from conferences to concerts—to the wedding that he was about to participate in.

"Smile," Bryce said, and Harry looked up at his cousin. Bryce snapped a picture and then sank on the couch next to him. "You seem pretty chill for your wedding day."

"I'm a mess inside," Harry told him with a grin.

He glanced down at the tiny infant in his arms—six-

451

week-old Matthew—who snoozed peacefully as if nothing was happening around them. "He's helping a lot."

"He's the best," Bryce said, plenty of fatherly love and fondness in his voice. "You think you and Belle will have kids right away?"

"I don't know," Harry said. "She's a little bit older than me, but I think it'll take us a little bit to figure out how to just get along with each other." He chuckled at the same time Bryce said, "Oh brother, you guys get along great."

Harry and Belle did get along great, and he loved her with his whole heart and soul. They'd stayed at Silver Sage Mountain Lodge last night, and he'd asked all of his family to be there by noon for a three o'clock wedding. That way, the lodge could clear the area, make sure the media wasn't there, and close the gate.

Harry had deliberately kept the date, time, and location of his and Belle's nuptials off social media, but internet sleuths and those who really wanted to know could find out almost anything.

In the family room, there was a foosball table and a pool table and a giant big-screen TV—enough to entertain kids for a while, which Harry and various aunts and uncles had been doing for the past couple of hours.

Belle's family consisted of her daddy and a couple of brothers and sisters-in-law, and they'd stuck together over in one corner of the room, probably cowed by the pure size of the Youngs.

He hadn't seen Ev or Belle's mom in the room at all, and he didn't expect to. Aunt Hilde and the other aunts had been in and out, all of them exclaiming about Belle's dress this or Belle's hair that. A pit opened in Harry's stomach, and yes, he couldn't wait to see her come down the aisle toward him.

The bridal suite sat on the second floor, and she would come down a magnificently carved staircase to the aisle and then toward him. She wasn't an extravagant woman, but as she'd planned the wedding, he'd learned that she did like nice things. He didn't care how much anything cost, because his money was just rotting in the bank anyway, and he wanted her to have whatever would make her happy.

Someone stepped in front of him, and Harry glanced up to look at his daddy. "Uh oh," he said, seeing the look on his father's face. "What's that look for?"

Daddy's jaw jumped, his teeth tight together, and his eyebrows had drawn down into an angry V. "Your mother is at the front gate," he said. "And she can't get in."

"I'll take him," Bryce said quickly, and Harry transferred the sleeping baby to his cousin's arms. He stood up and went with his dad, his own displeasure coursing through him.

"She didn't even tell me she was coming," he said.

"No?" Daddy asked.

Harry shook his head. They left the family room and found Boston standing there. "Hey, Harry," he said. "I've got your mom on the line."

He took Harry into an office, all the while with Harry wondering what in the world was going on. "She called *you*?" he asked.

"No," Boston said, cutting a look out of the side of his

eye. "But there was a slight problem with the catering that I was handling, and so when the call came in, the secretary grabbed me real quick."

"Problem with the catering?" He looked over to his father, who shrugged one shoulder.

"It's handled," Boston said, and Harry swung his attention back to his cousin.

"Yes, but why are *you* handling it?"

Boston swallowed and said, "I happened to be right there, and I knew what to do. If I overstepped—"

"No, no," Harry said, waving his hand. "I didn't mean that." He grinned at Boston. "You're a good man, brother. Thanks for taking care of me and Belle."

He looked at the secretary, who nodded to the landline. Harry hadn't used one of those in forever, but he picked up the black receiver and held it to his mouth and ear. "Mom?" he asked.

"Oh, thank goodness," his mother said in her rich, model voice, now slightly frustrated. "They are refusing to open this gate."

"Yes," he said. "Because you had to be here by noon. The whole facility is locked down for the wedding today. We bought it out, and we have every room, every event space."

He didn't want anyone on-site but those he had personally invited—and could be here by noon.

"Well, my plane didn't land until one o'clock," she said.

"I was very clear in my invitation," he said.

"Harry," she chastised, and he recognized the frustration in her voice. "I am your mother."

"Who's with you?" he asked.

"No one," she said. "I came myself."

"A driver, then," he said.

His daddy put his hand on Harry's arm, and he looked up. He couldn't believe he was seriously considering denying his mother the opportunity to be at the wedding. He leaned closer to his father as he whispered, "They can send someone out to get her."

He sighed and rolled his head, stretching his neck. "All right, Momma, they're gonna send someone out to get you."

"I don't see why they can't open the gate and let my driver bring me in," she said.

"Because I don't want anyone here who was not invited," Harry said crisply. "If you can't wait for them to come get you, then you can't come."

He didn't have the bandwidth for this today, and he handed the phone back to Boston. He fumbled it and then raised it to his ear as well. "Yes, yes," he said. "They're sending someone right now." He nodded to the secretary, who picked up another phone to take care of this.

Harry left the office and stood out in the hall with his back pressed to the wall, taking one deep breath after another. "It's fine," he told his father when he joined him. "She's one person. There's room for her."

Boston exited the office and said, "I can shadow her, Harry, make sure she's not going to be a problem."

"Where's the wedding planner?" Harry asked. "Shouldn't she be doing that?"

Boston grinned at him and drew him into a tight hug. "I'm kind of helping her out today," he said, and he bustled off down the hall.

Harry watched him go. "They should hire him here," he said. "I don't even want to know what other problems he's handled or what other fires he's put out today."

Daddy chuckled and said, "No, you probably don't."

"Come on, let's get back to the family room, because it's almost time for you to be at the altar." In the room, Daddy closed the doors behind him, and then raised both hands above his head and whistled through his teeth. That got everyone to settle down.

"Harry has to leave in a couple of minutes, and he wanted me to say the family prayer."

Harry stood next to Adam, who held Joey's hand, and they all looked at his dad. Shushes and murmurs of "Uncle Trace is going to say a prayer" moved around the room, and then Daddy took off his cowboy hat.

Harry hadn't put his on yet—and he didn't even know where it was—but he clasped his hands in front of him and bowed his head.

"Dear God," Daddy said. "We're grateful to be gathered here together as family in this beautiful mountain setting, to watch two people in love unite themselves as one. Bless both Harry and Belle to have clear minds and open hearts and to listen to the advice given to them today. We're grateful for the knowledge that we are Thy sons and daughters, and bless us to do good and to carry Thy name well. Amen."

His daddy never said more than necessary, but Harry added his "Amen" to the chorus of them moving through the room. The door opened as if on cue, and the wedding planner poked her head in and said, "I need the wedding party in the hall and the groom at the altar," in a crisp, no-nonsense voice.

Harry moved into action then, because he didn't want Belle to have to wait for him for a single extra moment. He hugged his daddy, who clapped him on the back and said, "I'm so excited for you. Try to listen to everything."

"I will," Harry promised, and he took the black cowboy hat from his father and positioned it on his head.

Then he hugged his grandmother and his grandfather, and moved on to Bryce and Codi. By the time he made it out of the room, the wedding party had lined up off to the side, and he had to hug every one of them, too.

Liesl and Cash, Corinne and Eric, Cole and Rosie, Boston and Beth, Bryce and Codi, Kassie and Reggie, and finally, Adam and Joey. He loved them both in unique ways, and as he clung to his former manager and best friend who didn't have the last name Young, Harry silently recognized in just how many ways Adam had saved him over the years. He pulled back and said, "Love you, brother," before he turned and went with the wedding planner.

She took him down the hall, then jogged to the left, and they went down another side hall and then through a door that ran through a narrow passageway and emptied into the big ballroom—where he was to be married.

Harry took his place at the altar with the pastor. He breathed in the grandeur of the place, with the high domed ceiling and the chandelier hanging down from above. Windows lined both sides and had pale pink stained glass with ivy running through them. The sunlight sparkled on the floor like someone had crushed up stars and diamonds together and sprinkled the dust about.

Every chair had been tied with a white ribbon, and the altar was similarly dressed with bows and flowers in the purest white Harry had ever seen. The staircase in front of him bore the same white satin, which felt rich and luxurious to him, with deep red roses positioned at the peak of every drape.

He stood there for what felt like a long time, nodding and smiling to the wedding guests as they entered in classic, traditional fashion—one couple or family at a time. His daddy had missed the memo, and he sent Keri, Clay, and Avery running down the aisle toward him, filling this reverent, beautiful space with their calls and laughter.

Harry knelt down and received his siblings into his arms, laughing with them. Then Ev called them back to her, and they sat in the very front row while Daddy hugged Harry again.

He hadn't seen his mother yet, but he watched each of his aunts and uncles enter and find a seat.

His former bandmates waved to him from further back.

Belle's family entered together—including her mother,

so she must be ready to go. His blood started to hum in his veins then, because he couldn't wait to see his bride.

The wedding party hadn't arrived yet, and Harry still hadn't seen his mother. Surely it wouldn't take that long to drive out to the gate and get her. Boston had been lined up with everyone else, so someone else must've been tasked with getting her.

He glanced up, catching movement at the top of the staircase. His pulse did back handsprings, because only Belle would be coming down the staircase.

He told himself he couldn't control what happened with his mother and her international flights and her refusal to honor his requests. He didn't want to be thinking about that right now anyway, not when his bride was about to walk toward him, and the love of his life was going to become his wife.

Pretty music started, and the crowd made a gasping, almost groaning noise as they stood and turned toward the back where Harry had been looking all along. Boston and Beth stepped down the aisle first, both of them dressed to the nines and beaming brilliantly, but Harry's eyes had caught on the movement at the top of the staircase.

Belle had to come down twenty-four stairs, and she did it one at a time while their wedding party moved down the aisle toward Harry in a slow—measured—steady—pace.

He watched her feet approach, and then the hem of her dress. It belled at her knees and then clung to her curves in a gorgeous mermaid style gown of pure white. Lace covered the whole thing, and pearls caught the sunlight coming in the pink glass, which made them glisten like pale, opaque rubies.

She carried a small bouquet of red roses that stood out among the snowy whiteness of her dress, and when she reached the floor, the aisle had been cleared of all groomsmen and bridesmaids. They'd separated and now sat in the second row of the congregation, and Belle alone stood at the head of the aisle.

Harry could not stop smiling, and Belle leaned into her father's kiss, and then they proceeded toward him. He'd loved living life with her, off the grid, out of the spotlight, and the whole world slowed down the way it usually did when she finally arrived in front of him.

"Wow," he whispered, taking her hands in his. "You are gorgeous, and I love you so much."

She half-laughed and half-cried, and Harry took her unto himself and turned to face the pastor.

The pastor smiled warmly at them and then addressed the congregation. "Dear friends and family of Harry Young and Belle Graves, I am thrilled to be here with you today." He had a loud voice that carried in the open space.

"We are gathered here today to witness the union of Harry and Belle in holy matrimony. Their love is a testament to the strength and beauty that two people can bring into each other's lives. Now, it is not easy to take two different lives, from two different families, and merge them into one. It will take patience, sacrifice, compromise, love, and faith."

He held up a finger for each thing he named. "I hope

you'll approach each situation you find yourselves in with those five things," he said. "Really try to see things from the other person's point of view, and take anything and everything possible to the Lord. He can help guide you both to a place where you can come together, counsel together, and build a life together."

He turned to Harry, who had done his best to listen to every word, the way he'd promised his daddy. "Well, I think it's time to get married, yes?"

"Yes, sir," Harry said, and his voice sounded like a boom in the great hall. Several people laughed, and Belle's low giggle was one of them.

"Harry, I believe you have vows for your lovely bride."

Harry took a deep breath, turned toward Belle, and centered himself by looking straight into her pretty eyes. "Belle, from the moment I met you, I knew you were someone special. You bring light and laughter into my life every day, and I promise to support you and stand by your side through every challenge and triumph. I vow to listen to you with compassion and understanding and to speak to you with encouragement and respect. I promise to create a life with you filled with learning, laughter, and love—and cats. I vow to honor and cherish you for all the days of my life."

He nodded. "I love you endlessly, and I want nothing more than this small-town life with you at my side."

Belle reached up and swiped quickly at her eyes. "I suppose it's my turn."

A laugh burst out of Harry's mouth. "Yes, baby. It's your turn."

She grinned at him, and he loved her steadiness. "Harry, you are my rock and my best friend. With you, I've found the love and care and compassion I needed in my life."

Sniffling sounded around them, but Harry kept his focus on his almost-wife.

"I promise to stand by you in life's joyous moments, as well as its challenges, to lift you up when you are down, and to always celebrate your successes. I vow to trust and respect you and to grow with you in mind and spirit. I promise to create a home filled with laughter, patience, and understanding. Today, I choose you and promise to choose you every day for the rest of our lives."

She nodded, and Harry leaned in and pressed his cheek to hers.

"All right." The pastor spread his arms wide and brought them back together as Harry and Belle turned back to face him. "Harry, do you take Belle to be your lawfully wedded wife, to have and to hold, from this day forward, for better or for worse, for richer, for poorer, in sickness and in health, to love and to cherish, till death do you part?"

Harry looked into Belle's eyes, his voice steady and full of emotion. "I do."

The pastor then turned to Belle. "Belle, do you take Harry to be your lawfully wedded husband, to have and to hold, from this day forward, for better or for worse, for richer, for poorer, in sickness and in health, to love and to cherish, till death do you part?"

Belle smiled, her voice soft but unwavering. "I do."

"By the power vested in me by the state of Wyoming

and the Good Lord Above, I now pronounce you husband and wife. Cowboy, you may kiss your bride."

Harry turned toward Belle, marveling that a few moments and some simple sentences sealed Belle to him and him to her.

He grinned and pulled Belle toward him. She smiled back, and Harry slid one hand along the side of her face and kissed her, the warmth and love of the moment enveloping him and Belle as their family and friends erupted into yeehaws and applause.

45

"I hope they have those pistachio croissants again," Joey said as Adam pulled into the Sip and Stay. He grinned over at her, wondering how much he should tell her.

It would all come out in the end, and he wanted it to be a surprise, so he simply said, "I hope so too."

But he knew they would. He'd asked Louisa specifically to make them for today and to make sure that she didn't sell out before they arrived for their mid-afternoon coffee date at two-thirty. He didn't expect the place to be busy at this time of day, and the parking lot didn't have very many cars in it. His pulse pounded at him because he knew there would be a lot of *trucks* around the back, and he knew Joey was observant enough to pick up on them if they'd parked out in front of the coffee shop.

He cut the engine, glared at the gray sky, and sent up

one more plea for sunshine, though it technically wasn't necessary for a proposal. He got out of the car, his hand automatically sliding into his left pocket where he kept the diamond ring he'd bought. He and Joey were flying to Tennessee tomorrow, and she'd meet his momma in another twenty-four hours. Adam did not want to take home a girl-friend. He wanted to take home a *fiancée*.

He glanced toward the coffee shop, didn't see anyone, and proceeded to open Joey's door for her.

"It's freezing out here," he said.

Joey smiled as she rose from the SUV. "You've even got your winter coat on, baby." She gripped his collar and leaned in to kiss him. "Maybe that will warm you up," she said.

"A peck?" he asked. "That doesn't warm anyone up." He chuckled and took her hand.

They started toward the coffee shop as she said, "Well, I'm not gonna make out with you in the parking lot."

"Maybe the Sip and Stay will be empty," he said.

She gave him a dry look. "We're not making out in there either."

He grinned at her. "I knew I should have just made coffee at my house."

She giggled again, quickly sobering. She'd been doing that a lot this week, and Adam squeezed her hand. "Are you nervous about meeting my momma?"

"Yes," she said. "I've never been to Tennessee, and I've never met anyone's momma."

"She's going to love you," Adam said. "I guarantee she'll cry."

"Is she gonna be worried about how old I am?" Joey asked.

"I don't think so," Adam said. "When I first told her about us, I told her you were young, and she didn't seem to care—as long as you weren't eighteen."

He grinned and reached for the door, holding it open as Joey walked in and Adam quickly followed her.

A single couple sat in the corner, their pastry wrappers empty, indicating that they'd been here for a while. Adam didn't truly care, though he had hoped to do his proposal only for friends and family. Joey went right up to the counter where Louisa pushed out from the swinging black door that led into the back.

"Oh, you've got the pistachio croissant," she said.

"Yes, we do." Louisa looked at Adam, so much knowing in her eyes. "You want that, dear?"

"Yes, please," Joey said. "And I think today I'll take...." She trailed off as she looked up to the menu. "I don't know. You order, baby."

Adam cleared his throat. "Extra-large Americano, please." He glanced over to Joey. "Didn't you want hot chocolate?"

"I did," she said. "But now that we're here, the coffee smells so good." She brought her hand up to her mouth and bit her nail, and Adam felt like doing the same, his own nerves rioting through him in an unkind way.

"You know what? I want a flat white latte," she said. "No, no, I don't."

He pulled his wallet out and waited while Joey looked at the menu again. "You know what? I want the hot chocolate with marshmallow cream."

"You got it, sweetie." Louisa put the order in, and Adam paid. She set the pistachio croissant on a plate, and Joey picked it up and turned to face the café.

Adam didn't care which table she picked, as the whole place held about fifteen of them, and he was planning to fill the space with people and music before too long.

"Right here by the window?" Joey asked. "Look, the sun's come out a little bit."

"Look at that," Adam said, and he pulled her chair out for her before he sat down across from her.

Their drinks came quickly, including the agave packets that Adam liked, and he stirred them into his coffee, wondering how to start this conversation. He'd never proposed to a woman before, and he, Harry, and Bryce had been over several ideas before he'd landed on this one.

"Back to the site of our first date," Joey said.

Adam looked up at her. "Oh, so you're counting this as our first date now?"

"Yes, silly," she said, her smile infectious and her eyes so bright. "I told you, we can't have kissed before our first date. So that means the coffee date was our first date."

"Coffee and cowboy hat shopping," he grinned at her.

"It's not a bad first date, right?" Joey asked. "So let's make sure we get the story straight for your mom. I don't want her thinking that I just kiss everyone who manages to make it out of a snowstorm."

She giggled, and Adam chuckled with her. "Speaking of my mom," he said, though that wasn't what he wanted to talk about at all. He cleared his throat, his hand migrating to his thigh, where he felt the distinct outline of the ring in his pocket. He leaned back, because that was the first clue for those watching, and then he paused as the couple in the corner got up and started to leave. He sat forward again as Joey's brow furrowed in confusion.

"Speaking of your mom, what?" she asked. "Is there something else I need to know not to say?"

He'd told her about how she loved steamed broccoli and made a lemon-mayo sauce to go over it. Joey had blinked and said, "Wow, I've never heard of that."

"Try to act as normal as possible when you see her eat it," Adam had advised, and that had launched a whole series of questions from Joey about what she could expect about his mother.

"No, nothing like that," Adam said, as the couple finally finished cleaning up and walked by them. He looked up at them so as not to have to say something else. The very moment he heard the bell on the door chime, he leaned back again.

"I've just been thinking," he said, raising his voice. "It would be way better if I could take home a fiancée instead of a girlfriend."

Joey blinked, "I...what?"

Adam grinned at her and stood up. He heard footsteps

behind him, and Joey glanced that way about the same time that Harry said, "Here you go, buddy." Adam turned and took the guitar from his best friend, the man who had literally changed his life by bringing him to Coral Canyon and introducing him to the Young family—including Joey.

Adam positioned himself next to Harry on his right, while Bryce came up on his left. The fact that Adam thought he could play the guitar as well as either one of them was a complete joke, but Joey had been asking him if he would ever play for her, and he figured a proposal was as good a time as any. He'd only been taking lessons for three months now, but he knew enough to pluck out a few chords and sing a few lyrics.

Harry had written the song for him, and it was only thirty seconds long, and Adam told himself he could do anything for thirty seconds if the prize was kissing Joey at the end with a pink diamond ring on her finger.

"We're waiting on you, buddy," Bryce said jovially.

Adam swallowed, took a deep breath, and looked Joey straight in the eyes—hers were wide and impossibly blue— and he reminded himself that he loved this woman and wanted to spend the rest of his life with her. That got his fingers to start moving, and he plucked through the simple notes like the novice he was.

Joey smiled, and that only encouraged him to keep going.

"Meeting you changed my life," he sang.

"In this small town, you're my light,

With flour-dusted hands, we bake our dreams,

Joey

Side by side, through the highs and extremes."

Bryce and Harry joined in on the chorus, their three guitars and three voices suddenly stronger and better together. Adam's confidence grew when he wasn't singing alone, and he really belted out the words.

Oh Joey, my sweet Roo,
My heart beats only for you.
Through fields of gold and skies so blue,
I promise, baby doll, I'll always choose you.
When the days are hard and nights are long,
Together, our love makes us strong.

When they reached the end of the chorus, Harry and Bryce backed off on their playing once again, showcasing Adam as he sang the second verse.

From cupcakes to sunsets, I've found my home,
With you, I know I'm never alone.
We'll face the snow, the wind, and rain,
'Cause a love like ours will always remain.

Then they all three started to play toward the chorus again, and then again, and then pure relief rushed through Adam as more guitars joined them.

He watched only Joey, his own fingers forgetting to play as her eyes widened, her mouth dropped open, and her hands came up to cover it.

Luke, Gabe, and Morris came in the front door of the coffee shop, while Tex, Trace, and Otis came up from behind with Mav, Blaze, and Jem stumbling out of the restroom, where Adam hoped they hadn't been hiding for too long. They all started to play the intro to the chorus again, but none of them started singing as Joey's aunts and cousins started to fill the space.

The front door opened again, and Adam somehow heard the chime above all the guitars twanging through the space, and he glanced over as Cecily escorted Jerry inside, and Gloria shuffled along with Lauren. He nodded to a table across from Joey, where they all sat, except for Jerry, who took a guitar from Mav, looped the strap over his shoulder, and started to play with them.

Joey cried openly now, and Adam joined back in on the intro to the chorus as Otis himself stepped forward and led them all into singing it.

Oh Joey, my sweet Roo,
My heart beats only for you.
Through fields of gold and skies so blue,
I promise, baby doll, I'll always choose you.
When the days are hard and nights are long,
Together, our love makes us strong.

With only a couple of words to go, Adam stepped away from this group of good examples of how to be husbands and fathers and men. He handed his guitar to Georgia, reached into his pocket, and pulled the pink diamond out. He dropped to both knees in front of Joey, glad her eyes stayed glued to his.

"I love you," he said as the voices faded and the guitars quieted. "I love you with everything I have and everything I am. I love your sense of responsibility and duty, and I love your hard-working spirit and how you set goals for yourself and go after them. I love how you take care of those around you, and I love having you in my life. I love the things you cook for me, and I love your love of pink, sparkly things."

He held up the diamond, which was pink and sparkly. "I hope this is the most amazing, bestest, brightest pink sparkly thing you'll ever own, and I would love it if you would be my wife. Will you marry me?"

Joey's eyes dropped to the ring, where her smile only widened, and when she looked at him again, she raised both fists into the air and said, "Yes!" Then she leaned right over that pink pear-shaped diamond and kissed him.

Her family started to cheer, with cowboys clapping against their guitars and making hollow, discordant sounds to go with their voices. Adam laughed, the kiss sloppy, and he took Joey's left hand and steadied it in his before he slid the ring on her finger. He kissed the knuckle above it and below it, and then inched a little closer to her so that he could kiss his fiancée properly.

"I love you," he whispered against her lips.

"I love you too," she said back, her smile wonderful and glorious. "You staged this whole thing?"

He grinned. "The Sip and Stay is ours from now until closing, and Louisa made a half dozen pistachio croissants for you."

She grinned. "The mob is pressing in," she said. "So kiss me one more time before we get separated."

Adam did, and then Joey stood and got swept into her mother's arms while Adam let Harry and Bryce help him back to his feet. The first person he came face to face with was Otis, who grinned and grabbed him, pulling him into a hug as he said, "You take good care of her."

"I will, sir," Adam promised. "I love her."

"Yeah, I know," Otis said. They both looked over to where Joey held out her left hand for Rosie, Liesl, and Corrine to admire the diamond. "And she loves you too."

Read on for a sneak peek at **BOSTON**, the next book in the Young Brothers series. Oh, something is going to go down at the Silver Sage Mountain Lodge and Resort...

Preorder BOSTON by scanning this code with your phone:

Sneak Peek! Boston, Chapter One:

Boston Simpson couldn't wait to get back to his apartment, even though it was small, and loosen this tie. Abandon it in favor of a T-shirt and his pair of cowboy boots, so he could go horseback riding in this glorious summer sunshine.

"Have you met her yet?"

Boston looked up from the digital checklist for an upcoming wedding at the Silver Sage Mountain Lodge and Resort. He'd been working here for four months now, after stepping in to help with several issues during Harry and Belle's wedding and getting noticed by the customer service manager.

"Not yet," he said to Julie, the woman who did his job when he wasn't at the lodge. They worked well together, and Julie was always willing to coordinate with Boston to trade shifts. They had each other's backs with their boss too —a woman named Mae Silver.

This lodge had been in her family for three generations, and it hadn't taken much to woo Boston away from his job in Jackson Hole. Silver Sage paid better, had better hours, and was far closer to where Boston really wanted to live: Coral Canyon.

He missed Cash, but his cousin trained for the rodeo relentlessly. If he wasn't at the gym, he was at the arena, training with his coach. And if he wasn't there, he'd be working with his horse.

Boston had enjoyed living with his cousin, and they still texted every single day. He'd gotten up and gone to church with Cash, and the two of them had helped each other stay strong—and sane—without the support and strength of their families.

He looked at the list in front of him, and he typed in today's date for the follow-up email for the facility rental, though he hadn't sent it yet.

He currently managed the wedding details for Adam and Joey, Boston's cousin. He'd specifically asked to have this wedding, though he'd never done one before.

Joey and Adam had booked the lodge and grounds for their wedding in September, though they weren't renting the whole she-bang the way Harry had done.

Of course, Adam wasn't a mega-star country music star celebrity who needed to keep his nuptials off the Internet. Joey wanted something nice that she didn't have to think too much about, and that fit Silver Sage to a T.

In fact, Boston had been tasked to think through and coordinate all the details—and he loved it.

Joey and Adam, he typed out on the laptop he'd been assigned. *You are ninety days from your event, and we can't wait to have you at the Silver Sage Mountain Lodge and Resort for your wedding!*

At this time, most couples book a slot on the grounds for their engagement pictures or bridal photos, and with summer here in Wyoming, it's a great time to pose for the perfect picture for your event.

We have a list of professional photographers we can provide for you, should you desire that, and if you'd like to book a photo shoot at Silver Sage, in one of our beautiful gardens, the orchard, or the gorgeous National Forest, please click this calendar and choose the time that works best for you.

Boston pasted in the link for the photography calendar, and quickly typed out the rest of the email about the costs, and what facilities would be available on picture day.

I'll be following up next month to make sure we have your final menu solidified and we'll schedule a walk-through with a mock-up of your event then too, to ensure we have time to make any changes you want to make your special day absolutely spectacular.

He typed his name and sent the email he'd said he'd already sent, and leaned back in his chair.

He glanced over to Julie, who'd buried herself in her computer too. "Have *you* met the new boss yet?"

Julie looked away from her work instantly. "I saw her

come in, yes." Her bright blue eyes shone with all the tea, but she didn't spill it.

Boston grinned at her. "And? Don't hold back."

"She was wearing stilettos," Julie whispered the last word like it was dirty. "And skin-tight jeans, and a tank top that looked like it had been made of feathers and clouds."

Boston grinned and grinned, reaching up and stretching his arms high above his head. "So she's a total city girl."

As suspected.

To Boston, it wasn't a suspicion. Mae's oldest daughter had moved to and had been living in Miami for the past decade, and what Boston spent his time speculating about was whether Cora would know what she was doing.

Her mother had told the staff here at Silver Sage that Cora had been running a hotel in Miami, and she'd know how to manage all the pieces of the lodge.

Boston wasn't so sure about that, because Silver Sage was a hotel, yes. But that was only part of what the lodge was. They hosted several events every month, and they led outdoor wilderness camps and expeditions. They had acres and acres of grounds that had to be maintained, and nothing he could even imagine in Miami looked like the sprawling, wooded facility that was Silver Sage.

They had three separate gardens, one of which held seventeen sculptures done by a local artist in Rusk, and a beautiful apple orchard where they held weekly cider tastings.

"She carried a huge bag too," Julie said. "Like, as a purse, and she had three people helping her with her luggage."

"You would too, if you'd moved here from Florida." He didn't know anything about the Silvers, as Mae had two daughters—twins—and they were several years older than Boston. They also hailed from Rusk, a tiny community about an hour north of Coral Canyon, with this land about ten minutes from both Rusk and Dog Valley.

"Hey, did you still want to meet Ottie?" Julie asked, and Boston sighed heavily.

"I don't know," he said. "You've set me up with three women now, and I'm starting to think you don't know me at all."

"Hey." She nudged him with her elbow. "I know you, and Ottie's fun."

"You said that about LucyAnn too," he said. "And she took one look at me and immediately made up an upset stomach." He chuckled, though that had not been a fun night.

"I think I'm going to pass on any more blind dates," he said. "There's got to be a way to meet women in other ways, right?"

"Sure," Julie said.

"How did you meet Callen?" he asked.

She grinned at him mischievously. "My sister set me up with him...on a blind date." She laughed, and Boston joined her, though he shook his head.

He groaned as he stood up. "Well, I have to go ride the Wicker Road Trail for that group I'm taking out tomorrow."

"Okay." Julie went back to her computer. "Walk real slow past Mae's office, and text me if you catch sight of her."

She made Cora Silver sound like a zoo animal, and Boston didn't go down the hall toward Mae's office at all.

He turned in the other direction and headed to the staff living quarters—a nice, two-story building that sat out of the way, out of sight of the guests, where he had a one-bedroom, one-bath unit on the second floor.

The sunshine outside helped Boston breathe a little easier, and he really loved the mix of his job from inside, desk work to outside, get-dirty work.

He walked along the immaculately kept gravel road, moving past the guest lodges and cabins, listening to the sky be blue and the wind whisper through the pine trees. Around the corner and past the tall Ponderosa pines waited the staff quarters.

Boston sighed and smiled just seeing the building, and he couldn't wait to get to the stables, which stood with the horses on the other side of the road.

He stepped into the air conditioning of his little space, relaxing and settling into the peace that always came with going home. As he unknotted his tie, he pulled out his phone.

I'm riding the trail for tomorrow's group, he sent to the stable manager, a man named Cotton. *Who should I saddle for that?*

He stepped out of his slacks and stuffy shirt and into his regular cowboy clothes. He hung his dress hat on a hook and picked up the cowboy hat he wore when riding or working outside.

He sprayed sunscreen on his arms, so he could tell his

momma he had, and he grabbed a bottle of water and started drinking it on the way over to the stables.

I'm at the stable, Cotton said. *I can go over tomorrow with you. The group is one of our return, Gold Status Groups, and I don't think you've worked with them before.*

Boston's pulse bumped a little harder, and he wondered why he'd been assigned to this ride with a group who surely someone else *had* worked with.

He found Cotton driving a wheelbarrow toward their compost pile, and he joined him with a "Howdy, Cotton."

The older man smiled. Cotton was nearing forty, and he was one of the strongest, kindest men Boston had ever met. "Howdy, Boston." He dumped the straw and waste he'd cleaned out of a stall, and reached to shake Boston's hand.

"Who do we have tomorrow?" he asked, needing this pit in the bottom of his stomach to be filled.

Cotton cut a look over to him. "The Silvers."

The hole fell out of his gut, and Boston sucked in a breath to fill it. "I'm gonna need the day off."

Cotton laughed, but Boston wasn't kidding. "You'll be fine with them. Mae's riding, with her daddy and her daughters."

"Is it some sort of test?" he asked, wondering if it was for him—or for Cora, who'd been called home to run the lodge reluctantly.

Boston didn't want to make judgments on the woman, because he wouldn't like it if someone came to learn about him through rumors and a single staff meeting where his daddy gave the highlights of his life.

His mother had taught him not to gossip, that doing so was like dipping his hand in tar and then trying to change a pillowcase without getting it dirty.

Impossible.

She'd told him that gossip and rumors didn't serve anyone but our own egos, that they made him soiled in his soul, and Boston had tried to keep his hands clean as much as possible.

"Have you met Cora?" he asked.

"Sure," Cotton said easily, but everything he did came out easy and calm. "I've got a list of horses for you to have ready. She likes Marigold."

"Oh, I love that horse," Boston said. "Goldie is really calm."

So it wouldn't matter that Cora hadn't been home in a year and hadn't ridden the horse in probably longer. Any of the horses here were used to strangers riding them once and never meeting them again, but when Cotton asked, "Who do you want?" Boston cocked his eyebrows.

"I can have anyone I want?"

"Anyone but Two Wolves," Cotton said. "He did a ride this morning, but everyone else has been grazing and getting fat." He threw Boston a grin. "So yeah, choose anyone you want."

"Coach," Boston said without hesitation. He loved the pretty bay with a gentle-giant spirit.

"Coach is yours," Cotton said as he moved over to the wall and lifted a clipboard off the nail there. "Your paper is here for the other horse assignments. Darren will need the stool, and Mae wants you to bring water and snacks and be ready to do a campfire and make lunch."

Cotton handed him the paper. "Everything you need is here, and the chefs know. They're expecting you in the morning."

Surprise streamed through Boston, because he'd never done a campfire or lunch on the Wicker Road Trail either. But he simply said, "Okay," and looked at the paper. On the back, a map had been included, and the spot for the campfire clearly marked.

"Thanks," he said to Cotton, and then he went to saddle his horse.

As he set out, everything inside him relaxed and soft now, Boston started thinking through where and how he could meet someone he might find interesting enough to date. He lived and worked full-time here, and he spent his free time driving down to Coral Canyon for family thing upon family thing.

Birthday parties, cousin nights, get-togethers for coffee and dinner and dessert. The Young family was huge, and Boston wanted to maintain and keep building those relationships.

It was the whole reason he'd snapped up this job closer to home.

But as he tipped his head back and drank in the blue, blue sky, he prayed, "It would be nice to meet someone special, though, Lord. So guide my feet toward them, if it be Thy will."

Sneak Peek! Boston, Chapter Two:

Cora Silver could feel eyes on her, though she'd left her cabin, where she'd been meeting with her mother, her twin sister, Kat's husband, and the three managers of the family lodge for the past few hours. She had been on the ground in Wyoming for a little over twenty-four hours, and she couldn't say she was happy about it.

The sun shone, but it wasn't nearly the same hot, vibrant Miami sun that Cora had fallen in love with and lived under for the past decade. She tried smiling, because she saw no reason to wallow in the situation longer than she had to.

She'd known she'd have to return to this sprawling piece of property where she'd grown up sooner or later. She kind of hoped that she would get married and start having a family first, but deep down, she knew that Katherine would win that race. She'd always known that.

Kat was married, with a two-year-old little girl and twins of unknown gender on the way. She had been working at Silver Sage Mountain Lodge and Resort in the years Cora had gone to college and then taken over a luxury boutique hotel in Miami.

She'd been telling herself for a couple of months now that the job here was the same, but the towering Teton Mountains in the distance told her it wasn't, and the scent of horse flesh and hay and manure also testified as much.

The fact that the walls of her home were made of blonde pine planks also told her that she'd left Miami in the rearview mirror. No more couches with zebra print, or flashy lights in the middle of a Wednesday afternoon, or little cocktail glasses full of pink liquid and umbrella straws.

She'd never really gotten into the beach life, though the hotel she managed sat right on the sand. She'd seen plenty of trouble come through the front doors, and truth be told, her soul needed something a little slower, a little quieter, and a little more wholesome.

She just wished it didn't come with a winter quite as biting as Wyoming's. "You've got six months until winter," she told herself, and then quickly amended it to four. Sometimes it snowed before Halloween, and it would be October in four months, and Cora would have to get a whole new wardrobe before then. She certainly didn't own any cold weather gear coming from Florida.

Her father had passed away several years ago, and while Cora's momma had always played a huge role at Silver Sage, she'd been leading the staff of over one hundred here ever since. She and Daddy had tried for ten years to have babies, and finally, through the miracle of modern medicine, they'd gotten two girls at the same time.

Cora was older by six minutes, and she'd known all paths led back to Silver Sage Mountain Lodge and Resort. She didn't have to like it, though, especially not on day one.

"You'll grow to love it," she said, only a touch of bite in her tone as she mocked something her mother had said when she'd first called a few months ago to tell Cora that it was time to come home. Kat was pregnant again, due at the beginning of November, and Momma would be seventy a few weeks before that.

Cora turned toward the good, earthy scent of the stables and walked down the gravel path that ran in front of them. She didn't see anyone, thankfully, because her emotions stormed out of control, and she had no idea if she would burst into laughter, break down into tears, or glare someone's face off if she encountered them.

She only knew she needed to be alone, and she ducked around the corner of the stable and pressed her back into the warm wood, which faced west. The sun shone down on her, casting a halo effect around the Teton Mountains and making her breath catch with the beauty of God's creations.

Yes, Cora had loved Wyoming at some point in her past. "And you will again," she told herself out loud. It would just take some getting used to, and no one could fault her for that. Truth be told, she didn't think they did, and she'd been so overwhelmed with the packets and folders thrust at her today that she feared she had put off a vibe that she didn't want to be here.

"Well, they're not entirely wrong about that either," she muttered.

She stood in the sunshine and simply breathed, and when she didn't feel like her own ribs would suffocate her, she went around the other side of the stable and found several horses with their heads hanging out of their stalls. Pure joy filled her, because Cora had been a country girl in her youth. Something deep and hidden yawned inside her, reminding her that she could become one again.

Every time she came home, her mother made her ride. Cora had hated it for the past several years, mostly because it felt like a manipulation tactic that Momma was using to get Cora to *volunteer* to come home.

Now she moved down the row of horses, lovingly giving each one of them a stroke down the side of their neck, though the animals scared her a little bit. They had such big heads and bodies, and her daddy had taught her to respect their space—and also demand that they obey her.

They'll take a mile if you give them a millimeter, he'd said, and Cora smiled to herself, pure missing and homesickness combining together into a terrible feeling that slipped through her blood like water over cliffs.

In Miami, it had been far easier to manage her emotions. Every little thing she saw didn't remind her of something amazing her father had taught her or said or that they had done together. She didn't have to see that her mother had aged and couldn't keep up with the lodge anymore. She didn't have to see her sister's sad face as she talked about Daddy and hosted birthday dinners in his honor.

Cora could experience all of that from afar, inside a very busy life. She'd lived with her best friend in a tiny, two-bedroom, one-bath condo on the outskirts of the city, and Cora could admit that she should have come home sooner.

"I'm sorry, Daddy," she whispered as she finally reached the end of the row of horses and found her favorite one—Marigold.

"Hey, my beautiful girl," she said to the pale yellow horse. She was technically a gray, and Cora loved the gentle creature with everything inside her. Her mother had scheduled horseback riding for tomorrow morning, where Cora was sure her training would continue. Jeremy, Kat's husband, had added several trails and riding expeditions to their excursions, and every employee at Silver Sage knew about and had personally experienced every offering provided to guests.

So Cora's schedule for the next several weeks looked like she was on vacation in the wilds of Wyoming, when really she was retraining herself to know everything that her mother and sister had built into Silver Sage.

Suddenly, she didn't want tomorrow to be the first time she had to saddle a horse—in front of everyone, no less. Acting quickly, she entered the stable and went into the tack room to get Marigold's saddle.

She struggled under the weight of it, as Cora really was used to lifting paper clips or a stapler and working on a computer. She stayed in the air-conditioned tack room and watched a couple of videos to remember how to properly saddle a horse. Then she brought Marigold out of her stall and threw the rope around the tethering rail in front of it.

It took her several long minutes, but she managed to saddle the horse and get herself atop her. "Look at that," she said to herself, joy and pride streaming through her now, chasing away disappointment of leaving behind a great job and good friends and, yes, a boyfriend in Miami.

She shook Tomas out of her head, because they'd technically broken up before Thanksgiving last year. Out of the pair of them, she was the only one who'd hoped they'd get back together.

Perhaps she'd left a broken heart in Miami and could have a fresh start here. She rejected that idea too, because Cora needed a boyfriend like she needed another hole in her head.

She had plenty on her plate just trying to get caught up with everything happening at the lodge—not to mention the cabin she'd been given to live in needed to be emptied from top to bottom, scrubbed clean, and put back together.

She clicked her tongue and gently pushed her heels back into Marigold's body. The horse moved forward at a slow, plodding pace, as she usually did. Hopefully, Cora would be able to get the horse saddled and get her moving like this tomorrow as well, and maybe then her mother wouldn't look at her like she'd made the worst mistake possible by asking Cora to come home and take over the operations of the lodge.

She walked the horse straight across the field that sat in

front of the stable, nearing the woods. A chill seemed to emanate from them, and Cora didn't want to go into the shady depths alone. Wild animals lived out there, and she needed to remember that.

With the property close to the Teton National Forest and Park and Yellowstone National Park, there definitely were more wolves and bears in the area than ever.

She turned Marigold, proud that she could pull a little bit on the left rein and get the horse to turn and walk parallel to the edge of the forest.

Some of this was their private land. If Cora hadn't been shown fifteen thousand pieces of paper today, she might remember the exact acreage. As it was, she knew it was somewhere in the vicinity of one hundred acres, and they took private hunting parties out during deer and elk season.

In fact, Cora could remember a time when she was nine years old and had come outside to feed the horses—her chore at the time—and come across a magnificent herd of buffalo bedded down in the snow in the very field she had just crossed.

"Some things never change," she murmured to herself, and this time, the feeling of nostalgia and being home struck a happy chord inside her.

Marigold's hooves made clopping noises against the dirt and snapping sounds in the underbrush where twigs and leaves had fallen. She relaxed fully, and the thought of *It's sure good to be home* had just crossed her mind when a loud, whip-like cracking sound filled the air.

Cora yelped, immediately tightening her hold on the

reins as Marigold also whinnied, rose up on her back legs, and took off running.

Her normally calm horse *bolted*.

"No, no, no, no!" Cora yelled, immediately and instinctively curling over the saddle horn and holding on with everything she had.

"Goldie, it's okay," she yelled. "Slow down. Whoa, whoa!"

The horse did not slow down, as horses were prey animals and their fight or flight instinct almost always defaulted to flight. Cora's teeth rattled in her head as they knocked together, and she had no idea how to slow this runaway train.

She heard another voice yelling, "Whoa, whoa, whoa there," but she didn't dare look left or right.

Marigold's hair whipped back into her face, and Cora actually closed her eyes and gripped the saddle horn tighter.

"Hey-o, whoa," the man yelled again, and something whizzed past Cora's head, and then miracle of miracles, Marigold started to slow. In fact, the cowboy brought her to a complete halt, her sides heaving, and him pressing in tight to her neck. "Hey, Goldie, you're okay. You're okay," he said in a calm, soothing tenor that worked as well on females as it did on equines.

Cora could not get a breath, though her nostrils flared.

"You okay?" the man asked, his voice guarded but kind.

Cora opened her eyes and looked into the gorgeous brown eyes of a simply stunning cowboy. He wore a frown, and he blinked at her. "What's your name? Are you with me?" He held up three fingers. "How many fingers am I holding up?"

Cora straightened, and her lungs finally expanded with a breath of air. She exhaled it all out shakily, her anxiety and panic striking together, like a snake—fast and deadly. She slid from the saddle and shook her hands as she paced away, tears dripping down her face.

"Hey, hey, it's okay." The cowboy's boots hit the ground and came toward her. He seemed to sense that Cora didn't want to be touched, and he let her pace away from him and then come back, all the nervous energy and the fear of being tossed like a sack of potatoes and hitting the ground and breaking every bone in her body flowing through her.

"Hey, it's okay," he said. "I saw her start, and I came right after you. It's okay. You're all right." He touched an open palm to his chest. "My name is Boston Simpson. I work here at the lodge. Are you a guest? I can get you back where you belong. No problem."

He took a step closer to her and held out his hand, almost as if she were a horse, and he wanted her to sniff him and deem him safe.

"Not a guest," she managed to say, and Boston's expression didn't change.

He simply blinked again. "Okay," he said. "I can still get you back where you should be. Why don't you tell me your name?"

Cora shook her head, because she was this man's *boss*, and she had no idea what he did here at the lodge. For all she knew, he worked raking bark or carrying luggage, and she would have four or five managers between him and her. She'd never have to speak to him again.

More importantly, neither of them could ever speak of this event again.

She catapulted herself onto Goldie's back, reached down and pulled the rope he'd used to calm her and stop her, and flung it away. Then she clicked her tongue and got the heck out of there.

"Wait," Boston called after her. "I'm safe. Do you even know your way back?"

At that very moment, no, Cora did not. But if she knew one thing about horses, it was that they always knew the way home, and *Goldie*—not the hottest cowboy Cora had ever laid eyes on—would get her "back where she belonged."

Mм, this is going to be fun! **Preorder BOSTON now by scanning the code below with your phone:**

Mav (Book 0): Meet Maverik Young, the cowboy country music star ready to hang up his guitar strings in favor of being a father.

Oh, and he'd like a good woman to settle down with in Coral Canyon too, please. :)

Tex (Book 1): He's back in town after a successful country music career. She owns a bordering farm to the family land he wants to buy...and she outbids him at the auction. Can Tex and Abigail rekindle their old flame, or will the issue of land ownership come between them?

Otis (Book 2): He's finished with his last album and looking for a soft place to fall after a devastating break-up. She runs the small town bookshop in Coral Canyon and needs a new boyfriend to get her old one out of her life for good. Can Georgia convince Otis to take another shot at real love when their first kiss was fake?

Morris (Book 3): Morris Young is just settling into his new life as the manager of Country Quad when he attends a wedding. He sees his ex-wife there—apparently Leighann is back in Coral Canyon—along with a little boy who can't be more or less than five years old... Could he be Morris's? And why is his heart hoping for that, and for a reconciliation with the woman who left him because he traveled too much?

Trace (Book 4): He's been accused of only dating celebrities. She's a simple line dance instructor in small town Coral Canyon, with a soft spot for kids...and cowboys. Trace could use some dance lessons to go along with his love lessons... Can he and Everly fall in love with the beat, or will she dance her way right out of his arms?

Blaze (Book 5): He's dark as night, a single dad, and a retired bull riding champion. With all his money, his rugged good looks, and his ability to say all the right things, Faith has no chance against Blaze Young's charms. But she's his complete opposite, and she just doesn't see how they can be together...

...so she ends things with him.

Gabe (Book 6): He's a father's rights advocate lawyer with a sweet little girl. She's fighting for her own daughter. Can Gabe and Hilde find happily-ever-after when they're at such odds with one another?

Jem (Book 7): He's still healing from his vices, and Jem has dedicated everything he has to his two kids. At least he's not mourning his divorce anymore, and in fact, he might be ready to move on. She's his former best friend, and once he breaks his wrist, his nurse. Can Sunny somehow rope this cowboy's heart?

Luke (Book 8): He swore off women when his ex told him he might not be their daughter's father. But a paternity test confirmed he is, and Luke Young has dedicated his life to his little girl and his brothers' band. There hasn't been time for a girlfriend anyway. He's tried here and there, and the women in small-town Coral Canyon are certainly interested in him.

But he's been thinking about his massage therapist for a while now. Can he ask Sterling out when all they've ever been is professional? Oh, and there's the fact that she's seen practically every inch of his body... Awkward, right?

Bryce (Book 9): Bryce Young has been broken and drifting for years. After giving up his son for adoption, he left Coral Canyon and hasn't returned...until now.

Harry (Book 1o): He's looking to make a change from his country music stardom, but the woman who's caught his eye isn't convinced he's permanent enough for her... Can Harry and Belle work out their differences to find a happily-ever-after?

Joey (Book 11): He's a renowned celebrity assistant, now taking over as manager for Country Quad, the legendary band of Young Brothers. She's a young cowgirl trying to find her place in life and her family. Can Joey take a leap of faith and land safely in Adam's arms? Or will small town gossip and expectations crush them both?

Boston (Book 12): Between planning exclusive events, navigating family expectations, and trying to keep their growing attraction under wraps, Boston and Cora discover that opposites don't just attract—they might be perfect for each other.

But can Boston overcome his fears of not truly belonging to the Young family so he can build his own? And will Cora find the courage to embrace both her roots and her heart without losing her inheritance?

About Liz

Liz Isaacson writes inspirational romance, usually set in Texas, or Wyoming, or anywhere else horses and cowboys exist. She lives in Utah, where she writes full-time, takes her two dogs to the park everyday, and eats a lot of veggies while writing. Find her on her website at www.feelgoodfiction-books.com.

www.ingramcontent.com/pod-product-compliance
Lightning Source LLC
Chambersburg PA
CBHW020514110726
47899CB00004B/1114